MW01268589

THE TATTOOED HEART & MY NAME IS ROSE

Published by Pharos Editions

Pharos Editions
1752 NW Market Street
308
Seattle WA 98107
www.pharoseditions.com

The Tattooed Heart
Text Copyright © 1953, Renewed 1981
by Theodora Keogh, all rights reserved

First edition 1954 by Farrar, Straus & Young

My Name Is Rose
Text Copyright © 1956, Renewed 1984
by Theodora Keogh, all rights reserved

First edition 1956 by Farrar, Straus & Cugahy

First Pharos Editions Printing May 2014

Pharos Editions version reprinted by arrangement with Sallie Free

Introduction Copyright © 2014 by Lidia Yuknavitch

ISBN-13: 9781940436012

All Rights Reserved

SELECTED AND INTRODUCED BY
LIDIA YUKNAVITCH

THE TATTOOED HEART & MY NAME IS ROSE

Two Novels by

THEODORA KEOGH

PHAROS EDITIONS | SEATTLE, WASHINGTON

INTRODUCTION BY
LIDIA YUKNAVITCH

DIGGING FOR MATTER

Lately, I've taken to digging up women.

What I mean is, I've become obsessed with going back and down and under to find women writers whose work made it possible for the rest of us, for the present tense of us, to "matter." I've developed this obsession in relation to finding the "market" for women writers in the present to be an abject abyss of dead tropes and formulaic forms, whereas the "matter" in the writing that came before us, even from dead women, remains astonishingly generative.

As my profound case study I give you Theodora Keogh, a novelist who wrote nine novels in the 1950's and 60's that, to be modest, blew the doors and windows off of what we mean when we say "women's writing." When we say "women's writing" today, unfortunately, we mean a subset of writing entirely dictated by market-driven gatekeepers of money-making products. Whereas Theodora Keogh's novels perform the act, the verb, the glorious excess of an *actual woman writing*. Writing through her body, to be precise. Without flinching or pulling punches.

Imagine that.

Her debut novel, *Meg,* is about a 12-year old girl who drifts away from her private school friends toward the streets where she is raped. She published *Meg* in 1950. That was where Theodora Keogh began. Think about that for a minute. From there she went on to publish *The Double Door,* a novel in which a cloistered teen heiress finds a secret door and ends up making love with her father's paid male lover, *The Fascinator,* where a young girl is seduced by a sculptor, *Gemini,* an incest and murder narrative about twins, *Street Music,* a story in which a music critic falls desperately in love with a child criminal, and *The Other Girl,* a fictionalized retelling of the Black Dahlia murder.

And it wasn't just her themes that ruptured the literary landscape. The formal moves she performed in each novel were every bit as daring as her contemporary male counterparts—which is probably the least interesting thing I could say, so I'll say this as well: her formal moves interrogated subjectivity from the specific site of a woman's body.

Like many of her characters, she also lived a full and novel-worthy life in France. She was dancer. She was friends with all things and people *Paris Review,* including the Plimpton. She was a designer, she worked for Vogue, she divorced and remarried, she bought a tugboat and married its captain, she lived in the Chelsea Hotel, she divorced and remarried again.

She kept a Margay as a pet; it nibbled her ear into a different shape.

And she wrote nine formidable novels.

So why haven't you heard of her?

It's a good question, isn't it.

With Pharos' re-release of *My Name is Rose* and *The Tattooed Heart,* we can turn away from the glitz and gleam of the market, away from "women's writing," and look back at what a *woman writing* looked like on the page. In *My Name Is Rose,* by alternating between first person and third person, Theodora gives us an unhappily married woman who writes her second self alive through a passionate affair only available in the pages of her journal. A passionate affair with an underage boy. What emerges is the crisis between two women—the women we are from the inside-out and the women we are told to be by cultural scripts of "wife" and "mother." Written in 1956.

Similarly, in *The Tattooed Heart,* a girl nearing adolescence spends a summer with her grandmother and discovers a younger boy in the wooded hills of the Long Island shore. The two revel in the younger boys childhood fantasies, almost as if it is possible to hover at the cusp of things, until the adult world around them shatters the possibility space of sexuality and creativity.

It's as if all of her novels meant to explore the form and content of passion—what territories of the body, life and language are available?

As Joan Schenkar wrote in her wonderful essay "The Late, Great, Theodora Keogh" which appeared in *The Paris Review Daily,* "But if passion is

Keogh's real subject, it's also the wrecking ball in her democracy of desire. In each of her books, passion equalizes class, age, race, and identity."

Thrillingly, then, we get a chance to go back, down, under. Like Anais Nin. Like Virginia Woolf. Like Gertrude Stein. Like Marguerite Duras. Like Djuna Barnes. Other *women writing* who I keep digging up to reassure myself that we always knew exactly what we were, and are, doing.

LIDIA YUKNAVITCH

THE TATTOOED HEART & MY NAME IS ROSE

THE TATTOOED
HEART

to
Hal Vursell

CHAPTER 1

TWILIGHT TURNED JUNE'S REFLECTION into a shadow. Slowly, as though by witchcraft, the mirror rendered back to her the hues of her flesh, the twin gleams of her eyes, the tawn of her hair, refused all but the nebulous outline of a young girl.

"Shall I turn on the light?" asked June aloud of the room.

But she was listless and did nothing, simply stood on there and felt the soft yet chilly night breeze contract her heart.

Half a year ago (how long it seemed!) June had been put to bed with one of those fevers that come from raw milk. She remembered herself quite well from those days: a thin, sinewy child, wild and rough as either of her two brothers. What had happened to that child? Where had she gone? Ah, she had vanished during those feverish nights and in those languid mornings she had disappeared, because the June who had risen lately could not have much to do with the June who had lain down. That homely drink of milk from which she had swallowed fever had contained, it seemed, another germ as well: the more ruthless one of adolescence. Yes, somewhere during the hazy aches of her illness, June's childhood had gone forever. It was unfair. She had had no chance to say goodbye, no chance to make ready for the next guest.

June was displeased by the shape in the cupboard mirror. She saw herself as thickened, softened and spoiled, without purity of line. Her legs, because of a new fullness in her thighs, appeared shorter, her waist too small above her hips. Then, too, the dark, changing flowers of her bosom dismayed her and rubbed against her clothes. June was still weak from being in bed and was not allowed out or downstairs, so she was free to contemplate for hours these differences in her person.

As darkness settled, June could see the little dormer window in her room begin to glow, and innumerable insect sounds belonging to summer filled her head like a buzzing of her own ears. Then the lights were snapped on and a well-known voice said cheerfully:

"How can you stay like that in the dark?"

June turned to look at the stranger who was her mother. "When will I be able to go downstairs, Mother?" she asked.

June's mother, or 'young Mrs. Grey,' as she was called, went over to the window and drew the blind. She was of the same colouring as her daughter: a dark blond with swarthy skin, but she had a thin, quick face and her figure was of the type known as smart. Before they had become strangers, June had really not known how her mother looked. Now she examined the woman furtively and closely, hoping that they were not alike.

"June," said her mother, "you are getting well now and your strong constitution has helped, but you must go quietly and slowly. I came up to talk about summer plans. We have never really discussed them."

The Greys had been preparing for a long trip which, in the case of June's father, was a semi-business one. They believed in including their children on such excursions and were indeed very dependent on them for amusement and pleasure. June's brothers were even now packing their bags. One could hear the sounds faintly through the thick old walls, a contrast to June's own idleness and silence.

"You see, darling," continued young Mrs. Grey, "you won't really be your old self again until the fall. I know it seems sad that you should be here without us, but you must get in good shape for school. Besides, you'll be such a pleasure to your grandmother."

The summer stretched out in front of them both now, different for each, filled with mystery and hidden fate.

"What about my lessons?" asked June, who had missed the winter and spring term at school.

"Your father has found you a tutor—or rather your grandmother has. It appears she got a letter weeks ago asking her to find one for another child, and so had already made inquiries in the village. Really your grandmother is remarkable!" she finished in the cross tones which meant in fact: 'She is secretive and sly.'

Young Mrs. Grey gave a bright smile and turned on her heel briskly as though glad everything were settled. She was about to leave the room when June asked:

"Mother, do you really think I will be my old self by winter?"

"Of course you will, darling. Why, you'll be allowed downstairs in time to say goodbye to us."

'I didn't mean it that way,' thought June resentfully as her mother's footsteps tapped sharply down the stairs, 'and she knew perfectly well what I meant.'

It was true. June's mother did know and she was glad to escape. She loved her children, but would she be able to love all of them, always? How oppressive the atmosphere had been in that darkened room! Something intensely sensitive, almost quivering, had emanated from the young girl's being. Despite herself young Mrs. Grey felt a cold dislike and was unable to summon a grain of sympathy. She would be glad to leave for the summer; glad to leave June whom she had nursed so carefully for the last months, and glad as well to leave this gloomy house with its Victorian inconveniences. She could feel here an atavistic draught blowing through stairways and corridors. Alien blood called here from other lands, thick blood with which her own refused to mingle.

June's mother was impatient. With her light step and quick, light, mobile thoughts, she longed for a country house of her own. She wanted chintz curtains, comfortable chairs and a fleecy bathroom. Yet so far they had come here every summer to live with an old woman on her hilltop where great, dripping trees darkened the windows.

Philip, nine years old, ran up to her as she reached the floor below. "Mother, I have no slacks and I need a real tie, don't I, if we're going anywhere?"

Philip had been a white blond, but each year his hair was growing darker just as his deliciously plump body was beginning to get thin. Now his whole face was twisted into an anxious, pleading expression. His mother smiled. She could see just the kind of tie he wanted: blue with a red stripe to turn him into a monkey.

"We'll have to go shopping in the village tomorrow, won't we?" she said in that complacent and motherly voice that is the balm of children. Silently she asked: 'Will you get strange and different too? Will you be on my side?'

Philip's blue eyes stared back at his mother as though to say: 'Pierce me if you can. It's still a secret.' Then the little boy ran thumping off in his brown, schoolboy's shoes.

And after all, reflected young Mrs. Grey, she felt no difference in Charles, and he was June's elder by two years. Perhaps this house, this atmosphere, would only claim one of her brood, and leave the rest alone.

Below, from the ground floor, an uneven tapping told that old Mrs. Grey, called simply 'Mrs. Grey,' was moving from one room to another. After dusk set in, the old woman sometimes became restless. It was as though she were expecting a great company of guests and were seeing to it that the house was in readiness. Yet she turned on no lights and did not so much as raise her hand to straighten a curtain. Over her shoulders she wore a lilac shawl and her face shone like parchment. At Philip's eager voice she turned her head upwards, but she did not smile for she disliked children as such, or rather, there were no children any more to whom she could give a place in her world.

'How nice it will be when they go,' she thought, 'and when I am left alone in my house.' Only June would remain, and June was no problem to her grandmother. She resumed her journey slowly, going out onto the wide veranda which overlooked both wood and water. Feeling the sweet night air she thought: 'How it used to make me suffer!' and she plumbed her breast for any sign of pain now. But there was none.

"Hello, Mother." It was her son, her only remaining child, back from the city. He sat down on the railing. "Well, we'll be off soon."

"All but June," said Mrs. Grey.

"Yes, I hate to leave her," said June's father.

"Well, you know," said the old woman, "I don't think she'll mind. She's at that age."

John Grey looked startled, threw away his cigarette and said: "I guess I better go up and have a talk with her now. There won't be time tomorrow."

He found June sitting on the bed, brushing the lion-coloured hair which fever had somewhat dulled. She was thinking: 'When they leave I can experiment with it,' or rather she had started in that vein before her father's step sounded on the stair. Then all reflections were cut off. Her body tensed and she waited.

As her father entered, June looked away and listened to his summer instructions while examining her hairbrush. She was to work hard so as not to go back a class. She was to remember that she was now fifteen. She was also to keep in mind that money did not grow on trees.

"But I won't spend any here," she said defensively.

"I'm not talking of spending," said John Grey. "You can't have been listening. I was saying that you must begin to think of the future; of what you want to do in the world to support yourself, and of how to prepare for it. Of course," he continued, making his voice stay matter of fact, "your mother and I hope you will marry. That's another thing I want to talk about. When we come back we must think of your wardrobe and appearance."

He was self-conscious by now and June felt cold with embarrassment. 'So he too sees the change,' she thought, and aloud she muttered: "I won't be fifteen for more than a week."

After her father had gone and while June undressed, she pondered on those remaining days in which she would still be fourteen. They did not count, it seemed. Her father had spoken as though they were over already. Yet she was sure he would never discount them in the other direction. He would never, two weeks after her birthday, call her fourteen. People hurried one along so fast, as though to urge one to catch up with them. And it was useless because their own spans ran on ahead. The talk of marriage was especially outrageous. How unbecoming of her father! How dare he speak of such a horrible thing? As if she, June, would ever marry! On the other hand the thought of preparing for some unknown job was equally alarming. The words 'support yourself' had a dry, routine, tedious sound.

June shook her head as if in this physical act to scatter her father's words. She released the blind once more and turned out the light. As she got into bed she could feel the summer evening take possession of the room again. Its throbbing insect song permeated the darkness. How quickly the summer would pass here on the peninsula—the last remaining months before she would have to think about life. June lay back with a sigh, and her hair, loose on the sheets, gave out to her nostrils a strange, womanly smell. This odour seemed to June in some odd way to answer the night sounds from her window.

Suddenly, down the hill towards the bay, a cry sounded: high, thin, melodious, hauntingly sweet. June had heard that same cry just after nightfall for the last week. Not knowing from what creature it came, she had imbued it with profound meaning. It was repeated a second and a third time. Vague longings filled the young girl's head and mingled with her dreams.

CHAPTER 2

JUNE WAVED GOODBYE TO HER FAMILY. She had been carried downstairs by McGreggor, the gardener, and stood on the porch while, with much confusion, her brothers, mother and father settled themselves in the car and drove off. She moved her arm up and down to them across the shimmering space of heat which widened as they circled a clump of bushes and then nosedived over the edge of the hill. Although she had never wished to go with them, June felt rather abandoned. "They might go away and never come back," she murmured experimentally, but no new sensation entered her heart. Then she saw McGreggor returning to carry her upstairs.

McGreggor, to go by his name, sounded like someone out of a children's book. Yet he was a dour man and June did not like him much. Rumour had it that he had been the suitor of Catherine, Mrs. Grey's one remaining servant, for twenty years. If so, his courtship was discreet. He lived in a cottage which was joined on to the rear of the stables and he came over every evening to sit for an hour on the back porch with Catherine. No one had ever heard them utter a word during these sessions although Catherine was talkative at other times. Occasionally too, in the late summer dusk, McGreggor could be heard playing his bagpipes to the woods. June had seen him standing on the far side of the stables, his face crimson with effort, hurling into the pipes at once his breath and his spit. Aside from these two diversions, he was a tireless worker, rising at dawn to brew his black tea. He had a team of horses and three fields which he rotated, one lying fallow. Although Mrs. Grey did not know it (or appeared not to) McGreggor made quite a good thing out of selling extra vegetables to the village. He sold butter and cream as well from the five cows. For this reason he disliked it that the son and grandchildren of Mrs. Grey came to stay with her, and thought of them as parasites robbing him of his just dues.

He came trudging around the corner with his dead pipe clamped in his mouth, his heavy hands hanging by his side. June, looking at him, did not want to be in his arms. How had she stood it on the way down? As he came close she became aware of his smell: mingled with earth and sweat, there was also the peculiar odour of a celibate and bad-tempered man.

"Let me try myself, Mr. McGreggor," she said. "Mother told me I could."

He shrugged and went off without a word.

The climb up the two flights of stairs was difficult that first time and June stopped often, drenched and trembling. The joints of her ankles, which she could not control, hit against each other and made bruises. There seemed not only a weakness in her muscles but also in her veins. They quivered like string that is pulled too hard. The exasperated nerves of convalescence made her want to cry.

Mrs. Grey's house was very big. It contained twenty-seven rooms, although most of them were now closed. Once, of course, all the rooms had been open and filled. Mrs. Grey had had three sons and a husband. Two of the sons were dead; a childhood illness had taken one, and the other had bled to death in a foreign land. Their faces looked down from the walls fresh and innocent, stamped with the righteousness of those who die young. Mrs. Grey's husband had followed the two boys. The money had dwindled. The servants departed.

June went up and downstairs every day after that and her muscular strength came back very fast. One morning, determined to conquer the lethargy which kept her indoors, she decided to take a walk. As was customary in the Grey family, she stopped first to bid her grandmother good morning.

Mrs. Grey was playing cards in bed as she always did between eight and nine at the beginning of the day. She went along as far as she could honestly, and then cheated to make her game come out. Although she was neither senile or foolish, she imbued the cards with a life of their own and treated them as sly, mischievous elves of whom one must get the better by guile. Her fingers, slightly swollen at the joints, darted down on this one or that. The old woman wore a lace cap on her head, which failed to soften the austerity of her features, and a linen nightgown of old-fashioned make.

The door was open and June did not knock. She had only just greeted her grandmother when Catherine entered the room. Catherine was a spidery little woman with eyes like sapphires. As the remaining servant, she ruled the house, vying for authority with its owner. She was getting on and the heavy work was now beyond her strength, so a cleaning woman from the village came once a week. Catherine, aside from her domestic talents, could drive and she owned an ancient car of uncertain make. She was proud of her car, for Mrs. Grey no longer owned one. But the old woman never left the peninsula and Catherine took this as a secret slight against her driving. She hoped that if ever an emergency of the right sort came about, the young Greys would not be there, then her mistress would have to swallow her pride in this respect. Not that Catherine wished her mistress ill; in their own way they loved each other.

Now Catherine said: "How sweet to see them both together! It's a real picture you make, the two of you."

She was ignored, and both June and Mrs. Grey felt drawn together in their disapproval of such remarks. Catherine, not at all nonplussed, proceeded to lay out her mistress' clothes. First, batiste undergarments, straight in shape and neatly darned, then intricately clocked stockings of strong silk, and finally a black dress.

"I don't want to wear that dress. It's too warm," complained Mrs. Grey, dealing out the cards afresh.

Now it was Catherine's turn for ignoring. She brushed the garment vigorously in preparation and said: "Isn't it grand to see Miss June up again?" Catherine emphasized the 'Miss' which she had not used before June's illness. "And it's different she is now, I'm thinking. More of a young lady."

"Is that an improvement?" asked June.

"Sure and you don't want to be a kid forever," said Catherine. "Now will you kindly step out and away while I dress your grandmother?"

June trailed out of the room, glancing up in passing at the portrait of her grandfather on the wall near the door. She had never known him and, despite this portrait and others in the house, she had no clear picture of the man in her imagination. The house too, which was outwardly his shrine, had secretly forgotten him. His robust footsteps had faded from the halls, and if the corridors had ghosts they were not his. Believing firmly in the harmony of body and soul, he had taken his spirit courageously with him to the grave.

June moved down the stairs, laying her hand against the banister. Beneath her palm the wood stuck and made a small, squeaking sound. She pushed open the side door, which was of screen, and held it deliberately ajar while a fly zig-zagged into the house. Then she walked down the veranda steps and onto the lawn.

Mrs. Grey owned all the peninsula of which the house was center and, except for a small corner, would neither let nor sell. She owned the acid, moss-covered lawns and the tangled woods. She owned the beaches with their bluffs, their stones, their quick-mud creeks. The unkept, rutted roads were hers. The taxes for these things took the place of the suburban villa and the comfortable apartment in town for which her daughter-in-law sighed. But Mrs. Grey would stay out her life here and ask no change.

June now wandered slowly between the trees on the lawn. The shade from their expanded leaves threw a tender light on her head, and beneath her feet fresh rings of moss were scattered here and there. These brilliant, soft circles of varying sizes were like secret signals, or an antique alphabet which no one could read any more. June and her brothers had played many games around them and had attached to them a hundred meanings. Now June looked down carelessly with abstracted eyes.

She stepped out of the shade. Had anyone been watching, he would have seen, in the instant the sun hit her, a gleam of future beauty. Just now June was only half formed. There was a lack of harmony about her; that soft, sliding, disturbing quality that is at once the despair of adolescents and their fascination. Her face was over-large for the skull behind it. The strong sweep of her jawbone met her ears as though surprised to come so suddenly upon these exquisite, small shells. Her eyes were yellow-brown; set deep with rough brows above them. Her forehead was too high. Only her nose, piercing through, so to speak, from behind the mask of her face, showed the same proportion as that dainty skull. It was straight, narrow, pure and of medium length. The nostrils were so thin that one could see the blood through, and they quivered with every emotion, giving her an angel look. Then too, softening the whole, were the rich, blond locks of her hair which fell wild upon temple, cheek and nape.

June kicked through the spiked grasses of the pasture and avoided the five cows with her eyes. She had never gotten over her fear of them and did not want to attract them with her regard. A few mushrooms which had sprouted in the morning dew now lay dying. Their rosy, pleated undersides were black. She reached the woods and started down the steep path to the bay. Occasionally her knees bent the wrong way from weakness and sent a sharp twinge along her leg. She had had the intention of bathing, but now she knew she would never have the strength to do so. She went on simply because it was downhill and had no idea of how she would ever get back up. The path wound around the trunks of trees like a cool, dark snake slipping downwards to drink in the marsh. Presently June could see the glitter of water through the branches and she came to a little dell at the bottom of the path where a spring burst out of the ground and ran away.

Someone was here already; a boy on a horse. He was a lad of eleven or so, with a dark mop of hair and his horse was drinking thirstily at the spring. June was startled. One might wander through these woods day after day and never meet a soul. Then she noticed that the boy had a bird on his wrist and, probably to protect himself from beak or claw, wore a leather gauntlet which reached up his forearm. The boy was regarding her, black-eyed, from a face which, even in repose, bore a mobile, nervous expression.

An unaccountable feeling of happiness came over June on seeing this child, like the pleasant recollection of a dream which one cannot really remember. She spoke first. "Do you live near here?" She neither smiled nor made any gesture of friendship, but the boy did not seem shy.

"Yes, over there." He jerked his head in the direction of the beach. His voice was in that fluty stage which not all boys have. So far no trace of manhood marred its tone although it was touched by shrillness. June, listening, thought that it reminded her of something. Then she asked, surprised:

"You don't live in the millionaire's boathouse, do you?"

She was referring to a large brick building which had stood tenantless now for years, yawning over the water. Mrs. Grey had rented the land over ten years ago to a rich man called Walsh. No one knew why and perhaps there was no reason. At any rate Mrs. Grey had never given one to her son. Walsh had built a house on it for his mistresses and his speed boats, but no one seemed to know what had happened to him lately. Only a caretaker and his wife remained, and they kept to themselves and were ignorant of the intentions of their employer. A high wall around the property kept out intruders, or rather wild animals, since forests and reeds had grown up on three sides and on the other the salt water slid beneath the building, in and out.

The boy, who had not answered her question, now stated: "My name's Ronny. What's yours?"

"June."

"You look rather funny," he said.

June defended herself. "I've been sick. It's the first time I've been out and I think I shouldn't have, come so far."

"I'm never sick," said Ronny with a look of regret. Then suddenly his face changed as though a secret thought had opened like a rose inside his brain. "I sometimes have headaches," he offered, looking down at her with that flirting glance which children sometimes give, a glance to which June could not respond. With a proud gesture he took the hood from his bird's head. The falcon fluttered for a moment and then lifted himself straight upwards. They watched in silence as his dark wings cut the sky above the trees. "He's a hunting hawk," said Ronny.

"Is he hunting now?" asked June.

"Well, he doesn't really hunt yet. I haven't got as far as that with him, but he comes when I call him home at night."

June started and looked up surprised. Ronny's horse, long finished drinking, was tearing at the foliage which grew near the spring. Now and then he stamped his hoof impatiently. A big fly with a brilliant green head was bothering him, giving him long, vicious bites so that his flanks quivered.

"Do you know," asked Ronny in his high, excited voice, "what happens when you put the leaves he is eating into the water?" With a kick he threw his bare leg over the horse's back and slid to the ground. Grasping one of the weeds from beneath the animal's nose, he pulled it up roots and all and plunged it into the water. He was like a magician performing a star trick and at once the leaves turned into precious silver, glittering as they bent beneath the water's current. Ronny crouched there in triumph by the spring and his black hair fell across his eyes.

"It's beautiful!" cried June, who had known about silver-weed all her life.

Ronny rose to his feet. "Where do you live?" he asked.

"In the house on top of the hill," replied June. "But I don't know how I'm ever going to get back there. My legs are so tired and weak."

"Get on behind," said Ronny at once. "Gambol will take you there." He led the horse to a fallen tree and they both climbed up. "I usually spring onto his back in a single bound," said Ronny, "but there's no point if you must mount too."

"None at all," agreed June, holding on to the boy's waist in order not to fall. She was overcome with lassitude and murmured directions as though in a dream. Once Ronny half turned around and asked:

"Do you think you could be called a damsel?"

"Certainly," June answered with a smile. "A damsel in distress."

Ronny was silent after that. He frowned in thought and swung his bare feet against the horse's sides.

CHAPTER 3

RONNY, THE LOVELY CHILD with his silky olive skin and tangle of hair, was a worry to his mother. Especially of late. The boarding school, to which he had been sent for the first time, did not suit his temperament. He failed in his classes, and his constant tension forced them to release him early. Even pretty, worldly Grace Villars realized that something must be done about her son. But Grace could not bear to give up her summer visits at fashionable resorts; indeed she could not afford to. So it was good luck when she came across Walsh at a party in New York that spring; Walsh who owned the boathouse on Mrs. Grey's peninsula.

"Grace," he said, "how nice to see you again after all these years, and looking as pretty as ever. How's Roger?"

"Roger's dead, Jim. Surely you must have heard," said Grace Villars.

"Oh, yes, as a matter of fact I did read about it." He put his rubbery face nearer hers so that she could look into his eyes below their heavy lids and asked: "How's the boy?"

"It's about time you asked," said Grace, shaking her bright curls and blinking her lashes against the melancholy power of his eyes.

"Now Grace, you know I've always taken an interest in the boy, even though we don't see each other," protested Jim, who had never been sure whether or not Ronny was his own son. He looked again at his companion. How strange it always was after a lapse of years to rediscover an old love! Their coy ways and the meaning which they unconsciously gave to every gesture mixed oddly with their added signs of age and filled him with a cruel pleasure. That he himself had grown flabby and gout-ridden did not disturb Walsh. He had never been handsome, nor young in any real sense; only, after a while, rich.

Walsh had decided tastes in women, although they had evolved slightly. When he had first been in a position to choose, show girls had been his choice; blond, with adequate experience and without tiresome, dramatic ambitions. Later, perhaps because this type was becoming hard to find, Jim had preferred women on the fringe of society: elegant but slightly flashy, women in their thirties, women who knew how to dress and how to set off a man's wealth without looking like a wife, women with thin, active legs, with long, tubular arms and bracelets on their wrists. He had never had a dark woman and he had never been in love.

A dozen years ago Grace, even if too young, had been a fairly good embodiment of his ideal. Married to a man whose money and career were slipping from his fingers, she had been looking around with those blue eyes of hers to find something different. By her husband Roger's trembling hands, his mute mouth and desperate gaze she knew that he was finished. Sometimes he had looked as though he wanted to beg her understanding, as though some sign must pass between them for their eight years together, their common meals, the darkness of their bed. Then Grace would cry:

"Roger, don't look like such an old bear! Take a drink! Do something! I must hurry and dress for dinner. I'm going out."

Her liaison with Walsh had lasted a little over a year and it was Walsh who had tired first; Grace could have gone on forever in the atmosphere of wealth which he exuded. Never mind, she had her twin diamond brooches, an emerald and diamond bracelet, a superb fur coat and the beginnings of Ronny. About Ronny she had not been so sure, and had tried several times in a haphazard way to get rid of him. But he clove stubbornly to her side and, after nine months and three days, emerged as dark as a changeling and yellow with jaundice.

Grace today was no longer too young. Her hair was bleached and she covered her face with a bricklike powder, in imitation of the ash blond curls, the peachy glow that had once been hers. Those little birdlike ways were showing a hint of the peckish; the nerves were rubbing through. Yet such details were only to be seen on scrutiny. Grace could still show a stranger that blond, dolly femininity for which men are supposed to sigh. The brave candid blue eyes glittered as though to say: "We at least are fearless, two stones unworn by tears."

Walsh looked into them now and smiled. "Well, he said, "what is it?" and moved his knee beneath the table.

At the feel of this thick yet knobby knee, matted, as she remembered, by black hair, Grace unaccountably thrilled. It was the thrill of wealth and ease and big cars, of a new dress for each occasion, and of jewels. Grace was not doing as well as she would have liked and Walsh was the best she had ever done.

"I don't want to bore you with my own problems," she said, "but I am worried about Ronny. My doctor says he's near a breakdown and mustn't be stimulated in any way."

"In other words you want to get him off your hands for the summer," guessed Walsh. "Quite right, a pretty woman like you has no business dragging a grown-up boy around. Besides, boys have their own tastes. Now if I had a son—"

* * * * *

It was as a direct result of this conversation that Ronny arrived at Star Harbour Junction one day in early June. He was met by Jeremy, Jim Walsh's caretaker. Jeremy was a pink-cheeked man with good health and a pessimistic outlook. He had come to the peninsula when the boathouse was first built and now lived there together with his wife Mary and

Walsh's horse, Gambol. They had all three been cast away, so to speak, and existed quietly enough. Although the couple's salary came regularly in the mail, they had never received money for the upkeep of the house nor any orders concerning its repair. Jeremy, with Gambol's help, dug up the ground beyond the wall and had made there a large vegetable garden. It was on Mrs. Grey's property but no word had been said. Then as a complete surprise, had come a letter from Walsh saying that a boy was coming to stay the summer; that he was to have Gambol to ride, and that a tutor had been found for him. Walsh had enclosed money and given Mrs. Villar's address in case of emergency.

Jeremy asked no questions of Ronny on the way home from the station. He did not pay much attention to this child who was to spend the next months under his care, and Ronny, as he climbed into the old Ford, felt lonely and abandoned. While they drove into the hills along the coastline, the boy stole sideways glances, not so much at his companion's face as at his square hands on the wheel and the black-booted feet on the pedal. Then he looked across at the woods, at the field of old and dying apple trees, and finally at the reedy marshes which fought the beaches along the shore. A sea smell filled his nostrils, stagnant and strong. It was low tide.

At last they drove over a space redeemed from the marsh, a filled-in area, which was ended abruptly by the boathouse. From the land it looked like any other house, conventional although somewhat shabby in its brick dress. How was one to know of the salt water which flowed like blood into its lower chamber? Ronny felt near to tears with dreariness, yet somewhere inside was a thrill of excitement. For a contrast he thought of his mother who would surely never come here if once she had seen the place.

"Well, how does it strike you?" asked Jeremy, carrying the boy's one modest valise.

"Fine," answered Ronny politely.

"Oh it's just a house, in any case," said Jeremy. "Houses are all the same; big or small, they can't prevent us from going to another one in the end, as narrow as our shoulders." For Jeremy could not conceive why he had been let live only to die in the end.

His wife Mary appeared now on the threshold. A thin woman, slightly shriveled and pale as her husband was rosy, her every gesture was kind, fussy and anxious. She hesitated, dried her fingers on her apron, and finally shook hands with Ronny.

"It's not much of a gay place," she said to him, "Not much company." She peered at the boy, slightly worried. Mary had always longed for children and frequently drove Jeremy into a rage by telling him they were something to live for. "Now if we had children," she would say, "you would have something to live for."

"What are children but men and women," he would cry, "born every one of them to go down into the grave?"

"They would be a comfort at the resurrection," Mary sometimes argued, picturing her bones scattered and vibrating in the final blast. Then Jeremy would give his wife a look of despair, but because of his pink skin, his round and jolly features, his expression carried no more weight than that of a clown who has been shot by a firecracker.

Ronny, despite his first impression, soon got used to living in the boathouse. Complete freedom and lack of interference were a novelty, a blessed relief. He was one of those creatures who are doomed from infancy to attract the emotion of others. It was partly his looks—the pure, almost cameo profile over the brow of which his black hair fell— but it was partly as well some illusive quality about him as though from another world; a wind blowing, so to speak, from lost dreams. It acted on them all—his teachers, the older boys at school, his mother's friends—and he could not respond to this host of urgent cries. They set his nerves on edge. Here, Mary was far too timid to make demands and Jeremy was almost indifferent. The couple took good care of him, however, and he adored Gambol. He had never owned a horse and had ridden seldom, but Gambol, although he might have lived up to his name seven years ago, was now a staid gelding with gentle ways. Ronny rode him without a saddle and with only a halter around his nose.

Ronny acquired his hawk quite soon after arriving. He had been riding out along the edge of the marsh early one morning when Gambol shied suddenly, rolling his eyes towards the edge of the path. A young hawk was lying there, stunned, with its feathers ruffled. Ronny jumped off his horse to kneel beside the bird.

"Are you dead?" he asked softly, and the hawk replied by giving him a proud, hostile look from its yellow eye. "You must come with me," said Ronny, "and be called Shalimar."

Ronny, as it happened, knew about hawks because one of Grace Villar's friends had been a hunter in Arabia and was versed in the keeping and training of falcons. The man had dropped out of his mother's life, but since then Ronny had longed for such a bird and had even named it in his mind. It seemed quite natural to him that here his wish came true.

Shalimar had hardly been a favourite with Mary for she was afraid of the bird. Nonetheless, she had made it a little hood of scarlet cloth, cut and sewn under Ronny's supervision. Jeremy had given him one of the old gardening gauntlets that lay in the tool shed. Having hooded his bird, Ronny put it in the box stall beside that of Gambol, and in a short time Shalimar had become quite tame. Ronny's natural love for animals had given him a way with them; dogs that were fierce with others would submit to his caress, and he had spent many hours taming squirrels and chipmunks.

So Ronny lived the life of the country child who sees no one; quiet yet excited, passing his days along the marsh and in the hilly woods. And then one morning he had met June. Her languid air and her solitude that matched his own attracted him. He felt as though he had never really looked at anybody before; as though she were the first person he had truly seen in the world so far. After he had ridden her to her home, June had stood for a moment gazing down at him over the railing. Then with a mockery natural to girls who have brothers she had said:

"Goodbye and thank you, little boy."

Her teasing manner stung him, yet refreshed him as well. Although she did not treat him as a knight riding a charger with a hawk at his command, her very mockery was an admission. "I know you are of chivalry," it seemed to say, "but I'm not going to admit it."

CHAPTER 4

RONNY DID NOT RIDE UP TO THE HILLTOP again that week, but June heard him every evening. The high, solitary cry of the boy calling to his bird mingled with other evening sounds: the fox, the night owl, the hurtling train. After day waned she heard them all. They were like personal messages thrown against her breast. Before, there had been no Ronny, and his call had been the night itself with its beating, secret lonely heart that reached out and sought her own. Now the voice had a shape, but June could never really believe that it was not she for whom the voice was destined. She wondered how Ronny spent his mornings, how he passed the heavy afternoons, and wondered, too, how she herself had passed them a year ago. The old pleasures were difficult to rediscover and she was bored.

Mrs. Grey was no companion for June. Hour by hour the old woman's tranquil habits unwound themselves so that there was no idle moment left in her day, and not many of these moments were devoted to her granddaughter either. After June's morning visit they would not meet until lunch and, after that, seldom until the evening meal. Sometimes Mrs. Grey was tired and did not even come down to supper, but at others she lingered afterwards and would ask June to read aloud to her from an enormous book of verse, marked and underlined by three generations.

One of the poems, a ballad about a knight lying dead in a field, made June think of the little boy she had met.

'I'll go and see him tomorrow,' she thought, looking up from the page. So the following afternoon she set out once more through the woods. By now June was stronger. A little colour had come into her face, tinting her ears and the high bones around her eyes.

After a while she took off her sandals and felt on her feet the damp, moldy earth of the path. She walked down to the edge of the marsh and then turned right until she came to the boathouse. She felt a little shy of its high gates which she had never entered before. They were silent, and around them, on the side from which she came, the reeds flourished like yellow spears. It was medium tide and the breath from the marsh made a haze in the air. On all sides were the trees, surrounding their stagnant ponds, their small and arid pastures. June tried the gate handle and then, finding it locked, pulled the bell chain. At once a loud peal echoed like a curse in the stillness.

'Why have I come?' she wondered. The locked gate was a rejection, the cursing bell an insult. Perhaps she had no right to penetrate these walls, for what if this gate were the door of childhood, closed to her now forever? This thought, which made her feel regret, had in it, too, a certain sweetness. She looked down at her bare arms rendered glistening by the sun. They were shaded by fine hairs which she had never noticed before and a breath seemed to pass over her body and contract the nerves against her spine.

Jeremy opened the gate to June, his cheeks flushed by the heat. With his blue shirt and brilliant health he resembled a laborer in a political poster.

"Yes, Miss?"

June was relieved to hear a human voice. Everything was ordinary after all; an ordinary country house, slightly run down, and a pink-faced gardener. "Is Ronny here?" she asked.

"He is," said Jeremy. "He's just finishing lunch."

"May I see him?"

"Oh yes, you may see him," said Jeremy. "He's there for you to see if you like." He turned on his heel and led the way.

June had never been inside the Walsh property before and, as she followed Jeremy, she was startled by the whiteness of the courtyard which was paved with oyster shells. Against their snowy welcome the house showed mouldering and dark. Ronny was in the kitchen, eating a piece of pie and talking to Mary. June could hear his fluty tones drifting out the doorway.

"As high as you are," he was saying. "Really, Mary! Cross my heart." Mary made the appropriate, soothing noises of fright. "Gambol just skimmed over it without stopping," said Ronny, and then he caught sight of June. For a moment he stopped eating, as children do when their parents enter the nursery. His mouth was still full, but he ceased chewing and regarded her impassively from his black eyes. Then he lowered his head so that his hair fell between them like a curtain.

"Hello," he muttered, offhand and sullen.

"Good afternoon, Miss, would you eat some pie?" asked Mary in her friendly, timid manner. She saw no difficulty here, only a nice girl paying a visit to a little boy. "Perhaps you'll have it later," she said as no one made a move.

"Is she staying here all afternoon?" asked Ronny, turning his face towards Mary.

"What a way to talk about a young lady guest!" Mary gave a deprecating smile at June.

June turned a slow, dull red. Her eyes blazed with anger and humiliation. "I was just passing," she lied, "and I can't stay. I must go home and read to my grandmother."

"I don't have a grandmother," said Ronny, "and I don't want one either. Old ladies kiss too much."

June had to smile at the idea of her own grandmother kissing too much. Her blush faded. She grew bored by this conversation. Childhood after all, was filled with petty statements and flat denials. She made ready to go, tugging at her cotton blouse which was too short and touching the locks above her temples with a new, unconscious gesture.

"Come with me," said Ronny suddenly. "I have something to show you." Getting up from the table, he slipped his hand in hers. At once the sensation returned to June of being in a lost country, a land whose shores it was perhaps dangerous to retread. For Mary's sake she smiled and agreed with nonchalance. But Mary noticed nothing in any case and only Jeremy, slouching in the doorway, remarked after they had gone:

"What a fuss over a year or two. As though it could matter! They'll be dead a million and it won't be enough."

Mary washed the dishes without answering. Such remarks had long lost the power to frighten her. At the sink, with her spindly legs and industrious arms, she resembled an ant. The giant stride could flatten her in an instant.

Ronny took his hand away from June's almost at once and led the way through the house, into a little doorway and down a circular stairway which came out onto the water beneath. The tide was coming in. Its lapping harried the dark air; a sucking, eager per-suasion. The sides of the cement landings, or quays, were still exposed. Underneath, one could see a muddy bottom pitted with the small holes of fiddler crabs. There were two boats here; a rowboat and a motorless speedboat. Both were rotted down into the slime and covered by the poison-green moss of the sea. At one end was an archway, which led out into the sunlit bay. It could be closed by a door that slid down from above. Standing open, it threw into this man-made cave a brilliant and painful glitter which slid over the air and did not lighten the gloom.

"Here was his dungeon," said Ronny. "He took his prisoners down here and tied them on those boats. Then soon the crabs came and ate them up, body and soul." He added in his soprano voice: "I would do it too, with all my enemies."

"Crabs can't eat the soul," objected June, feeling in this damp place the sweat growing cold on her body.

"Oh yes they can," he insisted. "Crabs can. They're only baffled by the bones." And he held up the white spine of a fish worn down by the tides which he had found that morning.

June did not contradict him and only asked: "Do you know him, the man who used to live here?"

"Oh yes, I know him," said Ronny (who had never met Walsh). "Mother thinks he's my father."

"You mean Mr. Walsh," cried June, "the millionaire?"

"Mr. Walsh, that's it, Mr. Walsh. He has a hundred houses, I guess, and fifty cars and a hundred motorboats."

"Don't you call him Father?" asked June.

"No," replied Ronny seriously, as though reflecting on this. "But you see he isn't my mother's husband. My mother's husband was called Roger and he died." Ronny nodded several times as though checking the correctness of these statements. Then a smile came over his face and brought out the twitch of his cheek. "My mother is a liar," he said. The word must have pleased him for he cupped his hands and shouted: "Liar, liar."

The echo came back to them several times from the imprisoning walls. It was like a bird who dashes itself to pieces trying to get free. Each time it was fainter and more plaintive. Ronny turned his eyes downwards to the murky water which was rising fast. All the mud had disappeared and the tide bit greedily into the rotten wood of the two boats. June followed the boy's gaze. A school of minnows darted into the boathouse and just as swiftly flashed out again through the arch. The green on the wrecked planks was as brilliant as emeralds.

"What will you be when you are a man?" she asked.

"Oh," said Ronny, scuffing his bare sole softly on the cement, "I shall be a knight. But as you know there are no more knights. Anyway it doesn't matter as I won't be a man very soon."

Just then they heard steps ringing out on the metal of the stairs, a town tread, cautious and sharp. "Ronny?" a voice called interrogatively. Then a man stepped onto the quay. When he saw them he advanced and said: "I am James Stevens. I am supposed to teach you, to get you up on your lessons."

"Mother said I didn't have to start until July!" exclaimed Ronny shrilly, dismayed and apprehensive.

"But you don't want to fall behind," said Stevens, "and have to end up the summer working all day. Besides, this is just a call to get acquainted."

James Stevens was a blond man who could still be called young. His hair thinned out at the temples over a narrow, high forehead and his mouth had a tight look to it caused by faint rays around the upper lip. He had grey, rather cold eyes. Now these eyes turned to June.

"Is this your sister?" he asked.

"No," said Ronny. "She's a damsel."

"I'm June Grey," said June, "and I think you're supposed to teach me too."

"Were you going to call on her to get acquainted?" asked Ronny, using Stevens' turn of phrase.

The tutor gave June a blank look. "I shall just be helping her catch up," he said. "It's not the same thing." He turned away again. "By the way, Ronny," he said, "are you a scout? If you are I thought perhaps you would like to transfer to our local troop." He waited, but the boy was not listening. He took June's hand again and looked up into her face.

"Damsel," he said again, "a damsel and a knight."

Stevens frowned. One could see the rays now plainly as he pressed his lips together. "That's a rather silly way of talking," he said. "You don't want to spend your time with girls, do you? You'll turn into a regular sissy."

Ronny lifted his heavy lids in astonishment until his eyes were almost round. "A knight is much braver than a boy scout," he cried. "There's no comparison! Just look!" Stooping, he reached down to one of the wrecks and came up with a crab in his hand. The crab was a fiddler and with its huge claw pinched at the child's flesh. Ronny's cheeks contracted. It looked as though he were smiling.

CHAPTER 5

RONNY'S HAWK GREW BIGGER and flew further each day, hunting over wood, sea and farm. He rose from the boy's wrist or from the stable door and his yellow eyes were fixed with the instinct to kill. Under the downy feathers of his upper wing powerful muscles stretched and knotted. He mastered the air. Sometimes, when he came home at night, falling towards that lonely, childish cry, his falcon's heart beat so hard inside his breast that it disturbed the rhythm of his wings.

"Shalimar," Ronny would call. "Shalimar!" The boy would look upwards with outstretched arm, waiting tensely until the hawk alighted. Nor could he repress a thrill of triumph when he felt those claws like wrinkled, primitive hands upon his skin.

Then Ronny would ask softly: "Did you hunt well, Shalimar?" And he would look for an instant into that serpent glance which remained unchanging; twin enemies separated by the hawk's deadly beak. Ronny often talked to his bird and asked questions of Shalimar about the day's journeys and Ronny was answered. At least that was the way it seemed, although when Ronny thought about it closely he could recall no phrases of those replies. Nonetheless, it seemed to Ronny that Shalimar told him of the thunderstorm catching him mid-air and throwing him this way and that between the heavy clouds, also of the sun which grew closer and closer at midday like another hostile, fiery bird. Or else it seemed to Ronny that Shalimar told him of hunting incidents, of the young rabbit who did not know enough to go to earth, of its piercing death squeal and blood-streaked fur.

Ronny found Shalimar's descriptions indescribably fresh. They weren't exactly talking, but—if they existed—they made talking ponderous in comparison, as though to talk were a tame and fussy way of doing things. Ronny conversed with Gambol, too, in this manner, but the horse, although more garrulous, was less interesting.

It was also a fact that June's presence severed this correspondence. Not only could he not communicate with Gambol and Shalimar when she was there, but even after she had gone they were mute for hours. One day, however, he tried to explain his conversations to her. They were on the edge of the marsh and June had just come down through the woods. She looked up curiously at the boy as he sat his horse. His profile was turned, out of shyness, as he spoke of these private things. Its perfect cut and the suave, rose-olive bloom of his cheek surprised her and she thought suddenly: 'I think him beautiful!'

How her brothers would have laughed at that description of a boy! But Ronny was alien in every way to them—to their blond, open faces, their sturdy limbs, their boyish scorn of everything that did not fit into their school world. She could not weld them together in her imagination.

"You are lucky to be able to talk to animals," she said.

"Oh they don't really answer me, you know." He frowned in regret of his confidence. "Only sort of." Unhooding Shalimar, he set the bird free. It was a stifling day and the high tide had just turned so that all but the tips of the marsh grass were covered in swirling water. The current dragged through the creek, a mirror for the pale summer sky. Ronny took off the leather gauntlet he wore to protect his arm and the skin beneath was drenched from the heat of the leather. On the moist back of his hand June could still see the marks made by the fiddler crab; small violet patches.

"I don't like James Stevens," said June.

Ronny slipped down from Gambol's back, careless of his bare feet in the undergrowth. "Oh Stevens doesn't know about anything important," he said.

"He doesn't like me," said June, trying to recall that only a year ago the thought of someone disliking or even hating her had been a gratification.

"I like you," said Ronny. "Didn't I prove it with the fiddler?"

"I didn't really know you were doing it for me," replied June and because his shrill, sweet voice stirred her, she gave the mocking, sisterly smile which her brothers found so odious.

"The wicked fiddler!" cried Ronny suddenly. "I'm going to punish him." And he ran to the edge of the marsh.

June followed and they stood side by side, peering into the creek. At first there was nothing to be seen for the tide had driven the crabs to their holes. Yet even as they watched, the water dropped. It raced swiftly through its channels to the bay and gradually, quarter-inch by quarter-inch, the mud reappeared; soft, black and reeking. An eel slithered down current, whipping its head from side to side, its snout pointed, its eyes blind as a mole's.

Ronny stepped down onto the creek bed and under his foot a clam spouted, throwing a liquid jet as high as his knees. The water ran in rivulets through the caking slime in which holes could now be seen, holes where one could just spy the frantic, jerky movements of the crabs. Soon they began to move, pushing in front of them their huge, single fiddler claws. The young ones came out first, active and shiny. The larger ones followed at a slower pace. Ronny took a jackknife from his pocket, although as yet he remained upright. Then, immediately in front of him an old crab, a veteran, scuttled sideways towards the bank. Its fiddler's claw, almost black with age, made the crustacean stagger and dwarfed its other limbs. Its hasty, almost obscene movements were too much for Ronny. June could hear his teeth grind as he released the catch of his knife and threw himself upon his knees in the slime. He thrust downwards and with a short, bitter movement severed the crab's claw from its body.

To June it seemed as though the crab gave out a sound of anguish, but perhaps that sound had come from her own throat. All was so terribly clear beneath the glaring sun. June felt sick with revulsion, yet another feeling, too, welled from the core of her body; a primitive force she dared not name.

The fiddler, bereft now of all its strength, of its weapon, of the very symbol of its virility, appeared to shrivel. Its remaining claws, frail as those of a spider, could no longer balance its body. It jerked forlornly and frantically sideways; a humiliated creature in pain and without hope.

Looking at those absurd struggles, Ronny had to laugh. It knotted his throat like sobs and doubled him into the mud. June, overcoming her fear of the marsh, ran and tried to pull him from his knees. She half dragged him to the bank where they both collapsed in the undergrowth. Ronny continued to laugh and, holding up the claw which he had kept in his grasp, went into fresh paroxysms. June looked into his face.

"How could you?" she demanded, squeezing his shoulder. "How could you?" The agony of the crab suddenly took on for her an unbearable meaning; the sin of the world. Yet now she, too, found herself laughing. They clutched each other and rolled on the ground. They were convulsed and helpless. Never had anything been so funny before.

But their laughter ended very soon, cut off as abruptly and as mysteriously as it had begun. Ronny turned over and lay with flat shoulders face to the ground. June sat up and regarded him. She arranged her clothes and brushed the leaves from her hair. The feeling of guilt returned to engulf her like a wave. Ronny could not feel it, she thought. He remained untouched, lying there with the sun on his shoulders. She forced herself to look into the marsh, to observe on its caked and parching surface the struggles of the now dying crab. The crustacean had been unable to make its way back to its hole and the sun dried up the flow of its crab blood.

Finally, after what seemed hours, it tipped over onto its back. The joints of its shell were visible on its underside; intricate and made by God. Ronny now sat up also. Dragging back the hair from his face, he turned to her naturally and asked in an eager voice: "Did you see me? Did you see how I fixed that horrible old crab? Where's the claw? I'll give it to you as a trophy." He searched around for it but it was lost amongst the grass and weeds. Then Ronny, too, caught sight of the fiddler lying on its back in the mud, its remaining claws still feebly stirring. His expression changed and he looked uncertainly at June. He jumped to his feet and ran to where Gambol was grazing.

"I thought you were lost," he said, putting his hand on the firm neck and locking his fingers in Gambol's mane. The horse lifted his eyes for an instant before he resumed his grazing and looked out onto the drying mud of the swamp. Ronny turned away and retraced his steps with a swagger. "I think I'll just dig a little grave," he said loudly to the air. "After all, that crab died honourably in battle."

"Not much battle really," observed June.

Ronny gave her a nervous smile. "It's all the fault of James Stevens," he said. He stepped down again into the marsh, sinking to his calf and fearful now of the other fiddlers who infested the mud and of the strange bugs, swift as lightning, that darted across the slime. With a shudder he picked up his victim, now motionless and rotting already beneath the sun. He made his way to the bank and then with his knife dug a little hollow in the ground beneath a tree. He put the remains in it, covered them and stamped once or twice on the spot. As a last touch he stuck his knife, blade in the ground, beside it.

"There," he said, "that will be his gravestone. The handle is ivory so he will have a monument from the tusk of an elephant. A gravestone from Africa, or India maybe, for this poor crab."

'What am I to think of Ronny now?' wondered June.

"I shan't pray," continued Ronny, "because I don't think crabs need it." He got up. The mud on him had dried green. It had smeared onto his shorts and his cotton pull-over. His hands and face were covered with it and it stank.

"You better rinse yourself at the spring," suggested June, leading the way through the woods.

Ronny followed without a word and, crouching near the water, dipped his arms in its small, fresh flow. June plucked a stem of silver-weed and trailed it in the stream. The forest sounds closed about them but they could still hear the seagulls mewing over the bay.

When Ronny was quite clean he rose and, with a wistful movement, came near June and leaned against her.

CHAPTER 6

OLD MRS. GREY SAT OUT ON THE PORCH, knitting. As evening came on, the fireflies began to flash around her and, above, the first star of evening stared down surrounded by the fathomless azure of the sky. Mrs. Grey's fingers slackened. She recalled how as a girl she had wished upon that star—Star light, star bright—Wishing gave such a lift to the heart. One believed at each moment of wishing that one's desire would come to pass. How many desires she had had! How many wishes! And now they were done.

Mrs. Grey moved a little in her rocking chair so that it swayed gently. She was dressed all in white; a white silk dress with long sleeves, and white stockings and shoes. Her shoes had old-fashioned heels, thin as a man's finger and curved in under her foot. They were pointed and small and she had worn them for years. Mrs. Grey, even in old age and with her cane, walked so haughtily that she never wore out a pair of shoes. The only untidy thing about her was her hair; of a harsh, grey colour which refused to turn white, it grew in wispy strands which escaped from her bun. She was forever raising a hand to tuck it in place.

'I wonder,' she thought, looking up once again at the evening star, 'if I would go through it all a second time were I given the chance.' Yet Mrs. Grey's life had been a happy and successful one. She had been wealthy and loved, the mother of sons, the friend of great men. Since the death of her husband, however, a sort of refining process had begun. She had gradually shed, so to speak, the fat of life from her soul. Despite the petty habits and quirks of age she was gazing now austerely in the direction of God.

Her son John would sometimes tell his wife: "It's really so nice for Mother to have us here in vacation time. How lonely she must be when we're away." But it was only the kind of thing people say to convince themselves, to make themselves believe they are wanted and necessary. Mrs. Grey was quite happy to be alone.

Now behind her the lower windows of the house were turned to a pale gold—Catherine, lighting the lamps. It would be supper time soon. Then Mrs. Grey saw June coming slowly through the dusk.

'She might be me long ago,' thought the old woman, and she wondered if June had yet noticed that the stars were for wishing and whether her breast were yet troubled by the wars of sensuality and soul.

June's voice had a strained note as she greeted her grandmother. "Am I late?" she asked.

"Not yet, my dear," said Mrs. Grey. "Come and hold my wool for me, if you please."

June obediently pulled up a chair and held out her arms. Winding steadily, Mrs. Grey said: "Mr. Stevens was here today and arranged for you to have your first lesson tomorrow."

"Do you like him, Grandmother?" asked June.

"He seemed a perfectly adequate young man," said Mrs. Grey, "although 'like' is a strong word."

"I mean did you think I would like him?"

"You must know," replied Mrs. Grey, "since you have met him."

"Did he say that?" June was not sure why she pursued the conversation.

"Yes, he did," Mrs. Grey said, and then after a pause went on: "I think it is nice that you have found a companion near your own age and within walking distance."

"Well, Ronny's not really near my age," said June as though she were giving the devil his due. "He's only eleven and I'm fifteen." As she said this June realized that her birthday had come and gone without mention. Suddenly her arms felt heavy inside their woolen chain. The darkness made her and her grandmother pale blurs to one another and the wool loosened and sped away in the night. It twined from her wrists like the magic skeins of old which led through labyrinths—as though her grandmother could, if she wished, teach her to avoid the central monster.

Catherine came and called them to eat.

The following morning at ten James Stevens was at the door. He wore a tweed jacket from which his thin, hairy wrists protruded, and grey flannels. He carried books in a dark green felt bag of which he was very proud, for it meant he had been to Harvard University. Actually he had only taken a summer course there.

During the lesson Stevens sat with his pupil at a big polished desk beside the library window. From there they could look out at the moss-covered lawns and into the forest.

June found the lesson tedious. She was in any case only a very moderate scholar. In her disorganized brain facts, fantasies, poetry and dreams were thrown pell-mell to sort themselves out as best they could. Stevens recognized at once that in some ways she was as advanced as he. In other circumstances it might have amused him to try to set in order the curious mixture of her knowledge. Her mind was supple and fresh, held at bay by her sickness and excited by long, feverish hours of reading. But she was at an age which he disliked in girls and he had always tried to avoid them in this stage of development. From his point of view they were ridiculous, almost nauseating. Nothing could be worse, he told himself, than a raw female who giggled and blushed and had spots on her face. Now as he sat beside June he thought she gave out a musky odor. It was not really true perhaps, but the idea of her girlish body, ill-cared for as a child's, unperfumed and unrecognized, made him almost unable to face her way.

When the clock struck twelve, June stood up with open relief. Stevens rose. "Well that's all for today," he said, and continued with a touch of malice: "I suppose it's near your lunch time, and as for me I've been asked to lunch with your friend Ronny, so I must hurry."

June was puzzled at the tone of his voice, but a feminine instinct made her answer: "Oh, Grandmother never eats this early!" Having indicated thus Stevens' lack of worldly hours, she went on: "Besides, I told Ronny I'd be down for a swim." She lifted her head defiantly and her face, too dramatic and positive for her age, jarred his nerves.

"You're not very good for him, you know," he said.

"Is he good for me?" asked June, her voice troubled with anger, surprise and shyness.

"You know that's not the point," retorted Stevens in the manner of a person really saying: 'Who cares about you!' He went on to explain with conscious patience: "Ronny is very high-strung. He is an extremely sensitive child and I want him to have every chance."

"I'm sensitive too, Mr. Stevens," said June in a dreamy voice, looking out at the woods as though at a far-off land. 'Now why did I say that?' she wondered. 'What is all this talk about?' At once her inner brain muttered a few stubborn words of reply that she could not quite catch.

'How ugly she is!' reflected Stevens, comforting himself with the disproportion of her head. Then he looked down at her hand which was doubled up on the desk. It was square, almost gnarled in places, and the knuckles were badly in need of scrubbing. Yet this unfeminine fist melted upwards softly and the skin above her elbow gleamed like thick brown satin as it disappeared into her sleeve. He was brought to a standstill by these contradictions and said with a faint smile: "Well, since you and I are bound in the same direction we might as well go together in my car."

June, surprised into being grateful, thanked him awkwardly. Looking back from the car window, she could see the head and shoulders of her grandmother, sitting in her study, writing. June waved but Mrs. Grey did not look up. She was answering letters no doubt, and June pictured the receivers:

old men with white beards, exchanging in envelopes the sum of their life's thoughts. Could that be better, she wondered, than swimming in the ocean? The beach had to be reached by a long, rickety and even dangerous bridge over the marsh. It was a sort of plank path held up by wooden supports sunk into the mud. Some of these had settled further than the rest, so that the bridge went up and down as though over hillocks. Many of the planks were rotted and both on them and on the broken railing could be seen the curious scrolls made by termites. Since the death of old Mr. Grey, before June's birth, no one had ever bothered to repair this bridge, but June, who was walking ahead, knew its every pitfall without looking down. Her feet sought out the firm crossboards automatically and she touched the railing in quick, light snatches lest the splinters run into her palms. A sensation high upon her back let her know that Stevens was nervous, afraid of falling into the marsh ten feet below. By jumping as she walked, June made the whole structure quiver.

There was a bath hut beyond, on the sand ridge, and from the marsh this hut looked terribly forlorn. Unpainted and blackened by the elements, it leaned sideways as though it longed to lie down and rest. A sort of lawn grew around it; reed grass that sprouted coarsely from the sand and was sharp as a knife. One had only to touch it to be wounded. Above, the seagulls mewed constantly, hovering over the tide lines in search of stranded sea creatures.

Ronny was already there when they arrived. He was astonished to see Stevens and would not speak to June.

"I thought I would join you for a swim," said the tutor, "since I am coming to lunch afterwards."

"Are you?" asked Ronny with polite interest, and then: "Is she coming too?"

"Now Ronny, you know, this won't do," said Stevens. "You must recall asking me yesterday afternoon when we had our lesson." This was only true in reverse so he hurried on: "We discussed it with Mary later. June, I presume, is lunching with her grandmother."

Ronny said nothing further and June, going into the hut, changed hastily into her bathing suit. When she came out Stevens entered in turn and found an old pair of trunks belonging to June's father. Ronny, who was already undressed, looked at June reproachfully and walked ahead of her to the water's edge.

"Well it wasn't my fault," said June. "He just came."

Ronny, judging from his back, seemed to accept this explanation and they waded out into the water together. Turning out of depth, they saw Stevens hobbling painfully over the stony sand. As he drew nearer they noticed to their delight that the hair on his chest, although sparse, was as long and wavy as feathers. It made up for everything.

CHAPTER 7

JUNE AND RONNY WERE HARDLY AWARE of the village that lay not five miles away because they could not see Star Harbour from their windows or from the beach. It was tucked in the curve of the peninsula and hidden by hills. Star Harbour had once been a thriving whaling town, but now its main industry was oysters, and many of its inhabitants commuted to bigger towns or even to New York. Aside from its port, it had like any other town its schools and its clubs, its residential section, its churches and its slums.

James Stevens had been born and raised in Star Harbour. He came from a good family, as measured by local standards, and although his father had died when he was young, his mother had given him a careful education. It was the kind of upbringing some mothers give to a son when they have lost or been disappointed in their husbands; the son must repair for them their lack. They sacrifice for him, work and worry on his account, and fret away the remains of their youth. And for each thing they do or renounce doing, they demand a counterweight from that young life.

Stevens sometimes reflected that he had obeyed his mother's every wish so far: school, college, his teacher's degree, even Harvard—almost. Each achievement had seemed at the time worthy of effort. Only now that they were accomplished, he sometimes had a flat taste in his mouth. Perhaps, had Mrs. Stevens still been alive, she would have found some further hurdle for him to leap. It was a last example of her will power that had placed him as master in the renowned St. John's after four years in an inferior and smaller school. Then she had died and he had come home to an empty house to wind up her affairs during his long vacation. It was Stevens' house now, standing a little away from the road, fringed modestly with trees and flowering shrubs. Inside it Stevens' taste had gradually supplanted that of his father, just as Stevens himself had supplanted his sire in his mother's heart. Nonetheless, a few relics remained to clash with the subdued walls and the uncluttered rooms.

Stevens had very little in common with Star Harbour because his whole life to date had been one of straining to get ahead of his environment. As a child, his friendship with most of the other children had been discouraged and those chosen few with whom he had been urged to play had not responded. They had had other pursuits: horseback riding, for instance, or sailing on the sound. In any event, he would have been lonely. His slender blondness, called aristocratic by his mother, was thought merely scrawniness by his fellows, and the faint accent with which his mother took such pains was ridiculed, even imitated, behind his back. None of these things had bothered him when his mother was alive. On the contrary it had made them feel superior and closer to one another than ever. He felt at her death as a plant must feel whose main, great, strong root has been cut away.

Yet the villagers, although they had no particular understanding or sympathy with him, tried to be kind to Stevens and respected his loss. The chance was held out to him of joining this or that committee and of making himself a part of them. His next door neighbour, in particular, had taken pains to solace him, orphaned as he now was. Lucy Philmore ran the village gift shop and had been, Stevens knew, very good to his mother during her last illness. It was Lucy, in fact, who had arisen from her bed one night to close his mother's eyes, and Stevens was grateful to her although at times her plain, thirty-year-old face depressed him.

It was due to Lucy that Stevens had accepted the Junior Scout outing class once a week. Of course he had been a scout master before; it had been almost compulsory in the teachers' college to which he had gone. Since completing his education, however, Stevens had preferred to spend the summer following courses or taking his mother on trips. Now he brushed up on his wood lore, breaking his nails on complicated knots and even succeeding in lighting a fire without a match. After his first outing Stevens had come home almost elated because it had gone so well and the children had seemed to like him. Tutoring jobs, too, helped fill in his time, although he never would have taken on June Grey if it had not been for his mother.

Even after her death he had been able to hear his mother's even, slightly flat voice telling him that it was impossible to refuse a service to old Mrs. Grey. Later Stevens did not know whether or not to regret taking this ghostly advice. After only a fortnight of their acquaintance he found his two pupils on the peninsula, or Grey's Neck as it was commonly called, occupying a strange place in his mind. The fact that he must think of them jointly exasperated him in particular. He became possessed by a desire to separate these two creatures, to sever them permanently and, having always considered himself aloof, even high-souled, he was humiliated by the pettiness of his actions. Yet June was like a seasoning without which his hours with Ronny would have had less taste, a constant irritant that excited his temper.

Being alone and introspective, Stevens had asked himself at once the meaning of his emotions and the answer was plain: duty. Mrs. Grey, acting indirectly for Mrs. Villars, had given him to understand that the boy was nervous, high-strung and overstrained. Surely there was nothing worse for a child in this condition than the company of an older girl, herself unhealthy and torn already by the struggles of puberty. June stimulated Ronny's imagination, Stevens told himself angrily, overpowered the boy with her difference in age and sex. One might almost say that she possessed him. Finally Stevens decided to be active in the matter. He told Ronny to come to his next scout meeting, ordered him as master to pupil. He planned to pick Ronny up by car early in the afternoon.

It started to rain on the morning of the meeting—those big, warm drops that fall in summer and drain the air or breath. From every street and alley in Star Harbour the water flowed downwards towards the docks. The trees drooped and on the ground the slugs came out to bloat their bodies with moisture. In bad weather such as this the scouts met in an empty gym which served at night as a sort of men's club. Here the scouts would spend the afternoon playing games, practicing their lore, and trying to look easy in their uniforms.

Stevens drove through the boathouse gate a little before three. Jeremy let him in, standing quietly in the rain while the car passed. Stevens saluted Jeremy with his hand, but the caretaker made no response. This was the sort of thing that happened to Stevens sometimes, and so now he tried to pretend that he had merely been smoothing his hair with his palm. He stopped in front of the house and blew his horn. Ronny emerged at once, clad in tight shorts which almost cut his upper thigh and with a woman's red silk scarf around his neck.

"Do I look like a scout?" he demanded in his shrill voice. "Do I?"

Something tense in his expression made Stevens say quickly as he opened the door beside him: "Don't worry, no one will care. You'll have fun, wait and see if you don't."

"I've had these shorts for three years," said Ronny. "They used to come all the way to my knees."

"They look fine." It made Stevens happy to be reassuring Ronny, to be handling him at last in a real, authoritative way.

Ronny leaned forward to wave to Jeremy at the gate. "Goodbye, Jeremy. So long." After a moment the boy spoke again without taking his eyes from the window: "Say, Mr. Stevens, we have to go to the Greys and get June."

"June!" exclaimed Stevens. "Really Ronny, you know these scout meetings are only for boys!"

"Oh she won't come there," said Ronny. "But her grandmother has some errands she wants done or something, so June can come and then go back when I do."

Stevens could not go against Mrs. Grey and with grating nerves he drove up the hill to where June was already on the porch stoop.

Holding a broken lamp in her hand, June looked today, with her locks of hair, her shirt open at the throat, like an archangel slightly out of drawing. She came down the steps and Stevens, piercing her with his cold, grey glance, reached behind Ronny and opened the rear door for her without a word. June climbed in rather clumsily, and just as Stevens pressed the starter he saw Mrs. Grey standing inside the open front door. The schoolmaster flushed. He felt that in his curtness, the rudeness of making the young girl sit alone in back, he had given himself away. Surely Mrs. Grey had noticed and was now judging him wryly, with an austere tolerance that made him squirm.

All three of them were silent as they skirted the water and drove off the peninsula. Presently, along the road's edge, the houses gathered nearer one another and turned the highway into Main Street. Stevens had meant to point out his house to Ronny as they passed it. Now with the girl in the car this pleasure was denied him. Also he found as he flicked his eyes sideways that the contours of his home displeased him. Under the rain it looked fussy and dark. He was ashamed, too, of the stones bordering the short drive. He had whitewashed them a few days ago. Now he hoped the rain would soon cleanse them. Was he never to rid himself, he wondered irritably, of these small-town tastes? The windshield in front of him clicked back and forth as though giving a negative answer.

Presently they reached the center of Star Harbour and turned down a side street to stop in front of a dingy building. A few boys dressed in scout shorts and neckerchiefs were on their way in.

"Be back here in two hours if you want a ride home," said Stevens to June.

"Yes sir," said June, and Stevens could not tell if the 'sir' was in earnest or if there had been a hint of mockery in her tone. He was angry because despite himself the address pleased him.

"Did you hear, she called you sir!" said Ronny. "Rise, Sir Stevens, I have dubbed thee knight!" Now the boy's voice was filled with an emotion which Stevens could not define. Nudging him to make him get out of the car, Stevens felt that the boy's hand was icy cold.

'He's afraid!' thought Stevens.

Stevens was right. Ronny was afraid of the boys he was to meet. Nervousness and fear made his fingers clammy and vague cramps squeezed his bowels as he tried to picture the games they would play. They had grown worse when he had been able to compare the real scout costume to his own. He dragged himself out of the car. June was already on the sidewalk, looking at the lamp she held with one of those vague, slightly surprised expressions that young people wear when they have been given something to do for their elders. Now that she was in the village, she could not imagine why she had come or what she would do with two whole hours. The rain fell upon her head in great drops and wet her white shirt. She started forlornly up the street and Ronny, although acutely aware of her going, bade her no word of adieu. To him, her aimless walk beneath the rain, her seeming lack of destination, was a freedom to be envied. She was not forced to enter into that drab building and to meet a score of unknown monsters.

Stevens said: "Come along, old boy. You'll like them you know, and they'll like you. Besides, we're going to play touch football. I'm sure you're good at it."

Immediately the picture of two boys rose up in front of Ronny's eyes: team captains choosing sides. They cracked names out of their mouths like bullets and, as they spoke, boy after boy detached himself proudly from the mass to stand with his team. Finally only one boy was left, alone and ridiculous in childish, striped shorts and his mother's old silk scarf around his neck.

They were inside the building now and from a large double door in front of them could be heard the joyous noises of the scouts at play. There was something repulsive to Ronny about that door. Its cheap wood, cheaply varnished and marred with a thousand scratches, spoke of the monotony of groups, of clubs, of the same sex gathered together with enforced gaiety and enforced rules.

Ronny, who was advancing with Stevens' hand across his shoulder suddenly gulped, ducked, and ran out of the building as quickly as a fox. His voice floated back to the astonished scout master:

"Be back in two hours—sir."

CHAPTER 8

STAR HARBOUR'S GIFT SHOP, run by Lucy Philmore, was a hodge-podge of the useful and ornamental. One could get almost anything one wanted here: china-ware, toys, cards, lamps, even dresses. Lucy was more like a hostess than a shopkeeper as she presided with a cheerful, pleasant manner.

When June came in that afternoon, Lucy greeted her kindly. She inquired after her health and the health of her grandmother and asked how June had liked the various presents sent up from the gift shop during her illness. It was Lucy who had chosen them for friends of the Greys. June thanked her and said she had enjoyed them all. In doing so and remembering the gifts, a flavour of her sickness returned to her. For an instant she recalled how it had felt to be lying there in bed.

"Do you know," she said, "I can hardly picture being sick anymore. It's as though it was someone else."

"Yes, things change when you are growing up," agreed Lucy sympathetically. "You are really a young lady now."

'I wonder if I feel like one?' thought June as she smiled politely at Lucy. That was the trouble about not seeing other girls for such ages.

"I hear you are being tutored too," said Lucy. "By Mr. Stevens. That must be very nice for you."

"Nice!" June was intrigued at this way of putting it.

"Well, Mr. Stevens is such an intelligent and cultivated person," explained Lucy. "You must have wonderful discussions about your studies." Her voice now sounded wistful. She would have given a lot to be in June's shoes.

"Do you know him well?" asked June, who was always surprised when people knew each other.

Lucy's cheeks grew a little pink. "Not very," she replied. "That is, until lately. But we are neighbours." Envy was a bad emotion she knew, yet she could not help envying June a little. Oh to have all in front of one again, to await sincerely the changes to come, changes other than the gradual settling of middle age. Even the secret hope inside her own breast was, thought Lucy, a feeble flame. The least wind would blow it out. She looked over June's head at the rainy street and gave one of those deep breaths that are not quite sighs.

"Mr. Stevens doesn't get along with me very well," said June, "or I don't get along with him."

June herself was now gazing at the door. She was depressed by Miss Philmore's empty cordiality. It emphasized a gulf she had lately begun to notice, an untraversable space between human beings. "Oh," she exclaimed suddenly, "there's Ronny!" Without a word more she hurried out of the shop.

Ronny was walking along purposefully, his rope-soled shoes leaving straight prints behind him on the wet sidewalk. His hands thrust into the pockets of his shorts made them tighter than ever around his sinewy thighs.

"Ronny!" cried June, catching up with him. "Why aren't you at the scout meeting?"

"I decided not to go," said Ronny, putting down his head to avoid her eye.

"What did James Stevens say?"

Ronny did not answer her. Instead he asked: "Do you know where I'm going now?" He did not wait but answered himself: "I'm going to the docks." He glanced at her doubtfully. "I suppose you could come," he said, "but it's not really for girls, not even grown-up girls."

"How do you know?" asked June, smiling down at his dark, wet, unruly head which came up to her shoulder.

"I just know," he replied shrugging. "I sometimes just know things that nobody told me." He slowed down a bit and turned towards her eagerly. "That's why," he said, making an effort to explain, "I often wonder—I mean about knights and all and Gambol and Shalimar. I couldn't be making it all up, could I?"

The rain was falling hard now and had gradually lost its warmth but Ronny was oblivious to it. The drops lay for a moment unbroken on his upturned face and then ran down his cheeks and neck. They gave his skin a luster and tangled the hair across his brow. He moved his body impatiently. The real meaning had not come. It was still inside him. He tried it from another angle. "If I were a knight I couldn't grow up," he said, "could I? Not when you really think about it, but if I were to be a sailor, for instance, I could."

"Yes," said June, "although of course there's no comparison. A knight is more glorious."

"That's just what you would say," Ronny took her hand. "No one else but you. James Stevens would call it unhealthy, wouldn't he?" Ronny was silent a moment and then exclaimed: "Shalimar is more glorious than all the scouts. I know he is. I know, I know."

They were both soaked to the skin by now as they walked down the sloping street which led to the harbour. Here the aspect of the town changed. There were warehouses, in between which were rows of broken down little shacks like teeth in a beggar's mouth. These were the slums of Star Harbour and inhabited mostly by Negroes. Dark faces looked out at them from the darker doorways and sometimes a snatch of strangely rhythmed song came to their ears.

Once an old woman staggered drunkenly in their path. Her face was so wrinkled and discoloured that it was impossible to tell her race. She stopped as they approached and with a grimace at Ronny pulled open the ragged, torn top of her blouse. One of her breasts leapt out at them like an animal; perfectly formed, pointed and white as milk. Her eyes leered into Ronny's, and in their wake her laughter was as harsh as weeping.

Ahead the dock stretched out over the water. Here fishing boats were being unloaded by men in thigh-length boots, while other men were shoveling oyster-shells into a truck from a huge, gleaming pile. Even in the rain a constant, important activity went on. It was the open gate to all the world. June and Ronny, standing side by side on the dock, felt a free salt breath enter their lungs and quicken their blood. The vast, unnamed possibilities of life made them smile. They were not afraid of destiny. Destiny was this rain-swept sea, these boats coming and going, and the far-off, nostalgic horizon.

There was a hiss. June felt a blow across her arm and shoulder, while at the same time an angry voice cried: "Look out there!" She had been struck by a painter thrown up to the dock from a boat, and she sprang back, more embarrassed than smarting.

"Don't you damn kids know enough to get out of the rain?" It was the same voice speaking, a voice with a faintly mid-European accent, which, despite the words, was soft with good humour. A swarthy man of middle age appeared over the side of the dock, his feet still on the ladder. He had an ugly, thick-featured face on which protruded several moles and he held his head far over on his right shoulder. His hands, grasping the top rung of the ladder, were crisscrossed by white scars and the fingers were as thick as sausages.

"Did she get you?" he asked June, who was rubbing her shoulder.

"Just a little," said June, but she was trembling.

"Standing around in this weather!" said the man. "No wonder you've got the chill."

"It's just her old fever," said Ronny, speaking for the first time. At his pure, high soprano the man looked at him as though cocking his head humourously. But of course it was tilted that way permanently.

"I don't know where you came from," he said, "but right now you're going with me. I'm Eddie, see?" There was something about Eddie despite his hideousness that made him disarming, even childlike, although June was of an age to find personal beauty very important. Now he led the way and they followed meekly. Behind them came a thin little man who shuffled rather than walked. It was to him the rope had been thrown. Skirting the water's edge with its hotel, its dance hall and its bars, they arrived at a grimy food shop called Snacks.

"Hey Ma," called Eddie, "you got customers!"

Ma, who was somewhere in back, came out, a thin, flat-chested woman with a nonchalant manner and curl papers in her hair.

"Give us four coffees," said Eddie.

They sat down in a grimy booth, the little man and Eddie on one side, June and Ronny on the other.

"Is she really your mother?" asked Ronny when the woman had served them and gone out of the room again.

"No of course not!" Eddie was shocked. The little man laughed. Eddie turned and looked towards the back of the shop as though its proprietress had given him an insult. "My mother was a beauty."

"Everyone's was," said the little man.

"Well you did call her Ma." Ronny spoke reasonably.

The little man laughed again and this time they all saw that he had no teeth. "That's just so as not to call her something worse."

Eddie turned to him. "Come on, Flo!" He winked at the others and explained: "Ma's coffee needs a little help."

Flo obediently drew a flask out of his hip pocket and poured liberal quantities in his and Eddie's coffee. He looked doubtfully across the table.

"Go on," said Eddie. "It's medicine, ain't it? She's caught a cold." Flo poured some of the liquor in the other two cups.

"Well, here's to you." Eddie lifted his cup and everyone followed him as though mesmerized by his soft, tenor voice whose accent was like a dim memory. The lukewarm liquid seemed to make a path in June's body and along that path all chill and trembling stopped. Eddie reached out and patted her on the arm. "There," he said, "you just drink that up." His tough, thick hand stretched from his sleeve so that one could see on the inside of his wrist a blue and red Christ on a cross, and above that, the four card symbols: spade, heart, club, and diamond.

"You're tattooed," said Ronny, almost with awe.

"Sure. I got many more,' said Eddie, and immediately unbuttoned his shirt to display a chest covered with designs. A full-rigged ship showed among his black hairs as though sailing through a forest, while beneath it a woman turned her profile with a padlock on her lips. Still lower a many-petaled rose wound its stem around his navel. These were Eddie's diary; the records of his sentiments and misdeeds, pricked out upon his skin with India ink. Encouraged by Ronny's admiring attention, Eddie now removed his shirt altogether.

Flo said: "I used to be a real tattoo artist on the other side. Here they got machines."

Eddie rippled his muscles; a woman on his arm danced with her hips and a butterfly flew. His thick, uneven lips, scorched by the salt wind, smiled. His face softened. "You're nice kids," he remarked.

"She's not a kid," said Ronny, pointing at June.

"All women are kids in America," stated Flo.

Eddie looked hastily at June. "Don't get rough, Flo," he said.

But June was not listening. She had been profoundly and secretly thrilled by the tattooing on Eddie's body. The images transferred themselves from his skin to stamp her mind. The liquor liberated her fancy. Her eyes gleamed and the drops of rain that fell from her hair were like pure round pearls on her skin. Beside her she felt the palpitating little body of Ronny with his bare thigh stirring against her leg. She turned to him suddenly: "Why don't you try, Ronny? I dare you!"

Ronny leaped to his feet, upsetting the remains of his coffee. A wave of emotion contracted the muscles of his cheeks. He looked at June with a sort of passion. "It's needles in the skin!" he said in his shrill voice.

"Yes," agreed June.

Ronny leaned across and plucked Flo's sleeve. "Can you do it, Mr. Flo?"

Flo smiled. It was as though he had been leading up to this all along, pulling at their nerves, guiding their reactions. "Sure I can. I'm an artist like I said."

Eddie smiled too. He had taken several raw swigs from Flo's flask which by now was cradled in his lap. "You're a funny kid," he said, not to Ronny but to June. "You've got all the makings, haven't you?" His eyes, reddened by sun and wind, concentrated themselves. June did not want to meet them, but her own vision was a little hazy so that she could not quite control its direction. 'He's ugly,' she thought as one repeats a charm or a prayer.

For a moment all four of them were silent and during the pause they realized that they were no longer the only people in the shop. Two clam-diggers in hip boots and sou'-westers were drinking coffee in another booth and at the counter some girls were ordering sundaes. June, hearing their noisy chatter, stared at them curiously. They were about her own age with brilliant, painted lips and permanent waves which split the ends of their hair. With every move they aimed uncertain weapons at the men in the room. Feeling June's eyes, they turned with one accord and stared back. Then, with derisive giggles, they wheeled around again to their sundaes.

June was very embarrassed. "Well," she said in a quarrelsome manner to Ronny, "are you or aren't you?"

"I am," said Ronny. He had grown quite still. All the vibrations of his body were suspended. "Mr. Flo is going to tattoo me," he continued slowly and almost with languor, "aren't you, Mr. Flo?"

"Sure," agreed Flo. "We have to go next door to the barber's, that's all. I got my needles there."

CHAPTER 9

THE AFTERNOON OF THE SCOUT MEETING decided Stevens to write to Ronny's mother.

"Dear Mrs. Villars:" he wrote.

"I am addressing you in some perplexity and after much hesitation. Please come and see your son.

That is as near the point as I can get. He is not ill. I simply feel he needs you."

Here Stevens got stuck. How to continue? He tried to conjure up a picture of Mrs. Villars whom he had, after all, never met, but an image of his own mother, faded yet determined, rose in its stead. Ronny's mother could in no way resemble it. He gathered she was rather young. That she was smart he was certain, perhaps racy. Did she love her son, that she had abandoned him in that mouldering boathouse? His own mother would never have done so.

Then, like one of those recollections which are merged with dreams, a past wish came back to Stevens; the wish to be free of his mother for a week. Dream or reality, he had been a boy then. Now he was a man and free of her forever. He sighed and a sense of oppression made his forehead ache. All the resolution which had made him write was gone. To stimulate himself he re-pictured Ronny as he had been that afternoon; Ronny, pale and sodden beneath the rain, clutching his breast as though his heart were ill, as though it would leap out of his bosom if he did not hold it in. The boy's hair had been streaming over his brow like dark water, and his teeth set visibly between his lips. He and June had both come walking down Main Street after Stevens had searched everywhere and when he was on the point of calling Mrs. Grey about their disappearance.

And how furtive June had looked! Her face had been exposed, almost thrust out; offered like a mask to hide those cruel, girl's thoughts behind it. Stevens had struggled to keep down the rage that shook him. He had not asked where they had been and it was only after dropping June on the hill that he had said to Ronny, trying to sound casual:

"Too bad you didn't come to the meeting. It was lots of fun."

Against the window of the car Ronny's profile was a pure, unbroken line. He barely moved his lips in answer. "I had fun too," he said.

Once again Stevens took up his pen. "There is really nothing more that I can say in a letter except that I hope you will come soon and that you will communicate with me if and when you do."

He examined his page. The thick paper from Lucy Philmore's gift shop looked impressive, his script impersonal and correct. 'Should I have typed it?' wondered the tutor. A business letter should be typed of course, but was this a business letter? Was it not rather an appeal, a cry for help? He thought of the scout meeting. Without Ronny it had fallen completely flat. He had been unable to keep the children interested because he had been on pins and needles. The two hours had seemed like two years. Later Stevens told himself that his feelings had been those of pure anxiety. He was responsible after all for the welfare of his charges. Yet at the same time a reasonable voice had demanded: "Why?" Surely in this country town children might come and go through the streets alone. What was it then?

As soon as the meeting ended, Stevens had gone out into the street where some feverish thought had led his steps to the gift shop. Once there, however, he hardly knew how to begin. Lucy's eyes had lighted and she had made him welcome with the special hospitality that was her asset.

"James! What a day to be out!" Had it been anyone else she would have added: "Lucky for me!"

Stevens had taken the hand she offered in a lifeless grasp. To his horror he realized that he was still holding it as he stammered: "I've come for some writing paper."

His stammer, the distressed inflection of his voice and his hand holding hers, filled Lucy with hope. Her pleasant, rather long face changed in expression and she said with a coy undertone: "Now James, it's hardly nice of you just to come here when you want to buy something."

Stevens by now had dropped the hand and tried to pull himself together. "Well, you know, Lucy, I'm not very amusing yet as company." Even as he said the words, Stevens had been disgusted with himself. 'What an idiot I am,' he thought. 'What a fool to play up to her!'

"Now that's not at all the right attitude, James," Lucy had replied, her eyes filling with moisture. "You may not know it but count myself as a friend—and not just a fair weather friend."

Wearied to the depths of his soul and unable to think of a reply, Stevens had bowed in acknowledgment.

For a moment Lucy had looked down on his fair, thin hair through which his scalp shone. How unlike other men in Star Harbour he was. How good-mannered and courteous. Perhaps after all she had not kept herself pure in vain.

For his part Stevens had, in bowing, looked down briefly on her straight, flat figure, respectably girdled and stockinged.

"By the way, James, I saw one of your pupils this afternoon—June Grey. She's growing into such a nice girl."

His pulse had leapt. Lucy continued mildly: "Yes, and she ran right out in the rain, after a little boy. Is he your pupil too? The one who lives in that house by the water? She was calling him Ronny."

"Yes," he had said automatically. Lucy had given him his answer. They were together. Perhaps they had even arranged it beforehand. Stevens had purchased his writing paper hurriedly and hardly recalled how he had finally quitted the gift shop to walk dejectedly beneath the rain.

Still thinking of that afternoon, he folded his letter and rose from his chair. It was not raining today, but a burning mist obscured the sun. He put the letter in an envelope and then weighed it thoughtfully in his hand. He did not have the address of Mrs. Villars and wondered how best he might obtain it. Lunchtime was over, and Stevens could hear from the back of the house a sound of dishes clinking. For an instant it was as if his mother were back there clearing up, but it was only Mrs. Russell who came for three hours every day. The difference struck him. 'Did I really love her so terribly much?' he wondered for the first time. As a revelation it came to him that he had never been passionately attached. Unlike some mother's boys, he had found his mother neither pretty nor seductive. He had never had a moment's jealousy on her account. It was only that their pale eyes, his and hers, looking into each others, could give a meaning to the world.

Stevens shrugged and left the house. The heat, as he drove towards the peninsula, lay at the side of the road like a parched beast. The shimmer of its breath burnt the grass. The trees were a dark, coarse green powdered over with dust, and the water as he skirted the bay looked leaden and unrefreshed. Finally he turned into the bumpy lane that ran through the woods to the boathouse. Now and then his tires spun on the dry sand which was blown into the ruts by the east winds. There was something desolate and still about these sandy woods.

Ronny, along with Jeremy and June, was in the stable grooming his horse. His bare feet made a squashing sound in the wet straw of Gambol's stall which smelled of ammonia and dung. He was curry-combing the animal's flank in a circular movement and then knocking the currycomb against the wall to make the dirt fall out. June sat on a pile of hay a little way off. She was wearing shorts which were unbecoming to her round, rather full thighs, and because of the heat had pinned her hair to the back of her head. This way of dressing it brought out the faulty proportions of her head, the small ears and skull masked by the larger face, with its straight, stern features and thick throat. As for Jeremy, he was repairing the lawn mower, which he used so seldom that it was covered with rust.

Stevens stood for a moment in the stable door, where Jeremy saw him although he made no sign. Finally Stevens walked forward.

"Good afternoon," he said to Jeremy. "I wonder if you could give me Mrs. Villars' address. I wish to write to her."

Jeremy looked up. "You'll be wanting to complain, I suppose," he said pleasantly but without jocularity.

Stevens stared at him coldly. "And I suppose that does not concern you?"

"How do you know he's going to complain?" asked Ronny, who had stopped work and was leaning against Gambol's side.

"Yes, how do you know, Jeremy?" echoed June boldly.

"June," said Stevens, "try not to imitate children. It is natural for Ronny to speak like that. In you it is neither amusing or cute."

June turned scarlet and for some reason was immediately conscious of her legs. The worst of it was that Stevens was right; she had been imitating Ronny. As yet there were no women's weapons which she could handle, and the old childish ones now seemed to be failing her. To her surprise Jeremy came to her defense.

"Well now, sir," he said putting down his tools, "I don't really see why you're making such a point of Miss June's being older than Ronny here. If we made such a fuss over a few years as that, none of us could speak to one another." He had scored his point, but now with his particular turn of thought could not help adding: Anyway I guess in a hundred years we'll all be saying pretty much the same things."

"You mean we'll all be ghosts?" shrilled Ronny.

Jeremy did not answer him, only gave him a quiet look whose meaning was concealed by his round cheeks and the bright health of his eyes.

Stevens, who had tightened his lips at Jeremy's rebuke, now relaxed them and seemed to take a new tack. Sitting down carefully on the slope of an old wagon tree, he smiled. His smile was unexpectedly youthful and charming, as the smiles of blond men sometimes are. He had nice teeth and a youthful, pink lining to his lips and gums. His mouth lost its faint wrinkles and his eyes grew warmer as they were drawn up by his grimace. "Well," he said, "now that we've had misunderstandings all around, we might just as well cool off."

"Go swimming you mean?" asked Ronny with the forced expression of one who is making a joke. He looked at June and they both giggled.

Stevens turned to Jeremy. "They are both laughing," he said magnanimously, "at the hair on my chest."

"I guess Miss June will get over minding that pretty soon," said Jeremy. Stevens looked shocked but suppressed it at once.

"I won't ever have hairs on my chest," said Ronny, "only a-"

"Only a what?" asked Stevens curiously.

"Only a heart."

"That would be in, not on," said Stevens mechanically.

"On, not in," said June.

"On and in, both, why not?" said Jeremy, and Ronny wondered if he knew. The other day, the day after, when his skin had been all sore and swollen he had taken off his shirt in the stable. Perhaps Jeremy had seen. He looked at Jeremy, but the caretaker had risen and, with his lawn mower now repaired, was leaving them.

"Wait a minute, Jeremy," called Stevens, "you have not yet given me Mrs. Villars' address."

"I can't seem to remember it," said Jeremy, giving Stevens a straight, full, slow glance. He continued on his way out.

Stevens controlled himself carefully. He stood up. "Perhaps your wife would know. I'll go and ask her."

Jeremy turned around again. Starting with the feet, his eyes travelled upwards bit by bit until they reached the lapels of Stevens' jacket. There they stopped and lost interest. "I don't know how it is where you come from, sir, but in my family the man rules the roost."

"You mean you refuse to give it to me?" demanded Stevens, who had grown rather pale.

"If you like," replied Jeremy quietly and almost to himself. He shrugged his shoulders as though wondering at his own complexity and went away. The lawn mower made a clicking sound as it wheeled in front of him on the stable floor, like a fussy conversation, a chattering, useless résumé of all that had passed.

CHAPTER 10

RONNY AWAKENED SUDDENLY from a long dream. The moonlight lay across the floor of his room but did not quite reach the bed.

"Nor the moon by night." The phrase came mysteriously into his mind. Where had he heard it? Why did it have for him now this submerged and rhythmic meaning, like a murmur of the blood in his veins? He tried to recall his dream but only a tangled and unreal impression remained. He rose and went to the window, drawn by those white rays. The moon was not at full; on the contrary, it was wasted as though by a disease. "Nor the moon by night." Again the words came into his mind. Then he recalled that they were part of a Bible verse which he had been forced to learn at school. Something about the sun not burning thee by day nor the moon by night.

Yet the moon was burning him as he stood in its rays; scorching the heart tattooed upon his breast. In the moonlight it stood out plainly: a blue mark, a valentine printed on him by Flo. He tried to read the letters underneath it, but bending made the skin wrinkle and they were lost. Besides, a slight scab still covered them. Never mind. They were easy to remember: JUNE. Flo had wanted to put an arrow through the heart as well, but Ronny had not let him.

Although the tattooing had really hurt more the second day, the making of it had been uncomfortable too. They had gone to the back of the barber shop in a space enclosed by a curtain. Here delicate operations were performed, such as hair dyeing or an occasional permanent wave—things that men like to have done in private. Sometimes Flo did a tattoo job here as well, although most people who wanted such ornaments went to New York and had them done electrically. Flo traced the drawing on a paper with soft charcoal and then pressed the paper on the boy's skin. When he took it off the drawing remained. Then he set to work with five fine needles wedged into a cork so as to keep them together. He moistened the needles first with his tongue and afterwards dipped them in his special Chinese ink. Then he inserted them obliquely into the skin along the drawing.

Ronny had been surprised not to feel more real pain. Flo, in fact, was the more nervous of the two. He was sweating and breathing hard as he traced the heart. Flo loved working on this tight, fine-grained young skin and did not want to have a failure.

"Just over my own heart, Mr. Flo," Ronny had begged, "a real heart just over my own." He himself could not say why he wanted this. Surely he had had a reason once, long ago, five minutes ago, but now he had forgotten what it was. Why not, as Eddie suggested, a rose for luck or a ship for hope? No, it must be a heart and over his own, with June's name underneath it.

During this time June had seemed to lose all interest in the proceeding and had gone to stand at the door of the barber shop, gazing out at the sodden dock. Ronny could not know that she was fighting nausea. Eddie for his part was covered with lather, being shaved in the front room by a round, good-natured barber.

When Flo had completed his work, Eddie and June came to take a look. Eddie was complimentary. "That's a fine piece of work," he said. "It's got no frills, but it's got class."

June gave an unnatural laugh—a 'ladies' laugh,' Ronny thought resentfully—and it was not until they had been on their way back through the streets that they had recovered their intimacy. They were brought together then by their common secret and the fact that they were late for Stevens.

Now Ronny wondered what time of night it was. One should be able to tell by the stars, or by the position of the wasting moon. Sailors could. But Ronny was ignorant of their laws. He felt for his clothes in the darkness and did not dare turn on a light for fear Mary should look out her window and see it. He had to rise. He had to go. A powerful magnate sucked him out into the night. Softly in his bare feet he descended the one flight of stairs and crept to the door. It was bolted and, pulling back the bolt, he found that it was also locked. With a smile of determination he opened the door to the boat garage and descended the spiral metal steps. When he felt the cement quay beneath his feet, he stripped and, holding his light clothing above his head, lowered himself into the water.

A rank stench from this enclosed space filled his nostrils and his splashings sounded deafeningly loud. To his dismay he could touch bottom and the thought of the crab-infested mud made him shudder and draw up his legs. The soft, corrupt wood of one of the wrecks touched his side like a living thing and he gasped. He made his way rapidly into the open and, half paddling, half touching, circled the building and came ashore in the reeds beside it. Here he redressed, shivering slightly. The moon turned the feathery tips of the reeds a leprous white and their crackling frightened him as he forced his way through. A sort of anguish possessed him. He would have liked to renounce his humanity, to become one of the small night creatures that surrounded him. Then humanity would trouble him no longer. He could obey quite simply the pull of the moon or the scurrying urge of fear.

Ronny went to the rear door of the stable which was outside the wall. "Shalimar!" he whispered softly to his hawk. "Shalimar, come with me." But the falcon was sleepy, huddled on his block and twice his size with pouted feathers. Gambol, on the contrary, nuzzled the boy's shoulder. He was ready, it seemed, for any wish of his master. Ronny felt guilty because he had so often thought his horse lacked spirit. He led Gambol out by the halter and left Shalimar to sleep.

Mounting by the gate, Ronny rode slowly through the forest. Here and there as Gambol made his way pathless up the hill, they came out onto a pasture ringed by trees and sown by the wind. These small fields were especially lonely. The wild wheat stalks rubbed against one another like sorcerers conversing and the surrounding woods were silhouetted in forbidding shapes. Ronny was crossing one of these fields beneath the crooked moon when a strange idea made him lay his hand upon his bosom. He fancied that his tattooed heart began to beat, a sluggish throbbing slower and heavier than his original pulse. Until that moment he had not thought where he was heading; now he realized that he was on his way to the big house on the hilltop. Every detail of the way looked new to him, covered by the mysterious film of night. Gambol must have felt the same way, for whenever he plucked at a branch or took a mouthful of meadow grass he chewed it in an astonished manner. He seemed surprised to find the same vegetable taste that he had known all his life, and acted as if he expected something completely different.

Ronny caught a glimpse of the house as he rode between the tree trunks. It was etched acidly against the moon and Ronny became a black paper figure as he rode around it. In what room, he wondered, was June asleep? He looked up at the windows, but they were opaque and blind, or else dark, cavern-like holes in the walls. And perhaps she was not sleeping at all and was looking out, leaning on the sill with her bare arms. Turning the corner, he saw two windows on the second floor lit up like bright squares. Someone at least was awake, but of course it could not be June. June would not turn on the light, would not fail him so utterly when he was riding for her sake in the dangerous hours of the night. No, it must be old Mrs. Grey. He had heard old women never slept. He rode on, passing the front drive and then the thicket which screened the kitchen porch, coming back at last to his starting point. It was then that he had an inspiration. Losing himself a little in the trees, he gave that far call with which he brought his hawk to roost, that boy's cry which was like the sound of some animal or bird:

"Shalimar!"

Afterwards Ronny was afraid. The stillness rushed back as though angry at being broken and pressed roughly against his ears. He waited for what seemed to him to be a long time and was at last rewarded by a faint, whispered "Ronny?"

Riding forward, he saw June in a robe, running silently out on the moss. When she saw him she stopped and waited, touching the trunk of a tree with one hand and with the other holding back the night tangle of her hair.

"Get on and ride behind," said Ronny, and even his whisper sounded shrill. He rode up to the veranda and she climbed the steps without a word and hopped sideways onto Gambol's rump. She was as yet half asleep, but the dew on her bare feet aroused her, sending through her body a sort of bell-like note. To Gambol's step she swayed her torso slowly and held Ronny's waist with her arms. The boy's flat back with its shoulder blades, its arching ribs, seemed to draw away ahead of her into the night.

'Shall I ever think of this moment later?' she wondered, and the question made her sad. 'I would never have asked myself such a thing last year,' she thought. Being taller than Ronny, she could look out over his head and see their shadows thrown in front of them by the moon. They rode from darkness to darkness between the trees and entered the woods directly, without crossing the pasture. It was the opposite direction to that of the boathouse and the ground here ran almost level to the edge of three tall sand bluffs which loomed above the sound. The vegetation was scrubby and short. A delicious odor came from its leaves; sassafras, laurel, bay, and the poisonous sumac. Thorns with shiny leaves caressed and stabbed their legs and soon there was nothing anymore between them and the moon.

All at once they were on the edge of the world, looking down over the pale water. They dismounted and, still with an intuitive silence, lay down together on the grass at the rim of the bluff. The ground was drenched in dew, but they did not mind. It cooled their skins made feverish by the close night or by the heat in their own veins. They lay side by side leaning on their elbows and gazing at the track made by the moon over the water.

"I was clever to think of calling you that way," Ronny remarked at last.

"Yes," agreed June, "very clever."

"I was like those troubadours who rescue people from prison by singing songs they both know."

For a while June mused on this in silence, comforted by the old dream that prisons are for the virtuous and that rescuers exist. Nearby, Gambol cropped at the grass and the contented sound of his chewing underlined their conversation.

"When we're both grown-up do you think we'll still be friends?" asked June, and despised herself for asking. Why this longing for permanent things? It was growing on her, yet it went against her sense of adventure and poetry.

"I don't know," said Ronny in the offhand voice of children who do not wish to be sentimentally drawn. 'Later' was not yet poignant for this boy. He said plaintively: "My tattoo still hurts."

"How brave you were," said June and smiled.

"You weren't even watching," said Ronny, but he was pleased and continued: "Tonight I felt as if the moon was burning it, like a sunburn." Talking about it made him feel his tattooed heart beating once again. "Sometimes," said Ronny in his pure, shrill voice, "I feel it will get really alive out there on my skin."

His remark had a questioning note and a sudden spiteful feeling made June agree: "Yes, it will grow stronger and stronger and draw all the blood and suck the other dry."

At the meanness of her voice, the voluntary cruelty of her reply, Ronny sat up quickly on his hip, but he did not pursue the subject and asked irrelevantly, pointing at the sky: "Can you tell the difference between waxing and waning?"

"No," said June languidly. "Which is it doing now?"

"It's waning. When it grows it looks much stronger and when it's full there are two faces on it."

"You mean one face." June was by now nervous and contradictory.

"No, two. Jeremy showed me. There is a skull kissing a woman on the mouth. Jeremy says that with each kiss the woman wastes away until finally only the skull is left and then it dies too."

June jumped to her feet. "Well, let's go. I'm all wet from the grass and I'm afraid Grandmother will notice I'm gone."

They were both angry now and apprehensive. 'What have we said?' they wondered, looking at each other, but their words lay inanimate behind them, bleached and meaningless in the moonlight.

CHAPTER 11

STEVENS, AFTER HIS FAILURE to get Mrs. Villars' address out of Jeremy, decided to ask Mrs. Grey. He knew that the old lady sat in the front room of the house while he was teaching her granddaughter. Driving away he often caught a glimpse of her, pen in hand, although she never raised her head. He decided, however, to approach her on an alternate day. He was somehow reluctant to mix his request with his teaching.

June's lesson hours were now stiff and almost silent. Alone with Stevens, she had none of the impertinence or daring she displayed in Ronny's company. She was slow at her studies and did her homework sketchily when at all. He, for his part, hardly bothered to rebuke her, only explaining in his dry voice the chapter in algebra or history through which they passed. June's face, thrust so strongly on her head and framed by its untidy, tawny mane would be sullen. Her eyes never met his and she hesitated, almost stammered, as she spoke. Yet, just as he would begin to feel himself the master, something in her presence would reach him like an electric current; the awareness perhaps of an adolescent girl sitting alone with a man. 'You see,' this current would seem to imply, 'everyone knows that men want girls.'

Aroused by this nubile aura, this innocent breath from an unconscious flesh, Stevens would grow uneasy. His voice would quicken; his glance would shift. At such moments he was glad to feel that Mrs. Grey was next door, pursuing calmly and serenely the correspondence of her old age.

He chose a Saturday for his request, driving up to the house at noon in the thick heat of the day.

Catherine opened the door. "Sure she's not in," she said. "She's out for a little walk, the darling."

Stevens was astonished to hear the stern old lady called a darling. Taking his silence for hesitation, Catherine volunteered:

"Miss June is out too." The manner in which she said this showed that Catherine really thought it was June the young tutor had come to see. The idea made him redden with vexation.

"It's Mrs. Grey I wish to find," he replied, pinching his lips and trying to repress a pulse of embarrassment which beat visibly in his throat. "I understood she was in at this hour because I have noticed her at her desk when I tutor Miss Grey."

"Sure and she's old-fashioned," said Catherine, giving Stevens to understand that Mrs. Grey had not trusted him alone in the house with her granddaughter. Catherine's manner also implied that personally she felt her mistress' precautions absurd. Thus Stevens was insulted from two directions and stood there with an air of having been slapped on both cheeks. Catherine took pity on him then because he was now drained of venom by her own strong personality.

"You'd be sure to find her if you walked towards the bluffs," she said. "Just follow that path there. It's her favourite walk because it's flat and she's getting old for the hills."

Stevens thanked her in his coldest tones and pursued the direction she had indicated. His heels, as he crossed the lawn, made definite tracks in the moss. Looking down he saw with a pang that a horse had passed this way, a horse carrying no doubt the boy over whom he fretted. The lawn with its black, moist, acid earth was like a record noting on its page the encounters of purpose and of chance.

The path changed soon into a grass-grown cart track which divided the scrub. A murmur of insects was all around Stevens, casting its spell upon his senses like a soporific drug. The birds, too, called to one another and flew about at his approach and the heavy sun glared down on his path. He felt all at once like throwing himself down on the ground with outstretched limbs and letting the noonday heat engulf him utterly. Perhaps it might then loosen in his brain the tight knot that had been tied there: the knot of Ronny and of June.

Stevens recalled that at night, while still a child, he had sometimes been seized by a fear of oblivion. At such moments he had been wont to range his thoughts and thus prove, as he had been taught, the existence of heaven and of God. These arguments, learnt at Sunday school and at his mother's knee, were like rocks flung into a dangerous morass, one by one. And at last they would form a foundation for peace, for sleep without fear.

Today Stevens felt that if he could only put together his reasonings in the same way, they would touch perhaps the bottom of his emotions and rob them of danger. Walking along he tried it, whispering to himself: "June is too old to be Ronny's companion." No, that wasn't enough of a beginning. "Ronny is nervous, overstrained in his imagination." There, that was true. Then: "June is—" But what was June and what was this feeling, this dark saliva in his mouth? Could he, a school master, a keeper of children, really hate a girl of fifteen?

At that moment, Stevens looked up and saw that he had reached the bluffs and that Mrs. Grey was there with her back turned, looking out over the ocean and leaning on her tall, man's cane. Stevens cleared his throat. "Mrs. Grey?" he called.

The old woman turned, surprised to see him there, annoyed almost, in a haughty way. "Yes, Mr. Stevens?" she asked. "What is it?" She came towards him a few steps but did not offer her hand.

In one of those rare flashes of insight Stevens realized that this woman was his mother's ideal, more, her vision, while he, Stevens had yet been in the womb. Those small blue eyes which never twinkled had a clear iciness, a true coldness beside which his own glance became counterfeit. The wrinkles around her sunken mouth mocked his own, faint, spinsterish lines. "I have got these through living," they seemed to say, "through chewing, through the conjugal embrace and the groans of labour. You, young man, have come by yours through fear of life."

"Is there something you wished to discuss with me?" asked Mrs. Grey. As he did not answer at once, she looked with a slightly bothered air into his face. But her mind was plainly still on other things.

"I am sorry to disturb you," he said, gathering courage. "I just wanted to ask you something. I wanted to ask you for the address of Mrs. Villars."

"You mean the little boy's mother?"

"Yes, Ronny's mother." He went on in an attempt to explain: "You see, I feel I should write to her."

His tone must have struck Mrs. Grey for she said: "I hope you are not having difficulties with the child, Mr. Stevens."

"Well," said Stevens, "not exactly difficulties."

"Of course, I should help in any way if I could," she continued as though she had not heard him. "I know June is very fond of him and he is company for her."

"That's just it!" cried Stevens, unable to stop himself. "Don't you realize, Mrs. Grey, that it is unnatural for a boy of eleven to be in the continuous company of a girl of fifteen?"

Mrs. Grey looked mildly amused. "When I was a little girl, Mr. Stevens, children were not so rigidly divided as all that."

Stevens gazed around him hopelessly. Here on the edge of the bluffs where the glittering ocean threw its glare into the sky, all his words sounded wrong. Flushing to the roots of his blond hair, he said in a forced voice: "But Mrs. Grey, your granddaughter is no longer a child."

Mrs. Grey gave that peculiar stare in another direction which severe people use to ignore remarks in bad taste. There was a pause and then, from a nearby bush, an invisible bird sang out so innocently and sweetly that they both turned.

"There he goes, the little one!" exclaimed Mrs. Grey in a benign tone. Looking at Stevens once again, she remarked conversationally: "It is hard to believe, is it not, that he is first cousin to the snake?" She held up her finger. "Hark," she said, "there he is again. Sing away! Sing away!" Her tone was completely unselfconscious. She tilted her head so that her face, sheltered before by the brim of her hat, was exposed to the light. The skin of her cheek was smooth where the grain stretched over bone, but in the hollows of her jaw one could see a thousand wrinkles. In these and at the sides of her mouth and eyes gleamed the humours of old age, the juices of her small, slight, shriveled body. She reached into a bag at her wrist, drew out a clean, folded handkerchief and passed it over her face. Stevens saw how her hand trembled.

'Heavens,' he thought, 'how old she must be! How can I possibly be afraid of her?' He was miserable because there seemed no way to get back to the original subject of the address. A fly settled on his forehead and, before he could brush it off, gave him a venomous bite from its poison-green head. He exclaimed angrily, and as though at a signal Ronny rode into view below, sitting astride Gambol, with June behind him.

The couple were riding on the moist sand at the water's edge and the rising tide slapped at the animal's legs. Ronny wore his gauntlet with the red-hooded Shalimar on his wrist. His soprano floated up to them through the air although June's lower voice was lost.

Stevens and Mrs. Grey were silent on the cliff top, watching this pageant from curve to curve of their short view of the beach. When it was finally out of sight, Mrs. Grey said absently:

"I hope Catherine prepared enough food for their picnic. She sometimes forgets young appetites."

Stevens made no comment. The force of that sight, of those two riders on the sand, had entered into his breast like an arrow. A terrible nostalgia darkened the sun for him and made his palms sweat. He would have liked to hold back his emotions and doctor them one by one as they crossed the depths of his soul, but they were gone too quickly, leaving only a sense of flatness and of regret.

Mrs. Grey spoke again, this time directly to him. "They are wandering," she said, "in the woods of Arcady. I hope they will be permitted there a little longer."

Nonetheless, when Stevens looked in his mail box the following morning, he found Mrs. Villars' address in an envelope written in an old lady's spidery hand.

CHAPTER 12

ALMOST EVERY YEAR A FAIR CAME TO STAR HARBOUR;
a double row of caravans that carried with them scenery and appurte-
nances of many sorts. The fair occupied a flat stretch of ground near
the village, beyond the port, that is, and along the edge of the water.
It attracted Ronny's notice one evening when he was coming from the
stable, because, although Star Harbour was out of sight, those winking
circles and squares were visible around the far bend of the shore. They
moved, so it seemed, upon the water itself. Their promise fascinated him
and he decided to go.

Entering the house, Ronny met Jeremy leaning in the door jam. "Say
Jeremy," said Ronny, "there's a fair over at the village."

"Is there?" asked Jeremy.

"Can we go? Can we go tomorrow?"

Jeremy drew on his pipe and said thoughtfully: "I've got instructions
you're not supposed to go to the movies."

"Movies!" cried Ronny. "Who's talking about movies?"

"Well, I guess the idea was it's not good for you to get excited."

"A fair's not the movies," said Ronny as though stating a profound
truth. He plucked at Jeremy's sleeve just as he was taking his pipe from
his mouth and a scattering of sparks flew from it into the dusk. Jeremy,

feeling that flutter at his elbow and looking at the bright sparks, almost wished that Ronny were his own little boy, that from his whole life and married years he had had the faith to erect one barrier against the night, against the terrible seas, the waters of oblivion. He shrugged. "I got my orders," he said.

"Who gave you the orders—Mr. Walsh or my mother?"

"I was never in touch with your mother. Mr. Walsh wrote me and told me what to do."

"Doesn't Mr. Walsh ever come here himself?" asked Ronny.

"Well, he used to," explained Jeremy. "Seven years ago a weekend hardly passed that there weren't a dozen people in the house. Champagne and whisky like water. Ronny, you should have seen those blonds. One just like the next, so you could hardly tell when one left off and the other started."

"My mother's a blond," said Ronny.

Mary came into the doorway, drying her hands on her apron. "I don't think blonds are a nice thing to talk about in front of a child," she said, tartly for her.

"His mother's a blond," said Jeremy.

"Yes, my mother's very pretty, but I think I like Mary better."

"You mustn't say that," said Mary, tears of pleasure coming into her eyes.

"Anyway," continued Ronny, "do we get to see that fair?"

Three days later they went: Jeremy, Mary, Ronny and June. June had walked down early to the boathouse so that they could eat together first. She was wearing a silk print dress of the kind mothers buy with a view to all occasions. But it had been bought before June's illness and fitted her no longer. The V neck was unbecomingly high, and beneath, her nascent breasts fought with the tight, childish bodice. The skirt was uneven, drawn up here and there by the new fullness of her hips, while her brown legs were thrust out beneath with a sort of indecent innocence. Ronny, who had never seen her before in a 'good' dress, thought she looked beautiful and took her arm proudly when they got out at the fairgrounds. "You are really like 'you know what' tonight," he said. He meant 'damsel,' but did not want to say it openly in front of Jeremy.

"Oh I hate this old dress!" cried June.

Ronny and June had a little over three dollars between them and for this could take their pick of the amusements. They chose the mechanical rides first, as though to exhaust the obvious possibilities of the fair and so pierce beneath its surface to its less apparent mysteries. Jeremy and Mary meanwhile strolled around and talked to the villagers. They did not come to town often any more, but Mary had been born in Star Harbour and Jeremy on a farm nearby, so they knew almost everyone. The fairground was noisy and bright beneath the warm summer evening sky. Occasionally a shoot of lightning crossed the horizon as though the earth were thrusting out a burning tongue. Everybody's face was glistening. The women's dresses clung to their bodies and the men's shirts showed dark patches of sweat.

At the far end of the fair the marsh with its reeking mud took over and lent a different quality to the entertainment, less mechanical. Humbler perhaps, but more free. The refuse of Star Harbour had been thrown into the water here for years, to build out and solidify the shore, but the mud refused to become real land. The water breathed against it, choking and sighing, a rank vegetation grew underfoot. Here the real being of the fair existed still, however humbly; the charlatan and fertile monster; the root, whose branches were theatre and church, circus and screen; a few poor wanderers tied together by uncertain crafts and bodily defects. All the benefits of modern life conspired to crush them. Mechanics had dried the sap of their imaginations; electricity had sterilized their hearts; social leveling had left them timid and ashamed—the sword eater, the snake charmer, the strong man and the freak. Their caravans were parked on the mud banks, just a handful of them, with platforms out in front.

June and Ronny, gravitating in this direction, saw on one of the platforms a bearded lady with a complacent, motherly expression. Beside her stood a woman with a doll coming out of her chest, feet first, as far as its waist. The woman pretended the doll was her twin sister and the rag legs moved and swung about as she turned from side to side.

"I call her Irene," she was saying. She used a tone and choice of words which she thought refined and pinched her mouth daintily as she spoke. "Irene is a great trial to me," she continued, "but I cannot help loving her as you do your little sister—or little brother," she added, turning to June.

"How can you love someone who's got no head?" demanded a scornful young man.

"Oh, but Irene has a head," said the woman very seriously and not at all angry. "Irene has a head and shoulders and arms, only they're all inside my chest. They just never emerged. She can think too, and she's very smart because I feel her thoughts right along with my own."

The young man said: "Oh go on!" and his squirming girl friend gave an artificial cry of repulsion.

Ronny piped up in his fluty voice: "Anyway Irene's just a rag doll."

The bearded lady who had been sitting quietly in her chair now smiled. She stroked her fingers through the soft, dark growth of hair which sprang more from her neck than from her cheeks. "I am a real freak," this gesture seemed to say, and she looked approvingly at Ronny.

After this they tried looking at the sword swallower who was lifting weights with a hook through his tongue. His open mouth was drawn down and there were tears in his eyes, so they did not stay. They walked to where, in a small, sawdust ring, a donkey shuffled stubbornly and slowly, carrying a young woman on his back. During the daytime it was children, but now he was playing an unwilling cupid. The girl on his back swayed continually towards the waiting arms of her companion, squealing and giggling, while behind them the adolescent donkey-boy strode along indifferently.

"Poor donkey," said Ronny. "How he must long to be a glorious horse. Then this never would have happened to him."

"Sad things happen to horses too," said June.

A hand on both their shoulders thrust them apart. A voice said: "Well, if it isn't my friends from the woods. Still together, I see." Eddie with his thick figure and cocked head now walked between them.

"This fair is not much fun," said Ronny.

"Why don't you come for a ride on the 'Arabella'? She's been out twice already this evening. Flo's doing the barking and you'd be surprised how good he is."

Craning their necks, they could see the dock and the "Arabella" moored in a respectable place with a runway leading down to her deck. Flo was there, wearing a bowler in the brim of which were spread the boat tickets. On approaching they heard his nasal voice strained almost to a falsetto:

"Step right up folks and take a boat ride. Enjoy the moonlight with the one you love. Come on folks, last trip of the evening only fifty cents reduced!"

"Do you think we should tell Jeremy?" asked June, who found she did not much want to go. The village couples disgusted her as they struggled down the gangplank two by two. The women clawed at the rail as their heels slipped and twisted. The men supported them arrogantly, holding them beneath their arms and around their helpless bosoms.

But Ronny was thrilled. "Oh they won't want to go home for another hour and we'll be back by then, won't we, Eddie?"

"Sure we will," said Eddie, turning his head towards June and giving her shoulder a little push.

In turn they scrambled onto the deck. Flo and another man cast loose and the engine turned over. The exhaust streamed out into the air with explosions that followed one another more and more swiftly until they merged into a steady noise. Beneath the "Arabella" an impure oil bit silently into the water.

The passengers sat amidships, prevented from going elsewhere by ropes. They did not want to move in any case. Some, leaning on the rail, looked at the heavens and were amazed by the number of the stars. Others threw themselves together in that frustrated embrace which forms the limits of virtue. Now and then these last would part exhausted, their faces swollen and almost featureless. Sometimes they, too, would catch a glimpse of the stars and be startled and look at each other as if to ask: "Who are we, after all?"

June and Ronny stood with Eddie in his little wheelhouse facing the prow of the ship while Eddie told them some of his adventures. The "Arabella" was not much to look at, with her squat lines, but she had been used, it seemed, for many purposes. Many a time she had bucked across the Canadian border; many a time had anchored in lonely Fundy, where the huge tides change the coastline from night to morning and where the bell buoys sound in the fog.

"She's getting on now," said Eddie, slapping the wheel affectionately. "I guess she'd just as soon take fishing parties and lovers."

Flo climbed up to the bridge after they were underway and asked rather shyly to see how Ronny's chest was making out.

"It isn't sore anymore," said Ronny, "and the little scabs all fell off." He opened his shirt so that Flo could see.

Flo was proud of his work but still thought it should have had an arrow through it.

"Then all the blood would run out," said Ronny, giving June a look. "June thinks it's a real heart," he continued with bravado, "but it isn't." Secretly he was not sure. Looking downwards, he thought it palpitated slightly like a wicked changeling draining his true boy's heart away. 'Or is it June who is wicked?' he wondered.

At that moment she spoke in a teasing voice: "You shouldn't have put my name under it if you can't take the consequences," and she asked herself angrily for whose benefit she was talking.

Ronny soon ran out of the wheelhouse and down onto the foredeck. Flo followed and from where she stood June could see them talking to each other and with the other man who was crew.

"Rather hard on him, aren't you?" asked Eddie, twisting his head around to look at her.

"Oh he's such a baby!" cried June, exasperated at Ronny and horrified at the sound of her own voice betraying him.

"Well he's only ten or so," said Eddie reasonably. "Why don't you go and get yourself someone your own age?"

"I don't want someone," June answered hurriedly, and pictured at once several of her elder brother's friends, all very handsome and all unaware of her existence.

"A good looking blond like you could just about take your pick," continued Eddie, pulling the "Arabella" around in a large circle.

This novel theory made June laugh, but the laugh was not quite natural. They were silent in the stifling little wheelhouse, watching the lights grow nearer on the shore, take forms and wax large and beautiful as the stars. Now there seemed something else in the wheelhouse with them, as though a musky, tense animal were crouching in the corner. June felt the sweat roll out of her hair, warm and persistent, wetting the silk neckline of her dress.

Just as they were approaching the dock Eddie sighed and said: "It's no use, see. I like you. You know that. But you're jail bait, kiddy, jail bait."

'Did I really understand?' wondered June, stupefied. 'Did he really think—' She would have liked to annihilate Eddie from the earth, make him disappear forever, at once, plumb down beneath the ocean. Yet at the same time the peculiar inflection of Eddie's voice as he said that word 'kiddy', its hoarse, tender softness, entered her blood like a disease.

CHAPTER 13

GRACE VILLARS, AT THE TIME she received Stevens' letter, was not having a particularly successful season. She was of that age where, if one is a lively blond both piquant and experienced, one may have a flock of young men at one's heels. But Grace was not interested in young men. She was interested in rich old ones and these were increasingly scarce on her horizon. It was strange that all her adult life had been spent making herself into their ideal and that now, when she had followed their every wish, they had rewarded her by disappearing. Did she not now have exactly what they had always pretended to admire? Was she not Grace of the blue starry eyes, dainty brown limbs and sunny curls? Was she not dressed smartly, but with that touch of coquettish bad taste that they loved—or used to love? This year, when she did get a glimpse of one of them, he appeared to be after something else. And surely that sulky brunette with the long, emaciated body, the big drooping mouth, the lank, falling hair could not afford him the same thrill. Ah, but men were stubborn creatures, and sheep to boot!

True, Grace was asked about a lot. She received more telephone calls than any of the three hostesses she had had so far that summer. She was in Newport. She was out every night and she played tennis and bridge every day with all her usual pert ardour. Nonetheless, she could see the change. All these occupations were merely frills; garnishings on the platter. When the meat was absent, they, too, were rendered useless. And the meat was definitely absent. Sometimes Grace wondered if she had not made a mistake in sending Ronny away, if perhaps his support would have been an advantage. He was surly, he wriggled, but he was handsome. His suave, olive darkness made her the more fair. She knew, too, that as she leaned her hand with its rosy nails on his shoulder and laughed down into his face, there was added to her aura another colour, a subtle incestuous shade.

So it was that on the morning Grace opened Stevens' letter, she contemplated fetching Ronny at once and letting him pass the rest of the season with her. Then she reflected further and thought of his sullen behaviour and his nervous manner which bordered on the eccentric. Besides, the tutor was so indefinite that her curiosity was aroused. Looking at the date at the top of the page, she got a flash of inspiration. Of course, Walsh! He and his yacht were due to arrive any day now. He had told her so and she knew it to be true from other friends as well. She would go to him with her problem. It would be an innocent link between them which she would know how to accentuate.

Sitting in the breakfast room of her friend's house and drinking her morning coffee, Grace began to dream. Who knew, she thought, if after all a happy ending might not come about? For if Jim could be made truly to believe that he was Ronny's father, he might wish to assume responsibilities. He was rich. He was old and childless. He would soon be lonely. Of course she would have to be subtle, and there must be no possible hint of compulsion. Walsh would never stand for that. Grace woke up from her reverie to hear her hostess of the moment saying:

"Grace dear, do look out over the harbour and see if that isn't dear Jim's yacht."

'Fool,' thought Grace. 'So he's dear Jim to you, is he? Why he wouldn't even spit in your direction, my girl.' Aloud she said: "Why yes, I do believe it is—or very like it." Grace added this last phrase warily because she had never seen Walsh's yacht. In her time Jim had not owned one. No doubt he had taken to the sea with age: to travel in comfort and spare his steps.

* * * * *

Two days later Grace had not only seen Jim's yacht, but was aboard her. Walsh was mixing drinks beneath a striped awning. He had once got it into his head that women—his women—liked a pink, sweetish gin drink and he had mixed the same kind for them ever since. He would have been shocked if they had asked for anything else—except champagne, of course.

Grace, after trying vainly to turn her back to the light, lifted her chin and made the best of it. Jim was getting on, she noted, watching him shake the ice and liquor together. Only his captain's cap hid his naked scalp, but his arms were covered by a grizzling mat which reached down to the knuckles of his hands. His face, on which the crude colours of the awning were reflected, was puffy, the features enlarged. Beneath his immaculate white flannels his great belly thrust itself out to strain against the cloth. He would surely not last much longer.

They were alone on the boat because she had asked for it that way and now, abruptly and with no further small talk, Walsh said:

"Well Grace, what's on your mind?"

"Why must something be on my mind to want us to have a little chat?" asked Grace in her pouting way, raising her blue eyes to his.

Jim laughed and poured her a drink. "What'll we talk about? The old days?" He looked at her straight on, and she saw that whatever else had vanished, those deep, hungry, Jewish eyes were left. For an instant she was startled by them, drawn into their humid and lecherous depths, but for all their promise Grace knew that they were as impersonal as her own china blue ones. She sighed.

"The old days! You can sneer at them, Jim, yet they were nice."

"Were they, Grace?" asked Jim. "Were they any nicer than other days? Oh I know you were a cute kid with cute tricks, but the world's full of cute kids, and full of cute tricks too."

"That's just it," said Grace quickly, "I was only a kid. Do you remember, Jim, how you always said I would be better in ten years?"

Jim tilted his glass and in one gulp finished his drink. "I'm an old man now," he said, "I guess I must have changed." He leaned forward and explained brutally and with coarse emphasis: "Because these days I like 'em young."

While Grace bit her lips and tried to control her mortification, Walsh continued to lean forward, examining her silently. This light, which was so hard on him, did not treat her as badly. She was made even more vivid by it. Her hair, eyes, lips and cheeks stood out brilliantly. Yet these distractions could not hide the rough skin on her throat and the few pale brown spots on her hands. She was right though; once she would have tempted him. Now there could be no more question of desire between them. He reached out and patted her hand.

"I had to do it that way, Grace," he said. "I know you scheming little creatures. I'm not a fool. I'm an ugly old man, but I'm rich."

"Oh," said Grace, lifting her eyes which were filled with tears, "why are you so unjust? Are you so sure of yourself that you don't need friends anymore?"

Walsh sat back in his wicker chair and spread his feet. His glance was now turned outwards on the sea. "I don't fool myself about friends either, Grace. I can have any friend I like as long as I'm paying the bill."

Grace sat up straight. Her eyes narrowed and an angry, scornful expression was on her mouth. "Poor little rich man!" she mocked. "What a trite mind you have for all your wealth! You can buy and sell a thousand silly creatures like me every day no doubt, but you can't make one new, honest observation."

Jim Walsh laughed freely. He was relieved in an instant of all his brooding philosophy. A grin flattened out his mouth. "Well, Grace, you must admit you started it, with your phony sentiment. Come on and have another drink and tell me how Ronny's doing. Does he write to you?"

Grace at once handed him Stevens' letter. "It's really what I came to see you about."

"Why me?" asked Walsh with quick suspicion.

Grace soothed him. "It's just because he's in your house and I thought you might have heard from one of the servants or something."

"As a matter of fact I did hear from my hired man," Walsh admitted, "but only to say that all was well." He fingered his lip thoughtfully. "I know, Grace, why don't you run up there for the week-end? I'll write that you're coming if you like."

"What is this Stevens like?" asked Grace. "You engaged him, Jim, didn't you?"

"No, not really, not directly. You see when I lived in that house there, after I built it, I got to know my only neighbour and landlady, Mrs. Grey, a widow."

"A merry one?" asked Grace, her blue eyes bright, tilting her head like one of those insolent little birds who pick up crumbs off the streets.

"Exactly the opposite," said Jim. "On the contrary, she's a severe old woman. One of the few of her sex one can respect and not buy."

"Is that so important, not to have a price?" asked Grace rather wistfully. The sweet gin drink, the sun through the awning, and the abrupt shifting of the waves were making her feel sick.

Walsh was not paying attention any more. "My God, what a crowd I used to have down there. Seven speed-boats shooting in and out of that damn boathouse, roaring away across the water and roaring back like so many water bugs, and the champagne and the whisky and all those naked legs in shorts and high heels. That was my Indian summer, Grace, before I bought the 'High Kick' here and had to take my pleasures one by one."

Forgetting Grace was there, or else forsaking vanity, Jim took off his captain's cap and passed his hand over his scalp. The skin on his head was notched and bumpy as though the various bones that held his brain together were buckling. It was mottled, too, and far paler than his face. Over it back and forth passed his hand, like a big hairy spider.

"I tell you," he continued, "I used to get sick sometimes of the whole bunch and then I'd go up and see old Mrs. Grey." It was true that Mrs.

Grey had refreshed him. She had seemed rather to like him too, and in her dim, cool house he had drunk port and sherry and talked of many things unrelated to blonds. He recalled with a half smile that she had even read him poetry. It sounded silly. Grace would laugh if she knew, but the words had had a ring that had made him think strange thoughts, or rather, that had brought a kind of rhythm into his body, a rhythm like the dreams a boy has before he starts to care if he is rich.

"What are you smiling at?" asked Grace in her light, coquettish voice that had slightly dried out in the last ten years just as her skin had dried out, and her small, flexible muscles.

"I'll tell you what," said Walsh as though she had not spoken. "You go down, Grace, and see your boy. I'll sail around at the end of the week and be there for the Fourth of July."

"Why don't we go together?" asked Grace.

"Because I'm otherwise engaged," he said dryly.

"And will your—guest—be gone by then?" Grace tried to make her question casual but failed to keep the curiosity from her tone.

Walsh waved his hand impatiently, dismissing the subject from their conversation. "You see, Grace," he said seriously, "I'm getting old. Sex is pleasant but it's not enough. No, don't look hopeful yet. I don't want a companion either. Still, I know what you've been hinting about. Perhaps it's true. I don't say yes or no, and you can't prove it either way after all this time. In court, I mean. Anyway I'm willing to give him the once over. I've no other children that I know about. Maybe he will be a consolation, or, as they say, a flower of my old age. I've always agreed to pay for my pleasures." He rose carefully and rang for his steward. "We'd better be getting you ashore," he said. "I must dress for dinner."

As Grace stepped neatly over the side, he reminded her in a kindly way: "Take it easy and I'll see you on the Fourth."

CHAPTER 14

THE DAY THAT GRACE ARRIVED at Star Harbour was the day that Shalimar brought down his first bird. True, he had killed others, but their bones lay in the woods or on the floor of the sea. This time he brought down his catch and dropped it at Ronny's feet.

"There," he seemed to say disdainfully and proudly, "if that's your desire I can fulfill it." Then he settled, not on the boy's wrist but on a branch nearby, and looked out fiercely from either side of his beak.

When Ronny saw the tattered thing on the ground, a breathless feeling swelled his lungs. The red, wet feathers gleamed as brightly as jewels and upon the small, open beak a great liquid ruby gathered and grew. Ronny trembled. He was standing near the spring, holding Gambol by the halter. The horse, having finished his drink, now turned curiously towards Shalimar's prey. Then, smelling the blood, Gambol jerked up his head and opened his soft, wide nostrils. He was an eater of leaves, oats and wild grass, and on his gentle breath there was no taint of meat.

Ronny, putting his hand against his side to control the sudden beating of his heart, withdrew it at once as though his palm were burned. He fancied that the dying bird made his tattooed heart leap with joy, drawing the other sorrowful one along behind it, as heroes once drew along their foes at the wheels of their chariots. Shrugging off his shirt, Ronny examined the mark, clear and perfect now, on his tanned skin. He looked up at Shalimar with despair and thought he heard the falcon say:

"What about the crab? You killed him."

"Yes," cried Ronny, "that's true." And he thought confusedly: 'But then all my feelings were not divided as they are now.' So as not to be put to shame before his falcon, Ronny stooped, picked up the bird by its claws and with a little string attached it to his belt. After this he mounted quickly. He rode on, forgetting his shirt which lay on the ground, warmed by the sun.

June was having her lesson that morning and her usual wish to be done with it seemed to be matched by that of Stevens. He looked constantly at the time. He wore his watch on the inside of his wrist, where it fretted the protruding veins, and to see it, hitched his hand forward out of his sleeve, closing his fingers convulsively. June was torn between desire to find out the time herself and repulsion at those thin, tendinous knuckles. Once or twice Stevens gave her a look which she could not understand; a sort of triumphant menace shone in his grey eyes as though to imply: 'Just wait my girl and you'll see!'

For Stevens knew, as June did not, that Mrs. Villars was coming.

Finally the hour was over. June leapt to her feet and with a parting mumble of farewell hurried out of the room. As her grandmother hated disorder, she gathered her books pell-mell in her arms and then, once in the dark hall, threw them into an empty chest. Stevens, from his car window, caught a glimpse of her on the lawn as she stooped to re-bind her sandal. The habit of maturity was still so new to her that, when alone, she fell into childish attitudes. Such poses, combined with the new softness of her line, were either ugly or intoxicating, according to temperament. Stevens stepped on his accelerator and the engine roared. June, startled, straightened up hurriedly and disappeared around the corner of the house, while Mrs. Grey turned from her desk with an expression of intense displeasure.

June made her way through the pasture, plucking the long grasses and chewing their stems. She crushed the resin against her lips and tongue and then spat them out and chose new ones. In front of her a swarm of insects was like an escort and her body prickled with the heat. She found Ronny on the edge of the woods, riding towards her, half nude, with the small, bloody carcass at his belt.

"How sad!" she cried. "The poor little bird."

Ronny was biting the inside of his mouth to govern his twitch, but he would not give in to her. "It's not sad. Shalimar is a hunting falcon."

"I think you're stupid and mean," said June coldly, irritated at his opposition. "It was doing no one any harm, singing and flying about. Grandmother says hunting is a sickness of the mind that men get when there's no war and they can't kill people."

"If it's a sickness and men have it," retorted Ronny, "boys have it too, I suppose, so why shouldn't I?"

"Have it if you like," said June, dropping back into her mocking tone and giving a shrug. "Perhaps it makes you feel heroic to kill a tiny animal." She paused and added slyly: "It's not the first time, is it?"

Ronny jumped off his horse and drew near with clenched fists. "Shalimar has a right to kill!" he shouted. "He's like a god. His beak is like the nose of God." Turning, he walked off down the path, kicking at the undergrowth with his bare feet.

June ran and caught up to him, leading Gambol. They were silent for a few minutes and then in a halting voice as though explaining something to himself Ronny began:

"I like things to be real. If Shalimar is a hunting falcon and wears a hood and isn't a free bird, then he must hunt."

"But it's not perfectly real to hunt with a falcon here and now," objected June.

"Don't you see," he said, frowning with the effort to explain, "knights do it, and if I am to be a knight—even only now, this summer—" His voice trailed off. He really did not know how to continue.

"I guess I do see," June answered softly, giving him a caressing touch on his bare shoulder. "It's like false button holes or flowers put into old-fashioned coffee grinders. It makes everything thin."

Ronny was not any too pleased at having his ideas brought to such a low level. June, however, continued talking, struck perhaps by what she was saying. "I think you are right to want to do things the real way. For good, I mean, for life and death. They are always saying we should not let our pastimes run away with us and become too important in our lives. But why do they say that? That would make them only hobbies. How I hate hobbies!"

"When you say 'they'," said Ronny, "you mean grownups," and he laughed because it sounded funny for her to be talking that way and he could not connect what she was saying with his own romantic thoughts.

"Yes of course. I do mean grownups," said June, stung a little by his laugh. "I know I'm almost grownup myself but I shan't be like them. I shall be something real, too."

She looked at him to see if he believed that she would be different from all the others and saw with a pang that it did not matter to him in the least. 'But why do I care what he believes of me?' she wondered with a feeling of pain. 'He is only a child still who does not have to think of the future.' Surely he thought of it just as she had once done: as a lump of time, somewhere long ahead, 'when I am big,' already moulded to the desired shape, perfect and complete. Now that this lump was upon June, she no longer recognized it. It had no more shape or perfection than the present.

They were passing at that moment a stagnant pond upon whose surface grew a brilliant fungus scum and in which the roots of a dead tree formed an island. The rotting, exposed roots made a soil for ferns and for red flowers, and from the bank it looked like a little paradise. June remembered how once she had begged her eldest brother to make a bridge to it out of logs thrown in the water. He had done so and she had stepped eagerly across, armed with sandwiches and a book, prepared to spend the day. But it had not been a paradise at all. The moulding earth had been damp and full of slugs, and the growth, so lovely from a distance, was coarse and harsh. There had been, as well, innumerable flies and mosquitoes. The stench of the pond had seemed alive in her nostrils. June had beat a hasty retreat and eaten her sandwiches on the lawn near the house.

Looking at the pond today, June, although she recalled her deception, was almost tempted to believe in the island once again. Where in all the world was a fulfillment of what that little island promised? Where were the virgin forests whose mossy floors invited rest? Where were the crystal fountains, the soft air in which no poisonous insect hummed? And if they did not really exist, why write about them in music and words, and paint them, too? Or perhaps they had existed only in antiquity. She had a sudden desire to go away; to leave these tangled woods with their marshes, and to quit as well this little boy who was their prisoner.

"What is your school like, Ronny?" she asked.

"Oh, stupid of course. Anyway I'm through with it."

She was impatient with the childishness of his reply. "Well I'm nearer being through with mine," she said, "but I can tell you I dread going back. I haven't seen any of them for ages and I can't imagine—I just can't picture, how they talk and how I'm going to talk to them."

Ronny had been disturbed by her mention of school; all those voices in his ears, those conflicting orders which he could never obey, those friends and enemies so indistinguishable from one another. "It's late," he said, "and I must go home because my mother's coming for lunch."

"Your mother!" cried June, opening her fine, rough eyes. She had never connected Ronny with parents who might come and see him.

Using a stone, Ronny climbed onto his horse (he had never made good his boast about springing onto its back in one bound). "Well, goodbye," he said, and kicking Gambol's flanks with his bare heels he was off.

He rode homewards slowly, looking up now and then to see if Shalimar was about. But the hawk was high up and far away. Ronny arrived at the gate just as Grace Villars, with a rather disgruntled air, was being driven up to it in Jeremy's old Ford. She had hardly expected a car so old nor a place so isolated and run down. She smiled, however, when she saw her son, and with a coquetry natural to her begged Jeremy to let her out. Holding open her slim arms and laughing gaily, she ran towards Ronny who was sitting on Gambol's back.

"Ronny, aren't you coming down to say hello? Have you forgotten me?" She spoke in a babyish voice which she used for males of all ages and it made Ronny realize that he did not want her to be here.

He slipped down from his horse so that his back was turned but, in landing, his hips twisted and she caught sight of the dead bird that dangled from his belt. Grace felt a thrill go through her. The desire for possession which is so strong in some women took hold of her; the desire not only to be loved by, but to own, this growing animal who would one day be a man, who had already lusted for blood. In a flash Grace saw herself five years or so hence, with Ronny tall and lithe and worshiping her beyond all others. Then as he straightened up she saw the tattooed heart which palpitated on his bare breast and read underneath the legend: june.

CHAPTER 15

JUNE, ASTONISHED AT THE NEWS that Ronny's mother was arriving, hastened homewards. She was troubled to find in herself a sensation of dismay. Yet this sensation withdrew on probing, or, like a down pillow, caved in to hump itself up on all sides of the question.

"Let me think," she said aloud (she often spoke aloud when alone), "What does Ronny's mother have to do with me? She will probably be very nice." But why had she come? Why had Stevens asked Jeremy for the address? Now there would be a stranger on the peninsula, and an interfering one.

June had lately discovered in herself an instinctive fear of other women. It derived perhaps from her fever. She had been isolated from her classmates at a crucial moment and had not been able to observe the changes that had surely come over them. Had she been able to follow these changes step by step, she could have been assured of her own similarity. Now there was no telling where she was, and there was nothing for it but to brazen the matter out. Mrs. Villars must be a first test.

By this time June had reached the house, where she washed and then entered the dining room. Mrs. Grey was already seated before her simple lunch. Catherine left the dishes in front of her mistress and then departed. The dining room table, as all else in the house, showed by its size and by the well polished nicks in its surface that it had been used for a long time and by many people.

June felt far away from her grandmother, as though the rim of the table were the rim of the earth curving, inexorable, between them; the turn of the earth, the turn of those years dividing them, thrown as they were at different times upon the spinning universe. Mrs. Grey in her white dress was cool and pale, but June was flushed. The ridge of a frown between her eyes made her face severe for all its youth.

"Did you met Mrs. Villars?" asked Mrs. Grey.

"Grandmother!" cried June reproachfully, "you didn't tell me she was coming. Do you know her?"

"No, we have never met," said Mrs. Grey whose manner implied: 'Nor are we likely to.'

"I didn't meet her either," said June, and after a moment she asked: "What do you think I should do now? I mean, do you think it's all right to go down there or do you think I should wait?"

"My dear," replied Mrs. Grey in a voice of mild surprise, "I don't think it matters."

But June was impressed by her own question. How was she to behave? Of course the normal thing would be simply to go down there, introduce herself and take her position naturally as Ronny's companion. But Stevens seemed to find it wrong that she, a grown girl, should be friends with a little boy. Also, how soon should she go? This afternoon would seem terribly hasty. Would tomorrow seem hasty, too? For the first time June became aware of her dependence on Ronny. How, for instance, to spend the rest of the day without him? The idea of waiting before going there filled her with dismay. And this very dismay caused in her an obscure feeling of shame. There was another question in her mind as well: Even if she waited would she be able to act naturally face to face with Ronny's mother? What was naturally?

In her room after lunch June stood in front of the mirror and practiced a casual air. Her frowning face with its straight mouth displeased her. She parted her lips and relaxed her forehead.

"How do you do, Mrs. Villars? I believe you are Ronny's mother," she said, and at the same time extended her hand towards the mirror. At once the old magic of her person blotted out her problem. Her hand was small, but the fingers were rather knobby, with short, pale nails. Did other girls at school have such hands? Were their wrists as delicate as hers? She couldn't remember, and anyway they were bound to have changed. Leaning forward she kissed the mirror, trying to watch herself closely as she did so. She saw the fluttering quiver of her nostrils and then her eyes crossed and her breath obscured the glass. Also it was well known that when a man kissed a woman, the woman closed her eyes. Thus it was really impossible to tell what one would look like when the great moment arrived. That is, if it did arrive. There were girls who were never married, never loved or anything until they died.

June felt hot and sticky in the attic room. On other days she would already be in the woods, wandering downwards towards the bay. It never occurred to June that Ronny might be riding there as usual. She pictured him only as shut up in the boathouse with the unknown woman who was his mother. Idly she pulled back her hair from her face and lifted it from the nape of her neck. At once the bones of her skull with its delicate, high-set ears put her face out of proportion. With a little twist of the mouth (which she considered attractive although she had never done it in public) June turned away and began listlessly to examine the books on the bedside table.

While she had been sick, many people had given June books and she had read them avidly. She would repeat passages that pleased her aloud in a singsong voice, and sometimes with a beating heart. She had extracted rhythm from prose or verse as one persuades gold from dross, and even the most illusive, harsh or unconscious melody had not escaped her feverish tongue. But today, throwing herself on her bed, she opened her books listlessly one by one and realized that for her their magic was over. They smelt of fever, of the dreadful monotony of illness. And after all, she was no longer interested in the words of unknown people, but rather in the mysterious depths of her own body. Its changes surely were more rhythmical than any poetry. Alone, she was constantly aware of this density that was she; this murmuring flesh between its bones. How it vibrated! How much glistening youthful sap, how much vital blood was thrown out of it as from a gyre. June was afraid of it and yet she loved it and did not want it disturbed.

The stillness of the room, in which the shade was drawn, oppressed her and she jumped up and went down one flight to the bathroom. Here she turned on the taps full force. They were both cold and the tub, surrounded by its wooden platform, was soon full. Yet she did not bathe after all. Halfway undressed, she leaned over and once or twice trailed her fingers in the water. Then, refastening her clothes and tieing the thongs of her sandals, she left the house and entered into the drowsy afternoon.

Mrs. Grey, with straw hat and basket, was on her way to clip the roses. Her heels, curving underneath her shoes, dented the ground less heavily than her cane. It was as though the cane were the crippled one and not she at all. June dragged in her wake and helped trim the bushes and pick the rose bugs off the flowers. McGreggor, still munching the remains of his tea, came out of his house. He could not bear Mrs. Grey to touch the roses but could find no way of preventing her. He walked watchfully in the rear and now and then, with an exasperated motion, straightened a branch as though his mistress had twisted it.

June realized on seeing McGreggor that she had not heard him play his bagpipes that summer, nor during the whole time of her illness either.

CHAPTER 16

GRACE VILLARS CERTAINLY HAD NOT EXPECTED Walsh's place to be as she found it. Where were luxury and wealth? Where the trained servants and the speed boats he had mentioned? Jeremy, who had fetched her from the station, had given a shrug to her questions and had smiled between his rosy cheeks. She had eaten her first meal in a huge room just above the water, overlooking the bay. Underneath, unless many people were talking, one could hear the waves lapping on the cement quays, and many people were not talking. There were only Ronny and Grace.

The room stretched around them, dwarfing the card table with unsteady legs which had been set for their lunch. Ronny sat opposite Grace, facing the light, since even with one's son one must be careful. He was sullen and brown as an Indian. A faded shirt was buttoned up to his neck and his hair was watered and combed back in such a way as to show either filial duty or resentment.

"Ronny," said Grace in her coaxing voice, "are you still mad at me?"

He did not answer but forked his food steadily into his mouth.

"I didn't mean to hurt your feelings," continued Grace, and seeing that he still made no reply she added: "But it really is ridiculous, Roddy."

The name 'Roddy,' his baby name, brought a dark patch to each side of Ronny's face. He looked up, his eyes black beneath the fine ridge of his brows. The light from the window, polished by the sun's reflection on the water, entered freely into those eyes. It was lost in them as in velvet or as in a well whose depths resist sounding.

Grace could not repress a tremour of uneasiness. What chemical was in those eyes to make the irises so dark? One could not define in them the circle of the pupil. They were heavy-lidded and dense. After her angry ridicule of Ronny's tattooed heart, the boy had not spoken, but now, seeing that he was about to do so, Grace turned her own eyes to her plate.

"Do we have to stay together all afternoon?" asked Ronny in his pure, high voice, which, coming from his somber face, startled Grace.

"I wish your voice would change," she said. "It gets on my nerves." Then as the meaning of his words reached her, she continued: "When you were a little baby, Roddy, you cried if I left the room even for five minutes and you were only happy in my arms." Actually, and Grace realized it as she spoke, Ronny had had a nurse in those days and she had seldom seen him.

"I don't remember that," said Ronny.

"Don't you want to be with me now?" asked Grace, with a pout.

"Well, I generally ride in the afternoons, and Gambol will wonder."

"Who is June?" asked Grace, crumbling a piece of bread with her fingers. She observed that her son's cheek was twitching and that lovely, quivering cheek with its dusk rose, its fine grain, almost softened her brittle heart. "She must be a very silly little girl," said Grace since Ronny made no reply.

"She's not a little girl," said Ronny and smiled as though his mother had tripped over a string.

A flood of unaccountable relief swept over Grace. 'It must be an animal,' she thought; 'But it's a disfigurement nonetheless.' Then with one of those irritating flashes of insight she reflected: 'If my name had been there I would have thought it fine.'

As though he had read her thoughts, Ronny said with eleven-year-old sharpness: "You just wish it had been your name written underneath instead of another lady's."

"A lady!" exclaimed Grace.

"Well, a girl really, but she would have been a lady in olden days. A damsel."

"Are you in love with her?" asked Grace, exactly as she would have spoken to Walsh or any other man.

But Ronny did not answer her question. He thought it foolish. Just what one would expect from a mother.

"What will you do, Ronny, when you grow up and go to a real preparatory school and have to leave fairy tales behind you?"

Ronny grinned. All his sullenness was gone. "Everyone wants to know that!" he cried. "Especially Mr. Stevens."

Mary came in. "Would you be wanting coffee?" she asked. Mary had a flustered manner because Mrs. Villars intimidated her. Before, when Walsh had kept open house, she and Jeremy had lived above the stables. She had never had anything to do with the guests, whom, in her simple, unresentful way, she imagined to be very wicked. Now, playing with her apron and hunching her back, she thought: 'She is my age I'm sure, but how different we are. Maybe we even had the same kind of mothers, and I was a pretty girl, too.' Where had she, Mary, gone wrong, to be old when this sister was still young, this sister who did everything God was supposed to frown on? Could God care so much as he was supposed to, or had he perhaps been on the other side all the time? Mary realized with a start that Grace was speaking to her, asking if Jeremy could drive her to the village.

"I'll ask him," said Mary. "What time would it be for?"

"Oh around three will do," replied Grace and, turning to Ronny, she explained: "I want to have a talk with this Mr. Stevens of yours. I came here for that." She tried to make these words into a reproach but the stifling afternoon heat entered her lungs and gave to her voice the quality of a sigh. She felt exhausted, drained, almost as though some secret vein in her body were open. This woman who for many years had never known solitude and who had considered the 'country' to mean fashionable resorts, now felt the flatness of sudden relaxation. Her dainty, slightly dry limbs were like dead sticks extending from her body, and she thought her cheeks must sag.

"Mother's sleepy," said Ronny to Mary. "I can see the white beneath the blue in her eyes. Say Mary, did you know that when a person sleeps their eyes roll right up in their heads?"

"You mustn't speak about your mother like that," said Mary.

"When you're dead you only stare," continued Ronny, "and your eyes grow hard as stones. That's what Jeremy says anyway. Shalimar loves the eyes of dead knights to eat and that's what a poem says, and do you know what Flo says? Do you mother?" A frown came into Ronny's face and he touched his mother softly and almost pleadingly on the arm, one of those anxious, timid touches which children use and which are often ignored.

Grace roused herself irritably. "No I don't know what Flo says and I don't know who Flo is, but I do know that you are being tiresome. You meet me with an ugly tattoo mark on your chest which you'll be sorry for one day. When I laugh at it, you have the nerve to sulk. Well, I had to have some reaction, didn't I?" She spread her little hands and opened her blue eyes.

"Yes, but it's about the tattooing that Flo said this thing," Ronny said eagerly.

Mary had left the room by now to speak to her husband, and Grace, feeling uneasy, got up and started wandering about from object to object. Behind her back Ronny's voice continued:

"You see, Flo says the only sure thing to take tattoo marks out is——" But Ronny found he could not say it after all. The idea was laughable, and he skipped out of the room as light as down.

CHAPTER 17

STEVENS PREPARED FOR THE ARRIVAL of Mrs. Villars by putting away the few last, genteel relics which he had kept so far for memory's sake. There was, for instance, a lace antimacassar on his mother's special chair. It was spotless of course, but frayed slightly by the hard, tight knot of her hair. He folded it carefully, feeling that curious mixture of love and distaste which was beginning to come whenever he handled these maternal things. He removed as well the semi-religious sampler from above the mantle, and the abalone shell from before the door. The shell had been his mother's ideal of beauty. It had taken that place in her soul which may be filled by the various artistic creations of man. Stevens hated the shell worse than anything else. He hated it even more bitterly because he still found it so beautiful and it was such bad taste. He put it in the coat closet where it remained in the darkness what it had always been: curled, rosy, shining, fair, murmuring about the sea whose miracle it was.

When Grace arrived in Jeremy's Ford, Stevens was polishing the mirror in the front hall with newspaper. He had his shirt sleeves rolled back over his thin arms and the afternoon heat had made his blond hair curly. He was startled by Grace, for the radio was on in the next room and he did not hear her coming. She stood in the doorway a moment, very small in her short, full skirts and tight bodice, like a doll with real golden hair. Stevens, who was balancing on a chair, almost fell off it.

"Hello," she said. "You asked me to come so I came."

He jumped down with a light movement that was one of his graces. Thus they were both pleased, as two adults must be when they catch each other in mutually youthful attitudes.

"Won't you come in?" he asked. "I hardly dare think you are Ronny's mother for you don't look old enough."

She moved towards him with her birdlike steps and gave him her bird hand. Then they went into the living room and in the different light from his mauve walls, Stevens saw that Grace was not as young as all that. Grace, for her part, saw a rather pallid man whose boyishness had lasted only a moment. But because of their first view they were smiling amicably.

"Before our talk," he said, "I shall order coffee for you. Will you have it iced?" He was proud of being able to ring for the servant even though she was fat and wore no uniform other than an apron.

"Yes," he continued when they were settled, "I really did think we should have a talk."

Grace was looking around the room shrewdly, drawing her summer gloves through her hands. The gloves were made of blue and white striped cotton, very pretty and fresh so that the eye followed them as they passed between her fingers. Stevens admired her immensely and could not help but compare her to Lucy, whose hands were large, red and always moist.

"I can see you are an artistic young man, Mr. Stevens," observed Grace, looking at the prints on the walls and at the colour tone of the room.

He breathed deeply: "Ah Mrs. Villars, it's rare, for anyone to notice things like that in Star Harbour."

"I was born in a place very like Star Harbour," said Grace, "and even now I shudder at the narrowness of my escape." Then she leaned forward and said coaxingly: "I didn't mean that as a slight, you know. It's different for a man. A man can make his own world anywhere, as I see you have done." The caress in her voice and its emphasis when she said 'man' sent a faint chord to vibrating in Stevens' body. He was flattered. His subdued virility stirred.

They began to talk about Ronny, but Stevens' obvious concern made Grace frown. "My," she said, "you do seem to care a great deal."

"It's my profession to care," retorted Stevens.

Grace looked down at her hands with a faint smile. What a prissy creature! She wondered if it would be amusing to disturb him. After all here she was, bound to wait over until the Fourth of July. A little romance would do the tutor good, and when had it ever harmed Grace Villars? Besides, and also just for fun, she reminded herself, it would be a satisfaction to rout this girl over whom everyone seemed so upset, this June who was intruding in her life. Grace was always courageous when faced with others of her sex and had never been afraid of women, old or young. She was like one of those small, fierce, petted dogs who will rush yapping up to a wolf.

The iced coffee arrived and Grace sipped it slowly, looking at Stevens over the rim of her glass. "I have sent the man Jeremy home," she stated.

"Oh I'll be delighted to take you home, Mrs. Villars. You see I was supposed to have a scout meeting this afternoon but when you called that you were coming I put it off. I thought our meeting much more important." He blushed and added hastily: "I mean the subject of our meeting."

Grace gave her clearest laugh, showing her little, white teeth. Then she said: "I just can't seem to picture you as a boy scout. You look such a man of the world, Mr. James Stevens."

At once Stevens saw that nothing was more absurd than a boy scout and with this realization came another: Grace Villars came from the very world he wished to inhabit. She came from the world of first nights and celebrities and clubs and amusing scandals. She smelt of those things. They were in her eyes, her manner, the way in which she pulled her gloves through her fingers. Stevens had always known such a world existed; that if one could only find the right entrance there was a brilliant, glamorous life behind the every day one. Grace Villars made it seem obtainable.

Had Stevens but known it, this was the element which made Grace fascinating to many young men more or less of his type. She had got away from a humdrum beginning and therefore could show them how to do so as well. Or at least so they hoped.

"Don't stare at me like that," complained Grace. "You make me think something's gone wrong with my face."

As a matter of fact she had a slight coffee mustache from the rim of her glass. Stevens choked with embarrassment, especially as she reached for her purse and took out her compact.

"You might have told me!" she cried, pouting with her eyes, but not at all displeased. The light brown mark curving from each side of her upper lip gave her the air of a little girl masquerading as a bandit. It pointed up her blond, merry looks. It was just the sort of thing older men found so cute—or used to find. She took her time to wipe it off, shaking out her perfumed handkerchief.

Stevens thought her stained mouth vaguely revolting and the idea of coffee mixing with her lipstick on the handkerchief offended his fastidious nature. Yet, all the time, she was holding the world out to him, a shining ball which it would soon be too late to seize.

"I must say I agree with you about June Grey," said Grace. "She sounds an unattractive creature. I'm surprised at Ronny. It isn't like his— father." She looked at him wickedly from the corners of her eyes and he comprehended that for her all this was a game. The curious weight that had been on his spirit lifted. It was a game after all, not a thing of moment or a thing of pain.

"Let's take her down a peg," suggested Grace.

"You make it sound such fun to do," he said impulsively, showing his boyish smile.

"I can't imagine what kind of women populate Star Harbour," parried Grace, "you seem to have things to learn."

Stevens wished he could say: "Won't you teach me?" but he could not bring himself to do it. Was she really throwing him a challenge? And if so, would he have the courage to accept? He tried to read a direction in her eyes and found them only blue and bold.

"Were you aware of the fact, Mr. Stevens, that Ronny has got himself tattooed?" asked Grace.

"Tattooed! How do you mean?"

"Yes, he has a heart tattooed on his chest and the girl's name is tattooed underneath it."

Stevens actually turned pale so that his skin showed a sparse sprinkling of freckles. The idea filled him with horror and drowned out all the previous lightness of their conversation. He pictured Ronny then with his olive skin, the black fall of his hair, the sweet animal glitter of his eyes.

"My God," he cried, "I know when he did it!" And this knowledge caused him the most unhappiness of all.

CHAPTER 18

FLO WAS REVOLVING SLOWLY around and around the dance hall. He did not look as though he were enjoying himself, but he had been here for an hour, turning and shuffling. His partner was a girl whose bulk seemed to be melting in the heat of the room. Small spirals of black hair fell from a white parting and left traces of oil on her cheeks. Her eyes, obscured by fat, roved moodily this way and that because, aside from Flo, no one ever asked her to dance. Her breath was acid from constant candy eating and there was a black, glandular mustache on her upper lip.

Flo could not explain why nearly every week he wore his shoes out with such a creature, nor why he sometimes took her to the "Arabella" afterwards. She was not a human being for Flo at all, and in her turn she despised him.

Jeremy, passing by the open door of the harbour dance hall, saw the couple wheeling grotesquely across his line of vision. He had come to town partly to see Flo, but now, finding him occupied, went on to the food shop next door to look in on Eddie.

Jeremy had known Eddie for ten years. So had Walsh, for Eddie had made himself useful to the boathouse. He had often rowed into its water doorway and had unloaded on its cement quays liquor and other contraband stuff. In those days Jeremy too, whenever he had an evening free, had come to the port to drink and to comfort himself with the spectacle of active life. Then he had come less often. The speedboats had gone. The peninsula with its lonely woods had closed him in.

Entering Snacks, he found it almost empty. Most people who wanted to eat went to a new place around the corner and those who wished to drink went to a bar. Only Eddie, Flo, the barber and a few others, stubbornly clinging to illicit ways, came here with flasks to eat and drink at the same time. This group considered itself apart, and only after close scrutiny would they accept a newcomer into their midst.

Eddie was there now, holding forth to the barber on past adventures in his soft voice. For all his ugly, thick, warty features, there was an attraction about the man. He seemed to caress the ears of his listeners and had a knack of making a brutal episode sound almost tender.

He looked up as Jeremy appeared. "Hello Jeremy. How's tricks? Still worrying about all those worms?"

Jeremy laughed and wondered why he came here so seldom. Eddie turned his obsession with the grave into a joke, a joke which could perhaps be shared among men.

Someone came to fetch the barber for a shave and then Flo arrived, holding his girl by the hand and pulling her along as a tug pulls a barge. "Well Jeremy, what do you know?" he asked as they sat down.

"You might at least introduce me," said the fat girl with an attempt at niceness.

"I might," said Flo, without doing so. "I don't know why I go with her," he complained to no one and with no expression. "I've tried and tried to think. Haven't I, Eddie? You heard me asking myself that question and I just don't get any answer. It's a mystery. Why, do you know Jeremy, I'm just the only man in Star Harbour that'll date Ruby here?"

Ruby looked at them with contempt. "Give me a chocolate marshmallow sundae," she called to Ma, and when it was put before her she ate it greedily, slowly but with a kind of lust, turning the spoon in her mouth and showing her tongue with every bite.

"You know we got a youngster up at our place," said Jeremy.

"Two, ain't it?" asked Eddie.

"You shouldn't have done what you did, Flo," said Jeremy.

"He wanted it." Flo looked nervous.

"Now I never saw Flo do a better job," said Eddie, "than on that nice kid from your place."

"His mother didn't like it much," said Jeremy, "and I must say I don't blame her."

"What's the matter with you?" asked Eddie. "It's not your kid."

"I know that but the boy thinks what Flo did is important. He hid it all these days."

"Well, it was bound to be kind of swollen at first and that little scab had to come off," said Flo. As he spoke there came into his brain the memory of working at his trade and of the pleasure of it: on arms stretched in bulges by muscle, on thighs twitching beneath the five needles, on hands to warn rogues of one another, on matted chests and on the smooth boy's chest of Ronny. That skin with its olive tan, its pure sheen, appeared before his eyes again. He would have loved to tie the boy down and work for hours upon him, pricking out all those signs and images he had learned. Such symbols were Flo's only learning. They represented religion and philosophy, romance and justice, poignancy and truth. Requested out of vanity, they were also records, as he well knew, of each emotional, each spiritual step in a man's life. His own empty little bosom bowed before them. He was proud to be a tool of their recording.

"I wish I could have used colour," he said.

"Any way I can't figure out your feelings on the subject, Jeremy," protested Eddie. "According to you, a skin don't last long, tattooed or not."

Jeremy had no reply so he swallowed several mouthfuls of Eddie's liquor.

"That's the spirit, Jeremy," encouraged Eddie. "We were getting so we didn't recognize you."

Ruby had finished her sundae and was gazing towards the open door where a handful of flies turned restlessly in a sort of loose ball. They were excited no doubt by the growing stench of low tide and their constant murmur was like a conversation. From outside, shouts of boys could be heard as they climbed down the ladders into the water or boldly dived from the dock end. The ferry's blast sounded wistfully out on the water.

Jeremy leaned back in his chair and lit his pipe. Eddie took a toothpick from his pocket and began to pick his teeth, carefully holding a napkin before his face. It, the napkin, was one of the few remnants of a mother's teaching in a far land and Eddie never made this gesture without a virtuous glow. He paid particular attention to his golden teeth of which he was very proud. His eyes, which could be seen above the cheap, white square of paper, wore the ruminating expression of those concerned with important bodily rites.

Ruby sat on and gave great sighs from time to time as though to lift her heavy bosom from her heart.

As Jeremy climbed back into his car half an hour later, he felt quite pleased. He had come to chide Flo and perhaps to ask him if there were not an easy way to remove the tattooing. He had done neither really, but the fact that he had wanted to was something.

CHAPTER 19

ON THE AFTERNOON OF THE FOLLOWING DAY June
received an invitation to the boathouse. She happened to wander down
into the front hall and there it was in an envelope on the round silver
dish that always stood there. No one left cards at the Greys' house so
the invitation might have lain there for days unnoticed, but actually it
had been left only that morning. After quitting his pupil, Stevens had
dropped it quietly into the dish. On the envelope in a sprawling hand
was written: "Miss Grey."

June took it up and at once felt that chill which the unknown brings
to skin and flesh, that lonely warning: 'You are mortal, you are frail. In
every future there is at least a death.'

The white, stampless envelope slid along her palm and at its contact
she hesitated; yet the note inside was reassuring, almost gay.

"Dear Miss Grey," it read, "Do not, please, stay away just because I
am here. Ronny is quite lost without you. Why don't you come for dinner
tonight. No need to reply, just walk in as always, Grace Villars."

All the words were run together so that June was puzzled by the "as
always." Did Mrs. Villars mean it to be the conventional ending of a
letter? If so, how odd. Mrs. Villars was not, as always, anything to June.
On the other hand she could have meant: "Walk in as you always do.

Walk in without being asked." June, at a most touchy age, felt that this ending spoiled the letter. She had been on her way out, but now went back upstairs to her room.

Heat, or else the violent cycle of puberty, was giving June today one of those headaches that put awry the very sutures of the skull. Her back ached below the waist and she felt as though she were about to get a cramp in the arch of her left foot. She sat on the edge of the bed and reread the invitation. It seemed to become a part of her discomforts. From the scrawling lines there emanated a female breath that put her out of ease.

The last days had been long and had brought back upon June all the heavy memory of her fever with its quality of languor and of boredom. Only now, to these ingredients was added the disturbing ardour of her dreams. Waking, she felt crushed by idleness. There was nothing for which her energy was enough, nothing for which it was worth while displacing her limbs or her entranced spirit. Then, when she lay down on the bed, a sort of half sleep overcame her in which her imagination and senses mingled. It was like being sucked down into a shallow whirlpool where, although helpless, she was not drowned. It was a sort of swoon.

Now, still clutching the envelope, June twisted around and threw herself face downwards on the counterpane. In this position she felt relaxed. By pressing her arms tightly against her sides she managed to protect the tender contours of her bosom. She raised the locks of hair from her nape and left them to lie upwards on the pillow, all twisted and damp with the heat. At once she fell into a doze and began to dream. This was not the submerged dreaming of midnight which is difficult to remember and comes from the locked chambers of the mind. It was rather a fantasy made of her substance; of her body pressing against the bed; of the dark tide rising in her womb.

Half awake, still conscious of her throbbing head, June found herself at the brink of the bluffs. Often in childhood she had run down their steep, sandy slopes with her brothers and now the uncontrollable urge took her to do so once again. As she took the first leap, (a leap which by its ease and length retold her she was dreaming) the whole aspect of the bluffs changed. Huge flowers spurted from their sands, coming into bloom like those sea gardens that are half beast, unfolding restlessly and greedily their thick blossoms. The stalks were filled with an oily juice which forced its sweat onto the petals so that the colours glistened.

Rising high above the flowers in her bounding descent, June caught sight of the donkey whom she had seen carrying lovers at the fair. He was grazing among the blooms, chewing the living petals one by one, stubbornly and with a sly expression. Her next leap brought her almost above him and she saw his genital organ thrust itself out of his body like a long, black sword. Yet he did not look at her. His yellow teeth kept on tearing at the petals. His sly stubborn face looked down.

With a start June woke up completely. She rolled over and put her feet on the floor. At once a black dizziness from rising abruptly made her sight dark. The room when it reappeared had a ghostly look which gave place gradually to its ordinary aspect.

'So that's what happened at the fair,' she thought. 'I knew something happened that night, but when I tried to think it went away.'

June passed her hand over the back of her head, pressing gently to quiet its throb. Yes, that was it.

The little donkey at the fair must have done the same thing as her dream animal only she had not noticed it at the time. He had been weary and thin. He had not even bothered to look at her. With his donkey mind and donkey heart he had ignored the marvelous weapon aroused beneath his belly.

'That's what they do,' she thought, 'pretending not to, just like that!'

But who were they? What made her think of them? June started to laugh, or rather to giggle, as she sat on the bed and held her head in her hands. She stopped when the note, which had fallen beside her, caught her eye. Whatever was she to wear? Once thought of, this problem appeared almost insurmountable. The normal thing would be the flowered silk, but she had observed herself in it the other night and knew it to be childish and ill fitting to a degree. Aside from that, what? In despair June looked through her wardrobe. Most of the things were completely outgrown, relics besides of a period in which she had given no thought to clothes. Mrs. Villars, coming from real places, would be sure to know what girls wore when they were fifteen. It was hopeless. Yet the problem of dress only reinforced June's determination to go.

"What if I were walking through the woods in my blue jeans," she thought, "and it became dark so that I was afraid of being late and was near there anyway?"

This seemed a good, although daring plan. But to her horror June found that her jeans which she had not worn for some time, no longer fit her. She struggled to force them over her hips only to see in the mirror their absurd effect. Loose before, now her forms were compressed in them so that she could neither walk nor sit. Angrily she peeled them off and threw them on the floor. There remained only her shorts.

After dressing, June yanked the comb through her hair whose rich locks were tangled and moist. For an instant her face in the glass around which this troubled hair fell was like the reflection of a stranger. June struggled to find a true appraisal of it, but before she could do so it was once more her own.

Ready, she plunged down the back stairs. "Catherine!" she called, knowing at the same time that she would never be answered. It was against Catherine's policy to answer shouts. June found the maid servant on the porch, accepting from McGreggor's hands a basket of berries as though they were a personal and compromising gift.

"Catherine, I'm going out to dinner at the boathouse."

"And what is there to shout about in that I'd like to know?"

"Well, we can't all be perfect like you," complained June, smiling at the same time to prove she was not embarrassed by Catherine's sharp tongue.

"That we can't," said McGreggor, but as he said it to himself nobody heard or appreciated his ready wit. Inside his head McGreggor had a hundred such remarkable observations stored away unused. Enough, surely, to have urged Catherine churchward long ago.

"Is it going in those clothes you are?" Catherine asked conversationally.

"No, I'll change later," said June, thinking: 'Well, I can if I feel like it.' But she got the impression Catherine knew better. Unaccountably the woman's eyes softened.

"Well have a good time for yourself," she advised, and watched June walking away under the trees.

June wandered slowly towards the beach. In the afternoon silence of meadow and wood a calm flowed into her breast. Her bare legs brushed lightly against the undergrowth while now and again, as a small branch was snapped or a leaf torn, there came to her nostrils one of those forest perfumes that are so filled with memory.

'Will I really leave here one day,' she wondered, 'and never come back?' The question with its tinge of finality pleased her because she was still so young and she tried to look around as though bidding her surroundings adieu. 'Would I feel sad?' she asked herself and then, like missing a breath, came the thought that her grandmother every day must look upon familiar places thus. 'How different it is for me than for her,' she mused with the dense, naive plainness that makes young girls disliked at times.

By now June had reached the edge of the creek and saw to her disappointment that the tide was at ebb. The green-black mud, covered with harsh rushes, was exposed and there was only a foot of water in the main channel. She traversed the crooked length of bridge, staring down over the railing at the marsh which was spread beneath her like a map of unknown lands. Yet she knew its every corner and was familiar with its monsters and its perils. The mud, for instance, was quick in patches. Icy springs flowed beneath and were choked so that a black jelly quivered above them. They could suck a man down in a perfectly deadly way, but June had known the position of the patches as far back as she could recall. Some of them indeed had lost their danger, since once one was over a certain height, one could touch bottom and stand triumphant on the freezing ground beneath. How passionately she had played here as a small, naked child! June shuddered at the thought and nothing would have made her step into the creek today.

She reached the beach, took off her sandals and walked down to the tide mark. There were a few sails to be seen lying aslant in the same breeze which played at the edges of her hair. Here it was no longer hot and the sun was sinking behind the hills across the bay. Soon she could see it no longer and the sky was left a deep, fathomless blue. No matter how far she stretched her gaze there was no end of it, nor could birds pierce it, nor any engine of man. June lay on her back in warm sand and looked up and thought of the sky and of God and listened to the seagulls mew and the lap of small waves against the pebbles.

After a while she rose and walked along the beach towards the boat-house which loomed up behind a forest of reeds. She did not re-cross the bridge, but waded through the mouth of the creek which was sandy and shallow with the tide's ebb. As she pushed through the reeds, June felt a veil of silence around her face as though she would never be able to speak again. A sort of sweet glue was on her lips, sealing them together. 'Soon,' she thought, 'I'll have to meet a strange person and say polite things.'

Surrounded by these dry, tall, solitary stalks it was hard to believe.

CHAPTER 20

JUNE PULLED FAINTLY AT THE CHAIN of the gate and then, irritated by the rusty response, pulled harder so that the noise shattered the woods and seemed to explode inside her head. Grace Villars herself opened the latch and June saw that her hostess, too, was in shorts. She realized at the same time that the older woman's slim, muscular legs with their tight knees, their smooth and modeled shanks, made her own appear unformed. She became conscious of unshaven down and of the dimples marked out on her thighs by puberty. What a fool she had made of herself by coming thus! Blushing, she presented her excuse and realized as she did so that it had already been made obsolete.

"It got late and I was walking so I didn't have time to change."

"Well I shan't change either," said Grace, taking June by the hand and drawing her towards the house. "Ronny will just have to put up with us like this for the evening."

June was intrigued by the mother's fashion of speaking of her son as though he were already a man. Through the corners of her eyes and with quick glances she tried to examine her hostess. In tight, pink shorts and a boy's white shirt, Grace was like a tomboy doll. True, her face was slightly raddled, the line broken around her jaw and the colour too high, but June was as yet uncritical of faces as long as they were pretty. 'I wonder if high heels would make my legs look like that?' she mused, and decided sadly against it. One had to have a boyish figure, the kind she, June, had lost already and which would surely never return.

As for Grace, she looked freely and merrily at June and could not understand. 'What an utter lump!' she said to herself. 'And just at that terrible age; gauche and no proportions.' Yet the strong, rather frowning girl's face annoyed her slightly.

"So you're the girl who's putting my Ronny into such a state," she said teasingly and showing her pretty little teeth.

June's colour mounted and she turned away her head and looked out over the woods where a few fireflies flashed in the air. These silent lights, hardly visible in the dusk, filled her with longing. They were like a part of her childhood which, at Grace Villars' tone, seemed infinitely remote. She wished she need never go into the house or see Ronny in this new atmosphere.

"I don't know where that dreadful man is who drives the car," Grace was saying. "I thought we could go to the movies after dinner. But you're probably a blue stocking," she added, turning to June with her impudent glance, "and prefer more serious pleasures."

June, who had not given the movies much thought since her illness, felt keenly the injustice of this remark. It was folly to say: "I'm not a blue stocking," because that would show she was afraid of being one. On the other hand to say: "Oh I love the movies!" would be utterly servile. The only right answer was a light laugh just touched with scorn; the glamorous, careless kind of scorn which is like bells tinkling. June gave her laugh, which sounded off key, and became more uncomfortable than ever so that she explained:

"You see, I used to love the movies, the kind my brothers like, but that was last year and since then I've grown out of adventure stories."

Now it was Grace's turn to feel unhappy. An obscure pain inside her, brought out by something in June's words, made her cry out sharply: "Nonsense, there is no such thing as 'growing out' of adventure films. I still love them best of all."

"Oh but it's different for you," said June. "You're older. I mean you're a mother and everything." What she meant was that once one was married and had children, romance could no longer be of any possible interest. One might just as well return to adventure stories. Yet could Mrs. Villars quite be considered as out of the way as that? June began to blush for her words. On the other hand the thought occurred to her that she was confronted by a loose, free woman; a fascinating idea.

They had reached the house whose open door showed black in the oncoming dusk. No lights were yet lit and one got the impression on crossing the threshold of being in a place afloat, half island and half ship. The tide had turned and June, hearing its urgent voice beneath, fancied the building trembled. She looked at Grace. Did this woman know that there was water right under the house? Would she care if she did?

Grace was calling Mary and running about, switching on lights. She did not feel the turning tide, yet the coming of night in this lonely place depressed her. She felt like crying and could not understand why she had come. There was nothing wrong with Ronny. He was just a boy, and as for James Stevens, he was silly and repressed. June, too, was nothing but a growing girl, hardly a rival. The whole thing in fact was futile. Then, because it was dusk and the house so gloomy, she thought: 'Yes, and when June is my age I will be old!' Grace shuddered at this terrible woman's thought for which there is no remedy, no poison strong enough to be its antidote.

"Mary!" she called in an exasperated voice. "Ronny!"

"You see!" she said to June, speaking with her lips drawn off her teeth. "Ronny is awful. He doesn't even come to meet his guest. You should train your young men better."

June stood quite still. 'Am I being insulted?' she asked herself in dismay.

Mary sidled into the room, drying her arms on her apron. It upset her that she must feed Grace Villars, for she had never cooked outside her home circle before.

"Oh Mary, for God's sake do bring in something to drink," begged Grace.

Mary's body at these words became slippery with apprehension. The problem of drink was exactly what she had been dreading most. Walsh had said in his letter: "Don't forget to buy liquor in case Mrs. Villars should want any during the week before I arrive." What did 'liquor' mean, in this case? Mary had consulted her husband.

"Well, the old man used to get in whisky, gin and vodka," Jeremy said.

Mary thought all these things sounded too manly. "Mrs. Villars is a lady," she protested.

"Yes, but I'm no butler and you're no ladies maid and the old man knows it."

"What about some nice wine or champagne?" suggested Mary soothingly. In the end Jeremy had got a selection, but up until this evening Mrs. Villars had not seemed aware that such a thing as alcohol existed. It was upsetting to have her suddenly ask for it now. It was probably insulting for a lady to be offered whisky, and did one drink champagne in front of children? Mary felt her nose growing red and her brow damp. All she could do was to stand wiping her hands and her wrists in her apron, as though awaiting further orders.

Grace came over and shook her gently, saying with a smile and in a sisterly voice: "Alright, tell me what you've got."

While they were talking, Ronny came up the boathouse stairs. For the last hour he had been crouching there on the quay, holding a line out over the water. He wanted to catch one of the eels which glided about the rotting timber of the boats. Mosquitoes tormented him as he crouched bare-legged over the half stagnant water, and the constant menace of their whine seemed like the thoughts inside his own brain.

He was squatting on his heels, and his knees, which thrust up in front of him, square-ended, were covered with warts. He had been getting dozens of warts lately on his joints; hard, pale growths which might be a message or a warning. In the dim light down here the mark of his tattoo appeared darker. As always when he was alone, he felt it to have a life apart: a heavy, hungry existence, like a vampire fastened to the pores of his breast.

Ronny was thinking about Shalimar and Gambol. That afternoon an incident had made him realize that his life with them and with all animals was coming to an end. The bird had arrived home without being called and with its feathers ruffled. It had been in some fight, a battle of the air, for there was blood on its beak. Ronny had been curious. He had smoothed the harsh plumage, talking softly. But something had gone wrong. There was a stillness, a sort of lack in the atmosphere. The bird, quiet under its master's hand, had gazed its yellow gaze to each side of its head, and there was nothing said and nothing thought between Shalimar and Ronny. The communications were cut.

'But of course I never did really talk to him,' reasoned Ronny now, peering down into the shallow green water and dangling his line. 'No, that's not true,' he contradicted himself. 'I must have since I knew everything.' Then a horrifying idea struck him. What if only his heart had spoken? They said the heart knew languages no tongue could utter; that it could leap the barrier from man to beast, a speech fashioned in the center of the blood.

And now Ronny's heart could speak no longer. It had grown feeble, drained as June had predicted by the sorcery on his bosom.

Ronny threw down his line and, leaping to his feet, ran up the circular iron staircase. He did not know that June had arrived and when he saw her upstairs in the big, gloomy living room, could not repress a start that was like a shudder of animosity.

CHAPTER 21

STEVENS HAD SPENT THE WHOLE DAY DOING NOTHING, or rather in yielding with an almost voluptuous pleasure to the hypnotic pull of the peninsula.

"Let us have some fun with June Grey," Grace Villars had said when last they met, looking at him like a wicked little girl. "I'll ask her to dinner and you must come along afterwards."

Stevens woke up early that morning. Standing barefoot in front of the kitchen stove, he brought a pan of water to the boil. He always drank tea in the mornings and the pot stood on the hob waiting to be scalded. Through the screened kitchen window the morning air poured into the room and refreshed his eyes. Stevens, because he slept without a pillow, had a temporarily congested look to his face when he woke up. It made him appear more full and virile. Yet there was no one there to see it. He always drank his morning tea alone. As alone, he reflected, as an old maid. Indeed, the other day he had heard himself called that by one of his scouts, repeated no doubt from the conversation of the child's elders.

Stevens prepared a tray and carried it into the living room where he sat down on the sofa. 'After all,' he thought, 'I am a desirable bachelor. Why do I think of myself as forlorn? I have only to crook my finger and Lucy would be at my side for life.' He pictured Lucy in her sweater and skirt, with her body that seemed to go in slightly everywhere, save at the elbows. How would she be as a companion, as the mistress of his house and of his bed? The idea was unwelcome and brought into his cold eyes a flicker of distaste. Yet he had found comfort in her admiration, and she had been the only one in town who appeared to appreciate his qualities and his taste.

Grace Villars had no taste at all. She had gone through it, so to speak, and come out triumphantly on the other side. It was only when one was struggling to become something that taste was needed. After that, perhaps, it could be cast aside, like a disguise.

Stevens ran his hand through his thin, tousled hair and looked ruefully around the room. 'Mother was right,' he thought. 'They would have loved this house just the way it was. It would have been an honest atrocity.' It was remarkable what a difference Grace Villars' coming had made and he hated to think how soon she would go away again. 'But after all,' he reflected 'she is probably no older than I am or very little. We could even marry and then I would be Ronny's father.'

This thought which had come boldly and clearly into Stevens' mind took him aback. A sharp sensation pierced his blood, whether of pleasure or pain he could not tell. He rose and began to walk up and down the room repeating to himself aloud:

"Yes, we could marry!"

Then, from the recesses of his brain, the rest of the sentence sent its echo to his heart. 'Then Ronny would belong to me—' The boy's face came before his eyes; that face at once too suave, too wild, too fair, too dearly loved.

It was night time when Stevens drove his car along the peninsula road with its deep, sandy ruts. Rabbits flew in front of his lights, unable in their terror to get out of the way, and a great moth came softly to die against the windshield. Above, the falling stars shot across the atmosphere to vanish in unknown skies. Stevens did not look up. He did not like the sky at night with its mocking blaze of planets and stars. Anyway, he had to concentrate and drive slowly because of the rabbits for he was tender-hearted.

The gate was open at the boathouse, with Jeremy leaning against it, smoking his pipe and gazing over the reeds at the glimmer of the bay. "Well, Mr. Stevens," he called, "coming courting?"

Stevens flushed at the man's impertinence. Why did menials all imply the carnal urge, he wondered irritably. Catherine, at the Greys, had had the same banter in her voice. Jeremy, standing in his path, forced him to slow his car to a standstill. "Move aside, Jeremy," he said in his coldest and most authoritative tone. "And please don't forget your place."

"My place and yours will be the same one day, Mr. Stevens," said Jeremy.

"I doubt we'll be buried in the same grave," said Stevens, and was pleased with himself for this quick answer.

"The whole earth is a grave," retorted Jeremy, but he moved aside nonetheless and wandered off into the woods, with his pipe glowing among the fireflies.

Stevens felt victorious as he drove around the shell-paved yard. He was greeted at the door by the still unhappy Mary.

"They're in the front room," she said, and seemed relieved to see Stevens.

"Your husband is certainly a gloomy fellow, Mary," remarked Stevens.

"Oh it's only talk," said Mary. Her voice was wifely and Stevens wondered if she were right.

Grace was sitting in a big chair, her feet tucked childishly beneath her and her sharp little bare knees pointing out over the edge of the cushion. She was balancing a cup of coffee on her thigh, and held in her hand a glass of brandy. Ronny was crouched upon the floor, occupied with a sharpened nail and a small ring. As for June, she was sitting in the middle of the room perfectly erect and looking in front of her with a smile on her lips. A slight movement as of a wind made the young girl's torso and head sway as she sat there. Stevens experienced that momentary sense of unreality felt by sober people on seeing drunken ones.

He greeted Grace. "Good evening, Mrs. Villars." And then: "Good evening, Ronny." June he did not acknowledge.

Grace smiled and held out her left hand in an intimate way. Ronny looked up briefly through his roughened hair.

"You never came before in the night," he said.

"Oh Roddy, is that nice?" cried Grace, smiling and pouting as though Ronny had paid her a risqué compliment, which perhaps he had.

Stevens had still not said a word to June, who was lifting a glass of brandy to her lips. His schoolmaster's instinct made him wish to demand: "Haven't you had enough to drink, June?" The words tried to force themselves out, but the presence of his hostess closed his mouth. He saw that she was enjoying the situation. Her frivolous little body was full of malice. In her posture, the movements of her head, and in the sharp twinkle of her eyes were the purest mischief. Stevens knew that to utter a chiding word would put him at outs with Grace forever.

Always before this, whatever colour had been given his words and actions by his secret being, Stevens had done and said what he conceived to be his duty. Now his silence seemed like a whisper in the depths of his soul, whether of relief or of regret he could not tell. In any case, he looked at Grace and smiled back and their two blond glances mingled, full of worldliness.

Then Ronny said shrilly without looking up: "June is drunk. Mother did it on purpose."

Grace laughed. "My little lovebirds haven't spoken together once all evening."

June held her glass by its stem and now a little of the liquor splashed on her legs. "Speaking isn't so important," she said. She spoke slowly, trying to control her thickened tongue and half frowning with the effort. Her tawny, uneven hair fell forward over her cheeks and big drops of sweat were forced out on her forehead by the brandy and the fever it had reawakened. Her skin glistened and was marred by red patches.

"If you're going to be a woman of the world, my dear, you must learn the importance of conversation."

"I'm not going to be a woman of the world," replied June, still in the same thick, slow tones.

"Oh? What are you going to be?" Grace winked at Stevens as she rose to get him brandy and coffee. June did not reply at once and Stevens, watching his hostess, reflected that he had never before seen a female who looked well in shorts. Those muscular, hairless little legs seemed to dance as they crossed the room and as Grace passed her son she brushed them against his shoulders. At the touch Ronny lifted his head and a sudden smile came on his face, full of masculine under-standing. Stevens showed his own boyish smile to Grace as she handed him the drinks.

"So I wasn't mistaken!" she said at once. Her airy voice with its frank inflections made a meaning clear to him; the gate, waiting to be opened between a woman and a man, was ajar.

"Mistaken?" He raised his brows whimsically.

"Yes," she said, moving away from him and speaking over her shoulder. "I thought I had found someone amusing in this hermitage and then I was afraid you might be stuffy after all."

"And now?"

"Now I think you needn't be stuffy," she said, laughing at him and curling up in her chair like a cat. Then deliberately she turned a great, blue, mocking gaze full on June.

June rose as at a signal and crouched beside Ronny. Her movements were full of a clumsy, soft, drunken grace which wrung the older woman's heart. Stevens could see this by the way Grace's eyes narrowed and a chord responded in his own breast.

"Ronny," asked June, "can I help you fix Shalimar's chain?"

"How did you know it was his?" Ronny looked at her with keen atten-tion. His animosity towards her vanished in an instant. "You can't touch it," he explained, "but you can sit right here and watch."

This did not suit Grace. "Come on," she said. "Let's all go to the movies." She jumped to her feet. "I'm going to put on a skirt. Shall I lend you one, June? Come along upstairs and try it on." She took June's hand, pulled her to her feet and whisked her out of the room, calling: "Get ready, boys. We'll be down in a minute."

Stevens felt a sensation new to him and thought it to be happiness. Yet perhaps it was excitement, admiration or even that ultimate emotion. 'If only this could be love!' he said to himself in a sort of prayer.

June did not want to go upstairs at all. In her burning hand whose edges seemed undefined, dissolved in fever, that other hand was sharp and cool. Those alien fingers curling around into hers were like supple knives and June fancied that they pierced the lines of her palm, that they marred her destiny. And how strong that sharp hand was! It lifted her to her feet, or one must suppose so, because June could no longer associate her feet with herself.

'Am I really drunk?' she wondered with a thrill. 'How wicked and daring I must be!' She stumbled on the first step. 'I am not one to be afraid of vice,' she thought. 'I knew I wouldn't be, since one must, after all, experience everything. One must drink life to the lees.'

"Don't you think, Mrs. Villars," she said as they went upstairs, "that one must drink life to the lees?" There! Surely after such a profound and courageous phrase, this blond mother of Ronny would treat her as a friend and equal.

"And what of the lees?" asked Grace; "Must one drink them, too? They're bitter you know."

"Yes, them too." June shook her head wisely and all of a sudden felt sick. The stairs curving up into the darkness were interminable and in the niche of them was a monster. It was a stone gargoyle which Walsh had brought back from Europe because he said it reminded him of his mother. Once it had stretched its stone neck to frighten the enemies of God. Now, with its protruding tongue and small, vicious eyes, it made June retch. She swallowed frantically. For a while the poison turned like a great wheel cold as ice between the feverish walls of her chest. She gulped back a sour mouthful which stung her throat. Then the wheel dissolved and sank slowly down again into her stomach. She was left grateful and almost sobered by her escape.

They reached Grace's room, and Grace, having opened her closet, had taken out a length of flowered linen and was twisting it around her hips. It became a skirt as if by magic, although one could still see a glimpse of her leg and the pink shorts on one side.

"Now let's see," said Grace, looking at June.

The young girl, too, looked down at herself, as though viewing her figure through Grace's eyes. She experienced at once that acute sense of unattractiveness which stains the adolescent's pride. It was hopeless, she thought looking down at her marvelous body, at the tender, eager, unviolated curves of her youth. Hopeless! She was going to be fat and ugly.

June's feelings must have been understood by the older woman, for Grace smiled. "Here," she said, "this is the biggest thing I have. I'm sure it would fit anyone." She handed June a peasant skirt dotted with small farm animals. While June put it on, Grace sat down at the old-fashioned dressing table and remade her face. She did this in a sketchy, happy-go-lucky way that was really meticulous. She spat into the mascara and rubbed her finger in the wake of her lipstick. Then she powdered her nose with a big, swansdown hoop and the powder scented the room.

June watched and admired her. Grace grinned in the mirror and then, half turning said: "Come here."

"Come on," she urged as the girl hesitated and she put out once again her small, sinewed hand. This time she grasped June's arm and pulled her around to sit beside her on the wicker-covered bench. When June was seated, Grace tightened her grasp.

"Look there, June," she commanded in a peculiar voice whose lightness could hide neither cruelty nor anxiety. Then, as June seemed to be gazing stupidly at nothing, Grace released her arm and twisted the girl's chin around to face the mirror. "Just look," she cried, "at the difference between you and me!"

For an instant that stretched for both of them out of actual time, they sat there hip to hip and stared steadfastly at the two reflected heads set so mistakenly together. Beside the older woman's vivid face, June's appeared sallow, troubled and pale. She saw that her nose shone, that there was a red spot on her chin and that the scrolls of Grace's platinum curls made her own hair colourless and dank. Oh to have small features, pink cheeks, and those blond curls!

Grace was laughing. All traces of anxiety had left her. "Isn't it funny?" she trilled, and letting go of June's chin she clapped her hands together. "How funny you look!"

It was the kind of thing a brother might say and one would forget it at once, thought June. Why then did she feel that she would never forget it now? She did not dare ask to borrow powder so she simply sat there smiling in a cowardly way until Grace got tired of the joke. Or perhaps Grace realized that the joke would not bear too lengthy an inspection. Anyway, she rose and they both went back downstairs.

Stevens was wondering why Grace insisted on bringing Ronny and June along to the theater. But that was her way. She liked crowds and she liked situations, especially if she were mistress of them. Also, she did not relish the idea of Stevens alone. To Grace it would be an insult were he not to make an attempt of some sort. Even Stevens would feel that. Yet with a man such as he, it was far too soon. It would be like eating a green apple. As a malicious stroke she said:

"I'm going to sit with my Roddy in the back." She flashed into the car, showing her leg and shimmying around like a fish to sit in the seat. Ronny followed her, silent and preoccupied. He had a dreamy expression and he clanked in his pocket the metal ring on which he had been working. June climbed in drearily and could not bear to look at Stevens as he started the car. Her fever which had flared up with her drunkenness turned now into chill. She shivered as the soft night breeze blew into the window. Against her neck the collar of her blouse felt cold.

They left the peninsula and the lights of Star Harbour appeared ahead. They had difficulty parking because it was Bingo night and every-body was at the movies, nor when they arrived could they all sit together although they were too late for the game.

Grace took Stevens' arm as they went up the ramp and they were placed almost in the front row, with two enormous faces looking down at them from the screen. Stevens was spurred on by the darkness and by the other couples around them. He let his arm, which was resting in back of Grace's chair, slip onto her shoulder. Did she move into it? He thought so, but it might have been a shake of dislike at his temerity. He pretended to have meant nothing and put his arm back down at his side. Then, at one of the climaxes of the film, Grace clutched him and, with a feeling of do or die, Stevens took her hand. With a slow, lazy movement, strange to such a nervous piece of sinew and bone, the hand turned upwards and unfolded its palm towards his.

Stevens almost mistook a thrill of excitement for desire. Soon, however, he began to worry about when their palms got warm. How would he remove his own gracefully and without lack of chivalry? And what if their hands actually became wet? Grace, as though guessing his preoccupation, released herself quite soon with a little squeeze and nestled close to him in such a way that he once more put his arm around her shoulders.

In no time at all the lights went up and whatever the story had been, it was over. Stevens became painfully aware of Lucy Philmore sitting with another young woman quite near them. He might have known that the whole town would be here tonight. The pain in those unguarded eyes made him self-conscious.

"Good evening, James," said Lucy when they were in the aisle. "What a bad picture. They always seem worse on Bingo night and I never win." Lucy gulped and blushed furiously because she had been about to say something about unlucky at cards. She hurried on with a strangled fare-well. But she had taken in Grace Villars to the last detail.

"Never mind!" said Grace, looking up at Stevens roguishly. "We can't all love whenever we are loved," and she added: "My, you seem to have found a heart to break even in Star Harbour!"

Stevens, as she meant him to be, was pleased.

At the doorway they met June and Ronny coming out. Eddie was with them, showing his gold teeth, his head to the side. "Hello, beauti-ful," he was saying quite clearly to June and his accent made of this cheap address something more poignant. June gave a smile of pure relief. After the events of the evening those words were like a balm.

Eddie caught sight of Grace and Stevens. "Well, I guess you're with company. We'll move on."

"They're not company," protested Ronny. "They're just Mother and our teacher."

Grace laughed her special laugh for Ronny's childish sayings. "Intro-duce us, Ronny dear," she begged.

"This is Eddie and this is Mr. Flo."

"Oh yes, the famous Flo," said Grace, looking at the little man who had been almost hidden behind his friend. "It's you who are the tattoo artist, isn't it?"

Flo shuffled his feet and eyed Grace's bright hair as though he were really seeing gold. Stevens took a step forward.

"Do you think it was an ethical thing to do, marking a child for life like that?"

"Oh Stevy," coaxed Grace, showing a new intimacy in her babyish tones, "don't be stuffy—remember?"

"Well," muttered Flo, "the kid wanted it."

"Sure," said Eddie, stepping forward with his hands in his pock-ets and speaking with a hard geniality. "That kid's so crazy about June here he wanted it put down." He added. "A man'll do a lot for a good-looking girl."

"*They* don't think she's good-looking," said Ronny, and he stole a look at June to see who was right. But when you had chosen a person you couldn't tell anymore.

The scene was finished as far as Eddie was concerned. He had nothing more to add. Turning on his heel, he went off and Flo veered like a ship's wake and followed after.

CHAPTER 22

RONNY WOKE UP ALL OF A PIECE, his eyes bursting open, fiery and dreamless. Outside his window the sun was wrapped in haze and threw a faint rainbow across the water. It was sure to be another hot day. Already all his body was moist and, as he thrust them from the bed, his legs shone beneath their childish down.

He was very unhappy and could think of nothing to lighten his depression. 'Until Mother came it was all right,' he reflected, 'or if it wasn't, nothing showed, and if things don't show—' But Ronny veered away from subjects like this. His mind nibbled at their edges and refused the core. He reached for his shorts and took from one of their pockets his handiwork of the night before. It was Shalimar's leg ring on which he had carved his initials. For Ronny meant to let the bird go. In the morning light his workmanship looked shallow and crude and Ronny gave a contemptuous smile. How much better Flo had done! He examined his tattooed heart. Did it look bigger? Was it only imagination when he fancied it swollen, or was it really filled with his true heart's juice? It bombed out and hid June's name beneath the nipple.

Ronny rose and dressed himself, pulling on his shorts over naked loins. He did not bother to wash and merely ran his hand through his tousled hair which was flaked with salt. Going downstairs, he met Mary with a tray for Grace. She gave him her timid, half plaintive smile for which she never expected a return.

"Do you want to bring the tray up to your mother?" This was a small sacrifice on Mary's part, but she need not have worried.

"No, I must go and feed Gambol," said Ronny, pulling the bow of her apron so that it came undone. In this trick Mary was perhaps the only one who found enjoyment although she said: "Oh Ronny!"

"Why don't you say, 'Oh master Ronny!'" said the boy. "That's the way you've been acting since mother came."

Mary did not know how to answer this and passed on in silence, her apron hanging from its yolk.

Ronny was about to leave the house when he heard his mother calling him: "Ronny. Ronny I want you."

Turning reluctantly, he mounted the stairs, stopping at the doorway of his mother's room. There Mary, having put down the tray, was retying her apron.

"I have a letter from Jim Walsh," said Grace gaily. "He's coming tomorrow for sure and I've decided we must have a Fourth of July party to celebrate. Do you think you can manage the supplies, Mary dear?"

Mary smiled nervously and immediately began pleating her apron.

As though she had assented, Grace went on: "Lots of scotch and gin." She held out her hand to her son. "Come and sit beside me, Ronny, while I have breakfast."

He came and perched at the foot of the bed, looking very impermanent. Mary left.

"Did you have a good time last night?" Grace asked, smiling with lips that were already rouged.

"I knew you wanted to talk about it," said Ronny. His high voice gave a sort of hysterical humour to the words.

Grace laughed. "You're such an amusing monkey," she said. "I can't wait for you to grow up."

"I can," said Ronny. "I don't care if I ever do."

"Don't you want to be a man and go to parties with me? I'll be so proud of my son. All the other women will be jealous."

Grace could see them now in her fancy. How Ronny would set her off with his dark skin and hair! They would be more like brother and sister than parent and child. No, she frowned, brother and sister was not quite right. Queen and courtier? That was better, although too dignified. Lady and amorous page? Ronny should appreciate that. She said aloud: "You'll be like my handsome page."

"Knights don't act the same way as pages," said Ronny, as though speaking to the window.

But Grace continued her reflections undisturbed by his reply. Not only women would be jealous. Men too would cast dark looks upon this handsome child for jealousy of her. Then one of those little chills came over Grace. How fast the years sped by! If only they could move for Ronny and stand still for her. But they wouldn't; not even for Grace, the youngest woman in all the world. At least that was how she had seen herself until recently. Now, she thought, shrugging her shoulders at the chill, even June Grey could make her stretch her claws.

"June is certainly a rather—odd—choice of yours, Ronny," Grace said aloud. "But I suppose there wasn't any other in this dreary place, my poor baby." As Ronny made no reply to this she lost her temper and asked: "Have you noticed she smells?"

"Yes, she does," said Ronny. "She smells of the sea and I like that much better than any old perfume."

At once Grace was all softness. Her blue eyes swam out at him filled with contrition. "Darling! Sweetest! I forget you're only a little boy. It's my silly way of treating you like an equal. You see I feel we're the same age, and soon we really will be. I mean, to all intents and purposes."

"But you think I won't ever be the same age as June," said Ronny shrewdly. His mother's words, or else his own reply now made him blush. His cheeks took on a dusky bloom.

"That's different," retorted Grace, and looking at him she felt a stir of some emotion that might have been love. "You see, we think," she said, trying to be honest, "that is James Stevens and I think that June takes an unhealthy interest in you. She's a girl, a woman really, and you are still only a boy. It's as if she wanted you to play the part of a man to her."

Ronny did not comment. His mother's words meant nothing new to him. He had known all such things already and perhaps more than Grace would ever understand.

"Roddy dear," asked Grace, vaguely regretting the whole conversation, "are you fond of James?"

"Oh, Mr. Stevens is all right," said Ronny.

"I know he's very fond of you." Despite herself the words once uttered took on their own inflection. Grace bit her lip.

"I must go to Gambol," muttered Ronny uneasily.

Outside in the yard the oyster shells had been ground as fine as flour. They caressed Ronny's bare feet, softer than sand, as soft as silk. Jeremy was washing his car, using a brush and liquid soap with a pleasant smell. He paid no attention to Ronny nor Ronny to him, but they were a comfort to each other. Ronny was reluctant to leave the yard for the stable where all was quiet and a sort of waiting hush was over everything. The chaff hung in the air disturbed by every breath and a musty beam of light fell across Shalimar's stall with its wooden block. The bird could not see this beam of light; its head was covered by the hood and it perched quietly with puffed feathers. Ronny held the falcon hooded while he snapped the ankle ring on its leg. Then he unhooded it and watched the eye on his side of the beak come to life. At first the pupil covered everything, but gradually as Ronny watched, the black lens contracted, the cruel gold of the iris took possession like a consuming flame.

Ronny drew in his breath. He no longer dared address his bird directly, so now he spoke of him, softly in the chanting voice children sometimes use when they are alone with animals. "Shalimar is so beautiful!" he murmured, stroking the ruffled feathers. "Soon he will fly away and live alone on the top of mountains. He will not mind his ring. Sometimes he will sharpen his beak on it and remember that we knew each other."

There was no answer in the stable. The falcon's iris grew larger as the bird glared into the sunlight. Ronny brought it almost to the back door of the stable before it opened its powerful wings and flew away. For a while Ronny watched it mounting into the sky, circling above the peninsula and the morning sea.

Ronny entered the stable once more and spoke boldly to Gambol over the break in his voice: "I suppose you are hungry." He took a pitchfork and began to clean the stall. The sharp smell of ammonia breathed into his fasting body made Ronny dizzy. The blood receded from his temples and he felt that instead of going back into his cardiac veins it ran into his tattooed heart like a traitor.

"Oh Gambol, did you ever speak?" he cried.

The horse munched at his grain contentedly and tore it sideways as though his teeth were a mill stone.

Now the false heart throbbed on Ronny's breast. He really had to put down his head between his knees to keep from fainting.

CHAPTER 23

MORNING ON THE GREYS' HILLTOP WAS A KING ascending his throne; a king surrounded by minions. First, in lieu of trumpets, the dawn breeze blew. Then a mist slowly permeated the air until the dusk gleamed like lead. Afterwards, crying harshly, a horde of crows flew over the peninsula, pursuing an owl. The owl flew slowly, hindered by his torn and bloody feathers and by the dawn which blinded his soft eyes. Other birds now broke into song and a heavy, red sun fought sluggishly up the sky.

June woke up reluctantly. Although she could not recall doing anything really foolish the night before, a guilt as though of some awkward memory sullied the new day. Dressed, she went down to her grandmother's room. Mrs. Grey had her cap awry on her wispy gray head and June repressed a laugh.

"Good morning, my dear," said Mrs. Grey, quite aware of this, but speaking blandly. She was laying out the cards on a tray in front of her and her fingers were glassy at the ends from constant use of a nail buffer. "Did you have a nice time last night?" she asked. "And is Mrs. Villars a pleasant woman?"

"Not very nice," replied June, "and I don't really like Mrs. Villars. She's just a little, blond, made-up lady." June as she said this was surprised. It was as though her grandmother's presence put everything in another perspective.

"Well, well, it's not everybody that can get along with young people or enjoy talking to them." Mrs. Grey spoke in a calm, almost self-satisfied way, but this might have been because she was pouncing on a card.

"Mrs. Villars doesn't consider me a very young person," said June.

Mrs. Grey put down her glasses onto the bridge of her nose and looked at her granddaughter over the rims. "I don't think one should go into things too deeply," she remarked.

This theory, so different from that of social workers, psychologists and doctors, had served the old woman all her life. June, who was at the self-probing age, turned restlessly towards the dresser.

"Well, look who's preening in front of the mirror," said Catherine, entering the room with a crackle of starch. It was as though only the stiffness of her skirts gave her body shape and substance. "It's last night you should have been preening," she continued severely, "instead of going out to dinner in your shorts."

"Well she was in shorts, too," retorted June, who had spent some time regretting her costume. "Besides, I hate all my clothes. Grandmother, how do you think up answers and comebacks and remarks?"

"I believe," said Mrs. Grey, "that if one reflects on the words of other people, one would just as soon not have said them."

"But then the other people get the upper hand."

"In that case you'd better consult Catherine," said Mrs. Grey. "She is never at a loss."

When June left her grandmother's room, she felt better, more as though it were possible after all to communicate with others. However, by the time she reached the kitchen her own isolation returned to her. The lower part of her body ached and a dark pulse dragged at her entrails. Opening the icebox door she was at once revolted by the smell of the new milk which had been set in pans. She shut the door again and looked in the cake box. But she had no sooner begun to eat a slice of cake than the thought of its ingredients disturbed her: butter from the cream in the icebox pans, and lard, like the greasy sweat of pigs. She put it down at once and taking a glass filled it partly with water. Then she poured in the same amount of vinegar and drank the mixture down in a gulp. She waited to feel the slight nausea before the liquid descended and became a part of her.

Stevens was waiting for her when June came into the library. "Good morning," he said, still sitting at the desk and looking out at the moss-starred lawn.

June replied apathetically to his greeting, yet inside her mind a whole silent controversy, as of puppets, was being enacted.

"Why don't you stand up for a lady?" asked the small puppet June.

And the puppet Stevens retorted: "If you acted like a lady I might."

Then the puppet June, made sharp by vinegar, had the last word: "And if you acted like a man instead of like a gray lily I might act like a lady."—No, it would never do after all; the school girl was in it thick as syrup. June sat down wearily at the desk.

Stevens bent his pale eyes upon her. He had expected her to look embarrassed or at least ill after last night. Because she must acknowledge that at one moment in the evening she had been really drunk. He noticed with irritation that June showed symptoms of neither. "June, I think you should know," he said in the authoritative voice which he had once found it so hard to acquire, "that your conduct is most immoral."

"Conduct?" muttered June sullenly. "But it was Mrs. Villars who gave me all that brandy—"

He cut her off. "I'm not talking about your lack of self-control in drinking. That is nothing to do with me. I'm talking about dragging a little boy into the underworld."

"Dragging a little boy into the underworld," repeated June without inflection, and then she understood that he was talking about Eddie and Flo. "You're just angry," she cried, "because—" It was no use. Her tongue was ignorant of all the things her mind knew. It lacked the knowledge and the art to utter them.

"Because?" Stevens urged with a slight smile. June's eyes were opened upon his. In their depths, palpitating and opaque, one could almost see the pulse of her heart. Then, throwing down her books, she ran out of the room.

Outside, June could hardly recall a word of the quarrel. The morning mist had gone except for a faint haze around the sun and it was very hot. A sultry wind blew across the hilltop, burned by the glittering surface of the water. She saw McGreggor trudging towards the back door with a basket of vegetables. They passed quite close, but June could not bring herself to greet him. Apparently McGreggor had the same difficulty, or else he did not see her. His narrow eyes, pushed close to his nose and half hidden by his cheek bones, looked straight ahead and did not waver. June stole a quick glance his way. What were the thoughts of such a man? What if she were to ask him:

"Is it true that you are in love with Catherine?"

She would never dare of course. He would probably rend her with his stiff, hard, small glance. Yet McGreggor must have a soul, or have had one once. She thought of the bagpipes which he had ceased to play. What had once made him bring them out at dusk and skirl their notes into the wood? And even more important, what had made him cease to do so? To cease to do a thing or to feel it; to have a thing be over, there was the mystery. Looking around, June saw that the leaves had a golden tinge and that their first, fresh green was gone, lost forever. Then from the far woods she saw a small figure advancing towards her. It was Ronny, on foot. June ran quickly forwards.

"Where's Gambol?" she cried.

"Oh I didn't ride him today," said Ronny, offhand. "He's just a horse, you know."

June was stopped in her tracks. Here was an example of her very thoughts. "Why do you say that now?" she asked, trying to sound as casual as he, although apprehension made her voice uncertain.

Ronny, if he knew, would not tell her. "Shall we go to the bluffs?" he asked. As of old he took her hand, and this act, always surprising to June because it was so unlike her brothers, now made her throat ache.

The bluffs when they arrived were also an ending, an edge to the world, as if the sound below were that river which only the dead may cross. It was easy to believe that there was no land beyond; only the whirling planets, the stars and the sun's roll. The morning mist still clung to the horizon and the sea was smooth as glass. It lapped quietly at the moist yellow sand of the beach below the bluffs.

"Let's run down," said Ronny. "We never have."

"Oh I've done it often," protested June. Once she would have devoured the steep sands like a tiger. Now, either because of her dream or because of a reluctance for feats performed in childhood, the idea displeased her. "It's awfully hard to get up again," she argued reasonably.

"We'll go around," said Ronny. "Besides there's a little path up the edge. Come on, June!" His high, clear, insistent tones, like a bird or like some rustic flute, now pierced June's ears.

"Don't you see," she cried, "that we aren't going to meet anymore?"

His eyes turned for an instant into hers. "What's that got to do with sliding down the bluffs? Anyway you're supposed to come to the party tomorrow night. Mother said so."

"What party?" asked June, but Ronny was off already, his brown legs making strange angles as he leapt down the bluff. He took big leaps, his teeth bared, his hair standing from his head and he gave yells of excitement at the speed and length of his stride.

A sense of loneliness, of desolation too great to be borne, made June follow him. Despite her distaste, the swift descent and its dreamlike ease exhilarated her and they arrived on the beach panting and almost side by side.

"Now which is beating the fastest," she asked to punish Ronny, "the real or the fake?"

"Eddie is going to bring me some mother's milk to take it away," he cried lightly, "and then I'll be just like before and when it's gone I'll never think of you."

June started to walk away along the beach, but Ronny followed her at once. "Wait!" he called frantically. "Wait, June!" He ran ahead of her and stopped her with his body. "Bend your head," he begged in an anguished voice. "Don't you see you're too tall?"

When they kissed their quick breath mingled and they tasted salt between their lips. June fancied, too, that she could feel on her own bosom the throb of Ronny's tattooed heart.

CHAPTER 24

"GRANDMOTHER," SAID JUNE ON RETURNING HOME, "they're having a party at the boathouse because Mr. Walsh is coming and it's the Fourth of July. Do you think I should go?"

Mrs. Grey was in her room. Although fully dressed, she was lying on the chaise longue and, for all the heat, her legs were covered with a shawl. She really did not feel well. 'I wonder if I'll die before John gets back?' she thought, but she did not much care. Her other sons, still laughing boys, were more numerous. She anticipated already their filial kisses on her soul. She made an effort to concern herself with her granddaughter.

"Go down to the village with Catherine," she offered, "and buy yourself a dress." She peered at June beneath the drooping lids of her eyes. "When you are old," she said, "you recall more clearly the first things than the later ones. I remember being your age perfectly."

"Do you, Grandmother?" asked June, who was both surprised and incredulous.

"I had a red setter puppy," said Mrs. Grey, "and I got a dress of the same colour, for when I took him on the leash. I'm afraid I was a very vain child."

"Now tell about an important thing," begged June.

But Mrs. Grey would say no more. Perhaps she had forgotten the important things, or perhaps what she had already told was of the utmost importance. Certainly it was a fact that when Catherine drove June to Star Harbour that afternoon the pleasure of buying a new dress was surprising.

* * * * *

Eddie and Flo received their invitations later. They had been out with a noisy family party who had taken to sea for no apparent reason. The women, three of them and very large, had lain around the deck so that Flo had constantly to step over them. They wore bathing suits from which the sides of their bosoms flowed out and turned painfully red in the sun. The men belonging to them, hairy and paunched, fished clumsily and with great good humour. Between men and women, fat children drifted like spawn in jelly.

Eddie was glad to get back and relax at Ma's food shop. Flo, as he left the "Arabella," could see Ruby sitting on the porch of her mother's ramshackle house. She was wearing slacks and fanning herself with a newspaper. Flo did not even wave, but followed Eddie into snacks for a sandwich. Ma handed them a note. It was from Ronny.

"Mother says to come to a party tonight at our place. She says to say 'informal' which means not to dress up and she says to bring your girls, only of course she means women and ladies. Also please bring some mother's milk. I have decided not to keep my tattooed heart."

Ruby, when Flo told her they were going to a party, wanted to change out of her slacks, but Flo said not to bother.

"You wouldn't look any better," he said, "and you might look worse."

"I got the figure for pants," said Ruby with an air of complacency.

"Oh Christ!" said Flo.

* * * * *

Stevens had known about the party all along, because after his fight with June he had gone directly to see Grace. She had been standing outside the boathouse gate in her pale pink shorts, staring helplessly at the woods.

"I want to pick some flowers for the party tomorrow," she said petulantly, "but I don't know what kind or where to find them." Becoming more aware of him, she continued: "Besides, they might be poison and make itches on my hands." As though to present their un-itched purity, she spread her ten thin fingers which were dyed scarlet at the tips.

"Party?" asked Stevens, leaning out of the window of his car.

"Yes," she answered in her gay little voice. "And you're coming and you must bring your girl."

"What if I don't have a girl?" Stevens said. He was annoyed that she did not ask him for herself.

"Don't be a spoil sport, James dear. How can a woman be at her best with no competition? She looked so nice, too." Grace said all this with the most coquettish air in the world, twisting and turning on her legs to show the dainty sides of her body. "Yes, you must bring her. It's a command, although I do hope you're not going to neglect me or call me Mrs. Villars in front of her."

"Can I help you get the flowers?" asked Stevens. He wanted to talk about last night, about June's behaviour which it would have eased him to discuss.

Grace, however, appeared to have forgotten completely about the flowers for she flipped her wrist, looked at her watch and said: "Oh, how did it get so late? How do you make time pass so quickly, James? What a dangerous man you are! I must fly." Then she twinkled into the gate and out of sight. Only her blond head reappeared for an instant. "Eight-thirty tomorrow on the dot," she sang.

Stevens had a hard time turning his car on the sandy lane, but his dismissal made it impossible for him to enter the yard and turn in front of the house. As he backed and filled, a nervous irritation soured his blood. 'Fly to what, pray?' he muttered, engaging into second so roughly that his gears ground.

* * * * *

Lucy Philmore heard about the party first from June. June would rather have bought her dress at some more flashy store. She was not sure the gift-shop dresses were right for a party at the boathouse. Catherine, however, was firm.

"It's your grandmother has the account there, so it's there we'll go. Besides, you'd have yourself looking like Sodom and Gomorrah if I let you be."

Lucy's dresses turned out to be very nice after all, and Lucy herself seemed unusually interested in the party.

"I suppose your teacher will be there," she said finally, just as they were leaving.

"Oh I hope not," said June from the doorway. "He's awful."

Lucy smiled sadly and wished she could think him awful in such a light-hearted way. She had never had him, and now she seemed to be losing him. The peninsula, like a hungry animal, had swallowed him up and devoured as well her slender chance of happiness. She recalled that only a few weeks ago it had seemed possible. She had even dreamed of their life together, had pictured herself discussing the problem of this or that child, or having one of his classes in for tea as she heard they did in boarding schools. Now these dreams made Lucy blush as though she had been caught out in an immodest act.

Lucy's shop was cool despite the heat. Customers gratefully remarked on it and stayed to gossip. She had two of them in the front room that afternoon when Stevens came in, and the more she tried to get rid of them the longer they wanted to stay. They must have known perfectly well that the man had come to talk to her. Both of them knew Stevens and had known his mother, yet they pretended not to notice he was there and when, as they were finally leaving, they almost tripped over him, they made surprised recognition an excuse for lingering.

"Mr. Stevens, what a tan! You look quite the movie star! Your dear mother would have been pleased to see you picking up like this."

"Mr. Stevens, my boy just loves his outings with you! My husband thinks they should do more sports, but I tell him: 'Henry, they learn manners with Mr. Stevens and that's just as important.'"

By the time Lucy and Stevens were alone they were both exasperated.

"How I loathe Star Harbour," said Stevens. "Thank God it won't be long. I've decided to sell the house."

"That's sad news to me," said Lucy simply.

Stevens forced himself to smile. "Yes, Lucy, and I'll be sorry not to be neighbours anymore. If all the village were like you—"

'One of me would be enough,' thought Lucy, 'if you cared,' but she said brightly: "You're right to go, James. You have your interests which the people around here can't understand. You have your career to think of, too."

"Oh I shall give up teaching," said Stevens.

"Give up teaching?" Lucy started and then pressing her hands together said: "Don't, please don't, do anything hasty, James."

Suddenly he knew she was thinking of Grace Villars whom she had seen at the movies. Her attitude, her long, thin body in its summer print, made him angry and his own pity hardened his heart. "Lucy, you must allow me to know my business." He waited an instant and then went on: "Besides, I didn't come to speak of these things. I merely wished to ask you if you cared to come to a party with me tomorrow tonight."

"On Grey's Neck?" she asked, using the old Star Harbour name for the peninsula.

"How did you know?"

"Oh, where else?" she parried gaily. "Where else?"

This bright gaiety of Lucy's, so out of keeping with her tight hands and the rigid set of her jaw, made Stevens more irritated than ever.

* * * * *

Jim Walsh drew in towards the boathouse around six-thirty the next day. He was excited and in an unexpected state of anticipation. From the beginning, that is from the party where he had renewed his friendship with Grace, something had been working inside of him. Sometimes, in fact most of the time, Jim did not think of it, but now and then into his old flesh crept the atavistic longing. 'Woman,' said this longing, 'is but a vessel and through this vessel there must run without a break the male germ, the miracle that is father and son.'

Now, as the "High Kick" neared land, Jim took out his binoculars and looked towards the boathouse. He had not so much as set eyes on the place for seven years, and with a sigh he acknowledged that those seven years had led him into old age. They had also sufficed to turn the boathouse from a deluxe oddity into a grimy and rundown building. In another seven it would commence to be a ruin. Already, through his lenses, he could see the crumbling walls that bordered the water and the wild reeds that were closing in everywhere. Had it not been for Jeremy and Mary, he supposed, there would be no staying in the place anymore. Even so, Walsh did not think the actual boathouse would be of any use for his landing boat. He observed that the slide door, green with mould, was half down across the opening and guessed that inside all must be mud and sea grass.

"You'd better land me on the beach, over near those high reeds," he said to his sailor.

Although, as Walsh had remarked, the water gate was half down, Ronny had meant to draw it down all the way. It had got stuck in the middle and would go no farther for all his straining.

It happened that Ronny had been left all alone on the afternoon before the party, while Grace had gone off with Mary and Jeremy to get last minute supplies in Star Harbour. The child had stood for a long time at the foot of the stairs, listening to the emptiness of the house, to the sounds of disintegration which were like groans in its bosom, to the constant sighing of the water beneath. Then he had gone out into the sun.

Ronny had formed one of those resolves, perverse and sometimes criminal, which have led men to the gallows; one of those decisions made even more terrible because they are acted upon calmly and in an ordinary way. It is as though the subject's own soul were hypnotizing his body and his brain, putting him in a trance. Something, at any rate, inside him whispers: 'Enough! Suffer as you will for it, flesh and sentiment, this must end.'

Now, without hesitating, Ronny led Gambol from his stall. The animal was munching a mouthful of hay and continued in this exercise as Ronny led him through the reeds and towards the water. The tide was ebbing and it was shallow all the way around to the water door, never more than waist deep. Gambol followed his master trustfully. He liked being in the water where the flies did not bite.

Ronny drove Gambol into the boat garage, but did not go in himself. Standing waist high in the water, he strained at the rusty chain which held the door. After a while the door, slimy to the touch, came down a little way. Then it broke from its groove and became wedged across the opening. Inside, Gambol waited patiently. Ronny meant the horse to drown when the tide came in, but if Gambol knew this he made no sign.

CHAPTER 25

TO THE BIG ROOM OVERLOOKING the bay Mary had brought many long candles. She was obeying Grace Villars although it seemed a silly waste of money. On a table at one end were laid out sandwiches, salty delicacies, and liquor. Jeremy and the sailor who had landed Walsh were acting as barmen. Out on the water the "High Kick" gleamed in the twilight. Her white paint turned her into a swan and she was only disgraced by the dingy "Arabella" anchored alongside. Both ships moved a little with the incoming tide as though resentful of their chains.

Eddie, Flo and Ruby had arrived at dusk, rowing themselves ashore, or rather, Flo rowing the other two. In landing they had seen Jim's speedboat lying high on the beach and half hidden by the reeds.

"This stuff's spooky," complained Ruby. For a minute they were hidden from each other by the hundreds of stalks rustling and dried of sap by the bitter salt sand in which they were rooted.

Ruby went on: "The guy's supposed to be rich, living in a dump like this?"

"Oh it's changed," said Eddie. "Before it was like a castle and you landed right inside it."

Ronny, who was sitting on a chair eating chicken sandwiches and watching the preparations, leapt up when Eddie arrived. But Eddie and Walsh were greeting each other.

"Son of a gun, Eddie! Still out of jail?" Jim clapped him on the shoulder. Eddie brought back poignantly those days when the fruits of wealth had still tasted sweet.

"It's good to see you're still a free man too, Mr. Walsh," said Eddie in his soft, tender voice, his head tipped sideways as though in mockery.

"Yes, I guess we're both a couple of rascals," said Jim. He look enquiringly at Flo and at the heavy girl in pants.

"We came to the party, Mr. Walsh," explained Eddie, reading Jim's mind. "Ronny invited us."

Jim was delighted. For some reason the fact that Ronny knew Eddie, had picked him out of the whole of Star Harbour, filled him with pride. And now Ronny himself was plucking at Eddie's sleeve.

"Did you bring it?" he asked.

"Hello youngster, bring what?" As comprehension dawned, Eddie started to laugh. Then seeing the tenseness of the boy's expression, he stopped and said seriously: "No Ronny, those things have to be done scientific. Don't they, Mr. Walsh?"

"What are you talking about?" asked Jim, who had been examining Ronny closely and almost furtively.

"Well, Mr. Walsh, Flo here is a famous man with the needles. I guess he couldn't resist practicing on the boy. Come on, Ronny, show Mr. Walsh what you got."

Ronny made no sign that he had heard. His expression was one of deep thought, as though his mind were a prism and he was trying to wrest the secret surfaces around for inspection.

Then Flo, who had been standing behind Eddie as usual, darted forward and pulled up the short sleeved cotton sweater from Ronny's waist. "Ain't it fine?" he demanded proudly, pointing at the tattooed heart.

Ronny, startled out of his thoughts, flushed. "They said something would take it away," he cried angrily. "I *told* them to bring it. That's why I asked them to your party."

"You're all crazy, I guess," said Ruby, and went off to the table to see what there was to eat.

"Who's June?" asked Walsh.

"Oh, nobody in particular," said Ronny in a hopeless voice. With a gesture of his hand he drifted off and sat down near the window.

"Well, I suppose it wasn't quite right to do it," said Walsh. "Those things don't come out easily." Then, feeling that perhaps he was showing a too paternal interest, he asked: "What did Mrs. Villars say?"

"About what, darling?" Grace came up and slipped her arm around Jim's waist, throwing at the same time her baby-bright gaze at Eddie.

"Well, I hear the kid got tattooed," said Jim. He felt self-conscious talking to Grace about her son in public.

"You do worry about that silly child," said Grace wickedly. "He got a tiresome crush on a girl called June, but he's getting over it now. I just threw them together."

"Good-looking girl." Eddie's voice was like a malicious caress. 'You're a pretty little kitten, aren't you?' it seemed to say by inflection, 'and I'll just stroke your fur the wrong way a bit.' Then, looking straight at Walsh, Eddie continued: "And that's a fine boy, Mr. Walsh."

"A manly little fellow!" mocked Grace with her pearly laugh. "Really, you two do seem to be growing maudlin. I better separate you. Mr. Eddie, be a gent and give me a drink."

As they moved off, Eddie said softly: "But I'm not a gent."

Either by accident or in answer to his words, Grace's shoulder brushed against the muscles of his upper arm and she fancied she could feel through his sleeve the great, twisting, swollen veins that bound them.

Jim was left behind. Eddie's remark flashed like a light before his inner eye and its shape repeated itself again and again in various colours on the retina of his mind. Eddie had looked directly at him. Was there, could there be, a resemblance? After all, Eddie had known him, Jim, ten years ago, when he was a younger man. And once, much farther back than that, Jim's hair too had been black and rough, his eyes shining and full of dreams. He looked at Ronny across the room, but the boy's face was set towards the window and towards the incoming tide. Walsh was surprised on turning back to see Flo's ratlike little face below his own.

"A man's got to practice," said Flo plaintively. "It didn't seem like I was doing anything wrong."

To Jim, who had forgotten all about the tattooing, these words were incomprehensible. Without replying he went off to find Grace. He would talk to her now without further delay.

Stevens arrived a little later. He stood with Lucy in the door of the room and looked around. Stevens was astounded to see Eddie and Flo, yet on an instant's reflection he realized that this was a master touch. Only Grace could be so sure of herself and of her social standing. Once in her power, no one was out of place, or rather, they were in the exact place she wanted them to be in. This was her empire: prince, slave, and fool. For some reason Stevens found himself thinking about the abalone shell and he resolved to bring it out of the closet and put it in its old place of honour.

Lucy, standing at his side, was utterly bewildered. Would no one greet them? It was already minutes that they had stood framed in the doorway. She put her hand nervously to her hair. Perhaps having it set was a mistake. It felt precise and flat. Anyone could see that she had just come out of the beauty parlour. The word 'local' came into her mind.

Then Grace ran up, dragging Jim by the hand. "Darlings! Or rather, darling, because I don't know your—friend, James, although I'm longing to. Jim, this is James Stevens, who's been so good to Ronny, and this is—?"

"Miss Philmore," said Stevens very correctly and bowing to Walsh. He would have liked to kiss Grace's hand, but was afraid of the older man's deep eyes.

"Miss Philmore. What a charming village name," said Grace, and just as Lucy was angrily thinking 'Bitch!' she added with an appealing simplicity: "I come from a village just like this one. Star Harbour takes me back to my childhood. James wants to get away but I tell him he is lucky." She tucked her arm into Lucy's and drew her towards the table. "I tell him he should marry a nice Star Harbour girl and settle down," she said.

The warm, childish voice, so open and sincere, flooded Lucy's heart with pain. It seemed to hold out such happiness, as though these words could make a dream come true.

From the back, where Jim and Stevens were following, the difference between the two women was grotesque. The doll-like silhouette of Grace with its twirling skirts was pointed up by Lucy's stooping back and her long, pear-shaped hips.

June arrived the last of all. She had walked slowly and carefully through meadow and wood so as not to catch her new dress on the bushes. A candelabra had been set in the boathouse entrance beneath a mildewed mirror. June coming in alone was startled by her reflection. Her sleeveless dress was open at the neck. In the flickering light the joints of her shoulders were polished and the rich supple cords of her throat. She was like a stern, honey-coloured angel.

"So I am beautiful after all!" she murmured, clenching her fists. "The main thing is not to forget it."

But no one appeared to notice her coming. They were all gathered around the window to watch the fireworks from Jim's yacht. Mary blew out the candles and the last of the twilight showed through the big window. Now the tide was quite high. Its voice surrounded the house. June felt as she walked across the room that her body was swayed by its rhythm, and it seemed to her as she stood beside him that Ronny too was captured by it, for his body trembled.

A bulb of light shot upwards from the "High Kick" and unfolded from its center a chalice which poured blue poison into the sky. In that ghastly light which illuminated the room, everyone stood rigid, as though to move were fatal. Then a great rosy wheel started to turn out there on the bay and, revolving ever faster, printed the watching eye. No one could tell at what exact point it went out because it kept on turning for each of them privately, and for several moments longer showered green sparks into their optic nerves.

June blinked as the fiery sparks pierced her brain, yet the feeling was not unpleasant. It was as though they were torches hurled into a cave. If only they would light the way, she thought, into those dark, twisting mind passages of which she was ignorant, discover in that maze the direction of her spirit. Once or twice she almost believed they did, but of course it was impossible. They went out too quickly, stifled in that airless cavern.

June wondered if Ronny felt the same way, or even if he were enjoying the fireworks at all. Certainly he was looking out towards the bay, but he had been doing so since June's arrival, sitting there quietly with, as she fancied, the tide vibrating through his body.

Suddenly the fireworks were over, leaving night in their wake. The candles glowed again and made the windows black in contrast, save for the penetrating, far-off glitter of the stars.

Grace Villars looked around the room and contemplated her guests. She had asked this gathering out of mischief, or rather love for situations which could make everybody uneasy except herself. Before the fireworks she wondered if she had succeeded in this aim. The idea of the party's being a failure entered her head like a sign of distress, a further whisper, as there had been all that year, of her own decline. Grace had seen June come in, mysterious in the candlelight. She had not greeted her guest and this very omission troubled her. Was she after all afraid of this awkward, unformed girl; of any girl? But of course it was only the candles and if they gave so much to June they must surely be doing more for her, Grace. In the dark she had moved away from Jim Walsh, away from Stevens and his poor, plain young woman, to stand again near Eddie, and it was Eddie to whom later she gave the first drink, curtsying as she did so. Then, turning, she clapped her hands and called:

"Now I want everyone to fill their glasses and drink to our host, Jim Walsh." She went softly up to Ronny who was still seated in his chair. "Have a sip of wine, Roddy," she pleaded. "Because you'll hear news tonight." She gave him a little champagne and tried to hold it to his lips. Her pretty, teasing gesture, as she bent over her sullen son, her blond curls so near his dark head, made the men in the room react. June, standing behind Ronny's chair, a little apart, looked at her hostess with wonder.

'How good humoured she is!' thought June, 'and how hard she works for her effects. That will always be the difference between us.' This reflection made her happy and proud. Yes *they* would have to do the work for her. June allowed her lips to form a scornful smile which she hoped was noticed by all. Grace, in fact, did see it, but she merely thought that the girl did not like the taste of champagne with its stinging bubbles.

Ronny had spoken to no one so far that evening. Now Jim Walsh, glass in hand, came up to the boy after his mother had left his side. A heavy, old man's flush had tinged his cheeks, and as he walked he straddled an imaginary line.

"Say, bring me a chair," he called to Jeremy where he stood talking to the crewman who had brought him from the "High Kick" to the beach. Walsh sat down with a wheeze and put his hand on the boy's bare knee. "Listen to me, son," he said.

Ronny turned.

"Your Ma and I had a talk," said Jim. "I told her I'd like it if we could share you."

"You mean, marry Mother?" asked Ronny.

"Good God, no," said Walsh with emphasis. He shook his head and thought that he would never be happier than at this moment with his hand on his son's knee. Because he knew that Ronny was his child. Somehow in this candle-lit room, discussing it with Grace, he had become sure. He would claim paternity in court, and Grace was only too willing to agree. She could have her son legally for half the year, like any divorcee, but Jim knew that money talked. With money, he could have Ronny almost entirely to himself. He would rescue the boy from this atmosphere, give him a boy's life. They would take long cruises and fish the powerful tunny from the sea. Ronny would learn to use a harpoon, to race the speedboat and to do what Jim had never done: fly an airplane. He would have something besides cocktail parties to boast about to his friends at school. He would become a man and, later, would know about wealth and its accumulation. Perhaps Ronny would even go into politics, although that was far ahead. Jim Walsh would never live that long.

Jim rose abruptly. He had meant to ask Ronny's consent, but now he saw that this was pure weakness. In life one must take what one wanted. "Get ready to leave tomorrow, Ronny," he said, and was about to walk off when he noticed June. He patted her shoulder without saying anything. June took this to mean that it was all right; that she failed perhaps now, yet would one day have her triumph. She resented this caress profoundly. Then Jim called to her: "How's your grandmother?" He did not even wait to hear the answer (he corresponded regularly with Mrs. Grey) but continued in the old man's way that was growing on him: "Fine, fine."

'What if I'd said she was dead?' wondered June, who felt suddenly like laughing. She was afraid to do so, however. The scratching throb in her throat might not be laughter at all.

* * * * *

All this time the tide rose. It stretched against the land and became high. Gambol in his watery stable did not mind. He had found that by standing near the rotten boats he was on a hill of silt, piled up there bit by bit by the drift of the sea. He did not think of leaving, although he could easily have done so. He simply stood with his back and belly quite dry and ruminated. Around him the air was pitch black but the water was alive with phosphorous so that every move he made was etched in flame. Beside him, and a little apart, a jelly fish made a globe of light. Its placid tide-rhythm was disturbed by the horse so that it rocked in the water. At first Gambol had been afraid of the jelly fish and had rolled his eyes at it, but he had got used to it after a while. This round, pure, swaying lamp brought comfort to his night.

Once Gambol's vigil was disturbed. Steps sounded on the staircase and the air echoed voices. It was Flo and his girl Ruby. They had stumbled on the door to the landing and now, turning on the light, came down there. Ruby stopped short on seeing Gambol.

"Didn't I tell you they were crazy?" she demanded righteously. "Keeping a horse in this kind of a garage!"

Flo was rather astonished himself, yet since he was down here for a purpose, he tried to pull Ruby into a corner. She resisted. Her lethargic nature was roused for once.

"Let go!" she said. "Do you think I'd do it here with that horse looking at me?"

CHAPTER 26

AROUND MIDNIGHT Mary helping clear the plates from the table said to her husband: "It's true, they do look better under the candlelight."

"Well, they won't look better tomorrow," said Jeremy, who had really enjoyed himself for once.

"They're getting a head on all right," said the sailor, nodding towards the other side of the room.

Mary turned to look and saw something strange. Eddie was sitting in a chair against the wall and on his lap perched Grace Villars. James Stevens was kneeling in front of them.

"Oh my!" said Mary.

The tableau caught thus at its peak had taken all evening to be assembled. From the time when he had walked with Jim Walsh in back of the two women, Stevens had made up his mind and determined to propose to Grace. He would make his offer tonight and it would be accepted. Stevens looked over to where Ronny sat. He noted the boy's tense head turned away from the room. How quiet he was! Stevens wondered what Ronny would think of the marriage. Would he be happy to have his tutor for a stepfather? With a dull feeling of pain Stevens acknowledged to himself that Ronny would probably not care either way. He was unaware of Stevens, whose comings and goings he hardly observed. That somber glance was set on other things. That heart held already another name. Stevens pressed his lips when he thought of Ronny's tattoo. When he and Grace were married, June would disappear from their lives and he would protect the boy from such influences. Yet her name graven on the quick of the boy's flesh would remain.

At this moment Stevens saw June come in and then, soon, the fireworks had begun. He swallowed nervously in the darkness as he tried to prepare a speech. Lucy's presence beside him irritated and put him off. Why ever had he brought her? What had he to do with this female who was suffering? Her constrained yearning was a tangible thing which revolted Stevens' nature. Grace was to blame, of course—by that wicked remark about settling down and marrying a Star Harbour girl she had given words to Lucy's desire. Lucy had reacted almost visibly and now her breath in the darkness was heavy, like continuous sighs.

Later Stevens drank to give himself courage and, while he drank, new groups formed. Jim, always a good host, came up and talked to Lucy. He could not pierce the mystery of her being asked, but he plied her with champagne and told her stories of his travels. He was so elated over his plans for Ronny that her expression escaped him, or seemed easy to wipe away. A few drinks were what she needed.

Flo and Ruby had disappeared. Grace was flirting with Eddie whose easy manner, contemptuous yet tender, filled her with a momentary excitement. Eddie, for his part, replied willingly to Grace's sallies. She was no chicken perhaps, but she was on the ball and pretty. When he pulled her onto his knees her little cork-soled shoes dangled against his legs and her light frame twitched in his arms.

"Come over here, Stevie," she called from the haven of Eddie's lap.

Stevens was not used to seeing women sitting in a man's lap, but to his flushed senses the situation became usual at once. He gave her his youthful grin and came over to stand in front of Eddie's chair.

"Say something new and interesting," commanded Grace, looking up at him impudently.

"Will you marry me?" asked Stevens, as though it were the least request in the world.

Eddie was convulsed. His moles were swallowed up in laughter. He thought he had never seen such an absurdity as this school teacher. "Well, Grace?" he urged, squeezing her waist.

But Stevens, having said that much, now became pale and in earnest. "Grace," he said, "it just slipped out and this isn't a very good time, yet I do mean it." Strangely enough, that Grace was sitting on Eddie's knee brought for the first time a twinge of amorous desire into Steven's blood. Eddie's thick, hairy wrist against that toy waist, his powerful thigh beneath the spread of skirt, awoke in Stevens the sleeping brute. He continued, almost stammering now: "You see, I've thought it all out. I'll give up my job, of course, and sell the house. It's enough to start something in New York and I have a small income, too."

Eddie suddenly thrust his ugly face from behind Grace's shoulder. "Why talk of money?" he demanded. "You should be talking of love. What are you anyway?" Turning up his hand from Grace's waist, he crashed his other fist into the palm. "Down on your knees, man!" he commanded. "That's the way to do it where I come from."

Eddie's soft tones, contrasting with the sound of his fist in his palm, made Stevens thrill with fear. The difference between that voice and the heavy sinews in his hand raised the sweat on the tutor's body. At once and without reflection he fell on his knees. The scene took on its final perfection and Grace was delighted.

"Now plead your case young fellow," demanded Eddie, looking sideways into the schoolmaster's eyes.

Stevens' glance grew rigid with fascination. "Will you marry me, Grace?" He said it almost in a whisper.

As though these repeated words were a signal, Eddie rose, spilling Grace from his lap. He had forgotten her in an instant and went over to talk to Jeremy and the sailor.

Grace straightened her skirts and was completely composed. Stevens shuddered as people do when they have taken a draught too strong for their palates. He looked at the little doll to whom he was offering his life and understood nothing. Her blond curls, the forced childishness of her apparel, bewildered him. The signs of age in her face held his attention for the first time. She was a fading toy, a columbine traveling the roads because her big-town days were over. Ah, but she had produced Ronny! This thought was like cool water on Stevens' brow.

"I mean it, Grace," he said. "Won't you answer my proposal?" 'And who knows,' he thought, 'if this disgust won't wear itself away.'

Grace had every intention of accepting Stevens. She had turned the idea over well in her mind. A husband of her own age would give her a new grip, set back the years a little. In partnership they could, as he suggested, start something, go into some enterprise; interior decorating, perhaps, or antiques. Her vast number of acquaintances, no longer of the most personal use, would become vital in another sense, and Stevens would furnish a basic capital. Yes, it would be a good move.

Grace put back her head. "Are we going to shake on it like two pals, or will you break down and kiss me?"

Stevens took her by the shoulders with a forced roughness that covered his indecision. The feel of her sharp bones in his hands, the sinews that twitched nervously in his grasp and the red paste like a greasy stain between their lips made his gorge rise.

"Jim," called Grace in her clear voice. "Come over here—and you too, Miss Philmore. We need congratulations."

She did not call to June and Ronny but left them together at the other end of the room, not as though she were unaware of them, but as though they were inanimate, two pieces of furniture whose attitudes she had already fixed.

"Well well!" remarked Jim, lowering his heavy lids sardonically. Yet his face was jovial. "Good idea, Grace," he said.

Lucy wondered whether the taste in her mouth came from the champagne or whether it were not some spinster acid fabricated in her own blood which she must swallow from now on. She merely said with her pleasant smile: "I hope you'll be very happy."

"Oh thank you, my dear!" Grace's teeth, small and pointed, gleamed in the candlelight. She touched Jim's sleeve. "Isn't it lovely of Stevie to propose just now, just when I was so sad about letting you have Ronny?"

* * * * *

Above the boathouse, in a tree overlooking the yard, Shalimar was huddled. The stable door was closed to him and he was no longer called home at night. Also, peer down as he would the livelong day not one glimpse of Ronny riding Gambol had showed through the trees. Shalimar made a small croak of distress. He was as disgruntled, as ruffled and as timid, as a hen left out of its roost.

The party had been like one of the fireworks. It had risen, unfolded, bloomed, given forth different colours and now was fading. The candles had burned down in their sockets leaving lumps of wax on the furniture. The groups had disintegrated and appeared not to recall why they had formed. June thought it was time to go and left as she had come, alone and without farewell.

The night breeze crossed her throat and her bare arms. Now and then a leaf touched her, cold with dew, and the chorus of the tree frogs grew shriller as she passed. Ronny was leaving tomorrow. He was going away with the millionaire. She would never see him riding through the woods again nor hear him in the evening calling to his hawk. Her family would return. They would relate their adventures and think them interesting. They would never ask her about the summer, since what could happen on Grey's Neck? They would never know about anything real; about the cry in the dusk each evening, or the tattooed heart.

And she could never explain. She could only say: "Once I met a boy who was only eleven and we played together."

To no one else would that sound important, neither to parents or brothers or school girls. Perhaps it was only important to June because it was first love and now it was over.

And it was important to Ronny, too.

MY NAME IS ROSE

For
Eileen Garrett

Bow down, archangels, in your dim abode:
Before you were, or any hearts to beat,
Weary and kind one lingered by His seat;
He made the world to be a grassy road
Before her wandering feet.

—W. B. YEATS
The Rose of the World

CHAPTER 1

MY NAME IS ROSE. It doesn't really suit me. I'm not the Rose type of girl; but I like it anyway. A rose—fresh as a rose—the flower of morning dew with the drops on its petals as clear as crystal, pure and immaculate as a rose—Rosemund, rose of the world.

Roses can wither, of course; their petals can grow black and sear. In this case one puts them in a bowl and they give out a musty fragrance that recalls grandmothers in country houses—or what one has read about them, anyway.

Did I say I was a girl? It seems to me I did. I get confused. I'm not a girl, you know (and by the way, who is *you?* Perhaps I'll have to go into that later on); I'm a woman. I'm nearing thirty already and I've been married seven years. The number seven always sounds magic, doesn't it?—like those stories in which children are turned into slaves by witches. They give the children a brew which tastes suave and transforms them into ugly shapes and there they are for seven years. When they get back home no one knows they've been away because living dolls have been put in their places.

There is a doll in this house, a bewitched doll who eats and talks and lies beside my husband in his bed. Sometimes he makes love to it and dolls don't like that. They aren't made for it, you see. Again that "you"! But who are *you*? Are you my father, dying away slowly on the Mediterranean shore? I think not. No, really, poor old man, setting up his final canvases and trying once again to pit himself against God. God? Well, perhaps that's who you are—or should it be "thou"?

I'm tired already and I haven't even mentioned the bugler. How his face quivered in the market place that day and how long ago that was! It's fall now, but it was spring that day.

No, I must tell you more about myself first: thy servant Rose. Do you know what I look like? So-so; not pretty and not ugly either. Or rather that's the way I was last spring. Do you remember? I had the same hair: short, black, girl's hair, with a barrette on one side the way I've always had since the age of one and a half. But my eyes were blue then, not purple-black the way they sometimes are now, and my skin was sallow, ivory if you like. It's not sallow any more, as you can see, with that staining flush on the cheekbone; a dull sort of flush that looks like badly put on rouge.

Anyway I live in Paris at 28 Rue des Grands Augustins and my father is American; an expatriate, as some people call them. That's why I'm writing in English, which nobody else around here can read. My mother was a concert singer; a Jewess with eyes the color of mine. But she was beautiful, beautiful! Her long, black hair came to her haunches, to her full haunches, which swayed as she walked. I've not inherited her figure. My own is (was?) tight and muscular and I'm small and compact. That's all, I believe, except that I married Pierre Flamand seven years ago when I got out of music school. He's a journalist and I ought to say a writer, too. Should I tell about him or does it feel too uncomfortable? Perhaps I could skip him for the moment and go on about the bugler. You see, I have to tell about *him* because when I saw *him* I was still one person—there was no doll or anything—and it's only by using him as a sort of landmark that I can see behind him to that united Rose Flamand.

* * * * *

ROSE ceased writing and rubbed her forehead fretfully. As she sat thus with a lined tablet in front of her, she looked more like a schoolgirl than the woman she claimed to be. Her flexible hand (her hands and feet were the most limber parts of her body) held the pen roundly and there was a home-washed sheen on her bent head. Rose led a double life. Sometimes the strain of it was like a rift in her brain and at other times she forgot about it altogether and simply lived whatever life she was in at the moment. It was only lately that these forgetful times had begun to make her afraid. Now she sighed and continued to write.

——————————— *Journal:* ———————————

On certain days, clear fall days like this, I try and think back to the moment when everything—my life and my head and my feelings—was joined. And I try to remember the bugler.

You see, it was the bugler who started the whole thing. No, of course that's not correct. He was *there* at the start, that's it. He was the first symbol, the first warning, as it were. Have you ever reflected on first warnings? I mean, how it's impossible to heed them because one doesn't know what they are warnings *against*. Or perhaps something inside, way down inside, knows. I dare say it does, but that's not enough for most people. I am like one of those antique heroes, Theseus I think his name was, who had to unwind a clue through a labyrinth. He wanted to discover and to conquer the monster at its center. I too am trying to hold a thread, but I must find it first, and around me on every side the walls of the maze are twisting and turning. Because *my* thread, unlike his, is already laid down; I laid it down myself. Now if I can only rediscover it in the darkness, isolate it, and hold it in my hand—why then, the monster will be there waiting for me. Pathetic or terrible, I don't care so long as I can see it at last face to face.

That's why I'm trying to think of the important things. And it's important for me to think of the bugler; how he stood in the brief spring sunlight with the rest of the band and blew.

I was coming out of the bakery when I heard the music. I had gone into the shop while it was pouring rain, but when I left it the sun shone and there was a band playing.

Do such things happen in all the market places of the world, or is it only Paris? Nobody was surprised. They never are at anything. They were busy hurrying to surround the players and to take their ease in the rare sunshine. I followed along and I recall trying not to march in step with the beat, but of course that's impossible. I even found myself marking time with my long stick of bread. I too was pleased with the sun. Anyone would be after a Paris winter, and I jostled myself into the front row.

The band was dressed in green; a uniform of some sort, although it was impossible to know whom they represented or why they were there at all. The bugler was standing a little apart from the rest with his cap on the back of his head. He must have been very young, for there was an adolescent boniness in his hands, and in his wrists, which were too long for his jacket. His thick hair sprang from his cap and he was straining his lungs. A hundred swollen veins quivered in throat, cheek, temple and brow. They lent a sort of gay mobility to his face. Only the eyes were rigid. They had a glassy look, as of someone in pain, and were tightly fitted into their sockets. And I thought those tight, stiff eyes were looking into mine. Of course everybody tends to think that. They want so to be signaled out and set apart in some safe way. But I really felt sure of it and even the play of his veins and muscles seemed to be telling something to me alone.

Then, as suddenly as they had started, the band stopped playing. The musicians smiled or bowed slightly and after a brief conference they moved off down the Rue Mazarin in the direction of the river.

As I walked home the clouds gathered again and my bread was half broken and felt all limp. Large, cold drops began to fall. It was as though all the sunlight, all the lovely feeling of spring, had been centered around the band and had followed them on their way toward the river. There was nothing left for me but to put up the collar of my coat. I have a camel's-hair coat and it's very soft. I like to feel it on my ears. I was rubbing alternately one side of my head and then the other against the collar as I walked along, and I wonder if any intimation came to me then.

Did something inside me stir as I went, first on the windy St. André des Arts and then on my own street, the crooked, the narrow Rue des Grands Augustins? Did something try to warn me that my path was dividing? Perhaps, but I was dense. I was thinking of my warm collar, of the icy drops of rain that had fallen on my nose. And yet the bugler was there now, fixed forever, a two-armed signpost in the middle of the road. Beyond him the same road seemed to stretch, broad and single. I could not see the hair-thin rift that widened slowly, slowly; the gap where, over the hill, grass would soon grow. No, not until *later*. Then I saw. Now, today, it's only by thinking of the bugler that I can picture once again the old Rose of last March. The Rose who lived and still does at 28 Rue des Grands Augustins, and who climbed to the fifth floor that day.

Bernice let me in. She's our maid and we've had her for several years. She's very nice and in those days we used to laugh together a lot—giggle, rather. She's a Celt, from Brittany, with short, reddish, haystack hair and she's one of those people whose face and body are of different ages. When you see her from the back, walking or doing something active, she's like a girl—an awkward-age, girl-scout sort of girl—and then you see her lined, weather-reddened face. Of course that kind of skin is too fragile to last without care and Bernice thinks a good scrubbing is all it ever needs.

I told her about the band. "It was horrid really," I said, "but it sounded nice when I heard it."

She agreed. "I know, it depends on the time and the place."

But now I must tell you that when she said that, those words about the time and place, I got a funny feeling, a sort of thrill, like when, as the saying goes, a wild goose flies over one's grave. Or perhaps it wasn't her words at all that gave me this feeling, but the sound of an accordion coming from one of the attic rooms, a sound which sets my teeth on edge. I hate that instrument as much as I love the piano.

I was still standing there at the door and feeling the remains of that thrill when Pierre came in with Simon.

CHAPTER 2

Journal:

Yesterday morning when I started writing this journal (but is that the word for it?), I did so with the express purpose of rereading it. You see, one has to remember what one has put down. There it is in one's own writing. I write a bold hand, I am told, not a very womanly one, but with traces of childishness in it. Simon analyzed it and of course you don't know who Simon is, or at least I haven't told you yet. You don't know much about Pierre yet either, except that he's my husband. He married Rose Latham seven years ago at the Mairie du Septième. That's our quarter.

Pierre was almost the same then as he is today except that he has a stomach now, not a big one though—and he always says it could go away in a fortnight. He was rather heavy-set to begin with; solid and fresh-looking like the country boy he is. I used to walk in the Luxembourg gardens with him hand in hand after we met. Do you know that garden? There is a fountain that blows slightly dirty water in the wind. I liked to kiss his mouth, which is rather soft. The lower lip sticks out a little and is red, much redder than mine. Pierre has pink cheeks, too. Why does that fact hurt me now? Can you tell me? I think of those trusting pink cheeks and my heart is squeezed, wrung with a protective pity, a regret too.

Regret! Ah, there's a word to write.

Anyway I can think back clearly to the time when I met Pierre. How comfortable I felt with him! I was still in the conservatory, planning to be a concert pianist, the way my parents had always wished. Pierre was just finishing at the university and he was going to write a book (he's still writing it, by the way). Marrying Pierre didn't seem like a break at all, just a continuation of life as I had always known it; the quiet, studious, wise life of an artist's only child, more liberal in one way than other children's, but sterner too, since one may not accept the everyday values and ideas of companions of one's age, nor those of the world either, for that matter. And of course one is usually with the grownups. One gets used to them and likes them better. Artists don't keep children out of their lives and they don't create a special universe on their account as do most other parents. They don't have to, I guess.

Anyway Pierre and I were going to continue living that life. He would write and I would go on being a pianist and we would have clever children, two of them or three. I pictured it that way. But now I see Pierre didn't even know what I was talking about. Perhaps he thought all girls spoke like that. Perhaps they do; I mean they *do* want not to change. Things just automatically get different. I realized it almost at once in my case. Yet today, *now*, is the first time I've admitted the real reason; or rather, I've not yet done so but I will. Here goes: Pierre is not an artist! He is a hard-working man whose job is with a publication. I think my father, Mark as I call him, knew this all along, but Mark would never tell me something like that. He would think I should make my own decisions as he has brought me up to do, and I suppose he thought that when it was a question of my life, my being wrong was better than his being right. When I asked him how he liked Pierre he said Pierre seemed very nice, very dependable.

Anyway being an artist or not isn't important in a marriage and although Pierre isn't one and doesn't consider me one either, we have been very happy. You know we have. We didn't have children as it turned out, but we might yet, who knows? We both want them certainly.

I am talking now as if that doll weren't there in bed with Pierre. Is that a vulgar way of putting it? My values seem to be lost or twisted, or perhaps I never had any but didn't notice before. Pierre's hair is soft and fine. It's not curly and crisp. Nor does he ever put cologne on it like ... But why do I say that? Heavens, how my head aches! Not in back—in front, between my eyes. I understand now why people frown—when there is nothing wrong with their sight, I mean; something contracts there and makes them. When I see someone with a heavy frown on their face coming down the street toward me I wonder if they feel the way I do: as though something were dividing that they had to keep together— solder, as it were, by the strength of their own muscles. It's a pity it aches so, because I want to write more. I want to write about Simon for instance. Oh don't misunderstand! Simon isn't the one that—the one who. . .

* * * * *

ROSE, who had been sitting writing at the table, got up abruptly and stared out the long window at the gloom of the courtyard.

The Flamand apartment wound snaillike around this yard. One might say that the large part of the snail's shell was the big studio living room in which Rose stood. The rest of the body was composed of the kitchen and of two small rooms looking out on the street. A terrace completed the circle by making a bridge from the inner back door to the outer one on the public stairway. Thus the visitor could stand on the landing and, without moving, could ring either bell, front or back.

Above the Flamands were three small, windowless rooms, which were not a floor at all, but simply carved into the roof of the building. To reach them one had to go up the stairs and out onto a narrow balcony. Heatless and waterless, they were illumined nonetheless by the first rays of the morning sun. Often, from the long window, or from the terrace still in shadow, Rose would look up in envy to see those three doorways aglow. Bernice slept in one of the rooms and beside her an old woman who was called "La Cigale" or "The Grasshopper" after Aesop's fable. La Cigale was supposed to have been a famous singer in her youth and to have had rich lovers. Now she was poor and, having no curtains, covered the glass top of her door with burlap.

The last and outermost room had been occupied for several months by a young man, an accordionist. He worked at night, but at other times one could hear the sound of his playing on and off throughout the day. It was sounding at this moment in an uneven way as though the notes were blown by the wind. But one could recognize the tune—an old favorite, "La Vie en Rose."

Rose listened for a moment thoughtfully. The day was waning and, reaching in back of her, she switched on a lamp. At once her reflection sprang out at her from the transparent glass like a stealthy tiger that has been waiting and twitching its tail in the darkness.

Rose, like many women, was wrong about her looks. True, she was, as she said, neither pretty nor ugly, but she was certainly not so-so. She had elements in her face of an unusual and timeless beauty. Her straight black hair lay shining along her straight cheeks. The short nose, too, was straight and the uncurved brows that faintly met above it, and the level eyes whose blue darkened into purple. Even the mouth, full but not pulpy, had no curve in its fold. Only the ends, now a little drooped, were mobile. Yet all these straight features did not make her look domineering or fierce or even mature. They had rather the stern and passionate innocence that certain children have just before they change into adolescents.

And now as she stood there some trick or faintness of the glass made a sort of wash over her form, as when an image in water is disturbed by a slight ripple; an equivocal softening and dissolving of all her body, reassembled thus more easily, more voluptuously, upon her bones.

After a while, inspired by a rush of thought, she went back to the table and continued writing.

Journal:

I was helping Bernice hang up our wash on the terrace last spring—well winter, really, before the bugler—when we saw our landlady crossing the balcony with a young man in tow.

"That's the new tenant," said Bernice, who always knows everything.

I was annoyed because I'd been trying to get that corner room for her. It's much the largest of the three, has two doors, a sort of private roof, and room for a stove. But that's the way landladies are and one never knows what distant cousin's husband's relative may be involved.

We stopped hanging the wash for a moment so as to get a good look. The young man was carrying a suitcase in either hand and had an accordion slung over his shoulder. He was short and compact and, even weighted down as he was, had a sort of preening walk. He was probably wearing his good suit. The jacket was brief and showed off the muscular arch of his haunches. It was pulled out of place, too, by the way he was sticking out his chest. Men's clothes are funny. They look best on people who have no figures at all—no muscles, that is. Even a paunch is better for clothes than a sticking-out chest.

Anyway I didn't much like that preening walk. We weren't used to having men up there anyway and it changes things. As the landlady passed La Cigale's door she gave it a scornful glance. She had probably seen the old woman's painted eyes peering curiously through the crack of the burlap.

"Some people love to know other people's business," she remarked to her new boarder, and added in the brutally realistic way common to people in a position of petty power, "At least you won't have amorous dreams about your neighbor."

The young man gave a laugh which was jarring in its lack of sensibility and which affected me unpleasantly.

"It's horrid to have a man up there," I said to Bernice. "What's more, that one looks unsympathetic."

"He probably works at something or other," Bernice said consolingly, "and he'll be out all day."

But the young man seemed to have no fixed job and would turn up at all hours, strolling across the balcony and glancing down at our flat with bright, hard eyes. In his room he would play his accordion ceaselessly and the tunes were almost indistinguishable one from another. "Musette music." You've heard it surely. There's a sort of febrile gaiety about it, a feverish monotony. "Look how short a time we have to live," it seems to say. "Behold our sentimental and our trivial dreams."

Music is sacred to me of course. Right after the war, when most people my age were behaving in the wildest way, staying out all night and driving their parents mad, I was sitting at the piano. My recreation was walks to and from various lessons. In other words I was continuing to be what I'd been up until then: the good child of artist parents. I don't think there are any children more good than that. Perhaps that's why I respected Pierre's book so much—the one he's been writing ever since we met. I was used to respecting work and it gave me a happy, confident feeling. At home, when I was little, I was always proud to tell visitors that Mark was in the studio and not to be disturbed or that my mother was rehearsing. As I told you, she was a singer and she died during the war. She was middle-aged, you see, and at a concentration camp—there was torture too. I often used to dream that I heard her screaming. It's just the last thing one could imagine her voice doing. She was a contralto. But she must have screamed. She never told anything and I'm not even sure that she had anything to tell. She was a heroine, if that helps. But I don't think it does, not for me anyway. And I don't think it helped Mark.

What happened to my mother made me shy of a certain kind of man. I can't exactly explain it, but anything callous in a man gives me a feeling of shy misery—an *aware* misery, if you know what I mean. Men in groups, for instance; I cross the street so as to keep out of their way. And the new tenant gave me that feeling. Our apartment is so open, what with the terrace and that big window. I hoped he would be gone by the time it grew warm enough to sun-bathe, or at least that he'd be occupied by then.

La Cigale disliked her neighbor. You could tell because, despite her burlap, she now nailed another stretch of material outside her door. But Bernice gleefully pointed out to me another effect of the young man on the old woman. Before he came La Cigale used to go downstairs in the morning without her fringe. Now she pins it on first thing. Bernice thought this coquetry funny, but it made me sad. La Cigale is old and poor. God knows what she eats or how she manages at all. Yet she hasn't given up; painted, bewigged, with a moldy fur on her shoulders, she sallies forth each day at dusk. I was unhappy to think that now she couldn't even go down to the yard in peace to relieve herself or to fill her jug from the faucet.

But that was long ago. That was in January and it's September now and I've still not told you about Simon.

* * * * *

ROSE made one of those abrupt movements with which people try to stem their own reflections. Leaning on the table she was surprised to note the appearance of her own writing on the page, which might almost have sprung there from a ghostly hand. The words seemed gibberish; a laughing matter. In fact she did laugh all alone as she was in the big studio room, and her laughter had the fresh sound that children's has when they enjoy cruel things.

CHAPTER 3

 Journal:

Well, I never got very far about Simon, did I? I digressed and then that song was playing and I had to go out—I had an appointment and I had to keep it. Yet Simon is as important as anyone else, not to me directly and not to Pierre any more either, but to *himself,* and that makes him impose upon this story. He hovers over it like one of those terrible birds with naked necks. He is a scavenger.

Scavengers are beautiful in flight. They even resemble eagles.

Pierre likes to have somebody around to admire, usually a writer. It completes him. That's not unusual if you think about it, although to think about it too hard is confusing. It makes me feel rather lost.

Simon is quite a well-known author, but it's hard to make a living in France just by writing and that's why he took a job on *Jouvence.* He was one of a series of bright young men employed by the magazine. It is expected (vainly of course) that these geniuses will save the magazine from its own policies. In such shifting sands Pierre's job alone seems steady. Without him I don't think any issue could ever get to the stands. He does everything and, instead of being jealous of newcomers, welcomes them with enthusiasm. He lets them pick his brains for their own profit and sees his ideas turned into theirs and relayed back to him by a capricious boss. In the end however they always make the mistake of really trying to redeem *Jouvence* from mediocrity and then they're thrown out.

I disliked Simon the first time Pierre brought him home, just after Christmas, and I wonder now if there was not a little jealousy on my part in the dislike. You see, the instant I met him I knew he would be Robert's successor. Not that I had much cared for Robert, or for his rather frighteningly intellectual wife either, but I had grown used to them and, in a way, they kept each other occupied.

Simon was a bachelor. It stuck out all over him that he could not bear real intimacy with a woman. Also that he tiresomely divided women into two classes; there were the glamorous and wicked ones with whom one slept but did not live and there were the good women with whom it would be boring to do either. I was of course relegated to the second category at once.

Another thing was that Simon repelled me. He was (and he's not changed) very pale with a long, sharp nose overhanging his mouth. The lips in that pointed shadow were pale, too, and sucked in over his teeth. Beneath the skin of his cheeks I could see his jawbones, which were constantly twitching in their sockets. Pierre's face in contrast appeared plump and, although they are of an age, Pierre looked much younger. His red mouth and stolid expression were lifted out of heaviness by his charming and boyish smile and by the enthusiasm in his eyes as he admired his new friend.

As I said, Simon arrived on the staff of *Jouvence* shortly after Christmas. He was the author of three books whose mordant dryness had won acclaim for them but had made them hard to read. Many critics called him brilliant and even genial and from this success he had acquired a world-weary air. I think personally that he was exhausted from frustration and lack of sleep.

I guess another reason Simon is important is because he was there from the beginning. He is a sort of glue. He knows me as the good woman, the one he despised but who did not bother him, and later he knew the other Rose which is me too. Sometimes I feel that Simon—and Simon only—could if he wished put those two Roses together. That's partly what I meant by his being a glue. The other, later Rose disturbed Simon. He seemed to loathe her and then not to loathe her at all. It's very confusing—enough to disgust one with men, as La Cigale is forever saying.

I remember that when Simon came for lunch for the first time I asked him what he did with his evenings. Then he looked at me as he hadn't before, balefully too, and said with that rather emasculated voice of his, "I *live*."

It impressed me, you know. It sounded silly and affected and it annoyed me, but now I can admit that it impressed me too. Pierre of course was delighted with anything Simon chose to say and I noticed that he offered me none of his usual and simple tenderness. He wanted to show Simon that he too knew a wife's place, perhaps even that he too knew how to *live*.

That evening he asked me what I thought of his new associate and friend, and I said that I had found him unattractive. That made Pierre mad. He protested at once, so I amended it: "Unattractive to me I mean," I said. "And maybe to women in general." It was true too. I had seen it and also that it was a big factor in Simon's character. It might even have been the reason for his writing those books.

Everything I am telling now is before the bugler and that's where I meant to start. But I like to go back further. It puts me together more solidly, as though I were a person who remembered everything as a whole. I did do that once and perhaps you recall that united Rose, the good wife who helped Bernice with the wash and who practiced the piano for three hours a day. Oh, I knew by then that Pierre would hate me to play in public. Besides, I thought being married to a writer was just as important as being something myself. Another carry-over from childhood you see; first the child of, then the wife of, an artist. I know now that's cheating. People have countries they betray only at their own peril.

Our house isn't centrally heated and in winter it gets very cold. Bernice and I heat our rooms here and we have different methods for each one. In our bedroom, for instance, there is a coal stove and in Pierre's study a petrol one. This room, the big studio, has a fireplace and when it's very cold I bring the petrol stove in here too. I wanted to use an electric heater since the new ones are very good, but the current won't stand it. This is an outmoded house as far as modern conveniences are concerned. Most of them are, in this section of Paris, and one would hardly know where to start if one wished to change. It would cost a fortune. Take the pipes for instance; they are terribly small and one couldn't change one in one flat without putting in a new one the entire length of the building. You see the complications. They run outside too and that's why they broke in the cold spell.

* * * * *

HERE Rose paused. Whether the mention of the cold spell brought too many things to mind or whether Bernice's key in the lock distracted her she did not know, but she closed down her writing pad and put it inside one of the portfolios of music which lay on top of the piano. In the old days, those about which Rose was now writing, Bernice, on returning from the market, would have come into the studio. In her boisterous manner she would have described the various events of the trip or made some comment about any of their neighbors whom she had passed on the stair. That intimacy, however, was over. No longer would Bernice stand with her hands on her hips or make one of her comic gestures while she gossiped with her mistress. Rose knew, however, by the glow in the courtyard that the kitchen light had gone on, and she no longer felt alone.

Then the telephone rang and Rose answered it with a sort of wonder. Here she was actually speaking. It was as if she had been a hermit for years. She listened to her husband telling her he had to work late on the magazine, as he quite often did before *Jouvence* went to press. "Why don't you go to a movie or something?" he suggested, and Rose in tones of exhausted surrender answered slowly, "Perhaps I will."

After she hung up she went to the kitchen door and called out, "Bernice, my husband isn't coming home until late so just leave the dish in the oven. Perhaps we'll eat it when he gets in." She wanted to go on and say that she was going to see a film, but already her effort was spent. Taking down her trench coat from its hook near the back door she belted it tightly and went out. Crossing the terrace she turned up the collar and with that change became another person; elegant, mysterious, and with a certain languor like that of chronic and recurring fevers.

A sigh made her lips tremble over her clenched teeth. Then, running down the dimly lit stairs, Rose went into the night street.

CHAPTER 4

As usual when it was time for Pierre to get up in the morning, he was terribly sleepy. He rubbed and rubbed his eyes. They were often puffy although he never drank much. His full, fresh-colored face was moist with sleep. He had stayed up late the night before at the magazine and he was tired.

Rose was still asleep with one arm up over her head. Her nightgown had slipped down to uncover part of her breast and Pierre pulled the sheet up over her. He did this not from solicitude but from modesty, and he thought that if his wife had been awake she too would have wished to hide herself from his eyes. That he was wrong in this thought made no difference to their relationship. They had never seen each other naked.

Pierre had banked the fire in the room before going to bed, but it had turned bitterly cold during the night. Winter, it seemed, was delivering a last stunning blow right in the teeth of spring. Keen shafts whistled through the cracks of the window which Pierre had left closed. This was against Rose's principles and the Flamands had argued endlessly on the subject. Pierre had been brought up to believe that night air contained a quality dangerous to the sleeper and in this theory he was upheld by many of his compatriots. The musty odor of the room did not bother him. Quite the contrary, it made him feel safe.

Now he looked around him to see that Rose or Bernice had put a big jar of weeping-willow branches on the mantel. The green of their buds was shadowy as yet, but brilliant in promise, like another light in the room. This room was entirely Rose's taste and Pierre was indifferent to its charm. There was something simple and girlish about it and this same quality was reflected in his wife's manner of dressing. In one way Rose's well-brought-up simplicity pleased Pierre. He felt *he* could appreciate it, but he did not consider that most people could. It was too subtle in his opinion and would merely be thought dowdy and plain. Her unpretentiousness, her very modesty, would be mistaken by the unloving eye.

Pierre glanced over at the Scotch kilt and cashmere sweater which were lying over the chair. In the book he was writing, his heroine Gloria would not have worn them. Gloria, through his seven years' acquaintance with her, had undergone many a mental change, but physically she was the same as ever and raised her curly blond head triumphantly over his pages. She was gamine and boyish, but she was very smart. Because sometimes Pierre longed for a glamorous and smart woman, a woman whom everybody—yes, even Simon—on the staff of *Jouvence* would admire. And his editor-in-chief would then say to him occasionally, "Well, let's ask your wife. Her taste is so chic, so sure; we can just trust to her judgment."

She would know all about literature too, this other, mythical Gloria-wife—modern literature, that is, not the outmoded or childish stuff on the shelves surrounding him. And she would talk brilliantly of world affairs. But Rose evidently considered that her classics were food enough for a lifetime, and as for world affairs, there she was worse than ignorant. He was ashamed. Pierre recalled a classic time when she had asked, and before Simon too, "Which side are you talking about now?" To her there was a strange similarity in the policies and actions of big world powers, and anyone with a grain of insight or conscience would be shocked by this. It was only because he, Pierre, understood her innocence that he forgave her.

But now suddenly Pierre repented of all these thoughts and of that other, worldly wife of his imagination. Leaning over he kissed Rose on her forehead. At once she opened her eyes and looked at him with a shiny, vacant stare. Her mouth turned down and quivered a little as though she were going to cry.

"What time is it?" she whispered tragically.

Then her eyes focused. The purple darkness, like that of a night sky, left them and they grew bluer. She smiled, and reaching out caressed Pierre's cheek, stroking it softly against the grain of his beard. A rush of tenderness invaded him so that he blushed. He would have liked to take her up in his arms, to rock her with the lullaby of his own male strength, to kiss those turned-down lips that had quivered so pathetically. But he did no such thing. Instead, rising quickly, he went to shave, first carefully donning wrapper and slippers.

Bernice was in the kitchen making coffee and its sharp smell was a spur to Pierre. The day and its, various occupations came close and as he shaved it was as though the razor were scraping away the night with its vague thoughts and half-remembered dreams to leave the smooth, shining, daily skin beneath ready for life.

Two hours or so later, Pierre was greeting Simon, who had just come into his office. Simon never bothered to arrive early and when he showed up it was with an air of furious exhaustion. Pierre had been almost annoyed with Simon lately, although his first enthusiasm was far from wearing off. What love affairs with women are to some men was replaced for Pierre by these friendly enthusiasms which came near to hero worship. They were perhaps the strongest emotional food in his life. Thus he admired Simon: Simon's independence, his venomous wit, his dry, trenchant writing that, like his voice, had an emasculated quality. He admired without envy and with a boyish enthusiasm. He was impressed too by Simon's version of his night life, his acquaintance with crooks and loose women, with so-called Existentialist types. Pierre, whose tender heart would wince at the sight of a drowning fly, could listen with admiration to sadistic stories told him by his hero, to callous and indifferent opinions on crimes and politics. The tree of hatred flowered in Simon's breast and its fruit, devoured inwardly, made his eyes glitter and sank his cheeks.

"Simon," said Pierre, "our chief's been asking for you. It's about that article you wrote on astrology. He says it's too obvious you were making fun of the readers."

Simon yawned. The sunken aspect of his mouth made one fancy he had no teeth, but now one could glimpse them, slanted inward toward his throat, ready, it would seem, to sharpen and poison the words that came out of his gullet.

Pierre's office was crowded. He was supposed to be alone in it, but the building was forever under repair and another desk had been put in with him. A tall girl who wrote articles on fashion and on social happenings about town was sitting behind it. Pretty only at first glance, she had actually not one well-shaped or handsome feature. She gave herself the airs of a newspaper reporter and dreamed of flashing her card at the scene of crimes. She annoyed Pierre by her way of putting her feet up on the desk, and he looked with dislike at the glistening line of her shin and the long, loose jointures of her knees.

Simon jerked his head at her. "So Marie is playing the American newspaper woman again," he said.

Someone came in from the pressroom with a problem for Pierre and then someone from photography. In front of him on his desk was a rough layout of the magazine with which he played as with a puzzle, trying to give it form and to please everyone. Simon remained in his office making occasional sarcastic remarks and apparently not even thinking of work. But somehow, somewhere, he would produce his contribution before the day was over. As for the request of his superior, he did not bother in the least about that. Pierre knew what would happen eventually, for such things followed a pattern. Having fired the ex-genius, and having hired the genius, the editor would spend a few months' honeymoon with his new acquisition. Pierre would hear his own suggestions scorned if they came from him directly, but in the same day they would be accepted with rapture when relayed by the genius.

"You see, my boy, you see, my dear Pierre, I was right; what *Jouvence* needs is a man like Simon, a writer of renown who can bring his touch to the most ordinary matter so that even the humblest peasant's wife— and the peasant, too, of course—can share on their lonely homestead the brilliance and glamour of our cultural tradition as it lives in our times."

Such were his speeches and Pierre accepted them quite seriously. He really did believe Simon could do this, just as the alchemist forever believes that gold can be made to spring from the baser metals.

Toward noon there was a lull and Pierre concentrated on the layout of *Jouvence*. He had a pile of photographs to choose from for spring clothes. The very idea of them in such weather was absurd and he shivered as he gazed carefully at these bare-armed girls. He knew most of them since they came to the building to be photographed, to get money or to complain. Simon, idly fingering the shots, mentioned one name or another with remarks as to their habits when not working. Under his venomous tongue the smiling celluloid faces, dewy with youth, turned into sweating drunkards, takers of dope, masochists and Lesbians. Pierre was as fascinated as a small boy gazing into a swamp. Only once did he protest half-laughingly, "Oh, but you can't mean Monique. She's a friend of my wife's. They were at the conservatory together."

"Oh, Rose is an appallingly good woman," said Simon. "I'm sure she can't be corrupted."

"You sound as if being a good woman were not a very desirable state," remarked Pierre.

"Well, it's all right I suppose," conceded Simon, "if you like that sort of thing. And she might make children although she hasn't yet. It's a problem for you though; after all, one does need stimulation."

"Come now," said Pierre flushing (as he did very easily), "that's going too far. My wife's a sweet, attractive girl. I shouldn't have married her otherwise." But he had the feeling that he only spoke from duty and personal pride.

Simon pinched his lips maliciously and Pierre, casting desperately around for something further to say in praise of Rose, brought out absurdly, "She has quite pretty eyes, you know."

Simon's own eyes now burned with triumph. "Has she?" he asked. "It's nice of you to notice—nice for her I mean."

"Well, I'll just tell *you* something," said Pierre, by now unhappy in his loyalties. "She thinks *you* are to be pitied."

"Of course. That's a natural protection," said Simon. "She wants you to feel sorry for me because I'm not domesticated like you."

"No, no, you've got it all wrong!" cried Pierre, but he was unable to explain further. And Simon had a knack of taking all the meaning out of life. Why *had* he married, after all? He could not understand now. He had been in love certainly, but such a phrase would mean nothing to Simon, would be contemptible. Pierre passed his fingers through his hair, which he had recently had cut short after the American fashion.

"And it isn't as if she could help you with your career," continued Simon as though divining the other's thought. "Why don't you fix her up a little, buy her some clothes, send her to the hairdresser's, give her some books to read? I'm sure she's never even opened Sartre, for instance. Or perhaps a drink of whisky would do it all, everything at once."

"She doesn't like whisky," said Pierre automatically.

"Of course not. She doesn't like anything which upsets her nursery routine!"

Simon's venom surprised Pierre and he felt ashamed of Rose and angry at himself for being so. At the same time he recalled exactly how she had told him she was sorry for Simon because he was unattractive and would not appeal to women. He had thought her remark silly then and incomprehensible, but now he thought, in the light of what Simon was saying, that he understood it in all its frailty. What she had meant was that Simon could not get someone like her and, more profoundly, that she knew such a woman as she could never interest a brilliant and satirical man, a writer of talent and thus of importance to his times.

Pierre felt a tender sadness for this wife of his, whose development had so soon halted. Simon was right; they should have children—three or four, in whose quiet, well-brought-up play her own level would be found. To watch such a family group would be a pleasure; even Simon would have to acknowledge its harmony. Pierre felt grateful to his friend for being one, for overlooking his dull life. Surely such a friendship would act as a stimulant to the book he was writing, just as the plodding horse starts forward under the lash of a whip.

"Are you coming for lunch?" he asked with the sweet smile which lifted his features out of heaviness.

"I might as well, I suppose," said Simon. "You have a fire."

Pierre called his home to make sure there was enough and Bernice answered. As he talked to her he could hear his wife laughing in the background.

It was as if a well-known coin were reversed to show on its other side an unexpected and forbidden face.

CHAPTER 5

Journal:

Now that I've described myself, the apartment and the people in and around it, I feel rather at a loss. There's the frame—or perhaps the labyrinth in which I wander. Do you think my life narrow? Are most people's lives more rich and full? Perhaps you want to know if I have friends or if we go out into society? The answer is no to the first part of the question. I was an only child and I don't care for friends much; that is, the kind of friends one went to school with and with whom one has long, intimate talks. I've heard that in America women go out with their friends to lunch and then they all play cards. They even go to bars, two women together in the middle of the afternoon, or so I've heard. I'm curious about America, but I don't think I'd like that much. Anyway, French husbands like to eat at home and I don't play cards. About society, I'm not so sure of my answer. Sometimes we have people for dinner and sometimes we go out. We go to the theatre too, and the opera and so forth. Pierre quite often has to review films, but I don't go with him then as they are never the ones I want to see.

I intend to write about the cold spell today. It's the last chance I'll get to talk about the old Rose, the flower blooming peacefully away in domesticity with a little music thrown in by way of soil food, and a few withered petals caused, no doubt, by the dry wind of Simon's talk.

As I write this page it seems to me that through all my words a soft breath is breathing. Do you feel it? In—out—like a man who is tired—*valiantly* tired, as they say—who rolls over and sleeps with his arm up over his head, whose temple is pressed by the round smooth muscle. Oh I've seen that, I can tell you, and it's a sight to melt the marrow of a woman's bones.

Anyway, the cold spell came when everybody was congratulating himself on having had an easy winter. They expected spring next. Then one morning it was freezing. The papers were full of it. They said it was the lowest temperature in generations and, according to their politics, blamed the atom experiments of Russia or America. Tramps were found frozen stiff in the streets, old people and babies died in heatless garrets and, as I've said, the pipes burst.

Here we spent a lot of time trying to keep warm. Of course we had no water, neither hot nor cold, and Bernice and I never came upstairs without bringing up a jug from the yard fountain. There the faucet always worked. I had a tall blue jug, a *brau* as it is called, which I used for our basin so that Pierre and I could wash. It was funny because before the frost I had filled this *brau* with weeping-willow branches for our room. They were just at that yellowish-greenish stage which goes away if you look too close and yet is the brightest thing you can imagine. It seemed impossible that winter could break the pledge of those branches.

I got another petrol stove too, but I returned it because the hardware-store man was out of petrol. Luckily we have a little cellar in the basement and a reserve of wood and coal, because the coal vendor was all out of everything too. So I banked the fire at night and I became expert at getting the most out of it. We roasted potatoes in the embers, but neither Pierre nor Simon would eat them. Simon said it was a nasty American habit but of course I am half American and I like that sort of thing. Mark— my father, if you remember—used to cook that way; fish and meat and shellfish; delicious. Anyway Bernice wasn't so fussy and she and I used to eat the potatoes together around six o'clock when for all our efforts the cold came in through every pore of the house.

On the second day, just as I was burning my fingers trying to get one of the potatoes out of the fire, I happened to look out of the window and saw in the failing light the burlap square of La Cigale's window-door. How grim and dark it looked and how icy! She didn't have electricity up there and the thought of her all alone in the bitter darkness struck me painfully. But as I think I told you—or did I?—I am rather timid. I hold myself back from many impulses because of it. That is, I used to; now I am bolder, much bolder.

Boldness! There's a subject to talk on. It's one of the qualities I most admire in the world. It gives me pleasure simply to know that it exists. A man should be bold. If he has no other virtue than that he is still saved. I don't know if Pierre is bold. Simon is insolent, but that's something else. What I have just written is bold because it betrays me. And it makes my heart ache. Do you know what that's like? They say it's not true medically, but I don't think they're right. I think they'll discover that they're wrong one of these days. Hearts do ache. It almost makes you sick with pain and then sometimes they beat and miss as though they were remembering a breathless thing.

* * * * *

ROSE laid down her pen. She pressed her hand over the heart in question. With one of those clear pictures that are different from reality only in time value, she reviewed the cold spell again in its minutest detail. Then, in a slightly larger and more flowing hand, she continued:

——————————— *Journal:* ———————————

Anyway, timidity prevented me from going up there that evening, but the next day was even colder so I took action. I wound a big plaid shawl around myself, went up to the balcony and rapped on the glass behind the burlap.

Inside, the old woman was sitting perfectly immobile on her bed. She might have been already frozen and fixed there to be found in the thaw. "Won't you come down and sit by our fire?" I asked with my own politeness sounding ridiculous in my ears, as though I were rehearsing a speech learned from parents. For a moment La Cigale made no reply and for all I know might have been too numb to do so. Then, breaking the icy silence, an accordion gave its first wheeze and she was brought to life.

"He has a stove, that one!" she cried hoarsely.

By way of answer a musette tango slid into the air and I saw La Cigale's eyes stand out from their sockets with a blurred shine as if she would have liked to weep but couldn't make the tears come out. I fought down a shudder of repulsion as I opened the door and held it for her to come through. She walked haughtily despite those unshed jealous tears and she came to our flat and sat at our fire. Her attitude was a curious mixture of condescension and suspicion, rather like that of a caged wild animal.

The cold spell lasted on and the papers now described it as a fight between Siberian and American winds. On the fourth day, and while the Siberian winds were still victorious, La Cigale had her revenge.

"He's run out of coal," she said when I came up to fetch her in the morning. Yes, she had to be fetched each morning and by me personally.

"Why doesn't he ask the landlady to lend him a little?" I asked without much interest.

"Because he hasn't paid his rent, that's why," said La Cigale, who was probably in the same position. Her lips, on which the dark paste had congealed, parted and she grinned. "He doesn't play his accordion now," she said.

Something in the way she said this made me respond in an unexpected manner. It was so spiteful and yet it had in it a primitive purity which lifted it above the kinder sayings of other people. To her surprise I shouted with laughter. But after a minute I stopped. "I must go and fetch him too in that case," I said.

It wasn't far to go and in front of his door, at the outer edge of the roof, the wind bit savagely at the room. Like a mountain hut, frail and exposed, it seemed to sway with the recurrent blasts. I had a sense of peril as one does in high wastelands and I felt dizzy so that I forgot to knock and just pushed open the door. He was standing up near his bed on which he had laid his instrument. His room, larger than the others, had two doors: one through which I had entered and which ended the balcony, and the other leading out onto a flat roof-top. The draft whistled through the cracks but could not animate the icy, still air of the chamber. I saw that his face was pinched and almost blue.

"You mustn't stay here," I cried. "You must come down to our flat at once. You'll get sick if you don't."

With numbed acceptance he prepared to follow me, first stooping to pick up his accordion.

"I'm sorry," I said, "but I don't like accordion music. You must come without it."

That brought him up sharp. A look of outraged masculinity crossed his features. "Oh, so it's like that is it?" he growled. "Well then, go back to your fire and leave me alone!"

What could I do? I was exasperated, but those hands red with cold and still faintly groping for his spurned instrument touched me. I had the impression he wanted to stamp his feet for circulation but was too proud to do so in my presence. "Oh come on then and bring it if you must," I said crossly, and I recall that I threw out my hand in a gesture of irritated surrender.

At this a winning smile showed me the triangular set of his bones. "*Tiens,*" he said, "I didn't realize that you were so pretty!"

CHAPTER 6

I wanted to show myself up a little, to expose myself, to make it easier for us both to recognize Rose. I thought perhaps the cold spell, writing about it I mean, would do it. Telling for instance about how I laughed at what La Cigale said about his being cold and how my father's neighborliness, which I've inherited, won out. Were there two sides to my nature even then? I realize that all my life I've had a special kind of sense of humor. At first it wasn't noticeable because I was still a child and all children have that kind more or less. It was only later that I noticed I still had it unchanged. I became aware of it through the reactions of other people. They were surprised. They didn't see why I laughed at *those* things and so unrestrainedly. It made them uneasy and it didn't go with what I seemed to be at all; with the studious Rose whose professors, although they thought she had promise, wished she would show a little temperament.

Pierre used to be almost shocked by my sense of humor and he was hurt by it. I recall one time, shortly after we married, there was a deep snowfall. We were still in the honeymoon stage and

one night when he had to work late I met him at his office and
we went out to the market place to have something to eat. You
know the central market of Paris, don't you? Les Halles, as it is
called. Enormous sheds with space all about them for the trucks
to draw up. Around this space are restaurants of all sorts and some
of them famous. It's a picturesque place to go to, what with the
various costumes worn by the marketeers. Butchers take the prize
in my opinion. They are dressed in white like charlatan surgeons
and stained all over with great red patches. They smell of blood
too, and that's sickening. Well, there was a whole group of these
butchers in the restaurant we chose, standing at the bar and drinking. One had to pass them to get to the tables beyond. Pierre is
fastidious about some things. Did I tell you? He can't stand dirt
and smells, which is strange when you consider he was brought
up on a farm. Perhaps that's why he left it. Anyway, just as he got
to the group the wind must have veered and he got a real whiff of
them. He threw back his head—literally, he shied like a horse. It
was very obvious, but what made it worse was that he slipped on
the floor which was tracked with snow. He fell sprawling with the
same bad-smell expression on his face.

I couldn't stand it. I laughed so hard I had to sit down. The
big veins on my neck felt as though they would burst and all the
butchers laughed with me just as hard. We were convulsed, and to
cap everything a little dwarf who is the doorman there ran over
and pretended to help Pierre up. Dwarfs are often clowns, I've
noticed. Kings were right about them. This one certainly was and
he made the most of the situation.

Pierre wouldn't speak to me afterward and do you know, I felt
horribly sad. Not because he wouldn't speak to me but for some
other reason that I don't understand. Perhaps you think that if
Pierre couldn't laugh too, he should have reacted in *some* way;
tripped me up, for instance, or waited until we got home and given

me a hiding. Was *that* why I felt so sad? Because of his lack of reaction? A laugh should be turned, I guess. But maybe it was something else—something in *me*. Anyway I lay awake for a long time that night and just sighed and I thought of the snow too as it lay on the streets and around Les Halles; so thick and white and so oblivious with its star-like flakes. I felt it falling, falling, covering up the grime of Paris, lying on the tops of cars and trucks and on the bloody shoulders of butchers and surgeons.

All this is only an example so that you'll know. And that kind of thing didn't happen often. Yet perhaps that was why, when La Cigale said that about her neighbor, I was touched. A responding chord had quivered in both our breasts.

When I came back with him La Cigale wasn't pleased at all. She gave us a baleful look and deliberately pulled up her chair so that no one else could get the full heat of the fire. She was reading, or looking at, a big scrapbook. She had been poring over this book constantly through sternly imposing glasses, but she never offered to show it to me. She acted as though each page were of absorbing interest; that is to say, containing long articles in her honor from her professional days. For all I knew it might have.

Now, as she sat square in front of my fire she muttered something about our having to put wax in our ears. My new guest took her up directly.

"It's as good as that caterwauling you used to do, grandmother, before I was born!" he said with a laugh, and he walked up to the fire with that preening gait I told you about.

She turned up her face to hiss at him, "Insolent animal!" And she continued in dramatic tones, "I was a concert singer!"

"Yes," he agreed, mocking, "concerts in cheap cafes."

I realized almost at once that despite the rudeness of their words there was no malice in them, not profoundly. They were enjoying themselves and each other in their own way and they understood. I felt happy to have them there, warm and quarrelsome like that, and I was smiling when Bernice came in from marketing. Her skin was blue-red from the cold, a sort of neon color.

"Ah, good morning, Jason," she said cheerfully.

When I heard that his name was Jason I was delighted. It made everything just right somehow, as though there were a little fair in the room; a *fête foraine* such as travels all over France. One could just see them, both with their trailers and their various claims to renown. Over his door would be painted: "Jason, Hero of ancient Greece, with his magic accordion." Perhaps it would go on to say that he had rediscovered the lost secret of Homer's art or had caused Helen's fall from virtue. They love to mix things up like that and talk about the high-sounding names of antiquity.

There's only one more thing I have to say about the cold spell and that's about the way those two behaved when night fell—when at last it came after so much waiting. But I don't think I can do it. I feel confused. That part of my brain I told you about, that rift—well, I feel it. They say we are all made in two pieces, sewn up the middle of our bodies; and there does seem to be a suture. It's traced by the spine, by the muscles, by faint lines of hair, by mistakes too: harelips and strange openings.

Yet only one side contains a heart.

* * * * *

FOR the first time that season Bernice had built a fire and Rose now went up to it, put her forearms up on the mantel and leaned against them the uncertain brow of which she spoke. Then what she could and could not remember burned there among the coals; what she wished or did not wish to forget, what cleared her head or made it spin, what eased her heart or made it ache. The coals pulsed and devoured her sensations in their midst, as perhaps they had devoured Jason's dreams or La Cigale's past glories when the two of them had sat there side by side last winter waiting for night to come.

After a while and with a grimace, Rose went to the piano and started to play. For an hour or so she abandoned herself, half closing her eyes and as if listening, not to the music but to some higher, thinner sound which the music might liberate. Upon her lifted face the heavy frown was partly smoothed away. All at once however, she rose and went into the kitchen.

"Bernice!" she called urgently.

Bernice was sitting at her table, sewing the hem of the kitchen curtains. She sewed like a sailor, as though she were using a palming needle, and when she looked up at Rose her eyes were blue stabs.

"Bernice, what did my husband say when he found those two in front of the fire during the cold spell?"

"You were there, Madame Flamand, you should know."

"But I don't remember," said Rose humbly. "I just know Pierre came in with Simon and that's all."

"Well, they had lunch here in the kitchen," said Bernice, "so your husband didn't see much of them and then in the evening you know how they were." Bernice spoke in a moody voice and she kept on plying the needle, using her whole arm at every stitch.

Rose stood there waiting apparently for more to come and after a while she was rewarded. Bernice spoke again, still moodily, in the voice of a woman whose ancestors have lived by the sea, who knows in her blood that there are powers one cannot fight. "Yes, I think you must know well enough how they were at night since you yourself—since I have seen that same look on you." For was the night not like the sea, a devouring magnet before which one could only submit?

As for Rose, these words must have been the ones for which she had waited because she hurried back to the studio, her body taut as though for muscular effort. She wrote:

Journal:

Those two stayed in this room together three entire days so I watched them. They were bored; warm but bored. Yet what would they have been doing otherwise? Neither went out much during the day. Jason played his interminable tunes and La Cigale stayed behind her burlap, presumably looking at her scrapbook. They didn't change their habits just for me you may be sure. Perhaps they were always bored in the daytime. It was only at night that they could live. They waited for dark, those two. They thirsted for it like birds with gaping beaks, and at its merest approach they would look at the window with eyes that were strangely alike. They shifted restlessly in their seats. Then, at a given moment, simultaneously but separate and distinct from each other, they would mutter their adieus and hasten out into the icy streets. They would go their mysterious ways in the dark.

CHAPTER 7

Today is one of those thrilling fall days. The clouds are a brilliant white and never cross the sun and the blue air mixes with the wind. I went for a walk this morning and it did me good. I walked by the Seine and saw the Garde Républicain trotting along the *Quai* on horseback. Behind them and bringing up the rear was a little boy astride a stick. He was the most impressive of all, with his wild eyes, and his imaginary horse was more beautiful surely than any of the real ones. A mysterious note was added because he hadn't quite decided whether he was the rider or the steed. I could tell this by the way he arched his neck and tossed his head and snorted.

Pretty soon a tired-looking woman called him to her side; monotonous and ordinary life that is forever calling her children in from their best games. But some don't obey; some, like the bugler, for instance. And like the gypsies Pierre and I saw a week later when we went out to lunch with his family.

It was rainy again and chilly; the endless drizzle of a Paris spring when it wants to show up the songs written about it. We were going out to my in-laws', which is a thing I detest. They are all so good, so heavy-jowled and earnest, and they turn Pierre into one of themselves so that he doesn't seem like a young aspiring writer any more or even a journalist—or even young for that matter. He is just another Flamand: fresh-colored, stout, and devouring the roast. His brother and his brother's wife would be there with their enormous two-year-old child all done up in white and everybody would once again try and understand Pierre's work and why he had chosen such an unhealthy profession. Meanwhile I would be expected to talk about domestic things with the women.

I sound horrid about them, especially as I know they try their best to like me. But they can't succeed any more than I can with them, since it's hard to like a vacuum and that's how we appear to each other. So I am just polite and respectful, that's all.

Anyway, we started out about ten as the Flamands live quite a ways out of Paris. Pierre has a little car and we went in that. It leaked over my ankles; icy drops which combined unpleasantly with the heat coming up through the floorboard. I felt as though I were catching a cold too. The Flamands live just outside a village and as we were maneuvering through its back streets a band of gypsies came by. They were breaking camp, I suppose. A horse-drawn van with slats for sides led the way, clattering across the railroad tracks. Through the slats peered various mournful animal faces and behind the van a pair of camels was being pulled along unwillingly. They were mangy and had disagreeable expressions, but then they always do as far as I'm concerned. Five or six riders trotted laughing in their wake with straight backs and legs dangling.

"They look happy," I remarked to Pierre, who had drawn up to the side of the road.

A few seconds later a last straggler came galloping along, riding bareback. It was a young woman with long, tangled, greasy hair and a sullen mouth. Her eyes, still full of sleep, glanced at us sideways.

Later, when I was sitting in front of my meat, I thought of them again and the words came into my mind, *"They* are like that." And it was at about the same moment that I realized that my mother-in-law had a distinct smell. She was serving us, stretching out her arm over the table, so that's why I noticed. It was a kept-in sort of odor that "good" material had altered. Gypsies must smell different—strong but different.

* * * * *

ROSE bit her lip thoughtfully as she looked down at what she had just been writing. Then she burst out laughing, showing to the empty room her small, white, even teeth. Yet as she laughed her eyes remained aloof from joy. Enveloped in their crystal waters they glittered between half-closed lids.

"Yes," she murmured, "but what's that got to do with it?"

Closing her journal she put it amongst the stacks of sheet music as usual and then sat down to play. But every note she struck sent an unpleasant shiver up her spine as though it were false. An almost unbearable desire came over her to play a certain popular tune. It was like an itch or like a burning spot somewhere inside which only the playing of this tune would ease. But when she finally gave in to it her face was contracted and a feverish flush came up on her skin.

Afterward she could not sit there anymore. She wandered past the kitchen where Bernice, stuffing a fowl, did not look up, and then into her bedroom.

Just opposite the back door to the terrace, this room was fairly small. With its sloping roof and checked curtains, it resembled in some respects the girlhood room in which Rose had spent many happy hours as a child. All her books were here, French and English, and she had only to look at their worn covers to find herself at that particular age when she had read the book for the first time. Some dated to the days before she could read and these brought back her mother's soft, accented voice and the thrilling fairyland in which children so perilously wander. And was not she, the grown-up Rose, wandering there once again?

Opening a volume at random, she saw a pressed flower in its leaves, but she could not recall having picked or put it there. Nonetheless a painful throbbing agitated her breast and her throat, and suddenly she cried out almost with horror, "It's the old woman's flower!" She brushed it off the page and when it fell on the floor, stamped on it again and again as some people do with insects.

As she was thus occupied, she heard a ring at the outer back door and, glad to escape her own sensations, she ran across the terrace and opened it. A thin, dark girl stood there with a sack over her shoulders. Black locks escaping from a scarf around her head gave her a gypsy look as did a certain sly expression in her long eyes. But her face was marked unbecomingly with large, pale freckles. In a whining voice the girl told Rose that she had come from Lourdes with sheets to sell. "Pure linen thread," she said vehemently and before Rose could comment she had stepped inside the door, undone her sack, and spread one of them out on the terrace.

It was an ordinary linen sheet of coarse quality and although as yet unbleached, it would grow whiter and softer with every washing. But the price, as the girl was now quoting it, was too high.

"I can do better than that right here in Paris," said Rose, although this was probably not true. As a matter of fact she was undecided, or, rather, incapable of making a decision. The girl observed this and said quickly, "Look, Madame, I will leave it with you for a while. I'm not leaving Paris until tomorrow."

"Oh, I wouldn't want to make you come all the way back up here," said Rose.

The girl smiled and the sly look of her eyes was thus accentuated. It lent piquancy to her unhealthy face which was like that of a young girl exhausted by a religious adolescence. "It's nothing," she said. "I'm staying with my friend up there on the top floor." She jerked her head at the attic rooms above them. "It's he who sent me," she said.

"Is that why you are asking so high a price?" asked Rose. "So you can share the dividend with him?" Her voice had a tight, flat sound as though it were being squeezed in her throat, and she found her words coming out with such slowness that she finished them mechanically. Their track inside her brain was already lost.

The girl shrugged. Her shiny, unhealthy, freckled face showed only the boredom of habit. She was used to insults on her wares. Most people bargained that way. "Pure linen," she repeated in a colorless tone.

"Go away," said Rose. "Go back upstairs and tell him you failed and that I'm not such a fool as he thought." With her foot she shoved the linen sheet aside.

Now the girl lowered her head and, stooping, folded up the sheet. Something humble in the curve of her back made Rose say sarcastically, "Will he beat you?" From her crouched position the girl glanced up, her eyes secret between the escaped spirals of her hair, but she made no answer. A religious medal on her breast swung free and glittered in the sun. Then she was gone and could be heard going down the stairway on whose threadbare carpet all steps sounded.

So she wasn't going up to report her failure! She did not need to, since beyond doubt Jason had heard everything from his room. Rose felt her heart beat stiflingly high up in her bosom. She leaned back against the terrace railing and slowly lifted her face. Jason had come out on the balcony and was looking back at her. His expression was hard and unchanging. Before its immobility Rose trembled. She clenched her fists impotently behind her back like a punished child. Then, turning, she ran quickly indoors.

CHAPTER 8

I wasn't able to write yesterday. I had a headache—no, that's not true—the *doll* Rose had a headache and her eyes were swollen too; dark underneath as though she'd been crying or as though— but it wasn't that. I'd have known. I have to know those things because she is my effigy. She has everything of me: my blood, my bones, my breath in her lungs. Does she have my soul? Of course you have no answer to that, and in fact so far you haven't answered any question of mine. I suppose you think I should find the answers by myself and that's just what I'm trying to do. Another thing: I still haven't decided who *you* are. Never mind. Perhaps when I come to the end of everything that too will be made clear to me.

As I said, the doll Rose had a headache and when she has one I have one too; a duller, more faraway one deep, deep down inside my head where dreams come from, if you know what I mean. And on the subject of heads: they *seem* fairly small. I look at mine in the mirror, for instance. It's a neat, round, black ball with a mask on one side of it. And there are passages behind the mask and teeth and strings to tie in the eyes. It's only what's behind all those things that counts. How minute a space for what goes on there; for the miles and miles of thinking and fancying that I've done since I was born. Yet there seems room for lots more. I often have the impression that there are dark caves there, caverns which echo dimly to my conscious self and whose imprisoned voices I can never quite catch.

There is a song which everybody sang in Paris last year about a diver; the lover asks the diver to sound the depths, first of his mistress's eyes, then of her heart and lastly of her brain. From the first two trips the diver returns and tells of the marvels he has seen, but from the last he does not rise. He is lost in the "profound abyss." I guess the song writer knew how it was although what the diver actually sees in heart and eyes is disappointing, not to say banal. Still, of the "profound abyss" he had nothing to tell. It was too mysterious even for a popular song.

Today I have to tell you about a trip I made to Montmartre. I wanted to buy some material for a summer suit and there are very good places there, one in particular. It's called the Marché St. Pierre and they have cuts and remnants from all the fabric makers of Europe. I found what I wanted easily. You know I like simple clothes; pleated skirts, blouses, and so forth. That's the way I dress. Simon thinks it's awfully dowdy, "the nostalgia of school days" as he calls it. Well, but I love good material and pretty colors and I do choose them with care.

Anyway I came out of the store with my package under my arm and stood for a moment outside the door to get my bearings. There was a soft, clear, gray light over Montmartre, whose summit, tipped by the Sacré Coeur, rose just above me. As you know there is a park running steeply down from the church and the Marché St. Pierre is just across from its base. As I stood there I noticed a couple coming down the last steps of this park and the man seemed familiar. When you've been in a crowded store your eyes get out of focus and it takes a while for anything to register. It wasn't until they had almost reached me that I knew the man was Jason.

I must explain that since the cold spell I'd not spoken more than a dozen words with my neighbors. We never met on the stairs, or if we did it was only a brief "Bonjour" on my part because neither of them had any definite word to say, only a sort of grunt. And now it was April and Jason was walking with his girl in Montmartre—very appropriate—and then, well, somehow she got lost or he left her and I found myself having a drink with him and we talked about nothing. I don't think we even talked at all and there was nothing of interest, nothing, nothing, *nothing*.

It's afternoon now. I wrote that last paragraph this morning, or someone wrote it. Shall I cross it out? No, I'll leave it because it's in my hand. But it's silly, just silly; even the writing slants a different way. No wonder I felt funny during lunch. More of the doll's tricks no doubt. Because that afternoon exists. It's in the world forever.

I'll start where I left off, at the material bazaar, outside it where I saw Jason and his girl. She came down the steps so awkwardly; Jason's sweetheart, as I called her to myself. Her cheeks shook at every step and her hair too, which was bleached brittle. Even her dress was shaken by the body fitted too tightly inside it. Jason, beside her, appeared very sure of himself. He walked lithely, holding her arm. He carried his accordion on his shoulder and was dressed in a coarse roll-neck sweater with a tight jacket over it. I was sure he'd seen me but he made no sign and, passing quite close, went on toward the boulevard.

I too walked in that direction, intending to catch a bus home from the Place Pigalle. The air was damp and beneath my feet the sidewalk sweated a dark oil. On the boulevard a drab crowd jostled one another and the strain of winter set a seal of anonymity on their faces. They walked clumsily as if the cold had cramped and paralyzed their limbs. No one seemed to notice me. They could have been a crowd of phantoms shuffling along and only the tapping of my own heels was sharp. I like high heels and the cobbler puts metal on them so I won't wear them down too fast. Listening to the sound of that clear tapping I wondered vaguely if I favored my left foot. They say most people do. It was some time before I became aware of the soft tread behind me. But after a while I realized that I was being followed and I glanced sideways into a shop window to see. It's an almost irresistible impulse. My follower turned out to be Jason and at that moment he touched me on the arm.

"You're far away from home," he observed in a cocky way.

"So are you," I retorted good-humoredly, although I did not care for the meeting.

"I'd like to offer you a drink," he went on. "Or at least a coffee."

The polite turn of his phrase surprised me as coming from a man who had always been surly to the point of rudeness. So he *did* appreciate my kindness after all, I thought, and I felt bound to accept his offer and show thus that I understood its meaning.

We turned into a café and sat down in the glassed-in terrace where we could still watch the passersby.

"What did you do with your girl?" I asked.

"Oh, she had to leave—and she's not my girl, as you put it."

"Why isn't she?" I asked teasingly. "I thought she looked nice."

He glanced at me quickly and for some reason that glance showed me his looks as though I were seeing them for the first time. He had the heart-shaped face that is unusual for a man: wide at the cheekbones and with a pointed chin. His mouth was fresh and boyish with a little cleft in the center of the lower lip. His brown hair was very bright and of the kind that would be curly when wet. Perhaps the most striking of his features was his reddish eyes, which hid their depths inside a small, black pupil as hard as stone. Now these reddish, foxy eyes looked into mine.

"Girls like that are a dime a dozen," he said. "They come easy and I make them go the same way."

So he thinks himself a killer, I thought, but in my heart I knew he was not boasting at all. It just *was* like that for him. Aloud I only said, "What are you doing way up here?"

"I came up about work," he answered.

"Work?" I was surprised.

He tapped his accordion, now on a chair beside him. "I'm to play in a ballroom, a *bal* near here called the O.K."

"I'm glad for you," I said. I had ordered Campari, a slightly bitter apéritif of which I am fond, and Jason had followed my example. He lifted his untouched glass.

"Here's to your health," he said with a smile. I too raised mine, but as I did so, I saw his smile fade and his usual surly look take its place. He drank and an awkward silence descended on us both. I began to feel foolish sitting with him like this; a man whom I neither liked nor admired and who in turn thought of me surely as a boring, middle-class housewife. Turning toward the window I was further dismayed to see the blond girl with whom Jason had been walking. The girl's face, which had seemed amiable before, was now contorted by jealousy and suffering. Her sharp nose was red and her mouth compressed. A deep line between her eyes showed the effort she was making to control her tears, and she was standing quite still with her purse clutched against her.

"Why there's your friend!" I exclaimed.

"I know," he said coldly.

"Why doesn't she come in?" I asked.

"I'd like to see her try," he said. "She'd soon find out!"

"Well, I must go in any case," I said and heard a quiver of anger in my voice. I buttoned my coat hurriedly and, with an effort, thanked him for the drink. I held out my hand and felt for a moment the surprising warmth of his palm.

"How small your hand is," he said. "I could crush it easily." And those boyish lips parted over pointed teeth. "I dream of you at night," he said.

Of course I made no reply, but just the same and as though hypnotized into doing so, I gave him a provocative look. I was furious afterward, and as I hurried out into the street I was blushing with irritation. I suppose women just can't help reacting to a compliment, even a doubtful one. What made it worse was that I now had to pass within two feet of the girl. I felt a burning look sweep me from top to toe. I even fancied I could hear a harsh, despairing breath. The girl was standing with her feet apart and her neck stretched forward. It was as though she were trying to divine the quality of my body through my clothes. And I think it was those very clothes that baffled her the most. "What kind of woman," she seemed to be wondering, "would wear a loose skirt when she could wear a tight one?"

I was miserable as I walked to the bus stop. "That girl thought I was a rival!" I said to myself furiously. "How shameful!" And then I thought further that they were probably fighting over me together right now, or even laughing. I was no longer in a daze. On the contrary, each former phantom in the crowd had been resurrected into flesh. I was painfully aware of each face and was dismayed by their expressions of anxiety and hate. The women seemed especially bitter since their beardless skins were less protected against the grinding monotony of life. How rarely one saw a smile or heard a laugh! And why should they laugh? Were they not mortal? Who knew what diseases lay inside them, body and soul?—inside them or inside me.

Once on the bus I sat near the window and, leaning against the glass, looked out at the street. This street would last longer than

I, Rose, who had been a child yesterday—or it probably would, though a bomb, a rising sea, or another planet could destroy it in an instant. There was an old man opposite me. I could see his reflection in the window: bearded, with dark, hollow eyes. "He's like a prophet," I thought, and I had the impression that he would suddenly rise and, with uplifted finger, tell of dreadful things to come. At the same time I could see through his reflection, through his eyes and his white beard to the twilight street beyond. And when, turning away from the window, I looked at him directly, I saw that his eyes that had seemed so deep were merely closed in senile slumber, while around his mouth the stained beard was wet.

CHAPTER 9

When I got home that afternoon from Montmartre it was to find Bernice fixing flowers in a vase. She was arranging them in her usual exuberant way, stuffing their stems roughly into the water.

"You look like a little girl, Bernice," I said. It was true—a good, happy, clumsy little girl. Her tow hair stuck up all around her head and had been shaven at the nape of her neck. Her feet toed in. It was a surprise to see her sanguine, forty-year-old face, whose innocent gaiety hadn't kept away the wrinkles.

"Some little girl," Bernice retorted and thrust another stalk home. "I don't much like your Monsieur Simon," she continued, "but he certainly sends expensive flowers."

"Simon!" I was astounded. True, I had been his constant hostess and he had been fed at our place on the average of once a day. But Simon had always accepted our hospitality as his due, or rather, as one accepts the doubtful conveniences of a boardinghouse. And then there seemed a strange discrepancy between Simon and flowers of any sort. One would think his look alone enough to wither them. I read the card which Bernice had already opened.

"I bought these flowers to send to the editor's wife," it read, "but the contrast was too terrible. It went against my artistic integrity. With you of course there will be no contrast at all."

"Very witty, isn't it?" cried Bernice. It had never occurred to her not to open and read the card itself. "It's a compliment," she went on to explain. "Monsieur Simon is saying that you are just as pretty as the flowers."

"Is he?" I asked, laughing, and then for some reason the grand piano in the corner of the room caught my eye. I had brought it with me at my marriage and it had once been my mother's. I fancied sometimes that it had an air of reproach. I knew I didn't play really seriously anymore and that my hands were out of practice. And I recalled promising my professor to work hard every day. He had been disappointed at my marriage. "Put the flowers on top of the piano, Bernice," I said because one always wants to soothe those gods one has betrayed. As she did so I went on, "I saw Jason up in Montmartre."

"Oh yes? I know he's found work up there now." Bernice went into an imaginary musette waltz, clutching an invisible partner. "I've been to the O.K. My last employers lived up in that direction. It's very nice; very chic."

As for me, I'd never been to a *bal* of that type and I could form no picture of it. Pierre and I occasionally went out with friends to jazz clubs in cellars where young people jitterbugged earnestly and with a sort of political fervor, or else, even more rarely, we went to night clubs. A *bal* would be different from either of these, with its nervous, tremulous music. "He was with a girl," I said.

"That's no surprise," retorted Bernice, and suddenly I couldn't tell her about the drink we'd had together. I'll tell Pierre, I decided. But when Pierre came home that night I didn't say anything about it.

Pierre was in a bad humor that evening in any case. His jaw had a heavy line to it. Something had gone wrong and by his attitude about the flowers I guessed what it was.

"He thinks he can do what he pleases," he said sullenly.

I understood. Simon's act was disloyal in my husband's eyes. He believes that a group working together on one project should be a sort of family. *Jouvence* fosters this belief. Personalities and ideas must be made to fit a standard just as the modes shown, the articles, and the short stories must all have a certain tone, a tone that will neither shock the readers nor exalt them. When individualists such as Simon upset this theory it's Pierre who suffers. He has to be the go-between and to explain why Simon must modify his writing, or, to the editor, why Simon's individuality is valuable. In the latter case, naturally, he is only repeating the editor's former words of enthusiasm. Poor Pierre, the struggle wears him out. It gives him perhaps an unwelcome glimpse of his own self. He'd probably spent all afternoon soothing Simon and translating his superior's commands as tactfully as possible. Now Simon, who knew Pierre hated disloyalty and disrespect, was paying this backhanded compliment to his wife.

"But why shouldn't he send me flowers?" I demanded, something perverse rising up inside me.

"It's not that he shouldn't send them," said Pierre. "It's what he says on the card. He's so insolent. He *knows* I don't like him criticizing his chief and to do it in a personal way makes it worse."

"Well, he could hardly pretend he thought your boss's wife pretty," I retorted. And now I really was piqued. I can't imagine why.

"He only did it to annoy me," insisted Pierre.

"I suppose it never occurs to a husband that someone could find his wife worthy of the least compliment," I cried. And do you know, I was sincere in my irritation. With another part of my mind I knew I was talking nonsense, but I was sincere nonetheless.

Pierre opened his eyes and looked at me as though he thought I'd gone crazy. Then he gave a shrug. "I never knew you were vain," he said.

"It's not vanity," I began, "it's—" but I couldn't explain. For after all what *did* I care about an absurd thing like that? But even as I wondered the phrase came into my head, "I dream of you at night."

Pierre was speaking in a conciliatory tone. "Well, darling," he was saying, "I always did say you had nice eyes. If you'd only pluck your eyebrows a little in the middle they'd be perfect."

"Perfectly mediocre like *Jouvence*," I retorted, but at his wounded expression I was sorry.

Later that evening Pierre worked on his book in the small room next to the bedroom which is his study. I was lying in bed and I could hear his typewriter starting and stopping. Sometimes he sighed.

I'm writing about Pierre today on purpose because there has grown a sort of mist about him lately. Oh sometimes he's crystal clear. It's when I try and think of how he was then that the mist comes up and envelops him. He couldn't have been much different. He's still working at *Jouvence* and on the same novel. I think his enthusiasm for Simon is just about over, but no doubt he'll bring a substitute back with him very soon. Yet that mist *is* hiding something. Here, I'll try to make it clear: When I was at the conservatory we went through a month of discussion as to whether a sound not heard exists at all. I daresay most students have that same discussion and they think themselves very clever for having it and it's rather scary too.

One pictures a sound: a marvelous chord perhaps or just a little grunt—and it happens in the wilderness, the desert most likely, the desert of the moon. It can have no life around it, no one, nothing, can hear it. So does it sound if no eardrum vibrates? How many times I've pictured that barren place and the chord, or the little grunt, *waiting* to sound. It's like that with Pierre. *Is* he the same now that I no longer throw back to him his former image?

That's why I thought I should write a few facts; I mean, about how I could hear him typing in the next room and how sometimes he sighed. I was reading a score. I enjoy that more than reading books as a rule, but that night I just couldn't concentrate. I lay in my bed in my once blue nightgown which Bernice's beloved Javelle water has faded since, and I looked at the score and instead of harmonies I heard the tapping of a typewriter and the rustling of paper and those few sighs. I wondered if Pierre's book would ever be finished. Simon writes one a year, but artists are different in that respect. I learned that early in life. One must never apply the rules of one to another.

I remember once, as a child, Mark taking me to the house of a young man who wanted criticism of his paintings. The young man impressed me by his odd clothes and his tender, fluttery manner. His work was all walls and houses with each stone perfectly drawn in. I don't know what Mark had to say about it, but before we left, the father of the young man came into the room. He was very proud of his son who wasn't going to be a wine merchant the way he was, and he treated him more as a mother would, kissing him and stroking his hair.

"You can't judge my son, sir, the way one would judge an ordinary painter," he said.

"What do you mean?" asked my father, puffing away at his pipe and giving me a wink.

"Well, others take only a day or two to complete a work, sometimes only a few hours. My son takes months. Why, I've known him to take a year over a single drawing."

"So?" asked Mark, putting his head to the side.

"Isn't it obvious," cried the man, "that he must command far greater prices for a year's work than for a day's?"

At that my father simply roared. He clapped the young man's father on the back and kept saying, "That's wonderful, wonderful! He must put how long it takes him on each painting."

The young man giggled and I thought it was nice of him not to be embarrassed for his father.

But recalling that incident now made me wonder if Pierre too thought actual time counted as merit. And I tried to picture how the book was written. I'd never read so much as a line of it. Pierre never discussed it with me. I don't think he considers I know anything about literature. Anyway, that night, trying to picture Pierre's book gave me an uneasy feeling. Then I heard a sigh heavier than the rest and Pierre's chair scraped back. When he came into the bedroom he was scratching his head so that his hair stood in tufts. He was swollen around the eyes. In fact, with his heavy step and with belt loosened he gave the effect of an older man. Yet his face was and is almost unlined. Only a few wrinkles bar his forehead as though to forbid his hair from coming lower. Habit made him stand warming his calves a moment at the unlit stove.

"I wanted to work tonight," he said, "but I can't seem to. I told Simon that I'd let him read it next week."

"Will it be ready?" I asked.

"No," he muttered gloomily with his eyes on the floor. He took off his jacket and his shirt and stood in the woolen singlet which he puts on religiously in the fall and which he keeps on until the first of June. I noticed how his arms were quite thin, too thin really for the heavy torso. He had already lost his boyish flatness and his body curved slightly outward at the middle. He took off his trousers and hung them up carefully in a press and then went off to the bathroom. When he returned he was in his pajamas and smelled of tooth-paste.

After he'd gotten into bed I asked him if he remembered the money which Mark had put in the bank for me when we married. He gave a sound which meant that he was interested with reservations.

"Well," I said, "I've been thinking. Why don't you give up your job and we can live on it for a while?"

"Give up my job!" He was so surprised that he sat up straight. "What for?"

"To finish your book, darling," I told him, and then I went on quickly about how the stuff they made him write must be bad for his real work and that his book was far, far more important than any job. It's the way I've been brought up, you see, but Pierre hasn't and he didn't even let me finish before he was shouting, "Are you crazy? Use up the money! And when it's gone then what? Really Rose, one would think you were out of your mind! Use up the money!"

Then I had to laugh. It was all his peasant blood boiling in his veins. "Don't you think it's dangerous to leave it in the bank?" I teased. "Don't you think we should bring it home and put it in a sock?" At his hurt expression I put my arms around him and kissed him, but do you know that even as I was doing this—and feeling very tender—yes, at this very moment I thought of the bugler.

CHAPTER 10

——— *Journal:* ———

I believe I'm feeling better today. I had a long sleep last night and a reassuring dream. I don't know if you've ever had a dream like that or even if you dream at all. I have troubled, or exciting, or anxious dreams. Sometimes I'm afraid when I wake up, or terribly depressed—especially when I dream of muddy water. You see, I dream that I am looking for a stream or a river that I used to swim in when a child. I search and search, but the landmarks have changed and usually some housing project has grown up there. When at last I do find it the water is a muddy trickle, a sewer that stinks. Anyway, last night it was the contrary. I was floating in water that was clear as green glass. When I awoke I felt soothed and refreshed.

Pierre was lying on his side facing me and I could feel his breath on my cheek. When I turned my head I breathed it and it had the hay smell of healthy breath. He was making little sounds and in the dusk (it was dawn) I saw how he had closed his eyes so tight that the lashes were sticking straight out of them and not lying on his cheeks at all. I moved and he said something to me but he was too much asleep to make sense. I couldn't understand. So I lay there with my feet beside his warm feet and shall I tell you that for a while, just a while, my heart felt light?

Oh, the bliss of those few moments; the peaceful and loving bliss! Do you notice that it was me there in bed, not the doll?

Enough of that; last time I was saying how Simon sent the flowers and how Pierre was annoyed. It showed that Simon's days were numbered both with Pierre and with *Jouvence*. Oh, it wouldn't happen right away or even very soon. *Jouvence* was clever. They wouldn't fire him until the end of summer. They'd keep him at his desk so that people like Pierre, people whom they really needed, could take a vacation and they'd not have to break in anyone new. But he'd go in the fall and that's now. He's already gone from his pedestal inside Pierre although so far there's no replacement. But I heard they hired a well-known painter and he is supposed to change and elevate the whole appearance of *Jouvence*. He's fat and has a beard. I know that much and no doubt I'll soon know more.

I notice I had only gotten as far as April last time and next comes May and there really isn't much to tell about May. Simon came to lunch and supper and afterwards he went out, presumably to "live." Often Pierre and Simon worked late on the review and I think Simon tried to persuade Pierre to "live" too, because Pierre grew quite dissatisfied with me in May. I could tell by the way he criticized me in little things. But he did it tenderly and sadly as one might do to a child whose possibilities are limited through faulty blood.

Paris grew warm and lovely with racing clouds. The chestnuts blossomed on avenue and *quay*. Today their seeds have all blown off and lie in great mounds rather like mattress ticking. There are piles of them near the Seine. When I see them I get a feeling that if I turned on the right switch I could make the whole reel go backward like people do in funny movies. I could lift the mattress ticking from the ground and scatter it in the air and let it waft back up to the trees and be drawn inside them and so on back to the blossoms of last spring. Perhaps then my life would be reeled back along with it. But I don't really know if I'd want that or not.

One day La Cigale came down and knocked at my door. She too had put out blossoms for spring in the form of a new turban, a bright orange one. The color tinged her face. I could see then clearly how once she'd been handsome; a big, square-boned, handsome woman, the kind they liked in those days, as one gathers from old postcards. And out of that square, muscular chest, it seemed, had come a light soprano voice. My mother's voice on the contrary just suited her looks: dark, pure, liquid, passionate. There was something fierce in it too; an humble sort of fierceness, like a beautiful, favorite slave. But then as you know she wasn't a favorite in the end. Why did they think she had secrets to tell? Or did they just *want* to think it?

Have you ever considered with all your mind the cruelty of man? People like Simon and even Pierre are forever talking about this or that injustice and cruelty, but they act as if it were only one side that did it, one political group. Or rather, that when the side they don't like is the victim it's good. That makes it the worst of all.

La Cigale had something she wanted to tell or to ask me, but she couldn't get started. I told her to come in and she wouldn't do that either. She just stood there at the threshold of the front door and smiled. I told you that the apartment wound around the courtyard so that the front and back door are cheek by jowl. La Cigale had actually rung the back-door bell. I can tell the difference in sound. There was something pathetic about that. She had such a proud, insolent nature. She must have been impertinence personified. So she must have loathed to abase herself thus. For my mother, of course, back and front door would be alike. Her noble and natural humility made them so. And there I am again comparing my darling, my beautiful mother to that old woman. I wonder why?

As I said, La Cigale stood there and smiled. I noticed that she was holding her scrapbook. Her smile was a slit, ingratiating and false, and it did not suit her at all. After a lot of hemming and hawing it finally came out that she had written an article on her life with some of her old photographs as illustrations and that she thought Pierre could get it published in *Jouvence*. Well, for all I knew so he might and I told her this. Then at last she came in and, sitting on the edge of the sofa very primly, she opened her book and shuffled through the pages. First of course she put on her glasses. It was impossible, it seemed, for her to find what she wanted, which I thought strange, seeing she'd come down on purpose to show it to me. Or perhaps she could not quite decide to let her life into my profane hands. While she was looking, the light from the studio window fell full on her face and I noticed that her glasses didn't reflect it. There was no glitter. In fact they were only empty rims.

I suppose you think it was cruel of me to laugh. I can't help it. I had to hold on to my stomach. When I laugh hard like that I have a sort of coarse, harsh, exuberant feeling and yet—and yet—

When I finally stopped and looked at La Cigale I saw she had taken off the spectacles and was holding them with two fingers right through the rims. She was grinning like a clown. *"C'la donne toujours un peu de ton,"* she said.

After that she had no trouble at all finding the papers she wanted. They were the only loose leaves in her scrapbook and she handed them over to me without a word. When she had gone I saw that a pressed rose had fallen out of the book onto the floor.

* * * * *

ROSE put away her journal with a smile. She really did feel better that day and as Bernice was doing the week's wash, she decided to go to the market.

It was noon when she got there, the busiest hour. The market occupied two streets and formed a sort of cross. Besides the actual stores, there were outside booths and carts lining the gutters. Rose walked along with her basket thinking of La Cigale, whose actual presence now gave her no surprise.

The old woman was holding a few small, withered apples sold in the humblest of the carts. She put them on the scales herself and then argued ferociously with the vendor over their weight. The vendor, another old woman, finally gave in, and as La Cigale turned away Rose thrilled to the gleam of triumph in her eyes.

"Madame la Cigale," she cried, "come and have an apéritif with me."

La Cigale turned and looked Rose up and down. "What are we today?" she asked; *"la femme bien,* the correct little wife, or—"

"Or what?" demanded Rose, changing color. Her clear, ivory skin had suddenly a greenish tinge as though she were about to be sick.

La Cigale came closer, perhaps to savor Rose's appearance more fully. "Oh, I think you can supply the missing words," she said.

They went into a small bar where market people forgathered, and ordered beer. When the two lukewarm draughts were set before them La Cigale raised her glass. "To life," she said, "to *la vie d' bohème!"*

Do you still drink to that now that you are old and poor? wondered Rose to herself. La Cigale as though to answer her unspoken question said, "Oh, I know you think I am a miserable old woman. People despise me for the money I let slip through my hands—if they remember about it, that is—but better let money slip through than life itself. I *lived* life."

Why do they all talk about living? thought Rose with irritation; how can one help but live if one's alive? But aloud she only asked, "And was that worth the years from now until you die?"

"Ah, that's another story," said La Cigale. "One can work and be serious all one's youth or one can sing and dance like this poor grasshopper. In the end one will be old. Not all the money in the world could make that up to any woman." She looked at Rose full-face with her handsome old bones deserted, so to speak, by the frailer flesh above them. Downing her glass she got up and held out her hand.

"Thank you for the drink, my lost and abandoned child," she said.

Rose stayed on there a few more minutes. The door of the café was open and the gusts of air that blew into the bar were warm and soft. Yet they were tinged prophetically with the breath of snow.

CHAPTER 11

When, on the first of June, Pierre went to Italy on a business trip, Simon called Rose up. The timbre of his voice made the wires vibrate. He asked her out to dine but she refused.

"My father is in town," she said, "and he's coming to supper." She added in her polite manner, "Please, won't you come too?"

This particular, grave politeness of Rose infuriated Simon so that he accepted. He was using the telephone in Pierre's office and on putting down the receiver he turned and looked at Marie's long bare legs which, as usual, were on the desk. "You need a shave," he said.

Marie nonchalantly reached out and felt them. She shrugged and continued rolling the gum she had in her mouth. This habit secretly repelled her and the bubbles forced into the gum by constant chewing hurt inside her chest and made her burp, but she sternly repressed her weakness for appearance's sake.

"Your act just doesn't go over," said Simon, rising.

"What's the matter, isn't Madame Flamand having any?" asked Marie, who had a reporter's nose despite her affectations. Simon's jawbones twitched. He could think of no reply that was vicious enough because what he wanted to do was blow a breath on Marie and have her calcify on the spot. He often wanted to do this to people and as so far he had not found out how to do so, he contented himself with dipping his pen in his own gall.

Mark, the father of Rose Flamand, pleased Simon. His leonine head whose shaggy locks were still thick, his straight, square features and his air (common to so many painters) of the workman, soothed this nervous man Simon. Latham however was only a shell now. He gave his daughter intent, ponderous looks that were dumb as an animal's and it was hard to tell whether the tearful brightness of his eyes came from sorrow or premature old age. He spoke slowly in his French that had never lost its accent and, although his every word gave the impression of sense, even of nobility, he said nothing.

Nonetheless, in Simon's eyes, Mark lent a certain stability to Rose. It was as if she had been wandering frameless until then. The presence of her father placed her, and even her clothes which Simon had so detested took on elegance. She was wearing tonight a pleated dress of silk whose boyish collar set off the dark, round, neat head. Other women by comparison now seemed diminished by fussiness, by cheaply won maturity. Yet Simon had suspected this all along about Rose. It was why she had made him angry and, partly, why he said sly things about her to Pierre. Actually Simon looked down on Pierre. He used him and people like him to make money if possible, but he did not respect him and in insulting Rose was only showing his disrespect for a man who was too stupid to know his wife's quality. As for Pierre's honest heart, his tenderness that was almost powerful, Simon hated those traits which gave him a sense of his own lack. He himself could not afford them despite all his talent, all his perception and brains.

At supper with Mark Latham and his daughter, Simon rested a little. Mark drew from him his venom, or rather, made its fabrication unnecessary. Mark did not know reflection and conclusion as Simon knew them. He had instinctively felt and had put his feeling on canvas in a harmonious way that was full of strength and meaning. Sarcasm, even satire, that crutch of the weak and the oppressed, was foreign to him. If a thing was brutal, ugly or ridiculous he put it down in that essence and drew no conclusions. The work spoke. He let it and was himself silent.

"Are you staying here with Rose?" asked Simon.

"No," said Mark with a still youthful smile, "I'm a dated Montparnassian and faithful to my old haunts. I'm staying up on the Boulevard Raspail."

"Well, why not come out and have a brandy with me? And Rose too of course," said Simon. "Besides, she must profit by her grass-widowhood, must she not, *Maître?*"

Mark, still smiling, turned his dumb, bright eyes on his child. "Yes, yes," he said, "I see she must. Have fun, my dear. Have a little fun. The rest comes soon enough." He got heavily to his feet; a burly, workmanlike figure and yet a shell for all that. "I'm tired," he said. "It's exhausting to arrange an exhibit and that's what I'm doing in town. I don't know why, either. Any fool can buy a gallery these days, but I suppose it's habit."

It was significant that neither Rose, Simon nor Mark himself thought of the possibilities of *Jouvence*. Mark could have had his photograph there or that of one of his works. It would have been publicity, the desire of the age. But they did not think about it. Latham in any case had no desire other than that of returning to his hotel where, once asleep, he could be happy. They walked with him to the crossroads of Saint-Germain des Prés where he took a taxi. The evening was warm and a light still lingered in the sky. They watched the taxi lurching around the corner and disappearing unevenly in the haze of its exhaust. Then, with a look at the crowded café tables, they turned into the nearest bar.

"What would you be doing, Simon, if you weren't being polite to me?" asked Rose when they were seated. "Would you be 'living,' as you put it?"

"I am living now," said Simon, looking at himself in the mirror doors of the cloakroom. His bitter mouth moved uncertainly in its shadowy place like a hungry animal which fear chains to its lair. But his feverish eyes pleased him. He looked at their points of light as sharp as needles.

Then, in the mirror, he caught Rose's glance violet with unlived dreams. "Let's have another drink to cheer us up," he said. He rapped on the table with the back of his hand so as to make his signet ring resound. At this gesture his sharp looks took on an aristocratic severity which put him in another light.

As they drank, the bar began to fill and several people came over to greet him. The men shook hands, but the girls kissed him, their hair falling across his face. Rose was silent and perhaps these wild-haired young girls made her shy. They seemed to live more like boys than like girls, drifting into the bar alone and, if they saw no acquaintance free, drifting out again. Although carelessly, even offensively dressed in greasy pants and shirts they had a certain charm. Some of them were beautiful. The ungrateful age—that is, mid-teens—had skipped them. It was as though debauchery had said, "Pass on. I am here already." And because they were so young, debauchery had made them beautiful, had rounded and softened their cheeks and their breasts which would have been hard as apples, had made their eyes heavy so that a glance full of premature knowledge was imprisoned in their lids. And in their walk there was the displacement, the loosened muscles of women long accustomed to men.

Simon, examining his companion, wondered what she had been like at that age; a prim child doubtless, who looked at the world without seeing it and whose dolls were still neatly arranged around the bed. A pang went through him, rising from some unused space inside his breast. What was there about Rose, he wondered, that could give him this pang? It made him resent her and he could not quite decide if he had felt it before.

"What do all those girls do?" she asked him.

Simon shrugged. "They come here, as you see. If they are lucky someone buys them a drink. If they are luckier still, someone with a bathtub asks them home to bed." And he added, looking at Rose, "The sex doesn't matter." He was hoping almost fiercely that Rose would show some disgust or astonishment, but the straight, ivory mask of her face did not change nor her jewel eyes. She only blinked her lashes as people do to show polite attention when they have no comment to make. These lashes were so thick and black that in profile they had a life of their own. They were rather like overturned insects with black, shiny, innocent legs.

"Where are their families?" she asked after a moment.

"Oh, in the provinces or in some other country; and by the way, they will all tell you that they are actresses or singers or models. Sometimes it's true and sometimes one of them blossoms into celebrity and leaves this quarter altogether." To satisfy her curiosity he called one of them over. "Heidi, come here," he commanded.

The girl was sitting at the bar, her legs mingled with those of the bar stool. She turned around, glanced at Simon and obeyed. Blond, with raggedly cut bangs over painted eyes and a pale little mouth, her small, exhausted face had barely emerged from childhood. No one had bothered to straighten her teeth. She slumped down beside Simon and held out a grimy hand to Rose.

"Sit up straight my girl and behave," said Simon. "Madame Flamand is hardly impressed by bohemianism." She made a face at him but did as he ordered. Her glance at Rose was brief and dispassionate. Such a woman was too respectable to bother about.

At this moment a little boy appeared in the open doorway of the bar. Standing alone with the night black behind him, he had a self-sufficient air. He might have been nine or ten years old and was dressed in shorts and a clean white shirt. His appearance, denoting a good mother at home, was made charming by his own fantasy; he had forked a bunch of cherries over each ear and their scarlet darkness made his eyes shine. He held three wooden bottles in his hand and now, smiling pleasantly, he advanced into the bar and started to juggle. The waiter tried to stop him.

"Hey, young man, you know that sort of thing's not allowed."

The child made no reply, but without stopping his act looked up smiling into the waiter's face. Afterward he passed a plate around. Simon gave him twenty francs. He heard Rose ask in a low, eager voice:

"Will you take me to a *bal musette?*

"Whatever for?" he demanded, genuinely surprised.

"I've never been to a popular ballroom," she said.

"But they're only tiresome," protested Simon, feeling as he spoke that Rose had put her hand on his arm. The hand made its own plea and Simon had to force his muscles not to tense. Just the same a pulse beat in his cheek.

"There's a good one in Montmartre," she continued. "At least a friend of mine said there was." Simon, who was staring at her, saw that the mention of this friend had made her blush, but she went on hastily, "It's called the O.K."

"Really? The O.K. How New World and up to date!" he said sarcastically. "I didn't realize, Rose, that you had pretensions of being one of the people. It's the most revolting snobbism." Rose was silent at this, merely taking her hand off his sleeve. "Well if we must—" he said. "Come along, Heidi—and why don't you change that sickening name—free drinks elsewhere."

When they stepped out of the taxi at the Place Pigalle they found it ablaze with lights. It might have belonged to a different city altogether than Saint-Germain des Prés. Both were centers of activity and both teemed with life. The crowd sought pleasure in each, sought entertainment, drink, women, drugs and perversion. Perhaps the difference was simply that where Saint-Germain was amateur, Pigalle was professional. If Heidi would go to bed for a drink, her sister in Pigalle had her price in cash, had her beat and her protector.

Simon and his two charges stood for a few moments bewildered and disoriented. The journey had drained them of spirit and what they had come to do seemed worse than futile. Heidi's small mouth drooped. She had not had enough to drink and now wished herself back in her own quarter. People looked at her tight jeans and laughed, remarking *"Zazoo! Art bum!"* and shrugging contemptuous shoulders. And they did look absurd here, emphasizing the pear-shaped bottom from which her thighs turned rapidly into a child's thin shanks.

They found the *bal* with the aid of a policeman and climbed toward it in the twisting stairs and streets of the hill. The door of it was open to the warm air and in front of them a group of girls flocked in together like stocky little birds. These were not the professional beauties of the Place Pigalle below, but servants and workmen's daughters who were set to enjoy a night out. Their faces were lit with enthusiasm. An innocent gaiety rendered them almost pretty despite their ugly clothes, their short, red, bare legs and clumsy shoes. But it struck the eye that the men were better looking than their partners on the whole, clearer featured and more finely made. Perhaps an absence of badly permanented curls helped, or perhaps it was only the physical drudgery which thickens women's limbs but leaves a man's slim loins intact.

They were shown to a table, however, by a man whose hips were enormous and who had the disturbing aura of one with a secret deformity.

"It's going to be horrible," said Simon, who now wished he had not given in to Rose's whim. He noticed, however, that everybody was laughing at Heidi, and the quality of their laughter, filled with obscure jealousy and coarse intentions, put him back into humor. He watched Rose who was looking down at the table as though she were afraid to meet the eyes, curious or admiring, that were examining her. A musette waltz was making the dancers spin on the crowded floor. The uneasy motifs of the accordion were threading the music through, like a brook running over a troubled bed or like the voices of those animals who sound almost like men. Plaintive and hurried, it was the expression of the dancers themselves; their brief youth, the smallness of their desires and their taut nerves forever on the stretch.

A youth in a checked shirt came up and bent over Rose. At the same time he threw out a perfunctory, "May I?" at Simon. But before the latter could consent or refuse he saw Rose get up and move off in the stiff embrace of her partner. He watched ironically as they circled the room and saw them pause beneath the bandstand where the accordionist sat. Rose, with a gesture startling in its suddenness and grace, looked up at the player. Simon noticed the arch of her back, the swan curve of her throat from which the hair had fallen free. Then, above the music, her laugh rang out clear and fresh. Its mocking undertone made that curved throat palpitate. It transformed her entirely from the woman Simon knew.

"Your friend has met a friend," said Heidi.

"Shut your mouth or I'll throw this glass in your face." Simon had a nasty expression in his eyes. His jaws felt knotted in his cheeks. He was furious with himself, with Heidi, with Rose and with Jason, whom he had recognized.

CHAPTER 12

——————— *Journal:* ———————

You know how I said there was a thread, or that I thought there was a thread, for me to follow in all this? I only hoped for it then. It's come out since, hasn't it?

Now I'm going to tell about my evening with Simon because so many things happened that night which fitted, which spun out the thread. To begin with, I didn't much want to go out with Simon. Pierre goes away on short trips fairly often and I'm not a bit lonely or afraid here by myself. But that time Mark was in town and he upsets me. We upset each other really because of Mother—the way she died. It seems so shameful—like a vice in *us* almost, although I don't know if you'll understand that. I get dizzy when I even *think* of torture, but she had to feel it and to live it and in the end it was all her life.

Well, as I was saying, she is always between Mark and myself and although at first it's wonderful to see him, after a bit a shadow grows in his eyes and he casts it into mine. So I was glad to go out with Simon and I guess Mark was just as glad to go home to bed.

I swear I never thought of the O.K. ballroom before the juggler came into the bar. In fact I was planning to go home myself soon, especially as a young girl had joined us and I'm not very good with strangers. She made me feel funny, the young girl, I mean. She was so much younger than me and yet so much more *used* and there didn't seem to be any meeting ground because being used was life to her and she neither knew nor cared about anything else. To her there *was* nothing else so that I didn't even exist in her eyes. I could tell by the way she looked at me, just once briefly, and then wearily away.

How refreshing it was to see that child in the doorway! There I sat with those two exhausted creatures and then he appeared with his cherry earrings and his clean shirt. He smiled directly into my eyes and it was as though he said, "I'm glad you're here." His smile at the bartender who tried to stop him was something else; polite and tough and devil-may-care and all the time he was juggling away, never missing a catch. Everybody gave him money and I had some ready in my hand. But he didn't pass the plate to me. He just smiled with his twinkling, manly eyes and I smiled back at him. Then I asked Simon to take me to Montmartre.

I suppose you want to know why. Do you? Well, I don't k*now* why. It was something to do with the child coming in but I can explain no further. Perhaps you can figure it out for yourself. Would you tell me if you did? Me, Rose. Rose with the blackening leaves, Rose blasted beneath a black sun, rooted in the waterless sand?

* * * * *

HERE, as though to belie the words she write, a drop fell on the page. Rose looked at it astonished. Was it a tear? A drop of sweat from her bent brow? She did not know. Yet surely its source was somewhere in her head behind her heavy and her constant frown. Bright, winking, it lay upon the glazed surface of the paper. One would not expect such clarity. With her hand she smeared it across her last words. She looked up to listen. It was dark outside and Rose was alone in the flat. The room was brightly lit and she was expecting guests for dinner. Simon, perhaps for the last time, was to be among them. Rose, recalling this fact, started writing again.

Journal:

I'll tell you a disturbing thing that Pierre doesn't know: Simon has asked me if he might dedicate his present book to me. Why? The idea frightens me, like the feeling one gets when a policeman looks at one. I asked him the title and he said it was to be called *La Vie en Rose.* How absurd! Is it a joke? And if so what's the point? I almost know but not quite. In any case I have started reading his other books (relegated now to the top shelf in Pierre's study) and I don't care for them. They are like his eyes and his jaws and we women certainly don't get much of a chance. But he told me this was to be different.

"*You* are making it, not me," he said.

Simon wasn't very happy about going up to Montmartre that night. He considered it a bore and personally I agree. One has to have a reason for doing things like that and then they become the most exciting places in the world. Any place, I mean; even a street corner, or a bare little cafe without any atmosphere—I know what I'm talking about!

Anyway so far I didn't have a reason. I knew that our neighbor Jason played his accordion up at the O.K., that was all. I thought it would be interesting to go and see what kind of a place it would be. I regretted asking to go the minute I'd done so although I was relieved when he invited the girl, Heidi, to come along too.

In the taxi, as we were crossing the Seine, I thought of Pierre. "That good Pierre," Simon called him apropos of some remark

I made. Simon, whom I thought so far beneath my husband. It made me angry to have him spoken of like some shaggy dog who lifts his head for a pat. And then a habit of Pierre's came into my mind; that when he was—is—very tired, he winds a cowlick on the crown of his head, winds and rewinds it around his finger and at the same time purses up his mouth. It's an infantile remainder, I suppose. But when men like Pierre have such habits, normal, everyday type of men, it makes them touching. One fears for them despite their solidity, as if they had exposed something of themselves to peril; laid visible, perhaps, the secret and childish goodness of their hearts.

Yes, I recall thinking such thoughts of Pierre that night as the taxi rolled over the bridge, and something hurt me inside like the first twinges of an illness.

I spoke quite vehemently. "Pierre's book will be finished soon," I said.

"Oh books!" cried Simon, moving his head on the back of the seat. "If you only knew how I despised them."

"Except your own I suppose," I said (and it wasn't worthy of me). To my surprise he put his hand over mine. I could feel those rigid fingers, icy cold.

"I am diseased, my dear," he said. "I spit my germs up on the page."

Heidi said "Oo-la-la," in world-weary, sarcastic tones and after that they left me alone and bickered together.

Later we were walking around the Place Pigalle in silence. Men ran after us and touted erotic exhibitions of various sorts. One of these men was very insistent. He took me by the arm—really—almost as though he wanted to drag me into his den. I was startled and looked up into his face. Gold teeth flashed in its swarthy oval and I could almost imagine myself lured by him, by the perfidy of his smile and the stale ugliness of his wares. Or perhaps by something else entirely, by the idea of other lives which he was offering and which might after all turn out to be one's own.

Then Simon tapped him on the shoulder with the back of his hand. "Go easy my friend," he said. I must admit Simon did and said this very well.

There was another flash of gold and, above, a reptile's glance examined Simon. He dropped behind us with a bow.

Now this is the second thing that happened in the evening. I know so I'm telling you. That's why I think it's helping me to write this. At the beginning I don't think I'd have known and of course I still don't know why and maybe I never will. But in the end, after I've told you everything, then, after you have listened—and even judged, who knows?—then at last you might render me the answer.

Anyway we got to the *bal,* which was crowded with small-looking dancers taking small steps. A strange creature showed us a table and served us drinks. He put one off until one understood that he was a giant midget. He was that same shape and his face, full of wrinkles, had absolutely no trace of a beard. But it had its interest; each of its many seams was dredged with sweat. They glistened like those threads of water which shine on the steeps of rocky mountains. I've seen them in Switzerland. Was this man the third thing that happened this evening? I hope not. In any case once I had placed him as a midget I felt better about him. He could have been terrifying otherwise. Why is it so comforting to place people, to classify them and, snipping off an edge or two if necessary, put them away in files? I despise that habit really.

My eyes are very farsighted and keen. They say blue eyes often are. So the minute I came in I saw not only Jason on the bandstand, but La Cigale at a table in the corner across the way. I wished I were a thousand miles off. I looked at Heidi who was facing me. She resembled a vicious schoolboy, an English one, with her blond hair brushed forward as though the curls had recently been cut off, and her soft little mouth so used by lies.

Our drinks came—*fine à l'eau*—and I gulped some of mine. The brandy was terrible but it must have had an effect because when a man came and asked me to dance I accepted. I guess you know it's done at such places, but I don't think I would have consented unless—well I'll be honest, I have to be: I was pleased that I had been asked first rather than Heidi. Pleased because I knew Simon and other people in the room would note it.

That's base, but I can't bother about it. I must go and dress and comb my hair and look like Pierre's well-behaved (if unfashionable) wife. It's a pity I feel so sleepy. I feel like yawning and yawning and stretching the aching muscles of my head. Only the yawn never gets far enough. It always stops at my ears.

CHAPTER 13

―――――――――― *Journal:* ――――――――――

We had guests last night as you know and Simon's successor was there as well as Simon. The successor is younger than I thought despite the beard; a sulky, pouty little man. One can easily picture him having tantrums. But I don't recall much about the evening except that I laughed. Someone asked me if I ever tried composition and Simon said in a loud, spiteful voice, "No, only transpositions for the accordion."

That's why I laughed, only all at once it wasn't laughing any more. I thought Pierre noticed something from across the room where he was sitting with his editor's wife. He tensed. He was like those people who, sleepless, listen to the slow voice of a tower clock striking the hour. They have heard one chime and await another with uncertainty. They fear perhaps that the insomniac beating of their hearts will break the sound in their ears.

And while I remember I must write down how it *hurt* me to laugh last night—not at first but later—and other people felt it too as I could tell by their expressions.

Once when I was quite young father drove me to the vet's with a sick puppy. It was in the country and the vet lived in a shabby-looking house whose yard was filled with chickens and cats. As we were driving away again I suddenly saw a kitten playing in the dust of the yard—playing, playing so hard, twisting and leaping and rolling over. I laughed with pleasure at the sight. It was such a sweet little thing twirling around in the sunshine. Then, all of a sudden, it wasn't sweet any more. It wasn't a kitten playing, but an animal in its death throes. Mark had hit it, you see, while backing up the car. I had thought it was having fun when it was writhing on the dusty ground.

That's the end of that story and I think you'll know how to take it.

But then in those days, and until last night, it didn't hurt me to laugh at all and I loved doing it and I insist on that because the way people react is important.

Afterward, when the evening was over, Simon didn't even say good night to me. It's funny how he once used to look down on me for being a good, quiet, ordinary wife. He scorned me to the point of rudeness. But he's not at all pleased now. He suffers, in fact. But why? What is it to him? And how furious he was that night in the O.K. ballroom when I saw Jason on the bandstand. I laughed that night too and Jason grinned back. He showed his teeth, pointed and foxy as his eyes. They looked as though they might wound the pulp of his lip. He sprang to his feet, still playing, and beckoned to a man standing nearby.

"Replace me for a moment, Jacquot," he said. "I must dance with this *bel enfant*."

Well, I can't help it; the phrase, "handsome child," didn't displease me. Do you think that's vulgar? But I must be honest, mustn't I? So I'll tell you the truth. No, it didn't displease me; more, it warmed me. It felt like when I used to be given a lump of sugar with camphor on it after being out in the snow.

But dancing with Jason for the first time wasn't really any fun. Musette seems stilted to me. One is whirled around in a rigid embrace. There is no lilt in a musette waltz, no leaning back and swaying from the waist; only tiny steps and stiff whirlings. The pull of the turns is counterbalanced by even closer contact. I didn't do it right at first and Jason was quite rude about it.

"You're not dancing a solo," he remarked. "You're dancing with me."

"I'm sorry," I apologized. "I'm not used to this type of waltz, and it confines me."

"Oh, so Mademoiselle would like to let herself go," he said in a way that was meant to be witty and quelling. It depressed me and robbed me of all the pleasure I had felt before. I wondered why I had thus left myself open to affront, why I had come and what I had expected. Yet even as I asked myself, we were turning faster, his knee was locked with the inside of my knee so that our two legs were a pivot. They were merged into one limb.

After the dance Jason took me back to my table and when we skirted the floor I couldn't help feeling that La Cigale's eyes were on me. Although I just hated her being there, or perhaps just because of that, I had to go up to her table and bid her good evening.

She gave me her hand, a surprising touch. Her flesh is hard you know, and yet it seems completely loosened from the bones inside, in fact to have nothing to do with them. Her other hand was clamped around a glass and there were rings on her fingers. Like her spectacles, the settings were empty. No doubt she had long ago sold the jewels belonging to them. Her face was heavily made up as usual and it looked dark and powerful. A brown turban covered her hair save for the artificial fringe which lay dustily on her forehead. Her eyes escaped mine to send their lost glances into the throng. Then she signaled imperiously to the waiter. He was looking our way so I know he saw her gesture, but he turned his back. He was wearing a sweater instead of a jacket and his back with its enormous hips and narrow shoulders was thus revealed. It was expressive. It had an expression of anger and intense concentration. La Cigale seemed undisturbed by this attention. No that's not right; she was *glad* of it. There was a faint change in her mouth which straightened the lines of her nostrils. Perhaps having long ago renounced true masculine admiration, she was making this do, as mutilated soldiers must with artificial limbs. It served her and her heart was brave enough to use it.

"She comes every night," said Jason after we had left her. "Every night she comes—no doubt to put me off my beat."

I was angry. "And where else is she supposed to go?" I demanded. "Where will you go, Jason, when you are old and poor?"

"That's the first time you've used my Christian name," he said and I could see he thought my question silly. *He* was never going to be poor, let alone old. Other people perhaps, that was their affair, but not he, Jason, for whom so many girls sighed.

"Well, I know no other name for you," I said. But I did, from his mailbox downstairs, and it was Perin. He grinned.

"I'm not complaining, *ma petite Rose,*" he said and we were right in front of my table. Then before he left me he gave me a sort of friendly slap on the rump.

"So Madame gets cheap thrills when her husband is away," said Simon, his whole face twitching.

I didn't answer and for some reason I looked up carefully at the waiter who was collecting his money from our table. His beardless wrinkles contrasted with his fixed expression. Something frustrate to the point of perversion made his mouth bend cruelly. I thought it must be filled with angry spit.

As we left, the music started up again and the accordion seemed to sear my heart, to stroke it with heavy, hot strokes. The sound of it was like one of those repulsive human caresses, given furtively by furtive men to make young girls cry.

CHAPTER 14

Sometimes, when La Cigale awoke in the morning, she thought she must be dead already. She felt no blood flowing in her body, no juices from organ or gland, and her face was a wooden mask pressed to her skull and fitting ill. Even her waking sighs came out of her lungs like tissue paper. And it was summer, early summer, barely June. A time when the body must relax in the heat and drink in warmth against the future winter.

The sun lit La Cigale's room early and penetrated even the two layers of burlap over the top glass of her door. She never opened this door at night and there was a rank stench in the room; a smell of stale make-up, old, little-washed flesh and incipient disease. The room, smallest of the three attic partitions, was so cramped as to be almost a closet and it contained nothing but a bed, some boxes and a folding chair. On the wall, stained with damp, hooks held her clothing. These garments were of varied shades but the effect of them together was a dull brown. They were like those strips of clay that children get as gifts; in the box they are multicolored, yet when mixed—and just when one had decided to create a rainbow—the whole is miraculously transformed into dung.

Aside from the clothing there was a small mirror of irregular shape, the broken piece of a larger glass and found no doubt in a heap of rubbish. There was also a calendar from many years past, showing a fat girl stepping into a stream and looking over her shoulder with unbearable coyness. One would swear she was inviting a kick.

On all these things and on La Cigale as she slept, the sun poured in through the burlap. But after a little while it receded to the balcony outside and then, slowly, the old woman awoke. It took her a long time to gather her forces and with each morning doubt came into her heart; a feeling of futility and despair. Then, always and suddenly, a long groan broke from her throat. She was awake. She lived.

After that she got up and went about the lengthy process of her toilet. There was no water up on the top floor and La Cigale had to bring it up in a jug from the yard fountain. Thus she was as sparing of it as possible and actually, when she had dipped her old fingers into the basin and dried them on a rag, she was through for ordinary days. On Sunday she washed more thoroughly, but never, on holy or ordinary day, did she touch water to her face. Everybody knew that water increased wrinkles, and as for soap! But in any case she seldom could afford soap. So, having no cold cream, no soft paper or cotton with which luckier women remove their fard, she left her skin to fight as it could beneath its load of paint and grime.

On this morning in early June it was very warm; the first real heat wave of summer. The day had sprung on Paris without warning, up from the Seine whose sultry mists obscured the air. A red sun had climbed haltingly and as though with gaping wounds to pant over the rooftops. Its hot breath had seared La Cigale's room. At length she gave her waking groan and sat up. Sleep or bitter dreams had pulled her mouth awry and her eyes, between their penciled lids, were glossed with rheum. Yet beneath, inside, her undominated heart still beat; stern, forceful and eager for life.

Dressed at last, her false switch coiled above her brows and her own sparse hair concealed in its turban, she opened the door and went out onto the balcony. Bernice was hanging sheets over the upper railing to dry and to bleach.

"Good morning, La Cigale," she said cheerfully, wiping her bare arm over her face. As she spoke the sound of Jason's accordion broke from the end room; small, shrunken noises like yawns and then, softly and still uneven, a tango. The notes crawled out into the hot morning like serpents, shining and impure, who come to warm their blood on sunlit stones.

Below them Rose appeared on the terrace and glanced up languidly at the sky. Pierre, who left for work around ten, had just gone by way of the front door. The two women looked down on Rose, on her sallow skin, on her cheekbones which gleamed with sweat, and on the blue-black sheen of her hair. There was something touching in the sight of this young woman extenuated by the heat and by the secret roil of her own blood. She was wearing her husband's dressing gown and had folded back the sleeves. Thus her frail wrists were left bare as were the slender joints where neck and shoulder met. Only her calves and ankles appeared vigorous, protruding from the skirts of the gown and turning finely on their arched muscles. They were like the powerful roots of a delicate flower. In turn she looked up at the two women and lifted her hand slightly in greeting. Then without moving her head she turned her eyes to the end room where the tango, now fuller in volume, cleft the hot morning. She dropped her head.

"Poor Madame Flamand," said Bernice, "she's a pianist, a real musician. It's hard for her to hear that type of thing every time she pokes her nose outdoors."

"I've seen her when it wasn't so hard," said La Cigale.

Bernice gave the old woman a startled blue look. La Cigale was growing so eccentric that it made communication difficult. "Oh, Madame Rose is very polite, even to a silly boy like that," she said.

A short laugh came up out of La Cigale's belly, rather more like a belch than a laugh. Without knowing why, the servant looked embarrassed and awkward. She put her fists on her hips and moved them up and down there until she found the bones on which they could rest.

"As an ex-singer, Madame La Cigale, you should understand," she said reproachfully, but her only answer was the rigidity of the old woman's jaw, her half-open mouth through which the teeth real and false could be seen locked together. Giving a last, straightening twitch to the sheets, Bernice hurried off down the stairs and into the Flamand apartment.

La Cigale, equipped with a basket and an empty bottle, now went out to do her marketing, choosing those stalls that sold yesterday's produce at a cheaper rate. She bought three peaches whose rotten spots could be cut out, a small piece of horse meat and some wilted lettuce. Just in front of her house she had her wine bottle refilled from the cheapest barrel.

Once home, and having washed the lettuce in the faucet, she took some potatoes out from under the bed and prepared her one meal of the day on an alcohol burner. She drank deeply of the cheap wine whose acidity roughened the inside of her mouth. The room was a furnace, but she did not sweat. And perhaps the outer heat was as nothing to the fire of curiosity and dread that burned inside of her. La Cigale was waiting. She had come to live for it lately: this silent secret waiting for something her instinct told her would come to pass.

She sat in her room now on the bed with the door open just the least crack. She had finished her meal and her scrapbook was spread on her knees. From its page a robust young woman in tights and a top hat smiled up at her. The solid thighs sprang directly from a corseted waist and the bosom rolled up gloriously toward husky shoulders. The face, solid and fleshy like the figure, shone with impudence, confidence and good will. Many curls completed it on top. Taken as a whole the photograph was an example of music-hall beauty in the nineteen hundreds. She had been sixteen at the time when it was made.

The afternoon wore on. Jason went out for an hour or so and then returned. Bernice came up to her room beside La Cigale's and changed her dress. She was going out no doubt, as she usually did every afternoon, to market or to do errands, certainly to flirt with the widowed hardware-store man who wanted to marry her. The piano had been sounding from the Flamands' but the young woman down there must have been put off by the heat for after a bare hour there came the crash of petulant discord and then silence. Bernice went out humming, her basket jaunty on her arm, her face a rich cyclamen. La Cigale could not see her but she imagined her well enough; cotton sweater, flowered cotton skirt and that cyclamen face beneath the pink straw hair. Bernice was neither pretty nor young, yet her girlish exuberance was so definite that it obscured all other facts about her.

La Cigale heard the steps going down the stairs and, as they receded, she felt something approaching faintness. It might have been the heat or the red wine or her own pulse hammering in the pit of her stomach. She counted its beat and now that beat was keeping time to another sound outside her body. She tensed. Her hands clasped each other above the smiling girl in tights. Then, through the crack in the door, she saw a figure pass. The polished black hair caught the light and gave out a dense, sapphire flash. There was a fluttering of summer skirts. Then Rose was gone from La Cigale's line of vision.

From that moment La Cigale changed her attitude. She tried to breathe as softly as possible and her face had the strained look of one who is listening intensely. Never fear, not a sound escaped her; not the light tap on the door next to hers, nor the answering murmur scarcely audible from within. Nor those other sounds so well known to her, far away yet never dim; brutal and tender, terminating in sighs.

La Cigale's own breath was wrung in her body. She opened her dark mouth to gasp softly and the tears she could no longer shed cut into the passages of her eyes like crystal stones.

Later, long after silence had once more descended, after the figure had once again passed her door, after Bernice had returned and Jason gone out for the evening, she herself rose. A heavy old woman, bulky yet juiceless, she went down into the street.

"I feel weak in this dirty weather," she muttered aloud. La Cigale always spoke aloud when in the street. Perhaps other people talking

together made her do this. "I need a small drink," she concluded and
looked hopefully into the depths of her shabby purse. It was empty of
all but a few francs, not even enough for a glass of wine. She grimaced.
"They can keep their foul money," she said, but what she meant was that
she would have to raise some.

And La Cigale could make money. It was her secret and her shame
and she did it almost every evening. Thus tonight too she started on her
trip across Paris. She took the Metro and, coming up in a distant quarter,
walked to the nearest café. In this season many people sat outside and La
Cigale sang to them. She sang the songs of her youth and others that she
had learned since, and although her voice had left all but a vestige of its
volume behind, it was still surprisingly true: a small soprano like that of
a bird lost at dusk.

On this night La Cigale was preceded in her act by a man playing a
violin. He must have got hold of the instrument by mistake and it was
with the greatest difficulty that one could recognize what tune he had in
mind. La Cigale was outraged.

"Why don't they simply beg like honest men?" she demanded loudly.
"Why insult people like that?" And she was furious at the few grudging
francs given him.

Waiting a few moments to let his impression fade away, La Cigale then
stood square in front of the tables and sang one of the roguish numbers
that had once made her famous. Her dark and angry face combined
unpleasantly with the words and her listeners were unconsciously embarrassed and talked louder than ever. Next she sang a more modern song.
"Long, long after the poets have disappeared," she sang, "their songs will
wander abroad in the streets." But this too, coming from an old woman
soon to disappear herself, made the clients uneasy. They paused in their
talking and laughing to peer anxiously, first at her and then out onto the
wide street from whence approached the inevitable night.

To a habitual performer it was impossible not to see the effect she
was having, so La Cigale pulled herself up. In her third song she turned

herself into a clown. This song was about a lame man and she too walked up and down limping comically as she sang. Her face with its angry expression fitted the cruel humor of the ballad. Her wide mouth mimicked that horrified and permanent yaw of the mutilated and the disgraced. Ah, here was something anyone could enjoy! The people at the tables relaxed and began to smile. And why should they not when God had given the example, when, out of a handsome, lusty young woman, He had fashioned (presumably for his own amusement) this dirty and evil-smelling hag?

Afterwards La Cigale passed the plate.

CHAPTER 15

Journal:

I suppose you know what's coming now and that I went up one afternoon to Jason's room. Oh, the clue passes by there all right! I've tried to give the important things leading up to that afternoon, but there's always a gap. How could I, Rose, despite the bugler, the gypsies, La Cigale, despite even the little boy who juggled in the bar—how could I have done such a thing? And it's much worse, you know, because I didn't go up there like those worldly-type women (only I've never known any) who coolly and wantonly seek adventure. No, I was *driven* up there and once in his room—when I saw him stretched half-naked on the bed, when I saw his breast gleam … He sat up when I came in and put out his hand to me in the most natural way, as though he had been expecting me and I was on time.

Well, when I saw all that a dark web crossed my eyes. Would "caul" be the right word? It comes to mind. I could hardly move a step forward before falling on my knees. Yes, there it is, I threw myself at his feet. It was as though I had carried a heavy burden for a long time and had cast it down at last. I don't remember how he drew me up beside him on the bed, but he must have.

What did I feel like before I went up to his room and did I know in the morning what I would do in the afternoon? I recall going out on the terrace and hearing his accordion. How hot it was! And the notes stifled me. Then those two women looking down on me from above! I suffered because everything, the red sun, the music, those two suspended faces, was waiting for me to act. And I think, I really think, that in that instant I was lost.

I've heard it's always so; that there is a deciding moment, an instant when one can still go back on one's steps, can still look with confidence, not on the future, or even the present, but on the past. The past that changes with the recollecting heart, grows sweet or harsh, or else, as I, Rose, know, fills up with such regret. Heavens how it hurts! One can't bear it. It becomes taboo. A thrilling and a shameful night envelops it.

The morning I'm writing about was the last in which I could awake calmly, could look around my room and note the trophies of my life; of the serious and happy child, the intent young girl, the tranquil wife. What did I think on that last morning? I remember the shower water was lukewarm when I wanted it cold and Bernice's coffee wasn't very good. It never is. What foolish things, yet they hurt me now, trivial as they were. They are fast receding into the night of which I spoke. There is one more: as Pierre was leaving I put my arms around him and he brushed me off impatiently. It was too hot or he wanted to get to work, was already thinking of *Jouvence*. It's like when, without realizing it, one bids a last farewell. Everyone in the world I guess has known or will know that. One thinks to see the person soon again, in an hour, a week, a month; and yet that ignorant and trivial word must last forever.

* * * * *

ROSE threw down her pen and got up hastily. Her throat was constricted so that she had to swallow painfully. Her feet were cold. It was getting dark already and she had an appointment. She put on her coat and went into the kitchen.

"Bernice, I'm going out for a walk. I'll be back in time for supper."

Bernice put her hands on her hips and opened her mouth as though to say something important. "Will you bring home the bread?" she asked.

Before Rose left the flat she combed her hair in front of the bedroom mirror. Something in her appearance struck her but she could not decide what it was. Perhaps the flush across her cheeks which mounted onto her temples and which gave to her eyes a feverish and theatrical cast. It was not ugly and in fact suited the strong, slightly tragic stamp of her face. Leaning close she stared at her own forehead. It was as though she were trying to read the lines there as one reads a palm. For destiny was surely set upon that frown, the shadowed cleft which smote between her brows. She fancied the skin alone was hiding some mysterious opening in the rock of her skull. Within the cavern yawned perhaps the labyrinth of which she spoke.

Drawing away with a grimace, Rose went out of the flat and started to descend the dusty stair. Light fell eerily into the well of it and she was afraid of falling. Behind her, from the very top landing, she heard steps coming down. It was a man, for he was whistling and she recognized the tune. Had she not heard it often enough on his accordion?

Rose's body became rigid and she tried to hasten her own steps. Despite the damp chill of the building her face burned and she felt her legs tremble. He would be later than she at the rendezvous. He often was. But he would come. He too was on his way.

How dark the street was! How swiftly the long night descended! He could not see her now, she decided, hurrying in front of him with her nervous heels. She put up her collar and for an instant icy fingers touched her cheek. Are they *my* fingers? she wondered. And are they really that cold? Were they not rather fingers of flame? She rounded a corner and soon went into a small bar which advertised wine and coal. The warm interior was smoky and there were only two tables. Several coal vendors were standing at the bar drinking wine. Their mouths and eyelids were red and moist in their smeared faces. They greeted Rose politely and in the manner of acquaintances. They were used to her.

Jason should be here by now, she thought, recalling the step behind her on the stair. Then the idea struck her that he had not been coming to meet her at all, but had been bound for a completely different place. At this notion the blood surged up into her head. It stung her veins. An agitation took hold of her which only women in the grip of physical passion know at its flood. She did not care if the men saw it and her lips quivered. But at that moment, still whistling, Jason entered. Immediately Rose's uncertainty turned to anger. As he came over and with a casual caress sat down, she pushed his hand away roughly.

"I suppose you think I'll wait all night for you," she cried furiously. "Well, I was about to go. In fact I'm going!" She got up, overturning her chair.

The childishness of her outbreak made him laugh, showing his pointed teeth. "Sit down and behave," he said.

"I'm going!" she repeated defiantly and desperately. "I'm going."

"If you were mine," he remarked, "I'd teach you a lesson."

Then Rose did sit down again slowly and with dark eyes half closed. "If I were yours," she repeated vaguely and her lips stirred as though on the point of saying something further, asking, perhaps, identification from this stranger beside her.

But he gave her no help. "Will you drink something?" he offered.

She nodded. "A red wine." They drank quickly. Rose had grown very quiet. She was trying to control the turmoil inside her body which was like a bucking and half-broken horse. She shuddered as the cheap wine filled her throat.

"Let's go," he said. They rose and with a nod to the *patron* behind the bar, Jason held open the back door which led into a coal-and-wood-filled alley. Here they entered the side door of a small hotel. The peculiar smell of it, of damp, of latrines and Javelle water and furtive cooking and more furtive love, washed over this amorous pair.

CHAPTER 16

—————————— *Journal:* ——————————

As I was crossing the Pont Neuf today I saw a newspaper blowing across the street. It moved a little, fluttered, quivered, paused and slid on again a few feet. It arrested me. I got the feeling it lived— it *knew*. I tried not to go quicker as I didn't want to seem to be escaping. But I couldn't help jumping when that malignant thing fetched up against my feet. I felt it on my instep and my ankle, dry, living, *néfaste*. It wanted me to look at it and at first I wouldn't. I just walked on, but it clung to me. I couldn't kick it loose and had to drag it along haltingly step by step. So I looked.

That's all. I couldn't really have seen what I thought I did. And newspaper photographs are notoriously bad. You know they are. Besides, it was dirty. No, I just saw a photo of someone who, at a distance, resembled me and in my imagination I read my own name in the caption. It's like when in a film a movie actress puts on perfume. You smell it before you realize it's only on the screen. Anyway that's how it must have been when I looked down and fancied I saw a photograph of me, a sensational-type photograph.

I'm not ever in the papers. They aren't interested in me.

I haven't written for several days. I've been waiting. The bugler seems like a signpost now with the road splitting into two as it hits him and those two roads spinning away farther and farther from each other into the distance. I like to think of him. I get a feeling of peace. Possibly I thought I'd never get as far as this, that before I reached this point all would have been resolved. But now I must go on.

After leaving Jason, that other, that first and summer afternoon, I went back to the flat. I lay down on the sofa and fell into sleep as if it were an abyss, struggling at first and then suddenly giving in. Falling head downward and dizzy. When I woke up I was drenched and my skin was cold. Then I tried to reflect on what had happened. I hoped perhaps (but I'm not sure) that it would turn into an incident such as many women experience. Why should it have been important after all? I was perfectly happy before—please believe me—in that long blood sleep from which I was aroused that day.

I was strangely concerned too with what Jason could have thought of me. Did girls in his experience always act like that? Kneel, shudder, groan and sigh? He was nonchalant enough, serenely awakening the sleeper from beneath her caul.

You see Pierre and the d— and I have a very modest relationship. We don't exactly hide from each other, but we turn our backs, close the washroom door and so forth. We turn the lights out too. I took Pierre's lead and it's always been that way. And the doll is modest too now, more than I ever was, furtive and sly. I hate that doll and sometimes I wish I could make an end of it. But then at other times its doll body slides into mine, its doll thoughts are mixed into my brain and we are one. That's what gives me these terrible headaches.

Anyway, as I say, I was much occupied as to what Jason thought and also as to whether or not he found me pretty; the whole of me, that is. I didn't ask him then or later, but I found out just the same, or rather I saw my rivals and I think that tells one as much as anything. I guess you know that I saw one just the other day, that freckled and consumptive girl with the sheets. And then there's the baker's daughter up the street, a fat girl in transparent layers of nylon, and I told you about the one I met him with in Montmartre. So judge for yourself. I had to.

No, there's not much hope along those lines of reflection, but then I may not be quite fair either. Jason might have other standards of which I am ignorant. All this might be nonsense from his point of view. Is he not the center, the pivot, a *man*? That's enough.

Oh you should see—or have you seen it?—the naked breast of Jason, the high ribs of Jason and his round limbs! And have you watched when he's asleep, how his eyes roll in the warm lids and how his mouth is pushed out by his breath?

It was several days before we met again after that afternoon and when we did it was in the hall.

"You're not very nice to me," he remarked with a grin.

"Why?" I asked. I was blushing for the stupid reason that I had not expected to meet him and did not remember how I was looking. But it was evening and the light was poor.

"You might have come again if only to thank me," he said.

"Thank you!" I exclaimed.

"I made you happy, didn't I?" he asked by way of answer.

And then I said "Yes." But of course "happy" wasn't the right word for it.

"Well then?" he insisted, and at that moment Pierre and Simon came in sight around the bend of the stair. I hadn't heard them and I don't know why but I think it was at that moment that the doll came. As though my shadow stood up beside me.

In any case I ran back up the stairs, trying as I ran to concentrate on all the facts of my path; the worn steps, the mildewed walls, anything to take my mind off the meeting I had had. When Pierre and Simon arrived at the apartment I was helping lay the table and for once Simon's sarcastic look did me good.

After that the sordid days came for me, the sordid and the thrilling hours. I never went up to Jason's room again though; only that one time. Guilty, I dared not return. I try however to recall exactly how it was, how the second door opened out onto the roof-top and from the bed one could see nothing there but the sky; a sky in whose blaze the pale moon wandered. And the bed was very large—or has grown so since—and besides this there was nothing in the room, or that's what I like to think; only the bed and the doorway and the moon-ridden sky.

How I'd love to go up there now and lie, just lie, quietly beside Jason on that big bed and look out at the moon, or perhaps I'd not look at the moon at all, but rest my head between his arms, rock myself to sleep against his lungs.

Sometimes I think it was being tired started the whole thing. I was exhausted with carrying that load inside me. When I cast it down at his feet I had to cast myself with it. Since the body goes with the desire.

* * * * *

ROSE, hugging her chest, went to the window. Looking up she saw the three rooms, and on the sunny balcony in front of them stood Simon leaning on the rail and facing down. She was not sure he could see her but, conscious or not, his eyes met hers in their tight depths and there was an expression on his thin mouth that might have been a smile. How like a dream things are getting, though Rose. Everything—the roof-top, the balcony and Simon leaning over it—seemed slightly out of focus. That is, they were clear enough, but in an unreal way as though floating in a finer, lighter ether.

Simon was wearing a dark, threadbare suit and his collar was open. He carried a folder in one hand and was once again the writer rather than a star journalist on *Jouvence*. He belonged up there on that top balcony in one of those tiny rooms with the cold winter coming on, each meal a struggle and a chalking up of debt. Yet his eyes, looking down at Rose, had an expression of reproach and of menace.

CHAPTER 17

Bernice was one of those people whom others envy for their happiness. If her face in repose was melancholy, nobody saw it in that state and if her underlying thoughts were touched with gloom, nobody was aware of them, she herself least of all. A mirror had been held up to her by the world and she had seen her image and believed in it. Born off the Brittany coast, the storms, the endless winds, the rain, had mixed a darkness in her blood, but it never showed and her visible heritage was the cheerful and weathered red of her cheeks. As a child, the youngest in the family, her life had seemed a constant round of errands: "Get the milk, run to the thread shop or to the grocer's or to fetch your father home." This last was the only errand she enjoyed. Then she would sidle shyly into the café and slip between the drinking men. The warm smoky air filled her with pleasure. She basked in it, especially in winter when, for the first time that day, the goose flesh would be smoothed on her chapped legs.

Bernice's father, with his flaming hair on end, would be holding forth to everybody—most of the time, that is. On a few occasions he would be staring belligerently at someone with raised fists, or even fighting. On even rarer evenings he was weeping, sitting at a table with the tears pouring down his face and his many friends gathered sympathetically around. Bernice did not care what mood he was in. He was always good to her in an offhand fashion and had hit her only once and that by mistake when he thought she was one of her brothers.

Sometimes he walked home all the way on his hands and then she was terribly proud and ashamed at the same time.

She was ashamed because the teachers at school pinched their lips whenever her father came in sight. He was oblivious of their disapproval however, and when he saw them he acted in a condescendingly gallant way as some men do to old maids.

Bernice was a dutiful pupil but the dull plod of learning did not suit her Celtic nature. She could only recall those things that stirred her and they were few in the school she went to. Later she stayed with a relative near Paris and had been in service ever since. She usually liked her employers and would not remain unless she did. She had numerous boyfriends although she was not in the least pretty and her weather-spoiled skin soon began to look old. But she was so gay and expressive that no one could resist her. They called her "Blondie" up and down the street. Bernice, however, did not really care for men except to laugh with and have a good time. She could do without the rest and only consented now and then so as to be a good sport.

She disliked Jason from the start and was horrified at what her mistress was doing. She knew because of La Cigale's hints but she would have known anyway. Rose had been her favorite of all her employers and Rose's calm relationship with her husband had pleased Bernice. She herself would have preferred something a little livelier but Rose was different. She wished they would have children.

She also knew around the first week in July that Rose was pregnant. After all they were constantly together. Bernice entered into many intimate details of Rose's life. And then right away there was a subtle change in Rose's appearance. No one but herself perhaps would notice it, certainly not Pierre who was working to get everything in order before he went on vacation. Bernice thought at once that it was Jason's fault and one day, shortly before Bastille Day on the fourteenth of July, she quarreled with him.

It was an afternoon when both the Flamands were out to lunch, a rare enough occasion. Bernice saw Jason sitting out on the stretch of roof beyond his room. He was sewing up a rip in the lining of his jacket and doing it (as he did all physical things) with grace and dexterity. Looking up he nodded to her and called out, "Hey, La Bernice, this is woman's work. You should come and give me a hand."

Bernice, usually so friendly, drew herself up and tightened the muscles around her mouth. She could not tighten the mouth itself because her lips were too thin by nature. They were like the indicative thread sewn across the face of a rag doll, a cheerful red thread as a rule, but they took on grimness now from the surrounding rigidity. "You permit yourself too many liberties," she said and her voice was trembling. Bernice was so seldom angry or haughty to anyone that she did not convince at all.

Jason burst out laughing. "And with better women than you, *n'est-ce pas?*" he asked sweetly.

"Don't you *dare* say things like that!" Bernice meant to shout but it was more of a squeak. Her breath was a ribbon in her tight throat.

"Like what, Bernice? Do you think yourself the best woman in the world then?" His pointed teeth showed against his lips.

"You know that's not what I mean," she retorted.

"What *do* you mean?" he demanded softly so that his words floated across the space between them.

"You know," she insisted, confused now and dismayed by her own indignation. She was ready to turn and flee, but before she could do so he gave a quick jerk of his head downward at the Flamand windows.

"Oh, you mean that!" he said. The suggestive vulgarity of his voice and movement sent the blood up into Bernice's face. She hurled open the door of his room, went through it, through the other door to the roof, and confronted him. Stooping she dealt him a ringing blow on the side of his head.

"I'll give you the hand you asked for!" she cried.

Jason sprang up still grinning and took her hands. He was not in the least annoyed although he shook his head a little. "Aha Bernice, so you are a woman of temperament after all!" he exclaimed. "And if you're not pretty you might be a good girl for all that."

Bernice tried to free herself so as to punish him again, but although she was strong and taller than he, she could not do so. And then something in those young tough, smooth hands on her own rough ones came into her consciousness. She had a feeling of regret as for something lost long ago. She looked into his clear russet eyes and into the pointed face with its wide cheekbones. So this is what *she* feels, she thought; what she feels and what she looks at. Who is to blame her? And without concrete words she reflected that life might have no better to offer than these smooth hands to hold and to caress, than that fresh mouth to kiss. A shining current reached up her arms and hardened the nipples of her breast. They stood out sharply against her work smock. Jason noticed them at once. He laughed.

"You're not so bad you know," he said. *"Tu n'est pas si mal!"*

But Bernice wrenched her hands away and rushed off back onto the neutral balcony. At a safe distance she turned and raged back at him defiantly, "Conceited little fool!"

His laugh followed her down the stairs and across the terrace to her kitchen. There was something strangely familiar about it that caught her attention, a sort of echo. She closed the window with a bang and commenced cleaning out the stove. This finished, she went into the studio room and to her surprise saw Rose sitting idly on the piano stool. Bernice started.

"I didn't hear you come in, Madame Flamand," she said.

"You were up on the balcony," said Rose.

"I was talking to that worthless Jason," said Bernice.

"Is he worthless?" asked Rose with a faint smile.

Bernice felt relief at being able to express her opinion of Jason, especially to Rose. "Oh he's not worthless in his own opinion," she cried. "Oh no, in his own eyes he's a real Don Juan." Protected by the comfortable wall of her indignation, she looked without embarrassment at Rose's smile and at her eyes whose stormy blue merged into the pupil.

"Does he try and make love to you, Bernice?" asked Rose touching a key on the piano.

"I'd like to see him!" scoffed Bernice, yet her voice did not sound quite right to her own ears. Against the clear lingering of the note Rose had played, its tone was rough and uncertain. Now she saw her mistress rise and, coming up to her, take her hands. As in a trance she looked down at the fingers whose cushioned ends were sanguine and which closed feverishly around her fists.

And Bernice never quite forgave Rose for the shudder that went up her arms and hardened her breast or for the laugh Rose gave as she released her. She felt the outrage of her violated nerves where, without her consent, those two had met and stamped their one desire.

CHAPTER 18

───────────── *Journal:* ─────────────

Before, long ago as it seems to me now, I used to bother no one. I was simply Rose whose life could be read at a glance (and who wanted to read it?) but whose secret thoughts weren't worth fathoming. I dare say there are other married women who can say the same. I myself wonder now what hopes the old Rose had. Children? But children are not an aim in life. One cannot anchor one's existence to theirs. Or one should not anyway, since they pass through us only and have their own destiny. They are people just as we are, and what we owe them, surely we owe ourselves.

Did I hope anything from my music? Of course I did in a way. I hoped that it would fill my soul and be enough. But most important, what did that old Rose expect from Pierre? Had she a right to expect it whatever it was?

No, that's all wrong—I mean the things I've been writing—because I think the old Rose was asleep: the slumber from which one afternoon she wakened and stood up. Do you know that when a woman awakes like that everybody gets into a panic? Yes, a real panic. Ah they hear that trumpet sound! They feel the trembling in their walls! Simon is listening with locked jaws. Pierre too looks from time to time at the doll who is near him with a strange expression in his eyes. I am not used to a look of interest in Pierre's eyes.

I want to tell you about how I was having a baby, but first I must explain something else. You know the way I keep going back to the bugler and say the road divides from him on? Well, really it is my head dividing, as I think you've gathered or I've told you. But from that day when I went up to Jason's a new thing began to happen. You see, although I had this cleft in my thoughts even then, both sides could still communicate. After that day they couldn't any more—or if they try, it gives me headaches. It's as if suddenly their languages had grown too different. And besides, everything got hazy. I began to forget. Sometimes when I was sitting with Pierre of an evening I would think about Jason, but he was like an uneasy dream to me. It was almost a story in my thoughts:

'Once upon a time there was a young woman called Rose. She had a lover whose name was Jason. He might have been a handsome man and it's possible he lived on a roof, but it's an old story and parts of it are lost.'

On the other hand, when I was with him, Jason, I could hardly remember Pierre at all—just as a sort of numbness somewhere, something that would hurt later, like a toothache with Novocain.

And why am I putting all this in the past? You know it's the same now, even worse. It's only when I'm writing this journal that things get straighter, that I can hold onto the thread and be a little sure.

Simon knew how it was from the beginning. He knew (or at least I think he did) that nothing confused me more than his constant references which only I understood. He should remain in one life with Pierre and with that good, quiet, well-mannered

Rose whose only fault is that she laughs a little too hard. But he won't and in a way I was the instrument since I took La Cigale's article to give to Pierre. Simon got to know her that way. He likes her and it's with her help that he crosses from one road to another, my roads you know, striding with his bony knees over the wasteland between. It makes my head ache and he rejoices. Simon is my enemy.

I told you I wanted children, but when I found I was pregnant in July I didn't want that. People always have the idea that one could have children with several men and the husband wouldn't know the difference. How can they think such absurdities? Already, formless inside of me, Jason's child cried out its father's name.

I was supposed to "come around" on the twenty-fifth or so of June and I've always been regular, early in fact. So by July I knew. I felt different too; my breasts burned and grew tight inside the skin. I've never been the voluptuous type and it makes a change. Also, right away I felt fat in the waist; as though I'd eaten too big a meal.

I was afraid. Whenever I thought about it I grew hot with fear. Have you ever felt that particular fever? It's like the first time one really understands that one must die. I remember it well in my case. I was fifteen years old. It was at sunset and I was just coming home from the beach. Looking up at the house, I saw a face in one of the windows. It wasn't the face of my father or mother, and aside from me they were the only people who lived there. It was just an unknown face, pale, blank and terrible. *The face of death*! I felt sick and in that moment I realized that I must die, that it was all a cruel joke; the olive trees, the blue, stretching sea, the familiar dwelling, all, all, since in the end was only death.

The fever mounted then, the blush of fear. I wondered how anyone could stand the terror of a death agony and yet everyone must—the coward and the hero both. There's no getting out of it.

When I looked up again the face was gone.

It was rather the same way when I felt afraid in July. Here was something quick yet fatal growing inside of me, a fact, and there was no getting out of it or pretending it wasn't there. I tried to think of all the things women do in such cases, but even if I knew *what* I didn't know *how*. There was no question of asking a doctor. I was certain no doctor would know. None that I knew anyway. They'd just say to go ahead and have it and that Pierre wouldn't know the difference. I've already explained about that. Besides, the Rose that lives with Pierre could never stand to bear Jason's child. It would tear her limb from limb. It would break her flanks like glass. So I was afraid and felt sick with fear and thought about nothing else.

It was approaching the fourteenth of July. Pierre and I always go to a party the night before, a literary affair given by an American woman who is a friend of Mark's and who lives on the *quai*. It's a good place to see the fireworks from and one drinks whisky. Afterward many of us went and danced in the streets. Pierre does this religiously once a year.

Paris was very pretty with the lights strung across the streets, and each little café had its music and its decorations. We went for several blocks dancing here and there and sometimes I would have as my partner someone vaguely familiar who would turn out to be the local butcher or the baker. I saw Heidi walking through the crowds of the Carrefour de l'Odéon. She was hand in hand with a curly-haired consumptive boy. They looked like two children who haven't long to live and must take their pleasures young. Once I saw them jitterbug languidly, fixing their eyes on nothing and with blank faces. They were dressed exactly alike in black sweaters and blue jeans and one could not really say who was the more masculine or feminine.

Near Saint-Germain des Prés we saw Simon who was alone. He was standing beneath the arching lights and staring around him eagerly and with venom. When he saw us he came up and asked me to dance.

"It's not the same, is it?" he remarked when we had moved two or three steps in the crowd.

"The same as what?" I asked.

"As dancing in the O.K. ballroom—as dancing with your friend there."

I didn't say anything but I could feel my heart begin to race. Simon may have felt it too. He stopped dancing. "Is there anything more sickening than women?" he cried loudly. "They are nausea itself!"

Something very like triumph welled up in me. I don't know why. I gave him a sideways look.

"Don't look at me like that," he said furiously. "I'm not your lover!" But I kept my eyes like that, sideways, until I could actually see him tremble.

"I thought you liked to *live*, Simon," I mocked him. "Aren't women a part of life?"

"There is no such thing as women," he retorted. "There are only whores."

"Men too are disappointing," I said, "when they make that kind of remark, and one might have expected a little originality from you."

I knew he hated me and that he would have liked to grind me down in that crowd until I disappeared, until I became the dust under his feet. Actually I understand his attitude although it's hard for me to put it into words. I think most men have it more or less and in this case it was aggravated because of Simon's not being attractive. He looked down on Pierre and on Pierre's wife even more, yet as I've explained, I think secretly I always troubled him a little. He couldn't fit me into the niche that he had prepared and that is so conveniently labeled "bourgeois." But it tortured

him when I too *lived,* as he puts it. It upset the whole balance of
his theories. He was supposed to admire me for it you see, and yet
he couldn't. Have you ever had a school friend, not a friend that
you truly love, but one whom you've known for years, and then
that rather dull child turns out to have had a hidden capacity,
becomes the world-champion figure skater, for instance, or writes
a book which people you look up to praise? Well, if that happens
are you sincerely happy about it?

Ha, ha, you see? Oh I know it's a bad comparison: innocent
glory compared to betrayal and shame and—but it's the best I
can do.

After shame I almost put "vice." But vice, in love I mean, is
something abnormal isn't it? Is the feeling I have abnormal? I die
in Jason's arms you know. I spin around into a whirlpool and at the
bottom is the most heavenly, the most blissful death. The cords of
my body tighten to the limit and then go slack. There is a winged
chaos like when a sailboat goes about in a storm. It's only afterward, when we are already dressing, that I become aware of the
sordid room, the greasy, dark walls, the sheets at which one daren't
look too closely. I'm afraid to be left behind and I pull on my
clothes hurriedly and with unsteady hands.

What has this to do with Simon? I'm confused. I really don't
know how to get myself out of Simon's arms and back home that
night. I'll just skip it I guess. We didn't see anyone else to tell
you about. But in a way I wanted to continue on the subject of
that evening because it was then that I reached the peak of fear. I
decided that I must do something at once and yet I hadn't the least
idea of what it must be. And all the time while I was smiling and
dancing and talking, the current of my fear was running like swift,
cool water through my blood.

When we got home the day was breaking. The stars faded as I
trailed across the terrace behind Pierre. I was exhausted and that

swift current in my blood seemed with each minute to reach new boundaries. First only the extremities had felt it; my hands and more especially my feet. Now my heart itself was chill. I pictured its chambers desolate with cold. How many chambers are there by the way for every heart? And how gracious they sound: scarlet and lofty rooms—but in them something palpitates and causes pain.

I'm cold now too.

* * * * *

ROSE was sitting, not at the table where she usually wrote, but at the piano with her notebook propped up against the edge of the keys. Dusk was already thickening the air and with the quickness of which she was capable, she leaped up and ran to the window, leaning her palms against the pane.

Just then, from somewhere out in the autumn darkness a small leaf blew against the glass; pale, moist, star-shaped, it resembled, in its helpless cling, the blind hand of an infant. It groped there for a few seconds, fumbling timidly yet insistently. Then, finding as contact only the cold glass, it dropped away again into the night.

Rose sprang back and laced her fingers together. "Is that the way it was?" she asked urgently. "Is that it?"

But in the empty room there was no one to answer.

CHAPTER 19

How shall I describe the fourteenth of July in a clear way? So many things happened on that day and yet it was shorter than others. I didn't get up until noon. Pierre was still asleep, his cheeks pink. I told you how that made me feel. He frowned when I left the bed, but he didn't wake up. I went out for a walk. I couldn't bear to stay in the house.

I don't know if you've noticed Paris on the fourteenth of July. The charlatans and mountebanks have taken over. In front of every sidewalk café the most extraordinary acts are performed; magic tricks, feats of strength, acrobatics, trained monkeys. There are even short plays whose art has bypassed the modern theater and whose gestures go back to another, a harsher and a holier time. In fact it's altogether as if these people came out of the Middle Ages. One can't imagine what they do the rest of the year. Certainly one never sees them. Perhaps they troop back silently into the air, into the foggy vapors of the Seine whose children they are. I can see them gradually mingling with the mist, their day of living over, looking ahead with their dark mist eyes toward their dim abode.

It's the same in the market place. The carts that only yesterday were stacked with fruits and vegetables are replaced by others with different wares: strange herbs and spices that are touted to cure all ills, powders from the horns of real and mythical beasts, mandrake roots, sired supposedly by hanged men in their agony and whose twisted forms assume the mortal shape. All this, superimposed upon the familiar street, gives the market a bewitched appearance. Someone has cast a spell over it. The same and yet not the same, it makes you want to rub your eyes.

On the day I was telling you about, the weather heightened my impressions. The sky was luminous, a silver-gray color, and a soft haze enveloped the near distance. I walked on for a bit, examining the charts on the stands, with their crude drawings and their extravagant statements. If what they claimed were true, one could buy eternal health and life here for a few francs. Such claims, despite all reasoning, give one an extraordinary feeling of hope. Perhaps after all modern medicine has gone astray and these people alone have the answer. One recalls reading of cures in jungles, of hypnotists and healers.

It came over me suddenly that any one of these people might have the answer to my own problem. I looked at them more carefully, at their hunched shoulders, their furtive and fluttering hands, their bony faces full of craft. I looked into their narrowed eyes.

There was a couple amongst them selling whole spices. The man's long, red nose and blotched skin gave him a brutal expression, but the woman's face seemed kind. She was obviously nervous and someone, probably her companion, just once had dealt her a blow on the side of the neck. It had destroyed her muscular control so that when she wanted to speak she had to hold her neck steady with her hand. Even so, her voice trembled.

As I came abreast of them the man muttered something and went off in the direction of the café. I stood in front of the booth and asked what she was selling.

"Cinnamon sticks," she said, "and cloves and saffron." After she'd finished answering me she took down her hand and I saw the scar. It hadn't been a blow at all. Someone had tried to slit her throat.

"Who did that?" I asked. "I daresay you're surprised at my asking such a personal question of a stranger. And it's true I'm not usually that bold." But when I spoke it was as though a voice inside me had dictated the words; another, a more desperate voice whose echo was my own. The woman wasn't offended although I think she blushed a little. Yes, I'm sure she did, and her mouth, which had a sweet expression, quivered.

"It's him," she whispered, looking fearfully in the direction of the café. "He was drunk," she added.

"And yet you stayed with him," I remarked. I was still speaking through that other voice and she gave me a glance full of such experience, such bitter and *accepting* knowledge of the world that I felt my own breast permeated.

"Who else would have me now?" she said and it wasn't even a question.

"Will you help me?" I asked. There was a sandy feeling in my throat.

"What do you want?" She seemed to have divined my thought, to have grown sterner. Her eyes were yellow beneath the silver sky. There was mockery in them. "So you want to escape!" they seemed to say. "So you want to bypass the brutality and the revenge of man! I didn't. Why should you?"

"Tell me how to do it. Give me something!" I could hear any voice stammering and I was so convinced that she knew my problem that I skipped putting it in words—or else I forgot I hadn't done so. At the same time instinct made me smoothly hold out a thousand-franc note in my hand, not openly, but so she could see it. When she did her whole attitude changed. Still with the same sweet expression (but I think it had something to do with the pull of her scar), she said softly, "Take this."

I was astonished. I use saffron in fish and I thought she was making fun of me. But in her quavering voice, very low, she explained what else I must get.

"If you take them together my little lady it's sure to work, but you'll be sick, very sick. That's your lookout." Her hand came out like the tongue of a lizard and the thousand-franc note cleaved to it. She thrust the money down the front of her dress just in time. Her companion was coming back wiping his mouth on his sleeve and giving me an appraising look.

"That will be one hundred and fifty francs for the saffron," she said with her hand back up to her neck. I hadn't expected to pay for the saffron at all, but I realized that the man probably kept count.

"Good morning, Miss," he now said with a leer and intercepted the money just before it went into her pocket. With the same gesture he pushed her roughly aside and took the king place behind the stand.

And these people too would disappear with their wares when the day was over and be seen no more all year. Already as I looked back their outlines were vague. The mist could hardly wait to dissolve their substance.

As for me, I felt as though a great load had been lightened from off my mind. I had complete confidence in what the woman had said. I was *sure* everything would be all right. You see I didn't think. . . I didn't know. . .

* * * * *

ROSE set her teeth. Turning in her chair she looked for a long time at the dark window where the leaf had clung, that small, groping leaf which had been blown away without a trace.

"Yes, that's the way it was," she murmured softly between those clenched teeth. "Yet how was I to foresee it?"

And indeed only a leaf endowed with diabolical cunning could have reached in through the window thus to twist her heart.

——————————— *Journal:* ———————————

When you're well it's hard to picture being sick. It doesn't mean anything, the word "sick." It didn't to me, in any case, on that day I was telling you about. I found a drugstore that was open and bought what the woman said to buy. I don't have to tell you do I? It's a bitter thing meant for fever and you don't have to have a prescription. But I thought the man looked at me rather hard. I thought I had to explain why I wanted it and I told him about how my husband suffered from malaria and how the attacks came back now and then. He made no comment and as he handed me the package there was such indifference in the way he held out his hand that I felt confounded. He didn't care what I did with the drug and if it was true about my husband and his malaria he didn't want to hear it.

So I went home where Pierre was reading the newspaper and drinking coffee. He takes a long time to digest the news and rereads each column. He looked so peaceful sitting there and pushing out that lower lip of his. One of his slippers was dangling, almost off, and I stooped and put it on again. I wanted to sit on his knee and tease him and prevent his reading, but I didn't dare. All those playful, innocent and wifely things which had once been my right seemed now to be forbidden me. It was hard to know what was left. The worst of it was that Pierre himself appeared not to notice any lack. Perhaps he was glad to be able to read his paper in peace, not to have me tease him anymore or mess up his hair or laugh at him. Perhaps he had only tolerated it before and had always disliked it and the things he really would have liked I never gave him. Well you see what I mean and I could not give him those other things now because they were already given.

So I went into the kitchen while Bernice was out, and boiled down the saffron and took it with the other just like the woman said, and then I waited.

By-and-by Pierre went out to a film that he had to review for *Jouvence* and I was alone. I lay on my bed and read one of the books I'd loved long ago and it was about half an hour before I noticed the ringing in my ears. It was deafening and I wondered how I'd been able to ignore it when it started. Again you see—that *moment* when things start and of which one is ignorant. Anyway I didn't get much chance to wonder about it as I began to feel very strange from then on. There was a sensation of loneliness, of being cut off from the world, and when dysentery forced me to rise I staggered without direction. My feet were weighted and yet the top of me was foolishly light. And I saw animals too. I think drunkards must see the same kind. There was a giraffe I remember with the face of a man who bent his tall neck to look me in the eyes. But his eyes were giraffe's eyes with long, dirty lashes. And there was a freak elephant with two trunks which he wound this way and that around my shoulders. They were all African animals. I wonder why? Is it circus recollection, that first outside thrill in most children's lives? Or perhaps those animals are the nearest to prehistoric creatures left on earth and the sick brain vomits ancient memories.

I wasn't afraid. I thought I was dying but I wasn't in the least afraid. It seemed all right to die in company with these strange beasts and only the wavering and distressed vision of Pierre standing near the bed disturbed me. At first I didn't think he was real, but then he kept asking me what was wrong and I had to answer. I was surprised to find myself able to speak and my voice too was that of a drunkard, slow and thick-tongued. What amazed me the most was my own guile. I told Pierre that I had eaten a little bag of shrimps in the market place that morning and that at the time of tasting them I had sensed something wrong. I get sea-food poisoning easily, as Pierre knows, so it worked. I think he did call our doctor and found he was out. Doctors are difficult to find on a holiday.

The cramps began soon after that and my head cleared. The blood when it came was startling in its brightness. For some reason I thought it would be black.

CHAPTER 20

In August Pierre took his wife away for a vacation of three weeks. They went south and stayed with Mark. Pierre did not like to stay with his father-in-law much, but Rose was run-down. She had not seemed to recover too quickly from her attack of ptomaine poisoning on Bastille Day and he thought a quiet place would do her more good than a resort.

Pierre did not understand Mark, whose sadness he mistook for disappointed conceit. His job on *Jouvence* had made him intensely aware of what was up to date. He could no longer (had he ever been able to do so) see the intrinsic value in a work. It had to be fashionable or, worse, "significant." Neither did he stop to reflect that what had seemed to him the only mode of expression a year ago was now dust in his eyes. Perhaps this flaw in Pierre's judgment was what made him so useful to *Jouvence*. He threw himself body and soul into each day's policy and was not divided as Simon was. Thus when he heard last year's viewpoint in any field still praised, he was sincerely indignant. Seeing a woman in the past season's dress, for instance, would cause him to exclaim, "How ugly she makes herself!" He would forget how he had applauded that very style, how he had explained it as the only possible flattery for a woman's looks.

Rose of course had no style at all, but he was dismayed to find that she had bought a bikini bathing suit.

It brought back a time just after they were married and were, as now, visiting Mark. Rose had disappeared into her father's studio for several hours a day and it was not until the holiday was almost over that Pierre had realized his wife was posing for her father naked.

"I don't look at you myself," he had repeated outraged and blushing.

"Well, you could," she had replied mildly. "Besides, it isn't the same thing. My father's an artist."

"Artist, artist—how I hate that word!" he had cried. "It's just an excuse for taking liberties of all sorts."

"I can't see it as a liberty," had countered Rose, "to paint the body you yourself helped fashion." The jewel-blue irises of her eyes had fixed themselves on his and she had added slowly, "I thought writers were artists too."

Pierre had said no more and had never mentioned the subject to Mark. One day however, when both the father and the daughter were absent, he had examined the painting furtively and with a curious fascination. So this was his wife; this young woman with her greenish shadows. He noticed how the start of her slight bones was belied by jet patches of hair. They lent a sensual atmosphere to the figure. Traces of the East. The Jew waiting patiently behind the flesh; the antiquity, the sorrow, the faithful and unvanquished blood. Pierre had not thought of it before and now an uneasy feeling took him by the nape. He had hurried out of the studio.

This half-buried incident returned to Pierre when he saw Rose in her bikini.

"Bikinis aren't being worn anymore," he said and even as he spoke recalled that in his novel Gloria always wore one. But Gloria and Rose had nothing in common. Gloria, with her sun-brightened curls, her small sunburned nose. She was, this girl of his creation, a boyish type of creature whose long, smooth, brown limbs looked just right in a bikini, whose body had a golden glint. The thought of her made him critical of his wife, of her total lack of blondness, her muscular line that had no boyishness to excuse or classify.

Then for a moment, with an almost mystic double vision, Pierre saw in front of him, not the quiet, neat Rose with her girlish dresses, her smooth hair, but a stranger vital with dark heritage. Her lean body seemed to him in that instant more voluptuous, more terrible than the roundest curves. And why were those eyes so heavy, those ocher shadows so far spread and that straight mouth so feverishly dry? What fever wasted the lips of his wife Rose? He shook his head like a spaniel and the illusion went away.

"I suppose it's all right for small beaches like this where nobody comes," he said. Rose smiled and touched his hand. Then, with a little sigh, she stretched herself on the warm sand and turned her face into her arms.

Pierre walked slowly along the tidemark looking down but not seeing anything; a heavy-set young man with the skin already scorched on his shoulders. Now and then he had to circle a group of bathers or ballplayers. Rose would never play with a ball on the beach and the very idea of such a thing sent her off into peals of laughter.

"Why not just run around in circles giving each other hearty slaps?" she would say. And of course it was true that people *did* get hearty on a beach. But Pierre rather sympathized. In any case *Jouvence* took these vacation games quite seriously and always ran a few pages on them. Before leaving Paris he had just seen the ones of this year; five girls in shorts illustrating healthy outdoor hours in front of a tent. One of them had been almost like Gloria, except that her thighs weren't right, and when one knew the model in question, so Simon assured him, one found her strangely uninterested in men.

Pierre was almost knocked off his feet by a child who was running into the sea. The child, a girl, was about twelve years old and of that extreme, wild beauty which reaches its peak at that age. Her wet hair, reddened and streaked by the sun, fell over her brows in straight locks, but as she collided with Pierre she threw back her head and exposed the pointed face that had been hidden. For a moment her eyes looked into his with the most savage abandon and then she was off again leaping and bounding as though her body were broken to the rhythm of her panting breath.

Pierre watched her throw herself at the water. She shrieked as the first wave struck her legs. Her piercing cry made him smile and yet something sad was at the back of his mind. Turning, he saw what must have been her family on the beach; an elder sister and a mother, an attractive group. The sister was sitting in the midst of small bottles and was giving herself a manicure. She might have been sixteen or so and resembled quite distinctly the child who had run into him. When she looked up, however, he saw that her eyes were quite different; the golden and bird-like freedom was absent, just as the tangle was absent from her short, waved hair. Beauty was gone and only decent prettiness remained to take its place. Pierre could see quite plainly that there was a copy of *Jouvence* open beside the girl's knee and the sight of it gave him an unpleasant reaction.

"Why I'm ashamed of *Jouvence!*" he exclaimed to himself. "I'm ashamed because it will turn that child into a replica of her sister, that child with all her promise!" Yes, that promise which seemed as boundless as the ocean in which she sported, would be cut down to size. Worse, she would cut it down herself and willingly. Soon, next year perhaps, she would leave her play and plunge without regret into the murky waters of adolescence. Self-consciousness would replace the abandon of today. Fear would steady her wild pace. *Jouvence* would wave her hair and paint her nails, would tell her what to think and what to hope for.

Yet if that's true, what am *I* doing? he wondered. Am I not a writer with a book to finish and bring out? He recalled that once Rose had told him he should quit the magazine and concentrate on his book alone. And how unreasonably angry he had been! It was as though she had urged him to jump off a cliff with a few feathers in his hands. But perhaps a few feathers were enough, or even the short, thrilling fall through the air. Enough, better, than the endless plod across the plain.

Such thoughts made Pierre's head spin and his rather puffy eyes opened in dismay.

The young girl thought he was looking at her and smiled at him invitingly. This was vacation and after all Mamma did the same. Her white-red smile changed Pierre's mood in a flash. Whatever had he been thinking? He could not remember. And how charming and fresh she looked with her neat, new figure, her high-lighted hair. How right that she should be gently waving her hand to dry her nails. How more than right that she should smile at him.

A breeze fluttered the pages of her magazine and then lifted it a few inches away from her. Pierre in two strides was over and had restored it. "I wouldn't like you to lose such a valuable possession," he said. Remarks of this kind are permissible on the beach and both she and her mother thanked him.

"But I've read it anyway," she said. "It isn't very good this time."

"Ah, that's because I'm on vacation," said Pierre.

"Do you work on *Jouvence?*" At his answering nod both women looked up at him with respect and he saw that the mother too took good care of herself. She hardly appeared older than her daughter, only a little brighter and a little harder.

"Mamma and I always fight over it," said the girl. The mother slanted her dark glasses at Pierre's face and gave a sophisticated twist of her lips.

"You'll have to allow that a woman my age needs it most," she said. She had to say it with that big girl by her side. There was nothing else to do.

"Why should one sister need it more than the other?" asked Pierre gallantly.

At this point the little girl came running back covered with goose flesh and with hair plastered down on her cheeks. The other two looked at her aghast and moved instinctively together. Who was this skinny, shivering child and what possibly could she have to do with lovely them?

"Don't drip on me!" cried one.

"Yes, do go away," agreed the other. "Really, my child, if you could see how you look with your hair like a wet dog's."

They shuddered and Pierre completely agreed with them. How could I ever have thought her beautiful? he wondered, looking at her sharp, child's face in which the lips were blue with cold.

After a few moments more of conversation and a tentative date for apéritifs that evening, Pierre walked back along the beach. It was getting late and bathers were preparing to go home. Some who lived near put on beach coats, others dressed nimbly and in such a clever way that one saw nothing. They wrung the sea out of their bathing suits and grimaced at the sand still sticking to their backs. Then, turning to give last looks at the beach where they had lain, they strolled slowly toward the sea wall.

Rose was lying on her back. She had been swimming and drops of water still pearled her skin. Her face was exposed and would have been serene were it not for the heavy frown between her closed eyes. It sprang from the meeting of her brows like a living thing, like a branch or like a cry for help.

But Pierre had grown used to this frown as husbands will and what he noticed was something else entirely: a dark shadow that ran along the insides of her thighs. Had it always been there? He did not know. A sort of soreness between the blades of his shoulders made him recall the portrait incident once again. He stood there for a few minutes more, looking down at his wife, and the confusion of his feelings was not unlike that of a man who is falling in love.

CHAPTER 21

After I had been with Jason, I used to feel empty. I couldn't care about anything and especially about seeing him again. Yet in a day or two, sometimes even sooner, a restlessness would come over me which has grown familiar since. I'd know that only Jason could cure it.

"One more time," I'd say to myself. "Just let me see him one more time." Who was going to let me, I wonder? Was it you?

I think that the fourteenth of July did more than anything to bind me to him although you might think it would be the other way around. It was as though every single thing that day was pointing in his direction. Did you notice that, when I was telling you about it? I mean that *other* population coming from a land that might have been my own dreams, that *other* market superimposed on the everyday one. Even my delirium later—yes, especially that—was a part of it. Oh, the fourteenth was thick with clues. It led on into the darkness. It darkened my brain.

Sometimes in those days, as I was lying in bed at night, the moon would rise over the terrace and a sliver of white would point into the open door of our bedroom. When it's hot like that we have to keep everything open; otherwise it's unbearable, even Pierre agrees. Occasionally, along with the moonlight, a tomcat would creep into the house. There are several of them on the roof, a tribe by themselves. God knows how they exist. I suppose they find birds. They can rove the whole block from roof to roof and they look quite different from the alley cats one sees down in the streets. They are paler, as though a hundred moons had bleached their fur, and they slink less. Perhaps that's because they haven't man to fear, or his civilization. Out on the peaked and barren ranges of the roofs they are alone with their desires, their hunger and their hatred of each other.

And when I saw those fiery eyes against the thread of the moon I started up. Oh the doll's heart ached then as human blood beat into it and the doll's eyes were burned in the glare. And I remembered Jason and I thought that if I didn't see him within the day I'd die.

We had a system which seemed to have developed by itself; at least I for one don't know how it started. It was a tune, "La Vie en Rose." Appropriate, not to say banal, and when one of us played it, it meant that in half an hour we would be at the rendezvous. At first of course we didn't have a rendezvous. Jason simply went downstairs and waited until he knew I was behind him. Then he walked off. He didn't need to turn around for he knew I was following. I recall that he was always smoking a cigarette at such moments, but smoking in a special way like in a spy movie. Sometimes it felt like an absurd game, not real at all.

Later, it was understood that we would meet at the coal vendor's. The coal vendor's is also a small bar. It always is in Paris although I've never discovered why. They have a sign up over the front of the door advertising wine and coal. Both warming products and I daresay theirs is thirsty work. The coal bar in our quarter is next door to a hotel and one can go from one to the other by side doors. It's very safe really, even though it's so near home. I'd always have the excuse, in case anyone saw me, of ordering wood or coal or else paying my bill. Even in summer it would work. And what more natural for Jason if he happened to be there than to offer me a drink, after my kindness of last winter?

The coal men know of course. There are several of them besides the *patron*. They take it in the nicest and most ordinary way and are very polite to me; much more so than before, in fact. Then too, they are all great admirers of Jason and of his accordion.

Nonetheless the first time was horrible. I'd never done a thing like that although lots of people must, judging from the hotel's attitude. Jason asked for soap and a towel. When we got into the room he pulled back the blankets immediately. I said and did nothing. I felt paralyzed. But I was happy to have come because it all seemed so crushingly sordid that I knew I'd never do such a thing again.

I knew it for three days and then I didn't know it any more.

But we didn't always go to the hotel, you know. Sometimes we walked along the lower embankment of the Seine or simply had a drink. Once we went to the Musée Gavin and stood in a room with mirrors all around and changing lights. The room was packed and we stood up close to one another. I felt Jason's heart beating against mine and I might have fallen down, I felt so weak, if the room hadn't been too crowded even to bend one's knees.

At other times, when Pierre was working late I used to go to the O.K. Ballroom and I'd see Jason there. I put it in the past. I put all these things in the past and in a way they are and in a way they're not.

I liked going to the ballroom at first because everybody knew I was Jason's girl and all the men asked me to dance. The regular girls were jealous and there were two of them there in love with Jason.

One of them was the girl I told you about before and the other was a robust-looking creature who thought of herself as the belle of the O.K. She wanted to make me a scene, but it was difficult because I was so quiet. Besides, I think she was a little afraid of Jason. I used to be friendly and polite to all my partners and I got so that I even enjoyed dancing musette. I don't know why I was so happy there, or rather of course I do. It was because Jason was the star and I was *the* one. I was new and I had nothing to fear. It gave me the most marvelous feeling of happy ease. I've never had that feeling before.

La Cigale was there often but we never spoke. She just sat and nursed her beer and even if all the tables were packed nobody ever sat at hers. Her recollections are being printed in *Jouvence*, by the way. It seems she really was quite a well-known music-hall artiste and knew other important celebrities of her day. She had photographs they hadn't yet seen of herself and others. Of course they wanted to change what she wrote and Simon fought with her all summer. After we got back from vacation Pierre tried to join in the battle but he's just not made to cope with somebody like that. You see, they wanted to hear about the celebrities she had known, little stories about them and so forth. But La Cigale (quite naturally) wanted to tell only about herself. *She* wanted to be the central figure and no mistake. They must have straightened it out somehow because the article's appearing shortly.

Anyway I was explaining how I felt there in the O.K. ballroom. Jason would notice me come in at once and the other musicians would nudge him and wink admiringly. His other girls would rove around the room like unhappy tigers. And Jason would be sitting there playing, with his hair still curled from the dampness of the comb and his knees spread in a powerful, graceful, manly way. Just as he's sitting at this moment—just as I'll soon see him.

* * * * *

IT was getting late and Rose was overtaken by the peculiar chill and pallor which comes at that hour to people who are alone indoors. It is a sort of shriveling, as though all life's juices were retreating to the core, leaving desolate the outer covering. She hunched her shoulders and then, rising, went slowly to her room. Pierre was away in Belgium for the night, supervising an article on Flemish culture, and he would not be back until the following day. His presence left no trace now in these dark rooms which were chilly with the first autumn fogs.

On her way out, Rose stood for a moment: on the terrace and looked up at the sky. The wind above the roofs made a pure sound that spoke out of the mouths of the stars. And the night took possession of Rose: the ritual, the quickening of night which pours its antique streams into the soul.

It was after midnight by the time she reached the *bal* and once inside she was halted by a feeling of panic. How *near* things have gotten! she thought, looking around her. She had an impression that her eyes were showing their whites as they rolled uneasily in their sockets. Perhaps it was because she had been writing about the O.K. that the feeling struck her with such force. A quivering in her nerves made her features stiffen in the effort of control and this lent a harshness to her face, forbidding and almost repellent. She felt her whole neck rigid and turned it with difficulty toward the bandstand. Jason was sitting there playing just as she had depicted. He had not seen her come in and was grinning at someone in the crowd. Then, noticing her at last, he made a friendly gesture with his head.

Over in the corner sat La Cigale alone as usual. It was as though the currents of her thoughts made dark, deep waters flow around her which no one dared brook. Only the waiter with his monstrous shape came near her and that was enough. They hated each other so much now that there was very little lacking in their lives—as good as love, really, for the woman who had had too much experience and the man whose deformity had left him chaste.

Rose tried to dance but the stiff movements of her partners aggravated her own condition so she sat down at a table and waited for Jason to be free. Other women passing on the arms of their men gave her hard stares. They were not taken in by this stranger in their midst and had always resented her. There was one girl in particular here tonight whom Rose had seen one day on the stairs of her house; a bold-looking red-head, almost handsome, with heavy lips and round, not very clear eyes.

When closing time was called this girl went up to Jason and took him by the arm. Rose, who had not left her seat, saw that the girl was angry. Jason merely shrugged. The hall was emptying fast. Even La Cigale was walking toward the door with halting steps while the waiter watched furtively. He kept pace with her on the other side of the room, doubtless to show that he did not trust her to be gone, and in this way they danced on slowly after the music had ceased. Rose was suddenly terrified lest Jason go out with the red-headed girl and abandon her to her fate. She felt herself incapable of movement and would stay forever in this dirty hall alone with the echoes, the darkness and the trap of her own skin.

At that moment however Jason came up and caught hold of her roughly. "Come *along!*" he said. "What's the matter with you? I can't stand around waiting all night."

"I didn't want to disturb anything," she said, at once mortified and relieved by the sarcasm in her voice.

He frowned. "I don't know why I put up with you," he muttered moodily. "I don't know what you want with me."

Rose made no reply. She did not know either answer.

CHAPTER 22

Simon and La Cigale could not exactly be called friends, but by the end of the summer they knew each other quite well. It was rather like the relationship of jailer to prisoner, only in their case no one could have said who was guarding whom.

Simon, fastidious as he appeared, was not put off by La Cigale's room or by her looks on close inspection. It was young women who had the power to disgust him or make him angry. This anger, which might have been a reaction to fear, absorbed him as far as Rose was concerned and he sometimes confided in La Cigale about it.

"What can she be doing?" he would cry. "And with a dirty little runt like that!"

"Ha, ha, you're just mad you didn't get there first," La Cigale would cackle in a truly witchlike way, looking maliciously into his face.

Being misunderstood in this preposterous manner should have irritated Simon, but instead it soothed him. La Cigale saw things simply between men and women although she might have experienced them otherwise. Had he protested that he himself had never desired Rose in the least, she would not have believed him. But Simon did not protest and, instead, continued as though she had hit it right. "I shall find a way to punish her," he said.

"What are you waiting for, my little one?" La Cigale would ask. "You have her in your hand." She put her chin on her fist and after a few moments' reflection continued, "Why not try and make a few remarks to her in front of her husband?—just enough to scare her."

"Oh but I do!" he cried. "She's cleverer than you think. She looks really as though she didn't know what I was talking about. Lately she's even seemed to *want* to know, like a child from whom one withholds a mystery."

"Perhaps it's not cleverness," said La Cigale, veiling her eyes so as to look deeper into her own meaning.

"What else then? Just the natural ability of your kind for deceit?" He spoke with a mordant bitterness that in another nature would have been replaced by tears.

La Cigale did not notice his tone. She continued sitting with her fist holding up her chin and her old eyes veiled. "Women deceive men, yes that's true," she said at length in her hoarse, conspirator's voice. "But they deceive themselves much more. They must if they are to keep on living. Oh I should know if anyone does." She gave him a glance. "If I'd had a man like you for instance, Monsieur Simon—because you were a power-ful journalist or some such reason—I would have pretended in your arms that you were the boy I liked and you would have taken my ardor for granted and been happy."

"Thank you," he said dryly, his thin lips smiling in their shadow.

"Your Madame Flamand is doing something like that I think," said the old woman.

Simon was so horrified by this idea that his voice rose. "You mean that when she's with Flamand—"

"Calm yourself," said La Cigale with delight. "I only said 'something like that.'"

"Then what?" he asked. His jawbones worked at the edge of his face as though with all his teeth he were chewing the narrow, bitter rind of his own flesh.

La Cigale lifted up her head. "Listen," she said holding up her hand. "He's stopped playing." All this time while they had been talking and as on most occasions when Simon came to see La Cigale, the accordion had been sounding from next door. It was now abruptly silent. "He played *their* song just before you arrived," continued La Cigale; "'La Vie en Rose.' No doubt they think it witty to pun before they perform."

Simon sprang up from where he was sitting on La Cigale's bed and went out on the balcony. The old woman's words propelled him as when a string is pulled on an outboard motor. Below him as he leaned against the rail he could see the big studio window of the Flamand living room. But as it was at right angles, the light hit the glass in such a way that he could not look in. Nonetheless he thought he glimpsed a face, Rose's face surely.

At that moment, with a muttered apology, Jason brushed passed him and went off toward the stairs. Simon on that narrow balcony could feel the other's body against his. It pressed against him for an instant; round, arched, muscular. It spoke a message to his rack of bones. A muffled shock somewhere inside him made Simon's legs tremble. He sniffed, moving the end of his long nose.

"That fellow must wash his hair with cologne," he said to La Cigale who had now come out to join him.

"He's a dandy," she said sarcastically. "After all, one owes something to one's public when one's an artiste."

"So *that's* what he is!" cried Simon. "Thank you for telling me." His sarcasm, which matched hers in childishness, pleased the old woman. She looked up at the pale blue afternoon sky and squinted. Soon (but never soon enough) night would fall. The long, weary day would be over.

"In my time," she said, "a woman of the world never appeared until dusk."

"Ah, but then they had candles and gas lamps. Fluorescent lighting is crueler than the sun."

She observed him with surprise. "You sometimes astound me," she exclaimed. "You are not a stupid man as far as women are concerned."

"Did you expect me to be?" he asked. He was aware however, despite this banter, of the repercussions of that shock inside him.

"Yes, or to be more—lucky."

"Can't you understand that some people don't want to be 'lucky' as you put it?" And now it was as though little waves were being thrown up against the walls of Simon's veins.

"Sour grapes!" she scoffed. Simon hardly heard her.

"Come on," he said, "let's take a walk."

La Cigale was only surprised for a moment. He wants to follow them, she decided; and he is afraid to do it alone. Poor fool, his case is bad.

They had to go slowly because La Cigale was unable to do otherwise. It was strange how, despite all the outward marks of it, she often made one forget her age. Automatically it was she who acted as guide to their direction. They walked down the street and around the corner. She jerked her head.

"They go in there," she said.

Simon looked at the little bar in front of which a high-wheeled and blackened cart proclaimed the coal dealer. At that moment the man himself came out, opening the door wide so that Simon could see the whole interior of the café. "There's no one in there," he said.

La Cigale shrugged and glanced up at the hotel next door whose small, dingy sign seemed trying to avoid attention. "But sometimes we like to take a walk," she said slyly. "Down by the river."

Late summer had already turned over the leaves of the trees near the Seine so that the pale undersides of them caught the light. They fluttered and twisted, making, even above the sound of traffic, a murmur of their own, lively and yet sad. Dusk was coming and another night whose chilly winds would dry their sap yet further. The cool sun was but a sham. Thus they spoke, one leaf to another, softly, desperately, asking no doubt the riddle of death which is always asked in vain.

Simon, hearing the wind in the trees and seeing the sun sparkle on the river, felt a revolt against the obscurity of his intentions. The old woman and the young man leaned together on the parapet between bookstalls. "Do you know that editing your article will finish my work on *Jouvence*?" he asked.

"You writers!" said La Cigale. "You act as if you want to write a person's own life for them. *I* know what happened. *I* know who was more famous than who despite what you say now. *They* just kept their banknotes or else they married the rich pigs who bought them champagne. I spent all and I lived my life for myself and for my loves. Why I remem—"

"Oh for heaven's sake," he broke in, "don't tell me about your disgusting affairs. I don't see that the oily gigolo is any better than the rich pigs you scorn."

"Who is speaking of oily gigolos?" she cried hoarsely. "Why he was an artist too—as beautiful as the morning—as beautiful as you'll never be—as you'll never know."

Neither of them spoke for a while after that and Simon, looking at his companion's eyes, saw them grow black with concentration. At length, in another tone, languid almost and dreamy, she said, "As beautiful as he is to her."

Something in the fixity of her regard (which at first he had mistaken for introspection) now arrested Simon and he turned his head to follow her gaze. About twenty paces off, the stone arch of the pont Neuf shadowed the lower *quay* beneath them and deep within that shadow a pair of lovers were locked in each other's arms. The girl was leaning against the wall and the boy, hardly taller than she, had his head bent across her face. As they kissed, her hand showed white on his hair. They had in their attitude a passionate, a desperate tenderness as if they hoped in penetrating each other's bodies to find another secret there than lust.

"As beautiful as he is to her," repeated La Cigale.

A sweet flow of saliva in his mouth made Simon fear he might be sick. But can I be sure that it is really she, he wondered, with her body fitted to his like water? And what about him with his knee raised like that? It's as though he were taking the temperature of her surrender.

Then the girl threw back her head and showed to the pale sky the deeper glitter of her irises. Simon moved quickly back from his post and, taking hold of the old woman's arm, took her with him. For an instant they looked silently at each other. Then La Cigale spoke.

"I'll tell you something," she said, "something that I have discovered. I didn't think I knew it until now, but I must have." She paused to put her thought into words for the first time. "You see," she went on "your Rose doesn't remember. That's her trick. I told you there was a trick. She remembers but she doesn't remember."

"Doesn't remember what?" Simon felt his brains like chips of glass in his head.

"Why, her *other* life, that's what," said La Cigale. "Whichever life she's living at the moment is the only one that seems real. That's how she bears it, a milksop like her. That's the only way she can stand it." Then the old woman put up a gray finger to her nose and winked. "But *you*, Monsieur Simon, could force both lives to come together—and we'd see what we would see."

CHAPTER 23

————————————— *Journal:* —————————

I read in a magazine that in some place or other they have a two-headed turtle and the turtle is perfectly healthy except that one head controls the right side and the other the left. The two heads don't think alike. They want to go different ways. So perhaps it's like that with me. Perhaps each side of my head wants me to tell about something else than the other side.

I keep thinking about one time when I was standing on the lower part of the *quay* not long ago. I was standing under a bridge, but it's hard to remember why. Was I alone, for instance? What nonsense! Of course I wasn't. You know it too. Anyway I do remember the feeling of damp stone at my back. And then I looked up and saw Simon staring at me. I could only see his head and part of his neck. It was as though the rest of his body were a broomstick; a head set up on a broomstick to confound me. I was dazed by it. I had a feeling like when one eats an unripe persimmon, but not only in my mouth—all over.

It was from that day on that I knew if I didn't get things clear by myself, someone else would do it for me and that would be worse than death itself.

Worse than death itself! You see what kind of phrases I use. How do I know what would be worse or better than that?

Anyway I went home and I started this journal or whatever you want to call it. I've tried to reread it entirely several times, but I can't. I guess I'm supposed to wait until the end. It did bring out a thread though, didn't it, just like I said? And I don't have to reread to remember every bit of that thread, like the bugler. He was the beginning, of course, and he is the spool and the thread unwinds and unwinds from around him—and the gypsies and the juggler and La Cigale and the *saltimbanques* on the fourteenth of July, even a little girl I kept seeing on the beach when Pierre and I were on our vacation.

Oh I can hold the thread all right. I feel it running through my hand, softly, softly, and I advance further and further into this labyrinth of my choice. And now my heart beats fast because everything is said, or almost all, or all I can think of, and soon I'll come out into an open space—I picture it round—and I'll discover the monster.

Perhaps you'd like to know more about *things*, but there's really nothing more to tell. Or you'd like me to clear up the question of La Cigale or of Simon. I wish I could. Do people become one's enemies just to divert themselves? Or is it because one disturbs them slightly in a way one couldn't possibly foresee and which, in the end, has only to do with themselves?

Last time I looked in the mirror I had a strange experience. There was something odd about my outline—a sort of haze; an aura would be a better definition. It eased my strict lines as with the grace of another softer, more voluptuous flesh. Then I looked at my eyes with that new heaviness they have and that ocher color on their lids. Where had I seen them before? And I recalled my mother's Oriental eyes that glistened always as though with a million unshed tears. Yes, mine were like that too and it was her body clasping my own in shadowy embrace!

Of course that's all an illusion and even if it weren't what would be the good? What good for the curse, the creative blood, to come out in the child? It doesn't stay pure through the generation. It only brings trouble. And if one denies it that's worse. I know. Certainly there's been a betrayal somewhere, but by whom? Against whom?

A while ago I heard a tune. I loathe the accordion, you know, but it hypnotizes me. The tune says, "In a little while you must rise up and go." And when the times comes around I obey. I rise up and I go. I can't help it. It's as though I were a puppet, a doll. There, you see—I *told* you there was a doll in all this! Perhaps I placed the doll wrong. I put it in Pierre's bed, did I not? Yet it's *me* that's here in this flat so it must be me in Pierre's bed too. No, the doll goes out to that other bed.

It's all very confusing. It's like those things you see best out of the corner of your eye. When you look at them straight on, you don't see them anymore. I have to go beside the point to make it even a little clear. If I went at it directly it wouldn't exist. You couldn't understand it at all.

Tomorrow I swear I'm going to read everything I've written— perhaps I'll read it aloud too—and then I'll throw this journal in the fire because I won't need it any more. Will I?

* * * * *

ROSE ceased writing. Somewhere a bell had rung. She recoiled visibly like one of those sea flowers that fold when the enemy approaches. Hurriedly, almost furtively, she went to the door and listened. But it was not to the Flamand apartment that a visitor had come for she could hear no stir on the landing.

Nonetheless the bell had left an echo inside her. An urgent need of haste made her wring her hands and turn around once or twice.

"I'll be late," she murmured in the distressed tones of one who is kept from an appointment. But there was nothing to keep her.

Outside it was cold and dark. A fine, icy drizzle fell on her hair and sought her neck inside the collar of her raincoat. She shivered. I didn't say goodbye to Bernice, she thought with a foolish stab of dismay. Yes, she distinctly recalled the servant standing there with arms wet to the elbow and watching her as she put on her coat. She felt that if she had only had time to decipher it, Bernice's glance would have held a message of importance. The blue glint in it had almost spoken.

When she reached the bar she saw that it was crowded, with coal men for the most part. Exhilarated by the warmth and the wine, they were arguing together with seeming fierceness. Their pale eyes were agleam in their black faces, their red lips were darkened by the coarse red wine. Rose sat down at her usual place and ordered a brandy and soda. Everybody looked at her as she did this for such an order was rare here. The *patron*, who was also the chief coal vendor, brought it over anxiously as though handling an unknown composition that might explode. At her command he also brought a small bottle of Perrier soda water. The idea of anybody using real Perrier instead of the ordinary charged water in the siphon impressed him.

"Mademoiselle is celebrating?" he suggested. It was a part of his discretion, when she came in thus, to call her Miss instead of the Madame Flamand he knew her to be and to whom he delivered wood and coal.

Rose shook her head. She had thrown off her coat and was wearing a thin silk shirt cut like a man's and opened low on her bosom. From its opening her breath seemed to struggle eagerly up the stages of her lungs and just at the base of her throat her skin was blotched faintly with excitement and anticipation. She drank thirstily.

There was no sign of Jason, but today for some reason she was not displeased by this and felt so certain of his entrance in a few minutes that it was as though she were already in his presence. So sure was she in fact that when the door opened she did not even look up.

Pierre and Jason were halfway across the bar before she noticed them. They were arm in arm.

CHAPTER 24

Simon, walking with Pierre toward the coal and wood bar a few minutes earlier, had recognized Jason's figure in front of them. The swagger with which the young man moved his shoulders, the ready arms at his side and the soft ease of his tread, all made him known. The street light shone on the half-curly locks of his hair and brought to life a red woolen muffler tucked inside his jacket collar. Simon snorted with his first head cold of the season.

"Why all this mystery, my friend?" demanded Pierre for the third or fourth time. "What have you to show me here that's so important? I had to leave everything in a mess at the office." Pierre's fresh voice had in it a note that Simon would never have heard a few months back.

"It's RESEARCH, my dear Pierre," said Simon.

"Research for what?" asked Pierre.

"Oh, for your book perhaps—that famous masterpiece to come—or else for mine. You'd want to help a fellow writer wouldn't you—even if he isn't good enough for *Jouvence*?" He took his friend's arm and made him hasten. "Don't talk, you'll be late," he said.

The bar was close now. A round ventilator above its door let out a steamy air into the street. From the archway of a porte-cochere a sudden movement made Pierre start and a grinning face peered out of the shadows.

"Good evening La Cigale," said Simon and at the same time he pushed Pierre forward. "Go into the bar—quick—now—there's not a moment to lose! See, that man is about to open the door—*hurry!*"

Pierre's naturally docile nature made him obey and besides, a nightmarish quality in the atmosphere mesmerized him, an impression of danger—something that he almost knew, perhaps *did* know, but which had been hidden from him by the thinnest of curtains. He stumbled a little with the unexpected force of Simon's push and had to take a few running steps to recover himself. These carried him into the door directly behind Jason and thus the two men arrived together.

How much that looks like Rose, thought Pierre, and then: But of course it is Rose.

Jason was still walking a little ahead of Pierre and to the side so that from where Rose was sitting they must have looked arm in arm. She blinked rapidly at them once or twice. A grimace that might have been a faint smile of greeting stirred the corners of her lips and for once there was no frown between her eyes. Her brow was sponged smooth and shone with a sort of blank attention.

Then, deliberately, she took up the Perrier bottle that was empty in front of her. With a dry, decisive movement she broke it on the edge of the table and rammed it violently into her chest.

"So it was me all the time!" she exclaimed, but in the turmoil no one heard her. "Yes it was me," she insisted softly—to her own wounds perhaps, or to her future scars. "*I* was the monster all the time!"

* * * * *

Later Rose was in the hospital and she had a dream. It might even have been a vision since she was under drugs and such fancies are obscure. In any case, she saw herself as part of the audience in a big concert hall where a full orchestra was on stage. The dream (or vision) opened on that pause which comes just after the music has ceased and whose quality measures appreciation more than the wildest claps and shouts.

For Rose this pause was warm, the pure catch of a collective breath and although consciously she had not heard the preceding music, it yet echoed in her ghostly ear and she was satisfied. She knew too that it had been a piano concerto, for the solo notes had not quite quenched their timbre in her blood.

Then the applause burst out and covered the musicians. The conductor, smiling, reached out his hand toward the soloist and from that moment Rose could see nothing else.

The soloist was a woman and stood gracefully away from her seat to make her reverence. She was dressed in the conventional long black dress which added to her height and set off her well-knit but voluptuous figure. Her head was pulled back as though by the hair whose heavy, ebony knot was caught at the nape of her neck. Thus her face was exposed to the light; serene, unsmiling, indifferent, it would seem, to the acclaim.

It was a face made to carry, to be seen from afar, and its looks were marred neither by middle-age, nor by the touch of sullenness or brooding that shadowed its straight bones. An almost super natural beauty was added at this moment by the glitter of her eyes which pierced the utmost corners of the hall. The composer's meaning seemed to fill them still and to rain from them like tears.

She bowed to the following waves of applause and had the gesture each time of putting her hand over her heart as the little boys of old-fashioned parents are taught to do. This gesture, formal and unexpected, was charming in the mature woman who in other ways appeared impervious to her success. But it was troubling too. One might believe almost that the heart was heavy inside her, heavy as a stone; that if she did not hold it thus it might roll forward to burst her chest.

Rose, who had been clapping with the rest of the public, now felt her arms weaken and dissolve. In fact everything around her was dissolving: the hall with its crimson and its gold, the black figures of the musicians, the woman bowing with her hand over her heart. There was just time in the advancing darkness to look at the program on her knees, to look and to read in the failing light and with drugged eyes the legend: Soloist and Monster—Rose.

Theodora Keogh, the granddaughter of Theodore Roosevelt, wrote nine novels between 1950 and 1962. A complicated and captivating prose stylist, her work has often been compared to Patricia Highsmith for its psychological depth and complex often morally conflicted characters. Appearing as they did midway in her brief career, these two novels provide a wonderful introduction to this overlooked author.

Lidia Yuknavitch is the author of *Dora: A Headcase*, *The Chronology of Water*, as well as three works of short fiction. Her work has appeared in *The Iowa Review*, *Exquisite Corpse*, *Fiction International*, *Zyzzyva*, and elsewhere. She received the 2011 Pacific Northwest Booksellers Award. She lives in Portland. More at www.lidiayuknavitch.net.

More Titles From Pharos Editions

The Lists of the Past by Julie Hayden
SELECTED AND INTRODUCED BY CHERYL STRAYED

The Tattooed Heart & *My Name Is Rose* by Theodora Keogh
SELECTED AND INTRODUCED BY LIDIA YUKNAVITCH

Total Loss Farm: A Year in the Life by Raymond Mungo
SELECTED AND INTRODUCED BY DANA SPIOTTA

Crazy Weather by Charles L McNichols
SELECTED AND INTRODUCED BY URSULA K LE GUIN

Inside Moves by Todd Walton
SELECTED AND INTRODUCED BY SHERMAN ALEXIE

McTeague: A Story of San Francisco by Frank Norris
SELECTED AND INTRODUCED BY JONATHAN EVISON

You Play the Black and the Red Comes Up by Richard Hallas
SELECTED AND INTRODUCED BY MATT GROENING

The Land of Plenty by Robert Cantwell
SELECTED AND INTRODUCED BY JESS WALTER